Praise for Liz Trenow

'What a delicious read *The Silk Weaver* is. I was
enchanted by this novel set in eighteenth-century
Spitalfields; meticulously researched, richly detailed, the
brilliantly structured story shimmered as the threads of
silk wound through its pages. I devoured it in two days
and was gripped from start to finish. The characters
shine too and Anna is an absolute triumph.
A fabulous book'
DINAH JEFFERIES

'I absolutely love the details about silk weaving . . . Liz
Trenow conjures up atmosphere concisely and brilliantly,
with not a spare word to be found. I felt enriched when
I reached the end of this gem of a novel, and can't wait
to read her next one'
GILL PAUL

'Push back the gorgeous brocade curtains of
The Silk Weaver's period detail and romance and
you find a window on eighteenth-century London
that, with its prejudice and divisions, is surprisingly
pertinent today'
KATE RIORDAN

'I absolutely loved *The Silk Weaver*. Liz writes beautifully, and I adored the characters of Anna and Henri – their love was so delicately and believably evoked. The background motifs of the silks and the floral designs, and the political/social context which made their relation-ship so difficult is also brilliantly done. I really couldn't wait to get back to it each evening'
TRACY REES

'Extraordinary, fascinating . . . deeply rooted in history'
Midweek, BBC Radio 4

'An assured debut with a page-turning conclusion'
Daily Express

'Liz Trenow sews together the strands of past and present as delicately as the exquisite stitching on the quilt which forms the centrepiece of the story'
LUCINDA RILEY

'Totally fascinating . . . a book to savour'
KATE FURNIVALL

'A novel about the human spirit – Liz Trenow paints with able prose a picture of the prejudices that bind us and the love that sets us free . . . Splendid'
PAM JENOFF

'An intriguing patchwork of past and present, upstairs and downstairs, hope and despair'
DAISY GOODWIN

IN LOVE AND WAR

Liz Trenow is a former journalist who spent fifteen years working for regional and national newspapers, and BBC radio and television news, before turning her hand to fiction. *In Love and War* is her fifth novel. She lives in East Anglia with her artist husband, and they have two grown-up daughters and two beautiful grandchildren.

Find out more at **www.liztrenow.com**,
join her on **Facebook.com/liztrenow**
or Twitter **@LizTrenow**.

Also by Liz Trenow

The Last Telegram
The Forgotten Seamstress
The Poppy Factory
The Silk Weaver

LIZ TRENOW

In Love and War

PAN BOOKS

First published 2018 by Pan Books
an imprint of Pan Macmillan
20 New Wharf Road, London N1 9RR
Associated companies throughout the world
www.panmacmillan.com

ISBN 978-1-5098-2508-0

3 5 7 9 8 6 4 2

A CIP catalogue record for this book is available from the British Library.

Typeset by Palimpsest Book Production Limited, Falkirk, Stirlingshire
Printed and bound by CPI Group (UK) Ltd, Croydon, CR0 4YY

Visit **www.panmacmillan.com** to read more about all our books
and to buy them. You will also find features, author interviews and
news of any author events, and you can sign up for e-newsletters
so that you're always first to hear about our new releases.

This book is dedicated to the memory of
Lt. Geoffrey Foveaux Trenow of the London Rifle
Brigade, who received the Military Cross for bravery
and died in Flanders in September 1917. His body
has never been found.

A note on the historical inspirations for
In Love and War

In Love and War is entirely fictional, but was inspired by real people, places and events.

The battles of Flanders left hundreds of thousands dead, swathes of land devastated, villages and towns reduced to heaps of rubble. Yet within months of the Armistice in November 1918 thousands of visitors travelled to the area to take 'Tours to the Battlefields' organised by church groups and companies such as Thomas Cook. Hotels in nearby towns were swiftly reopened and guidebooks were rushed off the presses.

These tours were controversial: some thought them distasteful and disrespectful to the dead, but it is easy to understand the desperate desire of bereaved families to discover where their loved ones died and where their bodies lay. Even today, a hundred years later, the remains of those listed as 'missing, presumed dead' are being unearthed, to be given proper burials. My husband's uncle, to whom this book is dedicated, is still missing and the only record of his bravery and sacrifice is the inscription we discovered on the Menin Gate at Ypres.

Just a few kilometres from Ypres is the small town of Poperinghe, which remained just behind the battle lines and was the divisional headquarters of the Allied command for the area. It was here that the army chaplain, the Rev. Philip (Tubby) Clayton set up his 'Everyman's Club' to provide rest, recuperation and recreation for all soldiers, regardless of rank. Thanks to the work of the Talbot House Association this building has been reopened for visitors, and its exhibits shine a remarkable light on the lives of soldiers caught up in this most terrible war. More at www.talbothouse.be.

The work of Tubby Clayton continues with the international charity Toc H, which seeks to promote reconciliation through group and individual acts of service bringing disparate sections of society together. See more at www. toch-uk.org.uk.

Outside a cafe in the square at Poperinghe is a statue commemorating 'Ginger', the youngest daughter of its owners, who became something of a celebrity among the troops for her extraordinary resilience and cheerfulness. Both she and Tubby Clayton appear in the novel, as does Talbot House, but the events in the novel, the town of Hoppestadt, the hotel and the rest of its visitors and inhabitants are entirely my own invention and bear no relation to any people living or dead.

ACKNOWLEDGEMENTS

This book would not have seen the light of day without the clear-eyed advice of my editors at Pan Macmillan, Catherine Richards and Caroline Hogg, and my agent Caroline Hardman of Hardman & Swainson.

Bereavement and reconciliation are tough subjects to tackle and each day of writing reminded me to be grateful that we live in times of relative peace and that family and friends are not expected to risk their lives defending us. Thank you to you all, David, Becky and Polly Trenow, and my friends, for your unfailing encouragement and support.

Last but not least, my thanks go to John Hamill, our own battlefields tour guide, who helped us understand the full scale and complexity of the tragedy that unfolded in Flanders a hundred years ago.

If you want to find out more about how I wrote *In Love and War*, please visit www.liztrenow.com. You can also follow me on Facebook.com/liztrenow and on Twitter @LizTrenow.

When you are standing at your hero's grave,
Or near some homeless village where he died,
Remember, through your heart's rekindling pride,
The German soldiers who were loyal and brave.

Men fought like brutes; and hideous things were done;
And you have nourished hatred, harsh and blind.
But in that Golgotha perhaps you'll find
The mothers of the men who killed your son.

'Reconciliation', Siegfried Sassoon, 1918

LETTERS TO THE EDITOR

The Times, June 1919

Sirs,

I wish to express my shock and disgust upon reading in your newspaper a large advertisement for a highly reputable travel company promoting 'Tours to the Battlefields', five-day visits to the Ypres and the Somme areas of northern France and Belgium.

The very next day you carried a report on the same topic in which it was stated that several thousands of visitors have already undertaken tours provided by this company and other groups. It was accompanied by an illustration showing a group of ladies taking a picnic beside a battlefield that was identified with a signboard.

Am I alone in finding it utterly distasteful that these sacred places where so many of our brave men lie, having given their lives for King and Country, are now being desecrated by the spectre of commercial tourism?

Yours, &c.

Sirs,

Your correspondent claims to be shocked by the thought of the battlefields of the Somme and the Salient 'being desecrated by the spectre of commercial tourism'.

Having just returned from such a tour, I must protest that our visit was the very opposite of such a thing. My wife and I undertook this pilgrimage with the greatest of humility and with the sole purpose of honouring the sacred memory of our two sons, both lost to war, and it brought us great solace to visit the places where they died.

In addition, visitors like ourselves are bringing vital income to these areas which will help support the almost unimaginable task they face in rebuilding the towns and villages devastated by war.

The sacrifice of our brave men must never be forgotten. We believe that tours to the battlefields are one way of continuing to offer a vital reminder of the importance of striving for world peace, in decades and centuries to come.

Yours, &c.

I

RUBY

July 1919

It was like the strangest of dreams, standing here on the deck of the steamship, with the blue sky above, the sun glittering off the sea like a million diamonds. To her right, the grey slate roofs of the little town huddled almost apologetically beneath those magnificent cliffs, so much higher and more brilliantly white than she'd ever imagined.

She could scarcely believe that she was about to leave the shores of England for the first time in her life. It was not an adventure she had sought, much less desired. Why would she want to cross that treacherous stretch of water, the English Channel, to visit a country so recently torn apart by four years of terrifying, tragic events? She was still only twenty-one and she considered that her short life had been tragic enough, thank you very much, without inviting further danger and heartache.

What she most wanted, now that peace was here, was to live a quiet, ordered life, honouring his memory by working hard and trying to be kind to others who grieved like her.

There were plenty of them, for heaven's sake. No family had been left untouched by the tragedy. She would keep herself to herself, would never allow anyone else to break her heart. *It's the best I can do*, she wrote in her diary, *the only thing I can do, when he's given his future to make ours safe from the Hun. How else can we make sense of it all?*

So when, after serving tea that early June afternoon, his parents solemnly sat her down in one of their overstuffed armchairs and presented her with the Thomas Cook brochure, she'd thought at first it was some kind of a joke.

'*Tours to the battlefields of Belgium and France,*' she read out loud. 'Why on earth would anyone want to go and gawp at the place . . . ?'

She saw Ivy wince, and the words faded in her mouth. Her mother-in-law was as fragile as cut glass, unable to accept that her only child was dead. Never an outgoing person, her health had been frail for as long as Ruby had known the family, which seemed like forever.

When they'd first started courting, she thought it odd that he rarely invited her back to his house. 'Mam's a bit poorly,' he'd say, or, 'She complains that I make a mess.' Now, Ivy was a feeble whisper of a woman, barely of this world, with a ghost-like pallor from lack of fresh air. She spent much of her time in bed, or at least in her bedroom.

***

Ruby and Bertie met at school and stayed friends until one day, when they were walking home together, his hand crept out and took hers. They did not pause, and neither said a word; they walked on in silence. But the warmth of his touch surged like electricity up her arm and she knew, then, that she would be with this boy forever. *I love Bertie Barton!!* she wrote in her diary that night, framing the words with a wonky circle of red-crayon hearts. She wrote it again and again, on her pencil case, her school notebook, the shopping list, the inside of her wrist. No one ever doubted that Ruby loved Bertie, and vice versa.

And then, shortly after this, tragedy. Her father, foreman at a boat-building company in their small Suffolk town, was crushed by a marine engine falling from a crane. He died instantly. She couldn't remember much of the following days – only that her mother seemed to be barely there, so hollowed out, so wrapped up in her grief that she had nothing left with which to comfort Ruby.

All she can recall, now, is that Bertie was always by her side, holding her as she wept, making endless cups of tea with plenty of sugar and taking her for walks to distract her with his stories of nature: which bird sang which song, what flowers liked to grow in certain places and how their flowering was so carefully orchestrated with the arrival of certain insects; which set of holes in the ground were badger, fox or rabbit. In her memory he grew, almost over-night, from a schoolboy into a man.

Hugs and hand-holding soon turned into shy kisses, fur-tive explorations behind the garden shed and, before long, his declaration of love. One evening when they were alone in the house he went down onto his knee and presented her with a diamond engagement ring for which, he admitted rather shamefacedly, his father had loaned him the money.

Bertie became her entire world. She never looked at another boy and knew she never would. He claimed she was the only girl for him, forever. *Bertie and Ruby, forever!* she wrote in enormous letters on a fresh page in her diary, encircling the words with yet more hearts.

They were the perfect fit in every respect: physically quite alike with curly dark blond hair and freckly complexions – neither overly good-looking nor too plain but just 'normal', as he loved to say. A matching pair of normal. He said her brown eyes were like ginger wine; she said his reminded her of hazelnuts. They both loved dancing, walking and sharing silly stories or games of cards in the pub of an evening with their close-knit group of friends. And of course, they were going to live happily ever after. She could not imagine that things could possibly turn out otherwise.

When the recruitment notices were posted on the town hall noticeboard she pleaded with him not to join up. But then the pressure became too much, all the lads were enlisting, so she made him promise to return safe and sound. True to his word, he did return twice on leave from training. He was changed: he seemed to have grown several inches and was certainly stronger, physically, with muscles she had never noticed before. Bertie the joker had disappeared; he was more serious and thoughtful, and struggled to make conversation in larger groups. Indoors, he was fidgety and uncomfortable.

Only when walking in the woods and fields with Ruby did he appear to relax. And yet, however gently she posed her questions, he still refused to talk much about what they had been going through. Only at the very last moment did he let slip that this would be his final leave for a while: they were being posted. He would not say where.

They married on the Monday before he left, a hastily

convened affair at a registry office. Her mother had been saving for years for this moment and when she saw Ruby in her wedding dress she burst into tears. 'War or no war, you'll have a day to remember for the rest of your lives,' she said.

And what a day it had been: bright sunshine, puffy white clouds in the sky, the smiles of many good friends and such joy that she felt she might burst. Those two nights at the Mill Hotel afterwards – their honeymoon – were the happiest of her life. Although at first shy with each other, she discovered in herself a new world of passion, of intense bliss, that seemed to have been waiting in the wings for all her girlhood years. She felt complete.

They spent the daytime walking the water meadows, stopping to watch the mysterious brown fish languidly swimming against the flow of the river, listening to the larks calling overhead and, once, spying the brilliant blue flash of a kingfisher.

'I never want this to end,' she'd sighed, giddy with gladness. 'Please don't go, Bertie. I can't bear to be without you.'

'I'll be back soon, I promise,' he said, and she believed him.

Even when he left Ruby refused to worry, determined to remain strong and cheerful. That's what he had asked of her, after all. He was doing his duty for King and Country and he'd promised, hand on heart, that he would stay out of danger. Of course she would miss him, of course she cried herself to sleep. But he would come home before long, she knew that for certain. Bertie never broke his promises.

So when, five months later, she received a telegram, followed by army form B104-83, dated September 1917 – *We*

regret to inform you that your husband, Albert Barton, is noti-
fied as being missing in action at Passchendaele – she refused
to consider that he was anything other than just temporarily out of contact. She built a hasty wall around her heart,
not allowing herself to contemplate any other outcome. *He's*
promised to come home safe and he always keeps his promises,
she wrote. *He'll turn up, soon enough.* She could even hear
him: 'Just popped out for a fag, officer. Didn't miss me, did
you?' At school he'd always been in trouble for his cheek.

She would keep calm and carry on, just as the posters
exhorted, forcing herself to get dressed each day, to eat the
meals which her mother so solicitously cooked for her but
which, to her jaded senses, tasted like cardboard. On her
way to work she nodded to the regulars on the bus and
exchanged the usual pleasantries about the weather. Once
there, she applied herself as efficiently as ever, pasting a
smile on her face for her colleagues and customers, hoping
none of them would ask her about him.

Word got out, of course it did. He was the boss's son,
after all, at Hopegoods, the men's and women's outfitters in
the High Street where she worked in haberdashery. After
the first round of sympathetic comments her colleagues
learned not to mention his name. This sort of news had
become almost commonplace.

But as the months went by and they heard nothing further, Ruby's protective wall began to disintegrate. She sank
into a chasm of grief and guilt that she experienced as real,
physical agony, from which she could see no escape. She
seemed to be in the bottom of a well, hemmed in on all
sides by darkness, with only a glimmer of light too impossibly high to reach and too exhausting to climb towards.

There were days when she felt she simply could not carry on and sometimes, walking by the river, she imagined wading through the deep mud and giving herself up to the cold, heartless current. But she never found the courage. Her mother, still struggling with her own bereavement just a few scant years before, did what she could to comfort her daughter, but nothing eased the pain.

In the face of Ruby's persistent refusals to go out with them, their once close group of friends drifted away one by one, and gave up inviting her, or even calling round. She stopped writing in her diary because she could think of nothing to say. She felt like an empty shell, the kind you find on the beach, bleached and whitened in the salt and the sun, hard to imagine that it had once held a living creature inside. She could not remember the last time she had laughed.

But how could she go on living otherwise? Without Bertie she felt like half a person, not really alive at all. She could gain no enjoyment from any of the things they'd had fun doing together: going to the pub, to the cinema, to dances, for walks in the woods. She wore only black, or occasionally charcoal grey. He had made the ultimate sacrifice, she reasoned, so how else could she honour him? It felt insulting to his memory, somehow, to wear anything cheerful. *This is how my life will be from now until I die. It's only right.*

Her dutifully regular visits to his parents only served to underline their mutual loss. It twisted the knife in her heart to see his mother so devastated, his father so grimly stoic. Afterwards she would emerge exhausted, as though carrying the boulder of their grief, as well as her own. Leaving the overheated fug of their house, she would look up at the sky and inhale deeply, trying to draw strength from the fresh air. *One step at a time*, she'd say to herself, *one day at a time. This misery will soon ease.*

Of course it didn't, not really. The grief was still so intense it sometimes took her breath away, and at work she would have to hide in the ladies' toilet until she could compose herself. She discovered, by trial and error, how to present a brave face to the world. At first it was an unreliable mask, so brittle that it threatened to shatter at the slightest unguarded word or prompted memory but, as the days passed, and then weeks and months, the disguise became more durable until now, two years later, it had almost become a natural extension of her real self. In fact, she was no longer sure who her real self was.

What she did know, however, was that she would never betray his memory. Not again. It had been a moment of madness with a man she'd never met before and had never seen since, but the guilt of it burned her heart with a pain she felt would never ease.

She viewed these twice-weekly visits to her in-laws as her duty to Bertie, a duty she would bear for the rest of her life. She was still his wife, after all, always would be. Mr and Mrs Barton frequently referred to her as 'our daughter'. Who else did they have, now that he was gone?

But conversation was always sticky. Ivy seemed as insubstantial as thistledown, liable to blow away at the slightest wrong word. Albert senior was unchanging, gruff and uncommunicative, but at least he was usually solid and predictable. But she could never have foreseen this moment, this little Thomas Cook brochure, their faces so solemn and expectant.

'We've some good friends who went on one of those tours,' he said, and she began to relax. Perhaps he was just offering her the brochure by way of conversation. 'They've recommended it to us. They found their son's grave, you see. It was difficult, they said, but it gave them a great sense of solace.'

'Are you considering it for yourselves?' she asked.

'We've thought about it, but . . .' He inclined his head fractionally towards his wife, who was silently dabbing her eyes with a lacy handkerchief. 'We wondered whether' – he paused a moment – 'whether you might go on our behalf?'

They've gone barmy, Ruby thought to herself. *Me, travel to the battlefields, by myself? Wander around the trenches looking for signs of him, along with a load of gawping tourists?* It was not just crazy, it was slightly distasteful.

Albert was still talking: 'To pay our respects, as a family. As we don't have a grave, you know.'

Oh, she knew all right, only too well. Bertie's body had never been found. That was one of the hardest things: not knowing how he died, not being able to imagine where he lay. She still had nightmares, fuelled by photographs in the *Illustrated London News* that she could only look at through half-closed eyes, about his body entangled with those of others, entombed and rotting in a muddy crater somewhere near Ypres. She turned back to the brochure, but the sentences swam in her vision. She loved Bertie, of course she did, and always would. But surely this was a step too far?

How would she ever survive seeing, for herself, those places of horror?

'My dear?' Albert prompted. 'Would you be willing?'

'I really don't think I . . .' she began, and then ran out of words. Surely they could not be asking her to go, alone, to this terrible place?

'You hear these reports, you know . . .' Ivy whispered into the silence.

It was a familiar refrain. For a few months after the armistice, with almost every visit to the Barton house, a newspaper cutting would be produced: photographs of men who had miraculously returned, skeletal but alive, having escaped from prisoner-of-war camps and walked hundreds of miles back from Germany, or who had hidden out in the woods of Flanders for months and even years, afraid to show themselves as deserters. She would be invited to speculate on what might have happened to Bertie – that he might have been taken prisoner, or just been injured and helped by a Belgian family who were keeping him safe – and on the possibility that he might just turn up one day.

Even though she knew it was infinitesimally unlikely, after these conversations she sometimes dreamed of it: a man walking out of the smoke of battle towards her, his face blackened with dirt, his uniform torn and his cap missing. And then that face would break into his beloved smile and she would gasp, unbelieving, running towards him.

She would wake, crying, watching the dawn rise through the curtains, hearing the birds tuning up for the morning chorus: a few tentative tweets at first, followed by a single territorial blackbird and then the rest, joining the full-throated refrain. The cruel world was still out there, she was still here, alone, and he was dead. The only way to survive was to harden her heart.

As 1919 drew on, reports of miraculous returns became fewer and fewer until, almost to Ruby's relief, they seemed to dry up entirely. At least now, she'd hoped, perhaps Ivy would begin to accept that he wasn't coming home.

But no. Bertie's aunt Flo had been to a séance a few months ago and asked about him. The medium had spoken some platitudes – Ruby's interpretation, not Flo's – about how he would always be with them, and this had been understood – distorted, in Ruby's view – as an indication that he was somehow still on this earth. He'd been injured, apparently, but was now recovering in hospital. Ruby didn't believe a word of it. If he was in hospital, they'd have heard by now.

'We thought perhaps you might be able to find him,' Ivy now murmured, leaning forward and taking Ruby's hand. 'It would mean so much to me, my dearest. I don't think I have the strength to go on living without knowing whether he is still alive, somewhere. Or at least to know where he rests.'

It was a ridiculous idea and there was no way that Ruby was going to agree to go to Flanders on her own. She had to find some way of refusing, gently, so as not to cause them further distress. But for now, just to seem willing, she flicked through the brochure.

'It's on page fourteen, the itinerary we thought would be about right,' Albert said, leaning over to help her turn the pages. 'Not too expensive, but time to get a feel for the place, and visit the places you need to see.'

'*A Week at Ostend*,' she read. '*With excursions to Ypres, and the Belgian Battlefields. Leaving London every Tuesday, Thursday and Saturday. Fare provides for travel tickets (Third Class rail, Second Class steamer), seven days full board accommodation at a private Hotel, consisting of* café complet, *lunch, dinner and bed; electric trams to Zeebrugge and Nieuwpoort. All excursions accompanied by a competent Guide-Lecturer.*' A detailed daily itinerary followed. The price for 'Second Class Travel and Second Class Hotel' was thirteen guineas.

'But that's a fortune,' she said. 'And the extras . . .' She did a quick sum in her head – it would add up to nearly three months' wages.

'Don't worry, my dear, we've already agreed.' Albert seemed to read her thoughts. 'We shall pay for you, of course, and the pocket money besides.'

'I couldn't possibly—'

'I called round and spoke to your mother this morning,' he went on. 'It seemed only right to let her know that we were going to ask you and I wanted to reassure her on every detail.'

For a moment, Ruby felt betrayed. Why hadn't Mum mentioned it? Then she remembered that she'd come here straight from work and she had not been home since. 'But I've never been abroad before, let alone on my own,' she said. 'I don't speak French, or whatever it is they speak in Flanders.'

Albert senior straightened his back in the chair, assuming his most assiduous expression. 'We understand that it's a brave thing we're asking you to do for us, my dear,' he said. 'But you are a mature, responsible young woman and will be in excellent hands. Thomas Cook is a most respectable outfit; you will travel in a small group with a guide looking after you at all times.'

She looked up from the brochure again, meeting his gaze, so earnest, almost desperate. Only then did she fully understand that he was deadly serious. She felt suddenly light-headed, hardly able to believe this was happening.

'I've been in touch with them personally, to make sure,' he went on. 'I shall accompany you to London to ensure that you are met by their representative at Victoria station. You will have all meals provided and will be looked after in every way. My dearest,' he said, leaning so close that she could smell his pipe-tobacco breath, 'we would never have considered allowing you to go had it been otherwise. You are too precious to us.'

'May I have a few days to think about it?' she asked, forcing her lips into a smile. She would talk to her mother, get her on side, ask her to dissuade them from pursuing this crazy notion.

'Of course, my dear.' Albert rose from his chair to shake her hand. It was the closest to physical contact she'd had with him since that terrible day of the telegram, when he had actually put his arm around her.

He turned to Ivy. 'Shall we revive the pot, dearest?'

After his wife had left the room he whispered, 'I would go with you, Ruby, but you know she is too frail to be left alone for a whole week. And she is desperate for some kind of news, good or bad. Without that I truly believe that she will fade away.'

'Perhaps I could stay with Ivy, and you could go instead?' she said, more in hope than expectation.

'Of course I've suggested that too, but she insists she

cannot manage without me. I'm the only one who understands, apparently.' He brushed a hand through his thinning hair, a gesture which, for the briefest of moments, betrayed his exasperation, his exhaustion, the heavy burden he carried.

Then he leaned forward, confidentially. 'Besides, we thought that going for yourself might offer you some personal solace, my dear. Our friends insist that it is a highly reputable company and it would be perfectly safe for a young woman on her own. In fact, there were several single ladies on the tour with them. They will give us a personal introduction to the tour guide, a former army major and a most excellent man, they said.'

This was emotional blackmail, Ruby knew, but she was powerless to resist. 'You seem so strong, and this will mean such a lot to her,' he went on. 'You do understand, don't you?'

She didn't *feel* strong. She could get by, day by day, doing the familiar things. But travelling alone to Belgium? Visiting the battle fields?

His brown eyes reminded her so much of Bertie's, gentle and pleading. She was never able to refuse that look when he was alive and it felt as though refusing his father's request might be an insult to his memory, perhaps even a denial of his very existence. In their different ways his parents were pinning their hopes on her, and the last thing she wanted was to cause them even further suffering.

'We will none of us recover, of course. But perhaps if you are able to bring back something . . .' Albert shook his head, lost for words. 'A memento of some kind, I don't know what, but perhaps a postcard, a flower, anything – it might allow her heart to rest. We should be eternally grateful.'

'When would this be?' Ruby asked. 'I've promised Mum we'll have some days out in the summer. She wants to go to the seaside and Auntie May has offered to lend us her beach hut.'

'It would be only a week, and I thought early July might be best, when the crossing will be calm. I'll have a word with Mrs T.'

She felt an urgency to speak up now, before she left, or it would be assumed that she had agreed. But just then Ivy returned from the kitchen with the pot of tea, poured her a new cup and handed it across the table with such an entreating smile that Ruby could not bring herself to say anything at all.

That evening she talked to her mother. A few years after being so suddenly widowed, Mary had managed to create a new life for herself: taking in sewing to supplement Ruby's modest income, joining the Women's Institute and making wonderful cakes, digging over her husband's vegetable patch and learning how to grow potatoes, beetroot, beans and salad vegetables to save on food bills.

Over the months and years she had become Ruby's closest confidante, her best friend, the one person, she felt, who could truly understand what she was going through: the daily pain of bereavement.

'I don't want to go, Mum,' she said. 'It feels a bit distasteful to me.'

'They're very set on it, you know.' Mary handed her a mug of cocoa. 'Mr B. called round this morning. I was in a hurry getting out for the bus, but he would have his say. Ivy's convinced Bertie's alive somewhere.'

'It's that wretched sister of hers, the one who went to the

spiritualist.' Ruby sighed, pushing aside the milk skin with the back of a teaspoon.

'It's your decision, love. I told him it was up to you.'

'If I have to go, would you come with me?'

'How could we ever afford that?'

'We could ask him to pay for you, too.'

'Shush, girl, I won't have us being in their debt. And anyway, I can't take more time off work if we're going to take up Auntie May's offer of the beach hut.'

'I'm afraid, Mum. Of the mud, and those battlefields, and all. Of finding his grave, even.'

Mary put down her mug and leaned over to stroke her arm. 'You never know, it might help, my darling.'

Ruby wasn't convinced, although she was starting to accept that she had no option but to do her duty by Bertie's parents. She would have to wrap that protective carapace of unfeeling tightly around herself, to harden her heart and concentrate on surviving.

As the date approached she tried not to think too much about it, but found it impossible to dispel the nausea of fearful anticipation in her stomach.

❧

It was after the wedding that Ruby had taken the job as a sales assistant at Hopegoods. Albert had inherited the business from Ivy's father and Bertie had worked there too, 'learning the trade'. It was always assumed that he would take over when his father retired.

'I can't just stay at home kicking my heels, with you going off to France,' she'd said to him one day. 'You won't mind, will you, if I get a job? I have to feel I'm doing something for the war effort.'

He'd smiled at her then, the heart-melting smile that lit up his face and crinkled the corner of his eyes, and pulled her to him, kissing her on the forehead, which was where his lips naturally reached.

'Dearest Rube, you must do what you wish. When I get home, and we start having little ones, then you can be a lady of leisure.'

She applied to become a clippie on the buses in Ipswich, but the places were all taken. She was offered a job in the munitions factory but her mother vetoed it. 'It's so dangerous. And I couldn't bear to lose you too, my darling. Why don't you ask Mr Barton if he has any vacancies at the shop?'

So for the past three years she'd been working in haberdashery under its redoubtable manager Ada Turner, a widow known to all as Mrs T., who was wedded to her job and appeared to have no outside interests. She never spoke about any family, where she lived or what she did on her days off, but she knew by heart the reference number for every one of the two hundred colours of threads, and the right yarn for each purpose: general stitching, heavy duty work, overlocking and serging, embroidery, quilting and patchworking, and the beautiful luminescent pure silk threads for very fine work.

She could guide customers to the appropriate fabric for their garment, advise them what stiffener to use, or which was the correct zipper from the dozens that they stocked, and help them to choose from more than a hundred styles, varieties and sizes exactly the right type of button. They loved her. If she was away from the counter for any reason, customers would linger over the pattern books until she returned. When she arrived back and took over a transaction that Ruby had already started it made her feel very much like second best.

At first Mrs T. and the other staff were wary and even mistrustful of Ruby, the boss's daughter-in-law. But she'd kept her head down and worked diligently to gain their trust and respect. Initially she felt bamboozled by all the information she was expected to absorb but as her knowledge grew she discovered that she enjoyed the work and getting to know her 'regulars'. The books of dress patterns were so enticing she couldn't wait to start trying them out herself.

She dusted off her mother's old Singer and started with modest items at first, petticoats and aprons, but soon became more adventurous, making skirts and even, most recently, a jacket of green wool serge, nipped in at the waist with darts at back and front. It was the first time she'd worn anything other than black since those terrible days of 1916, but it was sombre enough, she thought.

She was wearing it now, here on the deck of the ship, along with the black skirt she'd made to match, and a cloche hat, purchased at the shop with her staff discount. Over her arm was the summer raincoat that Alfred senior had pressed into her hands a few days before. 'You might need this,' he said. 'It rains in Flanders.'

It was, she could tell from the label, from a top-quality manufacturer, the very latest style in charcoal cotton twill, more luxurious and certainly more costly than she'd ever hoped to own. How proud Bertie would have been, she'd thought to herself, glancing at her reflection in the shop windows on her way home from work, enjoying the unaccustomed swish of the fabric around her calves.

Paradoxically, it was moments like these, brief moments of unexpected happiness, that seemed to bring home her loss more profoundly, rocking her stability, threatening to crack the mask. What always followed, she discovered, was an even deeper sense of despair and hopelessness, when the ache of missing him twisted like a knife lodged in her heart.

It was more than two years since she'd last seen him and, although his dear face still smiled at her from the photograph by her bedside that she kissed every night, she was starting to lose the most important memories: the sweet-clean smell of his shaving soap, the deep timbre of his voice that seemed to vibrate through his chest, the bubbling joy of his laughter. It was as though her mind was protecting her by blurring her knowledge of him, making him somehow less real. It seared her with guilt that the man she had loved for most of her life was slowly fading from her memory; that she was alive, and he was not.

But not as much as it did for betraying him while he was alive.

Bertie's father was as good as his word. On the appointed day he collected her by taxi, purchased rail tickets for both of them to Victoria station and bought her a cup of tea and a sandwich. During the journey he was more animated than she'd seen him for several years, pointing out landmarks as they passed, discussing his plans for the development of Hopegoods now that the shadow of war was lifted, and dispensing advice about how she should comport herself while on tour, in particular how she must be wary of approaches from strangers. He seemed to relish this interruption to the daily routine, away from the responsibilities of the shop and his tearful, fearful wife.

At Victoria station he quickly spotted the Thomas Cook representative.

'I'm Major Wilson. Call me John. Good to have you aboard,' the man boomed, shaking her hand vigorously with a bone-crushing grip. Then, turning to Albert, 'Don't you worry, sir. I will take the greatest care of your daughter-in-law.'

The major was a bluff middle-aged man with a kindly smile, not tall but with a bearing that left you in little doubt that he'd brook no impertinence. It transpired that he had spent twenty years in the army including several years in the trenches before being invalided out with a gammy leg.

'Hardest thing I ever did,' he told Ruby as they waited for the others to arrive. 'Leaving the lads there to face the Hun without me. Broke my heart. The army don't want a cripple like me, no ruddy use at all, excuse my French.' He grimaced, tapping his knee. 'So when Cooks advertised for guides I saw my chance. Escorting people like your good self to the battlefields to pay their respects to their loved ones is the best way I can think of to honour my old mates. You have to make sense of it all somehow.

'It's your husband, isn't it? Died at Passchendaele? A young man, I assume?' he added, after a discreet pause.

'Twenty,' she said, trying to steady her voice. The major

was waiting, watching, expecting more. 'He was only out there nine months,' she added. 'We'd just got married. They never found him.'

'God bless you,' he said simply. 'It's a brave thing to do, to visit the battlefields. I admire your courage. But I can reassure you that most people find it brings them some peace.'

Despite her initial wariness, Ruby warmed to his down-to-earth approach. She had been so busy just trying to put one foot after another, to get through each day, one at a time, that she'd forgotten to look up. The war was over but there was no relief from the misery: men returning were injured, often unable to find work or housing. Newspapers talked of strikes and unrest, food was still rationed. What had it all been for, in the end? But if, as Major Wilson said, this trip would help her make sense of it all, then it would certainly be worth it.

The group was soon gathered – around ten people, mostly older than herself – and shepherded onto the Dover train in a carriage that reeked of cigarette smoke and orange peel. A great weight of almost visible sorrow seemed to hang in the air. She glanced around at her fellow travellers. Most were couples, so far as she could see, speaking in low voices to each other, or just sitting in silence, drawn and sallow-faced. A man with an eye patch sat with his pale waif of a wife. She caught a brief glimpse of another single woman, tall and rather glamorous with a glossy brown bob, like a movie star, in a flame-red jacket and matching hat with a flamboyant brim. Red? To the cemeteries? How inappropriate. Happily she did not seem to be in the same carriage.

Being in the group made her feel even more alone and she wished for the umpteenth time that she'd found the courage to refuse Alfred's request. She found herself sitting opposite a couple eager to talk about their two sons, killed a year apart, in the fields of Flanders.

'They gave their lives for King and Country,' the man said. 'That is our consolation.'

'We want to find their graves,' his wife added, her voice serrated with grief. 'So we can tell them how much we . . .' She tailed off, sniffing into her handkerchief.

'Don't trouble yourself so,' the husband chided, squeezing her arm. 'I told you we must be strong.' It was like being with Albert and Ivy all over again.

By the end of the journey, Ruby had learned everything about their boys. She didn't mind, only relieved that the couple seemed so utterly absorbed in their own loss and pride that they never asked her a single question. Or perhaps they were just being polite. She was afraid she might not be able to retain her composure if someone showed sympathy. *This is just between me and Bertie*, she said to herself.

Now, as she stood on the deck of the ship in the sunshine, her heart began to lift. The weeks of waiting and the almost paralysing anxiety had almost disappeared. The sky was an unblemished blue, the water only gently ruffled by the slightest of breezes. The bracing tang of seaweed and salt that she'd first inhaled on stepping from the train was now overlaid with reassuring smells of fresh paint and varnish.

The last time she'd been on the water was at the artificial lake in Christchurch Park, when she'd found the instability of the little rowing boat unnerving. But this ship felt so steady beneath her feet it was hard to believe they were not still on dry land. A huge grey and white seagull landed on the railing just ahead of her, cocking its head to one side, interrogating her with a piercing yellow eye.

'Hello, bird,' she said. 'I haven't got anything to give you, I'm afraid.'

Men far below on the quayside began to wheel the wooden gangways away from the side of the ship. Great coils of rope, thick as a man's arm, were slung from either end and hauled in by waiting groups of navvies. Their shouts were drowned by a sudden ear-splitting blast of the ship's horn that seemed to reverberate through her body. The gull flew off, leaving a white splat on the high polish of the hand rail.

A single downy feather fluttered to the deck and she picked it up, turning it in her fingers, marvelling at its del-icacy. But then she recalled, at the start of the war, reading reports of women handing out feathers like this, shaming men into joining up. She shivered and dropped it quickly. She'd rather Bertie had been called a coward and come home with one of these than with his call-up papers. At least he'd have been alive.

Almost imperceptibly at first, and then more quickly, the ship moved away from the dockside. Beside her, fellow travellers waved to their friends gathered below, calling farewells. They gathered speed swiftly, passing through the mouth of the docks and into the open sea. As the breeze picked up most of the passengers retired below, but Ruby was determined to watch the land as it receded. This would have been Bertie's last view of England, and she owed it to him to look until it disappeared. What would have been in his mind, that day? Was he worried or frightened? Did he wonder when he would get to see those white cliffs again?

Or perhaps his mood was buoyed by the excitement of the journey, of the new sights and sounds. He'd have been with his mates, after all; they would have been jollying each other along and cracking jokes, of course. At school they'd called him the class clown. It cheered her to imagine how the other men would have come to love his impertinence, his generosity – always sharing his fags – and how he'd have made them laugh.

It was late afternoon and the intense whiteness of the chalky cliffs, illuminated by the sun, formed a wide luminous band, almost unearthly, along the edge of the land separating grey sea and blue sky. She stood, transfixed, as the ship pulled steadily away.

'Quite a sight, ain' it?'

The voice, with its unmistakeable American twang, made Ruby jump. She'd thought herself alone on the deck. She looked up into the eyes of the tall movie-star woman she'd observed getting onto the train. Bright scarlet lips smiled widely to reveal the largest, whitest teeth Ruby had ever seen.

'Alice Palmer. Pleased to meet you.'

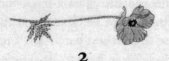

2

ALICE

Alice was weary. The transatlantic crossing had been peaceful enough but since docking in Southampton she'd been staying with her friend Julia, daughter of the American ambassador to London. Delighted to be together again, they'd gossiped late into the night, every night.

Despite the arrival of peace, London appeared so dejected and down at heel that Alice had found her own mood darkening. Even in the height of summer the weather here was more like winter in her native Washington: grey, cold and often rainy.

Her travel wardrobe of bright colours seemed out of place; most of the women they saw in the streets were still wearing drab, pre-war fashions, usually in brown or black. She was shocked to see war veterans reduced to selling matches on the street, and gaggles of haggard men with placards demanding the 'homes for heroes' they'd apparently been promised by the British prime minister. Her stay had been even more wearisome since she and Julia had curtailed planned sight-seeing jaunts, terrified of catching the Spanish influenza that had already claimed thousands of lives.

Although at the American embassy there were no such shortages, she was horrified to learn about the strict food rationing ordinary people had to endure. Even now, eight months after the armistice, just a few ounces of meat and butter were allowed each week along with horrible white bread that tasted of dust and barely any fruit or fresh vegetables. *We have no idea, back home, how much this little country has suffered and continues to do so*, she wrote her parents.

She loved Julia's company, but Alice was impatient to be on her way to Belgium, to the place where her kid brother, Sam, was last seen. There had been no reports of his death, nor even where he had been fighting; he had simply failed to return. She felt quite sure that, had he been killed, someone would have found a way to let them know. Somehow, somewhere, she reasoned, he must be alive. Perhaps he was too ashamed to return home, having joined up against their parents' wishes. Or his mind had been so shaken by the experience of war that he felt he could not face 'normal' life ever again; she'd read about people like that.

Her father had battled to trace his son, almost obsessively, for two years, using his considerable political clout as a congressman to pull every string he could with the Canadian authorities. But they claimed to have no record of a Sam Palmer. Was there any possibility that he might have signed up under another name, they asked? It wasn't unheard of for Americans to 'cover their tracks', they said, and Alice knew they were probably right.

'Surely when he registered they'd have asked him for some kind of identity documents? They're just being slack,' her father had railed. But after every avenue seemed to hit a brick wall he'd buried himself in politics once more. Her mother, usually so sociable and cheerful, had fallen into a well of hopelessness, refusing to accompany her husband to official events, even declining invitations from friends. She ate like a bird, becoming alarmingly thin, and barely left the house these days.

But Alice found that she couldn't let it go. The terrible truth was that, the night before he left for Canada, Sam had confided his plan to her. Shocked and disbelieving, she'd pleaded with him not to go. 'For goodness' sake, Sam, are you crazy? Don't you know what it's like over there? You could get killed.'

'I *have* to do it. For Amelia,' he'd replied, his jaw set in determination. 'I'll keep safe, honest. The Canadians aren't in the thick of it anyway. It's just that if I don't go, I won't forgive myself. We can't let those bloody Krauts get away with it.'

They'd argued long into the night about the rights and wrongs of the war, and whether the US had a moral duty to join it. In the end he just clammed up and she had to accept that there was no hope of dissuading him. Before they retired to bed, he made her vow, using their old child-hood oath – 'keep the lie or hope to die' – that she would never tell their folks. 'They can't stop me anyway 'cos I'm over eighteen, but just let me get a head start, won't you?' he pleaded. 'I'll write when I get there.'

In the morning, he was gone.

She'd kept the promise, but had been hugely relieved when his letter arrived, forwarded from an address in Ottowa, releasing her from the burden of his secret. It was the only one they ever received. She had it with her even now, safely hidden in a side pocket of her handbag.

Dearest people, it read. *I write to let you know that I am safe and well, happy at last to be here with the Canadians in Flanders, doing my small bit to fight the Hun.*

Forgive me for the pain I have caused you all. I could not share my plans because I knew you would try to stop me, and I am determined to do this for my dearest Amelia.

I simply could not go on living with myself while that idiot Wilson prevaricated. The Brits and the French and the Belgians are fighting valiantly, but we really do need US supplies and soon. Please do what you can, Pa, to make them see sense.

I'm on R&R at the moment behind the lines in a place they call Hops. You guessed it, they're brewers around here! There are kind-hearted people helping us, and we've got good beer and enough food. It's a little haven in a hellish war. So you mustn't worry about me. I promise to stay safe and be home with you all soon.

Best love to you all, Sam.

When the war ended and as the months passed he failed to return, she could not shake the thought that she should, somehow, have stopped him. *If only I'd told Pa, that very day, he'd have done something, anything*. But what could they have done, when Sam was so determined that he had covered his tracks completely, and had almost certainly signed up under a false name?

Even so, in her darkest moments Alice felt herself entirely responsible for the death of her little brother, her beloved only sibling. It haunted her, filled her dreams. The only way of assuaging her conscience would be to find out what had happened to him, and that meant going to Flanders.

'Over my dead body,' her father had fulminated. 'I suppose you imagine that you'll just bump into him on a street corner? It's not Washington, Alice. The whole of northern France and Belgium are one great muddy mess. You've seen it for yourself in the papers. Towns are destroyed, the people are still starving, crime is rife, transport simply isn't working. I will not let my daughter put herself through such danger and hardship. And that's final.'

She took her plea to her mother. 'If your father says no, it's a no,' she said. 'And anyway, what's Lloyd got to say about this plan of yours?'

Her engagement to Lloyd had been the talk of the town. The dashing young pilot with one of the pioneering US Air Force units was due to inherit millions as the only son of a well-established banking family. He was the most eligible bachelor of her generation.

She'd set her sights on him long ago, as a teenager, watching with awe as he vanquished the reigning tennis champion with a display of athleticism and power that left the spectators sighing with admiration. For Alice, it wasn't so much his skill on the court that caught her attention, rather the way his long tanned legs seemed to glisten in the sunshine.

They began dating just after she'd returned from France

nursing a broken heart. Three years later, when she'd begun to fear the day would never come, he proposed. Photographs of the happy couple featured widely in society magazines, a lavish wedding was planned, and she genuinely believed herself the luckiest girl in the whole United States.

The accident changed everything, of course. Lloyd lost a leg after his plane flipped over twice on landing, and after that he'd become bitter and pessimistic, claiming that his life was over; he would never play tennis again or sail his yacht, and his career as an airman was finished. He would rather die than spend his life in a wheelchair at a desk in the bank.

Alice watched on helplessly as he wallowed in self-pity, wondering where their love had gone. Although she considered it more than once, breaking off their engagement was simply not an option. How could she, when he was already so maimed, so broken? How could she cause such heartache to her parents even as they grieved for their only son? It would cause such a society scandal; she would be forever tarred as the hard-hearted bitch who had deserted her brave hero in his darkest hour. Her father would never forgive her for bringing shame to the family and casting a smear on his political career.

So she'd gritted her teeth and set herself the task of bringing Lloyd back to life. It worked: over the following months he became more cheerful, more outgoing and optimistic, more like the man she had fallen for in the first place. All was well, she persuaded herself, she loved him and they would marry and live happily ever after. He was determined to walk her back down the aisle unaided by crutches, so they had postponed the wedding until he could be fitted with an artificial limb.

When she mooted the idea of going to Flanders to look for Sam, Lloyd had reacted with disbelief. 'On your own, to Europe?' he gasped, grey eyes startled in that handsome, strong-jawed face. 'When the war's been over barely six months?'

She stroked his hair and rubbed the back of his neck, which always seemed to calm him. 'I love my brother almost as much as I love you, my darling. Pa's done all he can to find him, but he's got nowhere. It's my only chance – and the longer we leave it, the colder the trail will get. At least that's how I see it.'

'Why can't your parents go instead?'

'Pa doesn't see any point, thinks he's done all he can. Besides, there's a little thing called an election next year.' The Republicans had been running around like headless chickens since Roosevelt had died and, what with the riots and economic problems, her father had been working all hours in the Capitol.

Lloyd brushed away her ministering hand. 'I'm not happy, Alice. It's a crazy idea. Wait till I'm out of this damn thing' – he thumped the arm of the wheelchair – 'and I'll come with you. I can't let you go abroad on your own. Who knows what kind of dangers you might have to deal with.'

'You forget I've been to Europe before, Lloyd. My year at the Sorbonne – we went to Bruges and Brussels and Ostend. I speak French, remember? Anyway, I'll be staying at the embassy in London each side, and the trip to Belgium is an organised tour with a very respectable company. They'll look after me.'

She showed him the Thomas Cook brochure Julia had sent her, opened at the page with the description that she now knew almost by heart: *Superior tour to the battlefields of Flanders: A Week at Ostend with excursions to Ypres, and the Belgian Battlefields. Fare provides for first class travel, seven days full board accommodation at a superior private Hotel, consisting of café complet, lunch, dinner and bed; electric trams to Zeebrugge and Nieuwpoort. All excursions accompanied by a fully qualified Guide-Lecturer.'*

He read it and harrumphed some more, and she decided to drop it for the moment. *Let him think about it, he'll come round.* In the meantime she telegraphed Julia.

A week later, at a candlelit table in his favourite restaurant – its wide doorways and no steps made it one of the few they could visit with his wheelchair – she showed him Julia's reply: PA SAYS THOS COOK VERY REPUTABLE COMPANY AND TOURS POPULAR STOP SEE YOU SOON JULIA STOP

He read it, frowning. 'You're not still on about that trip to Flanders?'

She nodded. 'Julia's father's a diplomat, remember? He'd be the first to warn us if he felt it wasn't perfectly safe.' She pinned on her most winning smile, the one she'd practised in the mirror, the one that seemed to work every time. 'I really want to go, sweetie. I couldn't forgive myself if I didn't do everything possible to find Sam, and this seems like the last chance.'

When she saw his face soften she knew she had won.

'Lloyd's fine with me going to Flanders,' Alice told her parents now. 'I'll only be gone a couple of weeks, after all. He'd have come with me but for the physio.'

'I don't see why you can't wait till after you're married,' her father grumbled. 'Then you could travel together.'

'I have to go *now*, don't you see? The longer we leave it . . .' She hesitated. Best not to harp on about Sam, in front of her mother. 'Anyway, we've decided to have a proper honeymoon, perhaps in the Caribbean, or Florida, somewhere nice and sunny where he can relax and get really well.'

She handed her father the Thomas Cook brochure. 'Look, you can see for yourself. These tours are all above board and very respectable, Julia's father says. And he should know.'

'Seventeen guineas! That's nearly ninety bucks just for that week, let alone the cost of the transatlantic steamer, which is not going to give you much change from a hundred. And with your wedding next year? How in heaven's name can you expect us to afford that?'

'I am not expecting *you* to afford it,' Alice replied. 'I have my own savings, and Lloyd's promised to help. I will stay with Julia in London so there won't be any hotel costs.'

'What do you say, Mother? We can't let her go, can we?'

Her mother shrugged. Her daughter was never one to accept compromise, even as a small child. 'If she thinks it's our only chance of finding out what happened, then at least we'll know we've done everything we can.'

'Well, I disagree,' he said. 'In my view it would be a scandalous waste of time and money. In the chaos of that country you'll never find anything. Far better to concentrate on tracking him through diplomatic routes.'

'But you said yourself it's like hitting your head against a brick wall.'

'Don't answer back, young woman. You're over twenty-one now and I can't stop you. But when you return without a dime to your name don't come whining to me about paying for your wedding.'

Alice didn't really care. She was going to Europe, no matter what. He'd come round in a few days. It wasn't only her desire to find out what had happened to Sam and assuage her conscience – if possible, to bring him home.

There was something else. Another thing, a crazy notion that made her heart race just thinking about it. She'd shared it with no one except Julia.

Hey, it'll be great to see you, her friend had written. *I need cheering up. London is sooo gloomy these days. I can understand why you think that going to Flanders is your only chance of finding Sam. They say it's still quite a mess over there, and people turn up every day. You never know. At least you will have done all you can.*

Boy, what a cheeky notion to get in touch with D. I ought to tell you off, but secretly I'm a bit envious. I'm sure he should be able to help you with local leads to find Sam. But don't for heaven's sake fall in love with him all over again. Promise?

Alice had imagined that travelling alone would give her a sense of freedom; she had romantic visions of chatting to strangers or reading in deckchairs, undisturbed by social or family expectations. Her life in Washington was so packed with commitments: her mother supported at least a dozen charities and because her husband was usually too busy with his politicking she expected her only daughter to accompany her to endless cocktail parties, dinners and launch events. Recently, her mother's frequent 'headaches' meant that she'd been increasingly required to attend these functions alone.

At first it was fun – Alice developed a taste for exotic cocktails and sophisticated dishes – but after a few years the novelty wore off and she began to crave something more demanding than tennis tournaments and bridge matches to fill her days. Some of her girlfriends, after leaving school, had taken jobs as teachers or personal assistants to chief executive officers, and their excited chatter filled Alice with envy. Of course, once they were married they would have to give it all up, but that didn't stop her longing to share their few years of fun: to meet people with interesting ideas about the world, to earn her own money, to have a life of her own.

'Absolutely no,' her father had said. 'I won't have a daughter of mine going out to work. People will think we're short of money.' That was absurd, of course. Her mother's handsome inherited fortune ensured that they lived in some luxury in a beautiful brownstone in the historic village of Georgetown. Pa was so old-fashioned, clinging to the belief that women should stay at home and devote themselves to good works.

But the reality of the transatlantic crossing was disappointing; in fact, it was rather lonely. The ship turned out to be half empty, her fellow passengers mostly dull couples and even drearier businessmen. It was nothing like her first trip to Europe, six years ago. She'd been eighteen, just out of high school, and Julia – whose diplomat father had recently been transferred from Washington to London – was about to spend three months at the Sorbonne to learn French.

'Come to Paris with me!' she'd said. 'We'll have a ball.'

The ball had started the very first evening on board ship as several handsome young men vied for their company on the dance floor, and on the quoits deck the following day. It continued in London which, after a whirl of cocktail parties, they declared to be the most glamorous city in the world – until they discovered Paris.

At the Sorbonne, both she and Julia became infatuated with one of their teachers, whom they thought the sexiest man they'd ever encountered. Floppy-haired, casually dressed, moody and usually late, he smoked untipped French cigarettes incessantly. His habit of slowly, sensually removing small strands of tobacco from a pouting lower lip would send them into paroxysms of delight.

Fortunately their attentions were soon drawn instead to a group closer to their own age – a multilingual band of English, American, French and German students. They gossiped, argued and flirted late into the night in street cafes, nursing expensive *chocolats chauds* or half-litres of pale fizzy beer. The girls swooned over a dark-eyed Belgian architecture student called Daniel, who seemed more articulate and well-read than the rest. Romances flared and faded. At the end of the course they all wept in each other's arms and swore to keep in touch.

Alice returned to America and shortly afterwards, in

August, Britain declared war against Germany, which put a stop to their letters. The promised reunion had never happened.

✿

Now, as she watched the white cliffs of Dover slowly disappearing into the horizon, Alice found herself smiling at the memories. What a different world that was, all now lost.

The cross-Channel ship, so much smaller than the transatlantic liner, was starting to pitch in the open sea. A stiff breeze whistled around the deck, threatening to unseat her hat despite the three pins she'd skewered into it.

Nearly everyone else had sought shelter below and Alice was about to do the same when she spied a drab-looking figure at the rear of the deck. It must be the plain-faced girl from the train from London whom she'd imagined to be the daughter of the couple she'd sat with in second class. Either way, she was most definitely a Brit: you could tell by the long skirt, the sallow complexion and that mousy hair dragged back beneath a black felt cloche like something her old nanny would have worn.

She was alone, clasping the railings with a white-knuckled hand while trying to hold down her hat with the other. Alice made a passing remark about the view and the girl turned, wide-eyed with surprise.

'Alice Palmer. Pleased to meet you.' She held out her hand in greeting.

At first she seemed flustered, but then gathered herself. 'Hello. I'm Ruby. Ruby Barton.' As she went to return the handshake her hat lifted and blew away, bowling down the deck like a leaf in an autumn storm.

'Holy cow!' Alice shouted, running after it. A flock of seagulls wheeled overhead, mocking her. The hat flew on, rising on the wind. *Any minute now*, she thought, *it will fly off into the sea, I'll have to apologise to the poor kid and she'll be bare-headed for the rest of her journey*. Then, just as she'd feared all was lost, the hat snagged against the canvas of a life raft and, with a final sprint, she managed to reach out and grab it.

'That was a close call,' she hollered, waving it lasso-style around her head.

The girl was right behind her. 'Thank you so much. I'm an idiot.'

'Here, borrow one of my hat pins,' Alice said, pulling one from her own head.

'No, really.'

'Go on. I've got a couple more.'

'If you insist. That's very kind. I never thought. It's my first time at sea.'

'You never went on a ship before?'

The girl shook her head.

'First time out of the UK?'

'Afraid so.'

'Was that your folks you were with on the train?'

She looked confused.

'Sorry, I mean your parents.' It was a constant mystery to Alice how English people frequently failed to understand the language they'd invented.

'Oh no. They're just other people on my tour.'

'Thomas Cook?'

The girl nodded.

'Gee, I'm with them, too. To Ostend and the battlefields? You travelling on your own, then?'

Another sharp gust threatened to dislodge their hats. 'What do you say we go below and get a coffee or something?'

The girl was hardly likely to be the most scintillating company, Alice thought to herself as they made their way unsteadily to the stairs which, she knew, would bring them to the first-class lounge. But at least she was close to her own age, and travelling alone. It was better than having no one to talk to.

At the entrance to the lounge Ruby held back. 'I can't go in there,' she whispered. 'I don't have a first-class ticket.'

'Don't worry,' Alice said. 'You're with me, aren't you? They never check. The other lounges are nothing like so nice. C'mon, I'm starving and it'll be hours before we get to the hotel for supper. What do you fancy?'

Alice insisted on paying for their drinks (coffee for her, tea for Ruby) and a plate of buttered toasted tea cakes, and watched her companion swallow them down like a starving child. Even though she looked barely old enough to be out of school, Alice noted the wedding ring.

'Do you want to tell me why you're on this tour?' she asked. 'I'm guessing it's not because you want to see the beauties of Bruges, or sun yourself on the beach at Ostend?'

The girl looked down into her lap and there was an uncomfortable pause.

Oops. Put my big feet in it again. 'Sorry, I shouldn't have asked. My English pals are always telling me I'm just too forward.'

Silence fell again. *Jeez, this was going to be hard work.*

'Would you like to know why I'm on the trip?'

At last, a response. The girl looked up with the wisp of a smile which Alice took for a yes. She took out the photograph of her brother, taken on his eighteenth birthday, five years ago. How young he looked, how happy-go-lucky, with Amelia by his side and not a care in the world. It seemed like a different age.

'He's very handsome. Was he your . . . ?' Ruby hesitated, flustered, her cheeks flushing. 'I mean, is he . . . ?'

'Oh no,' she said quickly. 'It's my kid brother Sam, with his girlfriend. Soon after this photo was taken she travelled to Europe to visit friends and see the sights, you know, and then the war started and she had to get home. The Germans blew up her ship, the *Lusitania* – you heard about that?'

A nod.

'We all thought the US would join the war after that but our great president dithered and poor Sam was devastated; he just didn't know what to do with himself. She was such a beautiful girl and he was dotty about her; we could none of us quite believe she'd gone. He quit his college and started talking about going to fight the Germans. He told me he felt there was nothing else to live for. Of course, Pa was right against it and my ma, well, she was having fits at the very idea. I guess they hoped Sam would get over it, and he did go quiet about it for a month or two. But then he just left home. Signed up with the Canadians, under a false name, we think.'

'How terrible,' Ruby said at last. 'When did you last see him?'

'Christmas 1916.'

'And you haven't had a word since then?'

'Only this.' Alice pulled out the leather wallet in which the precious letter was safely stored.

'Here, you can read it.'

The girl hesitated. 'Are you sure?'

'The more people know about him, the more chance I have of finding him, that's what I reckon.'

Ruby took the envelope and pulled out the single page of lightweight paper, reading quickly. 'Golly. He sounds so brave,' she said, carefully refolding and slipping it into the envelope. 'But if he really did sign up under a false name, wherever would you start looking?'

The sympathetic gaze of the girl's dark brown eyes – eyes which, now Alice looked at them properly, seemed to contain a world of sadness – brought a pang of self-doubt, a realisation of the ambitious, perhaps even hopeless task she'd set herself.

'All we have is that mention of Hops. I've done some research: it's what the soldiers used to call a little village close to Ypres called Hoppestadt. There must be people who . . .' Unaccountably, a lump in her throat blocked the rest of the sentence.

'I'm sure you're right,' Ruby jumped in. 'There are all kinds of reports about men still turning up safe and sound. Men who got stuck there, or got a bit lost, for one reason or another.'

'Even if I don't find him alive, at least I'll feel I have done everything I can,' Alice managed to finish.

'Do you want to tell me about him?' Ruby asked gently.

The girl was a good listener, sitting silent and attentive

as Alice poured out her memories of Sam, of their child-hood, the holidays by the lake, how she'd taught him to read, to ride his bicycle, the adventures they'd had together in their teens. Talking about him lifted her spirits. It made him feel real again. He must, surely, still be alive, some-where in this land which they were, even now, fast approaching?

'But you haven't told me anything about yourself,' she said finally. 'Why are *you* going to Flanders?'

Just then, the tannoy boomed, announcing their immi-nent arrival.

'Another time,' Ruby said.

'Okay, let's go up on deck. Get our first look at Belgium.'

As the ship drew closer to land the excited chatter of the passengers faded and then ceased altogether. As it came into view the once-grand seaside resort of Ostend, playground of the fashionable, wealthy and aristocratic, appeared almost abandoned. The beach was still broad and sandy, but littered with so much barbed wire, blocks of concrete and piles of rusting machinery that it was almost unrecognisable.

Alice had visited once before, that summer six years ago, when the sands were busy with families picnicking, chil-dren sitting under umbrellas, old men reading newspapers in deckchairs, young men and women playing beach tennis and, at the water's edge, curious wheeled huts called bath-ing machines from which people emerged down short ladders into the cold grey sea. The seafront was lined with grand hotels and cafes, their terraces shaded by brightly striped awnings, where you could while away a few hours taking coffee, cream *gateaux* and delicious *glaces à la vanilles*, watching the world go by.

All this had gone.

From a distance, the promenade along the beachside had appeared relatively undamaged, but now they could see that many of the buildings were derelict, ripped by shell holes. The old royal casino, once such a feature of the seafront with its curving facade and high arched windows, was almost crumbled away.

'Cripes, it looks like a ghost town,' she whispered.

❦

Their hotel, a grey, gloomy building in a side street set back from the seafront, appeared mercifully undamaged but the lobby, brown-carpeted and full of heavy, overbearing furniture, did little to reassure.

Upstairs in her suite, Alice paid off the bellboy and looked around. The two rooms were large enough and overlooked a street lined with plane trees, but that was about the best that could be said. The place smelled fusty and unaired, the upholstery and curtains were faded and threadbare, the bedroom dark and dominated by an enormous carved wooden wardrobe. In the corner a tap dripped, leaving a brown stain trailing down the side of a chipped white basin. 'I thought this was supposed to be a superior hotel,' she muttered to herself.

After supper they were summoned to the lobby by Major Wilson for what he called a 'briefing'. It was the first time she'd had the opportunity to take a good look at the rest of the group. Everyone seemed weary and anxious. Apart from her and Ruby, most were middle-aged except for a man in his early twenties with an eye patch and a vicious scar across his cheek whom they'd seen seated on his own at dinner.

As they waited for a few stragglers to arrive, she caught his eye and gave what she hoped was a friendly smile. She felt sorry for him: he appeared so downcast. How tragic that a young man who'd obviously once been rather handsome should be so dreadfully maimed. He looked up, distracted by something behind her: a young woman who arrived, flustered, apologising for being so late. She took a seat next to the eye-patch man and he whispered to her, solicitously. *Must be his wife. Thank goodness he has someone to love him, with that disfigurement.* She was petite and pretty, with shoulder-length curly hair the colour of ginger ale (Alice remembered her ma once referring to it as 'strawberry-haired') and freckles dotting her nose and cheeks, but her skin so transparently pale it was hard to believe any blood lay beneath.

Major Wilson stood before them stiff-backed and sharp-eyed, as though he were about carry out a kit inspection.

'Welcome, all,' he started. 'I trust that you enjoyed your supper, and that your rooms are comfortable enough?' There was a mild murmur of approval to which Alice did not contribute. 'As you probably noticed when we arrived,' he went on, 'Ostend was badly damaged by the fighting and I hope you will understand that hotel accommodation is a little thin on the ground at the moment, so please forgive any minor shortcomings in the provision.'

'I'm sure you are tired from your journey so I will not

detain you this evening with too much detail about our itinerary for the next few days. Tomorrow we leave for Ypres and the battlefields. Nine o'clock sharp, please. The weather is set to be fair, but bring rain garments and stout shoes just in case. We will stop for breaks and lunch, returning to the hotel late afternoon, in time for you to change for dinner.'

'You are all aware, of course, that this is not a tourist trip and you are not tourists. Some of the places we visit and the sights we see may be distressing but please be assured that I shall be on hand at all times to help and support you, and answer your questions. It may be more useful to think of yourselves as pilgrims, here to honour the sacrifice made by our soldiers and by the unfortunate citizens of these devastated lands. It is our duty to pay witness, and I know that you will be respectful at all times.'

He looked around the room.

'Any questions?'

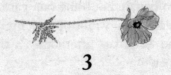

3

MARTHA

Martha was dreaming of food: soft sweet *challah* bread, made with real white flour, not the dry, tasteless *Kriegsbrot* filled out with plaster and sawdust. In her dream, the bread was mouth-wateringly aromatic and warm from the oven, its plaits shiny with egg glaze. There was another smell, too: coffee on the stove, the proper kind, not the *ersatz* variety made from barley, and on the table a jug of full-cream milk fresh from her brother-in-law's farm, from the cows she'd once known by name. She sensed the comforting presence of her husband Karl by her side and opposite them, with grins splitting their faces, their two sons, Heinrich and little Otto.

'Tuck in, boys,' she said.

A hand shook her shoulder and reality flooded back with its familiar ache of loss, hunger and despair. There was no family as she'd once known it, no *challah* bread, no coffee, no comforting candlelight.

'Mama! I need to pee,' Otto whispered.

'Can't you hold it?'

'No! I'm desperate.'

They were locked in a small, windowless cell lit by a single dim bulb. Scarcely eight feet square, with an oppressive smell of stale cigarette smoke and damp concrete, it had no furniture save the hard wooden bench on which she had, after many hours, succumbed to a restless sleep.

The train had arrived at the Belgian border around six o'clock in the evening. The connecting service would take just a couple more hours to Ypres and she had calculated that there would be plenty of time to find somewhere to stay, have a meal and make arrangements for their visit to the cemetery the following day.

But no one seemed to have informed the border guards about the Treaty of Versailles and the new freedoms of travel. As soon as they showed their German passports, Martha and Otto were roughly marched to a concrete building encircled with barbed wire and protected by armed men. There, they were told, they would have to wait to be interviewed by the head of the border security services before they could be issued with a pass into Belgium. They were led into this room and told to wait. The key clicked in the lock.

'Are we in prison, Mama?' Otto whispered. To survive during the harsh years of the war he'd learned to conceal his emotions. But with a mother's intuition she knew, just from the slightest expression, how much he was suffering inside, and he still turned to her for comfort at times like this. Having seen sights and lived through hardships no child should endure, he had a particular terror of men in uniform.

'No, they just want to make sure we have the right papers and we will be on our way,' she said, trying to sound reassuring.

Half an hour went by. She heard the whistle of a train and the rumble of its wheels moving off into the distance and knew that they had missed their connection. They would probably have to wait until morning for the next one. Another hour passed. They shared the last provisions in her bag: a crust of bread and a boiled egg. At last, Otto fell asleep on her shoulder. She laid him down gently along the bench and then curled herself up, as best she could, head to head. She had not expected to sleep.

Now, as she levered herself into a sitting position, every bone and muscle seemed to ache. Once upon a time she could have slept anywhere but, at forty-five, her body felt too old for hard wooden benches.

'I really need to go, Ma.'

'Knock on the door, the guards will come.' Her mouth was so dry. What would she give for that coffee she'd been dreaming of?

Otto knocked and called, shaking the door handle, but there was no response.

She stood stiffly and went to his side, calling through the keyhole in her best French. 'Please, sirs, I beg you, let my son use the toilet.'

When there was still no reply she took off her shoe and pounded the metal door. It resounded hollowly through the building, and she began to fear they had been abandoned. But at last they heard footsteps and the door was unlocked. Otto was roughly manhandled outside to do his business on the ground, and then returned with the threat that if he didn't shut up they would place him in a separate cell.

'How long do you think we will have to wait now?'

There was no way of telling in this windowless, airless

room whether it was night or day. 'Could you see the dawn?'

'The sky was pink.'

'It'll be a couple of hours more, at most. They will come to check our papers and we can be on our way.' She wished she felt as confident as her words sounded.

Somewhere out there, over the border, was her precious elder son, Heinrich. In her pocket she clutched the small green leather box containing the medal his great-grandfather had been awarded for bravery. Her husband Karl had pressed the box into her hands in his last hours. By that time his skin was already tinged with the deep lilac colour that, everyone knew by now, meant recovery from the deadly influenza was unlikely.

'Take this to Heiney,' he'd croaked. 'If I die, you must take it to his grave without me. It belongs with him. Promise me you will do this?'

They had planned to travel together, once the war was over. They'd had no official confirmation of Heinrich's death, of course; like so many families, they only learned the worst when their carefully penned letters had arrived back unopened with, scrawled upon them in red ink, the words *Zurück an den Absender*. Return to sender. Missing, presumed dead.

Fired by youthful idealism and nationalistic fervour, Heinrich, like all his college friends, had rushed to join up to serve the Fatherland as soon as he came of age. They were all so young, so talented, with so much to live for. But in their inexperience they had quickly fallen prey like game birds to the guns of French infantry and British riflemen.

The 'Massacre of the Innocents', that's what it later came to be called, a defeat the German authorities never admitted. But Heinrich's friends, returning with terrible physical injuries or the blank stares of the psychologically damaged, told their stories to nurses and teachers, who told others, who told Martha and Karl.

They had no idea where Heinrich had actually fallen except through stories from the families of the friends with whom he'd marched away with such optimism. It was among the gossip of bereaved mothers gathered in the bread queues that she first heard the word Langemarck, a dread place where, rumour had it, more than twenty-four thousand German soldiers, including those from Heinrich's regiment, had died in just ten days. Word was that they were all buried in a special cemetery there.

Karl's breath became shallow and laboured. It could only be a few hours now, and he was unlikely to live to see his dream.

'I'll find Heiney, I promise,' she whispered through her tears. 'He shall have Grandpa's medals.'

'*Tausend Dank*,' Karl managed to utter before succumbing once more to the harsh, uncontrollable cough that stained the sheets with bright red mucus. '*Ich liebe dich*.'

They were his last words. She called Otto to her side and they watched hand in hand as the man they both loved so dearly, the man who held the centre of their world, slipped into unconsciousness and drew his last breath.

That was back in October. The armistice came shortly afterwards but there was no peace in her heart, nor any in the country, either. Why had the generals caved in so suddenly, giving away so much when right up until that moment the newspapers had been full of German victories? No one seemed to know, or at least they weren't telling. The Kaiser, in whom their hopes had been vested for so long, deserted them. How would their proud new nation ever recover? What was the point of it all, of so many lives lost for the so-called honour of defending what was now a weak, defeated country?

The terms of peace seemed only to rub salt in their wounds: the financial reparations, the loss of lands and the relinquishing of arms, like a series of punishments. The Allies claimed this was the reparation Germany had to pay for starting the war.

Rumblings of discontent had already started, blaming the generals, the communists and even the Jews for the country's plight. Food and fuel were just as short as ever; families grieved, and bureaucracy failed to cope with the tide of administration for army pay-offs and disability pensions. Her beloved Berlin was a broken city. Thousands of citizens, their bodies weakened with malnourishment and the cold, succumbed like Karl to the virulent strain of influenza. It had been a bitter winter.

Still, the Treaty of Versailles had now been signed, travel restrictions were lifted and Martha was told, when she visited the *Auswärtiges Amt*, the Foreign Office, in central Berlin that there would be no problems crossing the border. Now she could make her pilgrimage to find her son, to carry out her husband's dying wish and perhaps, just perhaps, find some peace for her own troubled soul.

Karl's determination to find his son's grave had, she knew, been fuelled by the sufferings of his grandmother Else, who had never recovered from the death of her husband in the Crimean War. No amount of medals for bravery could help her accept his loss. Right up until her own early death – as the result, the family all believed, of a broken heart – Else's almost daily refrain had been, 'If only I'd been able to visit his grave, to tell him I loved him.' Martha had already resolved that she would not spend her own life carrying the double burden, Karl's and her own, of such regret.

She knew, too, that Karl had suffered a deep and unacknowledged guilt of his own. Of course he was too old to be conscripted and he had a gammy knee, but many other men of his age had signed up. He and Martha, along with many of their friends, had watched in horror as the country seemed to be drawn inexorably towards war. In their eyes, the assassination of the Austrian archduke was just a flimsy excuse for the warmongers.

Yes, their army was powerful, highly drilled and well supplied, and right up until the last months it seemed they were, by some miracle, holding their own. Now, everyone wondered how Germany ever believed they could match the combined powers of Russia, France and Britain. And who could have imagined the scale of the losses, and the hardship and hunger it would bring to ordinary people?

Even knowing all of this, Martha suspected, Karl must surely have reproached himself that his son had died on the fields of Flanders, while he had stayed at home.

The loss of Heinrich hit Otto hard, she knew, but at least the boy had the comfort of believing that his much-revered elder brother had died a hero trying to save the great German Republic. However, that his father should also die, just before the announcement of peace, had been almost unendurable.

His childhood had been stolen by the war and even now, on top of having to cope with the usual agonies of being twelve, of the acne that had started to pock his face, of the newly long limbs that seemed to have a mind of their own, there was the constant fear of violence in the air.

Gangs of unemployed, hungry veterans roamed the streets of Berlin, bitter at the failure of the Kaiser to fulfil his promise to create a 'country fit for heroes', and sometimes clashing with demonstrations by communists demanding the utopia they called Bolshevism. The pavements were lined with food queues and beggars, and it wasn't uncommon to encounter ordinary folk sent mad with grief and hunger.

Only last month she'd sat opposite a woman on the tram counting out loud as she held up her fingers one by one: *eins, zwei, drei, vier, fünf,* and then again, one, two, three, four, five. As other passengers began to smile between themselves, embarrassed by her eccentric behaviour, the man beside her spoke out: 'Do not laugh at my sister, ladies and gentlemen,' he said. 'I am taking her to the asylum. She has lost five sons, all killed in action, and her wits are gone.'

Sometimes Martha imagined that she herself was also losing her mind. Her body was starved, ever since the British had decided to win the war with their 'hunger blockade'. Even the peace treaty hadn't made much difference. Farmers continued to hoard food and only the rich could afford to pay their extortionate prices, made worse as the Deutschmark devalued, becoming more worthless by the day.

Much as she loved the Fatherland, it was no place to live at the moment. She tried to look into the future but could see nothing but bleakness. The private ladies' college where she worked as a part-time French language teacher had closed during the war and its doors had never reopened. Learning an enemy tongue was well down anyone's list of priorities, and would be for the foreseeable future.

Otto was all she now had left in the world, apart from a few cousins scattered across the country with whom she had never been close. Her parents were long dead and her own brother had emigrated with his wife to America in 1910. He'd prospered there, working for an engineering firm in Chicago, and had pleaded with her and Karl to join them. We'll come later, they'd promised, after the boys have finished school and college.

Then, when war was declared, all correspondence ceased. It pained her deeply that his adopted country had gone to war against her own and that its might and wealth had been the cause of Germany's terrible defeat. Since the armistice none of her letters had received a reply. She longed for his news, to hear he was safe.

It was only her concern for Otto's welfare that got her out of bed each day. He gave her a reason for living. In spite of her anxieties, planning this trip to Flanders had given her a goal. A small legacy from her father was probably enough to pay for both of them to travel, so long as they were prudent. At least then she could discharge her promise to her beloved Karl and perhaps help Otto understand, to give him something to remember of his brother.

They heard the tramping of hobnail boots. A key clanked in the lock and she found herself blinking in a shaft of harsh daylight as the door opened and three uniformed men entered.

The next half hour would decide their fate: whether they would be allowed into Belgium or sent back to Berlin, with her dream turned to ashes.

4

RUBY

Ruby collapsed onto the soft, wide expanse of the bed, grateful to be alone at last.

Her head was reeling. The day had presented such a cacophony of new sights and sounds that she could barely take it all in. It was as though she had somehow taken on the mantle of another person – the other Ruby was surely still at home in her small childhood bedroom with her neat suit and blouse, washed and carefully pressed, on a hanger on the back of the door ready for work tomorrow?

But this was a new version of Ruby, who had travelled to London and then crossed the sea to this tattered seaside town and an old-fashioned hotel with its curiously formal staff, its starched white napkins and bland food served with such pride. Who seemed to have attracted the attentions of a complete stranger: an American woman, brash, over-friendly and bold as brass. And here she was now, this other Ruby, with her small, battered suitcase, in this cavernous room with its dark wood furniture and tapestries on the walls depicting unsettling medieval scenes of knights and dragons.

The double bed felt enormous; she had never slept in one, save for the honeymoon. She shifted position, trying to make her neck more comfortable; the curious sausage-shaped pillow stretched across the full width of the bed but didn't seem to support her head at all.

Was she really here, in Belgium, the country Bertie had come to defend, where he had fought so bravely and where he had, almost certainly, died? At home, every step she took, every place she visited, every meal she ate and every person she met reminded her of Bertie. These were things they had done together for so many years that she could not imagine life without the presence that she felt of him, night and day. But it was only now she realised that although, as John Wilson had said, she was here to honour the sacrifice Bertie had made, she had barely thought about him since leaving Dover.

Guiltily, she went to her case and took out the photo-graph, the one of their wedding day that sat by her bedside at home and which she'd slipped into her case at the last minute. He looked so young in his army uniform, his curls shorn into a severe haircut beneath the cap; she was wear-ing the pale lace-trimmed dress that had cost a fortune and never been worn since. It was a beautiful garment, hanging flatteringly from her shoulders and draping in layers down to her calves. Her own slightly lighter brown curls were held back in a bun beneath a jaunty hat with a ribbon that matched the dress. They were both smiling, self-consciously, as bidden by the photographer.

Gone. All gone.

The next day dawned grey and muggy. Breakfast was a strange affair of coffee so strong and bitter that Ruby recoiled at the first sip, along with crispy bread rolls, thin curls of pale butter served in a saucer of iced water, and the choice of an anonymous red-orange jam or yellow sliced cheese.

'In France they do fabulous flaky pastries called croissants that you're supposed to dunk into your coffee. I was hoping for some of them. But no, here it's plain bread and cheese,' Alice complained, a little too loudly. She seemed to have attached herself, but Ruby didn't really mind. It was better than sitting alone, or enduring the self-absorbed litanies of sorrow from the other couples.

'I rather like it,' Ruby said, after a tentative tasting. The butter was creamy and unsalted, complementing the saltiness of the cheese. 'Makes a change from the fry-ups we have at home. Well, we *had*, before rationing,' she added, a little wistfully. On the rare occasions they managed to get hold of a few rashers, the smell of frying bacon never failed to remind her of her father.

She'd slept well, surprisingly. The heavy curtains in her room blocked the light so efficiently that she'd only woken when Alice had knocked on her door: 'C'mon, sleepyhead, it's eight. You don't want to miss breakfast.'

By the time they were outside the hotel waiting for the motorbus to arrive, she'd barely had time to think about what today would bring. A photographer arrived with a large black camera on a heavy tripod, and began to organise the group into some kind of order.

'Gentlemen at the back, please. You, miss, come to the front. I can't see you.' It must be a lucrative little sideline if

Thomas Cook had gone to the lengths of bringing an Englishman across the Channel especially for the task, she thought. 'That's right, a little further please, miss.' Ruby stepped forward reluctantly while Alice, so much taller, was encouraged to move to the side. Smiles were forced and positions held as still as possible until the ordeal was finally over. The prints would be ready for purchase at the end of the week. It would be something to take home for Bertie's parents at least.

Major Wilson shepherded his troops onto the coach via a set of steps at the rear. Ruby was relieved to see that the vehicle had glass windows, the lower half of which could be pulled up or down with a leather strap, for ventilation. She wasn't afraid of motion sickness, but disliked being cooped up for too long without fresh air. Alice manoeuvred herself to the head of the queue and secured a pair of seats at the front.

'Gotta get the best views, don't you think?' she whispered, as Ruby joined her. The wooden benches were designed for two people and supplied with flat cushions. Alice helped her arrange them: one for the base and one for the backrest.

Major Wilson took the seat opposite. 'Slept well, I hope, ladies?' he asked. After murmuring polite confirmation, Alice confided that she hadn't slept a wink. 'If you like a lumpy mattress and bedding smelling of mould, it would be just dandy,' she grouched. 'And it was supposed to be a superior suite. What a joke.'

Are all Americans so hard to please?

The major began to address them in a finest parade-ground voice that ensured even the deafest among them would not miss a word. 'Good morning, friends. I hope you are all feeling well, and ready for day one of our tour, a day that I confidently predict you will remember for the rest of your lives. We shall visit Ypres in the morning and a war cemetery in the afternoon, passing by the battlefields. As I said last night, it may be difficult at times for some of you. But I hope that it will help you to understand what happened over here, and perhaps to come to terms with your losses. Some call it bearing witness, but of course everyone has their own way of describing these things. One thing is certain, you will come away with a greater appreciation of what war really means – and hopefully a determination never to allow it to happen again in our lifetimes.'

'Hear, hear,' called a gruff voice from behind.

❀❀❀

To Ruby's relief, the countryside seemed perfectly normal at first, green and very lush farmland, flatter even than East Anglia, small fields bordered by canals and peppered with black and white cows that reminded her of the painted metal toys in her play farm long ago. This tranquil, misty landscape was punctuated by farmhouses huddled together with red-roofed barns, all protected from the wind by plantations of willow trees. Tall poplars lined the long, straight road, their silvery leaves glimmering in a gentle breeze.

They passed through a small village where black-clad women queued to buy vegetables from a stall, old men sat on a bench smoking pipes and children played in a school yard. Ruby began to relax. So far, so normal.

A few miles beyond this, everything changed.

They pulled up beside a collection of derelict buildings and large piles of rubble, and the major held up a photograph of a village square with an ancient town hall and church with a tall spire.

'Believe it or not, this was once the beautiful medieval village of Dixmude.' Gasps of dismay fluttered through the group. 'It was one of the first villages the French and Belgians defended against the German invasion in October 1914. The name Dixmude means "gate to the dyke" – that's the canal – so they were able to open the gates and flood the whole area, which stopped the German advance. The river became the frontline throughout the rest of the war.'

'What happened to all the villagers?' someone asked.

'They fled, like so many thousands did,' he replied. 'I'm sorry to say they weren't alone. As you will soon discover, this was the fate of dozens of villages along the front line, even major towns like Ypres. But the Belgians are resilient people; they're determined to return and rebuild their lives again.'

Among the rubble, groups of men were pulling out wooden beams and planks, piling them carefully according to shape and length. Others collected and stacked undamaged bricks and tiles, and a further team seemed to be salvaging metal gates and railings. They faced a Herculean task, battling to recover normality amid mountains of destruction.

'Where are their families?'

'They went wherever they could, to villages behind the lines, lodging with other families or renting barns, whatever they could find. Now, so they can get to work, they are building temporary homes.' He pointed to a distant corner, where yet more men were hammering wood and corrugated iron into makeshift shacks.

'Poor devils. Imagine having to live like that,' Alice said. 'I had no idea.'

They left the village and the road surface worsened, the coach slowing more frequently to avoid the potholes. Trees disappeared from the landscape and, in their place, reaching far into the distance, stood lifeless, blackened stumps like exclamation marks. The formal demarcation of drainage dykes had been obliterated. No more black and white cows stood peacefully grazing. Ruby shivered, struggling to accept the desolation her eyes were seeing. They had entered a place in which battles had been fought, and lives had been lost.

The landscape was barren, bleak, monochrome brown and grey, the only relief of colour provided by occasional clumps of wild flowers valiantly pushing their way through the ravaged earth: yellow dandelions and buttercups, pink ragged robin and bright red poppies.

Alice nudged her. 'Did you read that little poem about the poppies?' She pronounced it 'pome'.

Although Ruby couldn't remember exactly how it went, she'd heard people at work talking about how the poem, by a Canadian soldier, had inspired someone to propose the poppy as a symbol of remembrance.

Alice began to quote: '*In Flanders fields the poppies blow between the crosses, row on row . . .*'

Ruby felt her throat contract, aching with sadness.

'*. . . that mark our place, and in sky the larks, bravely singing . . .*'

She sniffed, fumbling for her handkerchief.

'I'm so sorry, I didn't mean to upset you,' Alice whispered. 'I'm such a fool.'

'No need,' Ruby said. 'It's just those larks, singing so bravely . . .'

'I guess you've lost someone very close to your heart?' Alice said.

'Please. I can't, not here.' Ruby swallowed. She hadn't reckoned on everyone wanting to know her 'story' and the prospect of telling it terrified her: it would mean having to lift her mask, cracking the cocoon that she'd wound to protect herself against the pain.

As they jolted along rutted roads the major did his best to describe the complex pattern of battles that had taken over this narrow belt of land, no more than twenty miles wide. They passed by lines of trenches, long, deep ditches zigzagging into the distance, sometimes separated from the enemy lines by just a few hundred yards of 'no-man's land', an area of mud so pocked with water-filled shell holes that it was almost impossible to imagine that this had once been green and fertile farmland.

He told them of triumphs and catastrophes, of territory lost and regained, only to be lost again. He gave them the numbers, always in thousands, of lives lost in each battle. He passed around maps with wiggly lines reaching from north to south, their colour denoting the relative front lines of the enemy and the Allied forces. Some places had changed hands almost every few months.

However carefully she listened, Ruby found it virtually impossible to take it all in: the unfamiliar names, the unfeasible tolls of casualties, the tonnages of shells, the magnitudes of explosives, the miles of trenches and tunnels made deep below the surface, the indescribable terror of poison gas.

She'd imagined that, in war, one side moved forwards, taking towns and villages, while the other retreated. But here in Flanders, it seemed the two sides spent months, even years, hunkered down in their trenches, firing bullets and shells at each other, releasing terrifying poison gas and tunnelling beneath each other's lines to set off enormous explosions. And all, until the very end, for little tangible outcome, except that thousands upon thousands of men suffered and died for the few yards of land gained or lost again.

What had been the point of it? When she'd begged Bertie not to sign up, he'd told her it was his duty. But what did that mean? His duty to whom? Why did the Germans want to invade Belgium and, in any case, why was Britain so keen to defend this little country? Why did so many lives have to be lost for these few miles of otherwise unremarkable countryside? If she could summon the courage, she'd ask Major Wilson what he thought. He'd told them, more than once, that coming here would help to make sense of it all, but right now she felt even more confused.

It was a further half hour before they finally reached the outskirts of a much larger town – or what was left of it – with a deep canal and some ancient fortifications, which the major called 'Wipers'. It took Ruby a moment to grasp that this was the place written in the Thomas Cook brochure as Ypres.

Beside her, Alice breathed, 'A whole city just blown apart.'

The coach picked its way slowly along streets of broken

houses and pulled up in a wide central square bounded by the ruins of civic buildings that had been toppled, as though by some clumsy giant, into vast piles of rubble. Ruby found herself squinting through half-closed eyes, scarcely able to believe what she was seeing. Even the ruined villages they'd passed through could not have prepared her – any of them – for this. Was this what people meant by 'bearing witness': seeing for their own eyes, written in the physical wreckage of a whole town, the terrible destructive power of war?

'This was once the Grande Place – the central square – of Wipers,' the major was saying. 'It stood for six hundred years, since the Middle Ages, but it took the ruddy Hun only a couple of months to destroy it. They never actually occupied the place, just blew it to high heaven.'

'That was the ancient Cloth Hall, the main market place for the ancient city's weaving industry,' he went on. 'The town's cathedral was over there.' He pointed to another ruin of which only a high Norman arch was still recognisable. Tall columns of broken brick and stone reached precariously and defiantly towards the sky, the remains of a tower Ruby reckoned must once have been the height of Norwich Cathedral. Stretching into the distance the other side, along what must once have been the town's central square, was a long row of derelict arches.

Here, just as in the villages and fields, men and women clambered over the rubble, salvaging, sifting and sorting household items: saucepans, books, boxes, and even carpets and curtains, which they piled onto horse-drawn carts. Steamrollers strained to clear a road, official-looking men in smart suits scribbled on notepads and one man had a camera tripod which he set up from time to time, disappearing under the black cloth to take a photograph. People walked purposefully around the square, some in army uniforms. Others just stood and stared.

Two or three motorbuses offered 'excursions to the battlefields' and, now she looked more carefully, Ruby noticed groups like their own, dutifully following guides around the square. 'I expect you'll all want to stretch your legs,' the major said. 'We'll have elevenses and then take a walk around together so I can tell you more about what Wipers went through.'

'Elevenses? What the heck's that?' Alice whispered as they climbed down from the coach.

'It's what we call a mid-morning break – tea or coffee and a biscuit usually,' Ruby said. 'But where on earth we'd get anything in this place . . .'

'Over there.' Alice pointed towards a makeshift stall advertising coffee and something called waffles. Tea was not on offer, it seemed, so Ruby asked for a weak coffee with milk.

'I'm having a waffle. Want to indulge?' Alice said. 'My treat.'

Ruby was about to refuse but the mouth-watering aroma of warm sugar was impossible to resist. The stallholder poured batter onto a hotplate powered by a small paraffin stove beneath the counter, and hinged down another metal plate on top. Within seconds the waffles emerged, fat pancakes with a chequerboard design wrapped in a white paper cone, dusted with icing sugar and presented to them steaming hot.

She took a bite, careful not to burn her tongue. It was

utterly delicious. Sipping her coffee, she looked around and wondered, all over again, what she was doing here, feeling guilty for being alive in a place where people had suffered such misery.

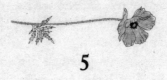

5

ALICE

As soon as he said the word Hoppestadt, she knew.

'We'll be taking lunch in a little town just a few miles from here,' the major told them. 'It was a main rail and transport hub and also headquarters of the Allied command for the area and where the troops came back from the front line for rest and recuperation. The Belgian name is Hoppestadt, but us Tommies only ever called it Hops.'

She could hardly believe her ears at first. 'That's it! Oh my goodness. Where Sam wrote his letter, remember?'

Ruby nodded.

'We're actually going there. Imagine, someone might remember him?'

She endured the rest of the short journey in an agony of impatience, scarcely able to contain her excitement. After the devastation of Ypres and the other villages, the place appeared almost normal. Most buildings were intact and the small central square, bordered by shops and cafes, was buzzing with activity. Bicycles, farm carts, cars and motor coaches clattered by on the cobbles and crowds of black-clad women gathered around market stalls.

The major shepherded them towards a cafe on the corner, busy with customers seated at tables beneath faded awnings. 'If you're in the mood, you can partake of their famous beer, and I can recommend the beef stew they make with it.' So that explained the bitter-sweet odour of roasting malt that pervaded the air.

A young waitress, no more than a teenager, slim and willowy with a head of russet curls, emerged to welcome them.

The major greeted her like an old friend. 'Ginger! *Ça va?*'

'Business good. Many tourists now.'

'Not tourists, Ginger. We call them pilgrims. It is more respectful of the dead.'

'Any name, so long as they spend money,' she responded genially. 'Heavens know, we need it.'

'Have you seen anything of Tubby lately?'

'I regret, no. We miss his big cheerful face, but the owner takes the house back.'

'Give him my best, if you see him.'

The waitress glanced at the group. 'You are ten?'

'Please. On the terrace, I think, now the sun's breaking through.'

'What you drink, Major?'

'The usual, of course.'

Alice listened, intrigued by this little exchange. The girl was surely local, and had probably been here right through the war. Had she served Sam, perhaps, or at least people who might have known him? And what about this Tubby character, for whom both she and the major appeared to have such great respect? Might he also provide a lead to her brother?

Faced with a menu entirely in Flemish, the group quickly turned for advice. 'I could order some of my favourite dishes for everyone to share, so you can taste different types of Belgian cuisine,' the major said. 'Would that suit?'

Delicious aromas began to float from the direction of the kitchen, and before long Ginger was ferrying plates to their table: white asparagus with chopped egg, a cheese tart she referred to as *flamiche*, stuffed tomatoes, a curious-looking vegetable called endive like a lettuce heart wrapped in ham with a cheese sauce, a sort of fish stew and several baskets of white bread. Finally, she brought a plate of cold meats and a kind of smoked fish that John Wilson happily informed them was eel.

'Eel?' Ruby whispered, frowning. 'Not for me, thanks.'

'Go on, try it. You might surprise yourself,' Alice urged, recalling how she had discovered, rather late in the day, the delights of continental cuisine. But Ruby was not to be persuaded; she picked at her food like a sparrow, contenting herself with bread and butter, a couple of tomatoes and a single spear of asparagus.

Alice lingered over her coffee and when John Wilson rallied the group for a tour of the town, said she would join them later. Ginger and a couple of other staff were already seated with their own meals at a table at the rear of the restaurant. As they finished eating, Alice approached. 'Mam'selle? Excuse me, may I speak with you?'

Despite her youth, the weariness of war was clearly written on the girl's face. 'Of course, madame.'

'My name is Alice Palmer. From America. Can you spare me a few moments?'

'My name is Eliane, but everyone calls me Ginger. Your French is very good. Please, take a seat.'

Alice took out the photograph. 'This is my brother. I know he was here in Hoppestadt because he wrote about it, but he hasn't returned home. I just wondered . . .' She faltered, suddenly fearful. Ginger studied the photograph carefully before passing it to the barman and her father, the chef, who had emerged from the kitchen in his tall starched white hat. They all shook their heads.

'*Je suis désolée*, I do not think we can help. We saw so many,' Ginger said. 'English, French, Canadians, Americans. Was he an officer?'

'I really don't know. Probably not.' How foolish she had been, how absurdly optimistic, to imagine that of the many thousands who came here they might remember one individual soldier.

'Is there anyone else I could ask?'

'There were two other places the men went, apart from the bars and whorehouses.' Ginger's smile was apologetic. 'Forgive me, but that was the reality of war.'

'I'm sure my brother was no angel.'

'There was the Church Army hut but it is gone, and the people.'

'And the other place?'

'Talbot House. The Everyman's Club they called it, on Rue de l'Hôpital.' She gestured towards the left. 'Many went there, all ranks, hundreds of them. But it is closed now.'

'What was this place?'

'It was somewhere to relax and meet friends. They could have a meal; they had a library and events, music and so on.

And a place to pray.' Alice found herself hanging on every word, her heart pounding in her chest. This was surely the place Sam wrote about: *There are kind-hearted people helping us, and we've got good beer and enough food.*

'Is it possible to visit this house?'

Ginger shook her head. 'The man who ran it, a priest, he's gone home to England and the owner has taken it back.'

It was so frustrating. This was the closest she'd come to finding Sam – or at least discovering what had happened to him. Gripped with the certainty, without knowing why or how, that this place would hold the clue to Sam's disappearance, she would not give up now. 'Can't I go there anyway? Could you introduce me to this owner?'

'I'm sorry. There were so many wishing to visit that he had to close the doors.'

'What was this priest's name? Maybe I could write to him?'

'Philip Clayton. But everyone calls him Tubby. Perhaps the army will have his address?'

'Thank you, mam'selle, for giving me your time,' Alice said.

'It was nothing. Good luck, madame.'

❧

She saw the sign immediately, on the opposite wall, as she stepped out into the street: *Rue de l'Hôpital*. It didn't take long to find the handsome red-brick three-storey town house that, although now dusty and neglected-looking, must surely once have been a grand residence. The shutters and heavy cast-iron gates were firmly closed, but above the doorway still hung the hand-painted sign: *Talbot House, 1915 - ? Every-Man's Club.*

She tugged at the bell-pull; it sounded hollowly but no one came to the door. She rang again, more urgently this time. Still no answer. She sighed impatiently. If only she could get inside she might get a sense of Sam's presence, when he had been here, what he had been doing. After trying a third time and waiting for several minutes more, she turned away, itchy with exasperation. Retracing her steps to the square, she tried to reason with her sense of disappointment: the priest had left, the owner had taken the house back. There was probably nothing left inside anyway; it would have been taken away at the end of the war. Besides, she had no proof that Sam had even visited it. There must be other leads to follow – she would ask Daniel.

She crossed the square to the town hall where Major Wilson had arranged to meet them, and entered the court-yard through the stone gateway. Over lunch the group had begun to get to know each other; a few beers helped to ease their reserve and the conversation had become light-hearted, even jocular. But now they stood in solemn, respectful silence, hanging on to his every word.

'. . . this building also had a more sombre role.' He pointed to a barred window in the corner of the courtyard. 'That is the prison where they held captured deserters, awaiting their fate.' There was a collective in-drawing of breath. Everyone knew that deserters had been shot, but no one wanted to ask how or where, and he was clearly not going to go into detail. It was enough to learn that when those poor souls were brought here, they must have known that they were never going home.

'Of course they may have been considered cowards, but in my experience half these poor fellows were literally not in their right minds, suffering from shell shock and the rest. I am sure you have heard of this? But what can an army do, in the cauldron of war? Discipline is the key to victory, and had it become understood that deserting was an easy way of escaping, then many more might have tried to follow.' John Wilson's voice was level, but Alice could see from the way he was holding himself even more stiffly than usual that he was working hard to hold his emotions in check.

She moved to Ruby's side. 'Imagine being locked up here, knowing you were probably going to be shot.'

'I can hardly bear to think about it.'

Alice boarded the coach reluctantly, her feet heavy with disappointment. She'd felt closer to Sam here than at any time since he'd left all those years ago, and she needed more time here to find out why. But then, just as the coach began to pull away, a familiar red-haired figure ran across the square waving and the major asked the driver to stop.

'Is American lady with you?' Ginger called, as he pulled down the window. 'I have news. Tubby Clayton comes in two days. Please can you tell?'

He turned to Alice. 'I expect you heard that? I'm afraid it'll be too late, if you were hoping to meet him.'

Back in Ostend, she went to the hotel bar and ordered a large glass of whisky. She'd grown fond of the spirit during her days in London, where Julia's father had taken great pride in introducing them to the embassy's extensive cellar. 'A good malt is the sign of a civilised nation,' he'd say. 'All enlightened people should understand its subtleties. Have another.'

This Belgian version certainly wasn't the best, but it slipped down surprisingly well. It was while drinking her second glass that it occurred to her, an idea so simple she almost laughed out loud. She would get a cab and return to Hoppestadt to meet this army chaplain. It was only a couple of hours away, after all.

She predicted stern resistance from the major, who would no doubt consider it improper for a woman to travel alone. Then she realised that the solution was right here, with her in this hotel. She would ask Ruby to come too. Surely he could not object if they had each other as chaperones? Hadn't she wanted to spend more time at Tyne Cot to look for her dead husband? Alice was sure she could persuade her, especially if she offered to pay. And if not, then hang it all, she would go on her own no matter what the major said.

It would mean a change of plan for that other matter, of course – although, now she came to think of it, getting away from the group might make it easier. Besides, if her geography was correct, Hoppestadt was even closer to Lille than Ostend.

At the front desk, she asked to send a telegram: IN HOPPESTADT TOMORROW TUESDAY CAN WE MEET THERE INSTEAD STOP A

6

RUBY

For a few confusing moments, hovering midway between waking and dreaming, Ruby could not remember what time it was or even *where* she was. A sliver of daylight slipped through a gap in the curtains, so it could not yet be night time. Besides, she was still fully dressed, and lying on top of the quilted coverlet.

Then, in a flood of painful recollections, she realised that she was back in the tall-ceilinged hotel room in Ostend with its dark furniture, wall hangings and strange sausage-shaped pillow. And it was still only Monday, the day they had seen so many terrible things, the day she had felt certain that she would find Bertie's grave, an opportunity she would now never have again.

Her mind wandered over the events of the afternoon, as the coach party left Hoppestadt for their return journey to Ostend through the battlefields. As they'd jolted along her gaze had drifted over the endless tracts of barren, shell-pocked land, punctuated only by twisted shards of rusting metal that had once been the deadly machinery of war, by writhing coils of barbed wire and dismal stands of blackened, broken trees. Mournful grey clouds hung heavily in the sky, freighted with rain. It was a landscape of nightmares. She longed for their view to return to normal, to feast her eyes on cows and sheep peacefully grazing, farmers setting the hay into stooks, women hanging out washing.

But they were not allowed to forget, not just yet.

'On our way back to Ostend we will visit Tyne Cot, which is one of the largest war graveyards in Flanders,' the major had announced as they left Hoppestadt. 'Of course, you'll have seen the crosses along the wayside. In the chaos of wartime, many were buried where they fell. The authorities are now planning formal burial grounds as a permanent memorial to those who gave their lives. There's a commission working on these plans as we speak, trying to decide what the stones should have on them, whether it should be a Christian cross, or just the names, and so on. You might have read the letters in the press – feelings are running pretty high. But one thing's certain, they are not going to bring them home and, hard as it might be for the families, I think that is the right decision. They died here, fighting for this piece of land together with their fellow men, so this is where their souls should rest. Tyne Cot has been identified as one of these permanent sites. Here are buried men of all nationalities who fought and died in one of the most costly battles of the war, the battle to capture the Passchendaele Ridge.'

Passchendaele. The word sliced like a blade. Where Bertie had gone missing. Although she knew that many thousands had never been identified, or even found, she'd heard that comrades would sometimes just place a simple stake in the ground, marking it with whatever came to hand. As the coach trundled onwards, closer and closer to this place, she found herself clasping her fists so tightly that the nails left marks in her palms.

'Although many men gave their lives in this battle,' the major was explaining, 'the Germans pushed back and occupied the area until September 1918, when the Belgian army recaptured the ridge in the final push during the last weeks of the war.'

A tangle of emotions jangled in her head: excitement, anticipation and, above all, fear. Much as she knew that finding Bertie's grave was important for herself and his family, she could not imagine, now that it was a real possibility, how she would cope with the reality, the finality of discovering where he lay, in the ground beneath her feet.

They'd seen plenty of roadside crosses and memorial stones on their way to Ypres, but nothing prepared her for the sight of Tyne Cot. As she gazed out at the thousands of wooden crosses stretched higgledy-piggledy across the field, way into the distance almost as far as the eye could see, the breath seemed to stop in her chest. Some were of smooth sanded timber, identified with expertly carved inscriptions or stamped metal plates. With a sick, chill fascination she also noticed that many were simply rough planks hastily hammered together with lettering scratched or burned onto the wood, with garlands of dried flowers tied to them, an identity tag, a belt buckle, an army cap.

The major led them forwards along a pathway of packed mud into the graveyard. Every now and again he would pause, straightening up a cross carefully and reverently, pushing it more firmly into the ground.

'I know some of you may be looking for the graves of loved ones, and we have an hour now in which you can do so. Please take care of your footing, *never* stray from the pathways, or touch or take anything from the ground. There is still a danger of unexploded ordnance, or something personal which may lead to an identification. Either way, you must not touch. Do I make myself clear?'

Ruby wandered from cross to cross in a kind of trance, barely aware of time passing, reading the inscriptions and willing her eyes to see his name yet at the same time terrified of doing so. There seemed to be no order: officers lay next to infantrymen, regiments were all mixed together, there were French names, Belgian names, English names. All the differences imposed in life had been erased by death.

Smith, Merton, Bygrave, Freeman, Augustin, Travere, Marchant, Tailler, Brown, Peeters, Dubois, Janssens, Walter, Fellowes, Villeneuve. Perhaps some of these men had known Bertie, stood by his side in the trenches, shared their rations, spoken of their longing for home, for their sweethearts, wives, children? As she stumbled along the rows, gripped by a fierce determination to find her beloved, her eyes began to play tricks. Any name beginning with a B seemed to halt the blood in her veins. When she found a cross with the name Barton inscribed upon it, her knees threatened to buckle beneath her. But it was Michael Peter. Not Bertie.

If she looked long enough and hard enough she would find him, stand at his grave, tell him she loved him, ask for his forgiveness, and be able to live the rest of her life in peace. She could almost sense the relief of it already. And yet, the further she walked, the more that certainty began to waver. Many crosses bore only the simple inscription *R.I.P., Known Unto God* or, saddest of all, no mark whatsoever. So many thousands of individual, personal tragedies, so many of them anonymous; a visual representation of mass slaughter.

Keep breathing, just put one foot in front of another, she told herself. *Hollander, Frost, Blundell, Taylor, Kelly, Schofield, Allen, Carter, Meredith, Brown, Pullen, Masters, Wade, Francis, McCauley, Titmuss, Archer . . .* the parade of the lost went on and on.

And then, the worst shock of all, gripping at her heart like a vice: dozens of crosses with German names. *Müller, Schulz, Schmidt, Schneider, Fischer, Weber, Becker, Wagner, Hoffmann, Koch, Bauer, Klein, Wolf, Schröder, Neumann, Braun, Zimmermann, Krüger, Hartmann,* lying cheek by jowl with their enemies.

Had one of Bertie's bullets killed the man now lying by his side? Had the shell they fired, shouting 'For King and Country', or hailing the Kaiser, blown to pieces the men now their neighbours in death? So many husbands, brothers and sons, all now gone. What an absurdity, such a terrible waste. And all for what? What further evidence could ever be needed of the futility of war? Far from making sense of it all, she was becoming more bewildered by the hour.

'We're going soon, Ruby.' Alice's call threw her into a panic.

They *couldn't* leave, not yet, not until she had found Bertie. This was her *only* chance. She might never, for the rest of her life, have another opportunity. She must find his grave, to tell him she was sorry for not being a better wife, for not honouring his sacrifice, for continuing to live while his body lay in the ground in this desolate place, to ask for his forgiveness. She quickened her step. *Tolbert, Frencham, Smith, Smith, Marks, Aaron, Middleton, Jacobs, Willems, Dupont* . . .

'Mrs Barton? I am afraid we must leave now.' The major's voice, from somewhere close behind, brought her feet to a halt. As she raised her gaze across the forest of crosses, far too many to count and certainly too many to check in a single hour, the darkest of sorrows seemed to suck the strength out of her. She felt sure she would be able to find him, if only she looked hard enough for a few more minutes, or perhaps an hour or two. But now, even though fate had brought her to the very place where he had died and where he might indeed be buried, her dearest wish would be denied.

She felt a hand cupping her elbow. 'It's time to leave,' he said gently. 'And it's starting to rain.'

She hadn't even noticed. 'But I need to see his grave. What's the point of coming all this way if I can't find him?'

'It is not always possible, Mrs Barton. You have to remember that more than one in four casualties were never identified.'

'What do you mean, not identified?' Even as the words left her lips she already knew the unpalatable answer: their bodies had been so badly mangled or blown into so many pieces that they were unrecognisable. But one in four? A quarter of all those thousands of men? The truth was unsayable. 'So I'll probably *never* find him?' she managed, in a ragged whisper.

'Never say never, Mrs Barton. But please take some comfort from understanding that although you cannot find a grave, your husband's body will probably be here somewhere, if he died at Passchendaele. You may have been close to him without actually knowing it.'

It felt like cold comfort, but he was doing his best. She nodded, to please him. The pressure of his hand on her elbow increased and obediently, reluctantly, she followed him, legs moving automatically. Each step felt as though it was ripping her heart in two, and half of it would remain here forever in this gloomy place.

Alice was waiting for her outside the coach. 'You look as though you've seen a ghost. Did you find anything?'

Ruby shook her head miserably. 'Any one of those unmarked graves could be my Bertie. But how will I ever know?'

'Bertie? Your brother? Your husband?'

'My husband. Went missing in action here, at Passchendaele. Whatever can I tell them?' she wailed.

'Them?'

'His parents. That's why I'm here. They wanted me to come, to find him, or at least find his grave. How can I? It's impossible.'

Alice put her hand on her arm and was about to speak, but Ruby moved away. Any sympathy would unravel her completely. 'I'm sorry,' she said. 'I just need to sit down.'

'No problem,' Alice replied. 'Thought you might like these.' She thrust into her hand a small bunch of wild flowers – poppies, ox-eye daisies and harebells. 'Keep them safe, and press them into a book when you get back to the hotel.

You can take them back to his parents and it will comfort them just to know where they come from.'

She took the flowers gratefully.

There was a knock on the bedroom door. 'Ready for dinner, Rube?'

Ruby sat up, looking at her watch. It was already seven. Now she thought about it, she was really hungry.

'You go on down. I'll be with you in a few moments.'

After such a dispiriting day the familiar voice was curiously welcome. When Alice had so boldly introduced herself on the deck yesterday – was it only yesterday? – and then virtually forced her to take tea in the first-class lounge, Ruby had only gone along to be polite. She'd found the American woman's overt friendliness overwhelming; she was brash, nosy, liable to speak her mind on anything and everything, and patently so wealthy she could barely understand how others might not be so fortunate.

But now, in this foreign place, it was reassuring to know that someone was waiting for her in the dining room. At least Alice was always cheerful and upbeat, she hadn't pressed her for further information about Bertie, and her support and companionship today had been very welcome.

As she stood to brush her hair she saw the little bunch of wild flowers wilting on the bedside table. It *was* comforting to have something from that cemetery, something that had grown in that sacred soil, to keep with her. She would press them tonight.

'What a day. You were very kind. Thank you,' she said, as they waited for their meal.

'No problem,' Alice replied. 'You don't have to explain. Tell me more about Bertie when you're ready. I'm a good listener.'

'I hope you don't mind me asking: was it something very important, that message from the waitress in Hoppestadt?'

'It could be,' Alice replied. 'It was about a reverend who ran a club for soldiers during the war.'

'So you think this man might remember him?' Ruby felt her heart skip. Might he remember Bertie too, perhaps?

'Sam used to have a strong faith. He'd be drawn to a place like that. It's a long shot, but so far that's all I've got.'

'What a shame you missed him.'

'Well, you see, that's the thing . . .' Alice straightened her cutlery.

'The thing?'

'I thought I might go back. I've been to Bruges before and it's very pretty and all that but, you know, why are we *really* here? Not to visit tourist sights, that's for sure.'

'Go back? To Hoppestadt? But how?'

'I'll take a cab, and probably stay over. There was a hotel on the square. Who knows? There's bound to be some-where.'

'You'd go on your *own*?'

'Why not? We're in the twentieth century now, we don't need chaperones these days. Unless you want to come with me?'

Ruby was so astonished that she missed the question. 'I

didn't mean you needed a *chaperone*,' she stumbled. 'I meant you're brave travelling on your own in a foreign country.'

'And I meant it when I asked if you'd like to come with me.'

Thankfully, just then, the waiter arrived with their plates of grilled Dover sole, fussing around, briskly flapping open starched white napkins onto their laps, reverently serving the plain boiled potatoes from a silver platter as though they were precious jewels.

Would *mesdames* require anything further to drink?

'Let's have a glass of wine, shall we?' Alice said. 'On me.'

It would be rude to refuse.

For the next few minutes their attention was fully occupied with the delicate task of separating the delicious buttery fillets from the bones of the fish and consuming the surprisingly tasty yellow potatoes. Two glasses of dry white wine, expertly chosen by Alice, arrived and went down nicely, the perfect complement to the meal.

Alice finished first, placing her knife and fork neatly side by side on the plate.

'So, are you coming with me?'

Ruby finished her mouthful, took a small sip of wine.

'To Hoppestadt?' It was a ridiculous, reckless idea.

Alice nodded.

'I've got no money to pay for cabs and hotels and the rest.'

'You don't have to sweat about that, I'll pay.'

'I couldn't possibly . . .'

'You won't owe me anything. Honest. It'll be an adventure.'

'I don't think so, but thank you for asking.'

'Have a think about it and let me know in the morning.'

Back in her room, Ruby arranged the wild flowers between two pieces of blotting paper from the bureau and weighed them down with the Bible she'd found in the bedside drawer. She undressed into her pyjamas, cleaned her teeth and climbed into bed. It was already late but she could not sleep, her mind whirling over Alice's proposal.

Why would she want to return to that battered little town with the shadow of those poor executed deserters hanging over it? Did she really want to witness again the mud and devastation of the battlefields or the awful, tragic silence of those graveyards?

And yet, the more she thought about it, the idea was tempting. She could go back to Tyne Cot to look for Bertie's grave, and this priest Alice was meeting might, just might, have known Bertie, or at least men from his regiment. The alternative of traipsing around tourist sights was not exactly appealing. Neither was the prospect of spending the next few days alone with only those grieving couples for company. Alice might not be the usual sort of person Ruby would choose to spend time with, but she was at least someone to talk to. She sat up and turned on the light, feeling suddenly very alone.

Whatever was she doing here? Bertie's parents wanted her to provide them with some certainty about his fate. Only then would they really be able to reconcile themselves to his death, they said. She needed to bring them something more than a bunch of pressed flowers that could have come from anywhere.

Whispered questions stalked her mind, quiet at first, but increasingly imperative. What of herself? What did *she* really want? Until now, she'd believed that by shutting down her emotions and putting a brave face to the world, she could get through life without Bertie, albeit a life she would not, *should* not, enjoy.

If only she'd been able to find a grave she might have talked to him, asked his forgiveness. It might have helped release her from these overwhelming feelings of guilt and duty; allowed her, somehow, to accept that he was truly gone. Only then would she be able to look into the future without that terrible feeling of emptiness and dread. If one in four were never identified, that meant three out of four *were* found – the odds were in favour of Bertie having a marked grave. The only problem was that this afternoon she'd simply not had enough time.

She would not be able to forgive herself if she did not give it one more try.

Pulling on her dressing gown, she tiptoed along the corridor to Alice's room and knocked quietly on the heavy door. After a few moments Alice answered, tousled and sleepy.

'I've decided to come.'

'To Hoppestadt?'

'I want to go back to Passchendaele to find Bertie's grave.'

Alice's face, vulnerable without her usual mask of make-up, broke into the widest smile. 'That's great, Ruby. We'll speak to the major first thing before breakfast.'

Ruby hadn't considered this. He'd been so kind, she didn't want to hurt his feelings. 'Will he mind?'

'He'll understand if we explain why. Besides, it's our trip. He has to please his customers. Don't worry, I'll sort it in the morning.'

'So long as it's fine with him. Goodnight, Alice,' Ruby said. 'And thank you for everything today.'

Back in her big wide bed, she tossed and turned, head spinning with excitement at the momentous decision she had made. Mr Barton would have a fit if he knew she was leaving the tour but now the idea of returning to Passchendaele, having a chance to meet this mysterious priest and learning about his haven for soldiers all made perfect sense.

What an adventure.

'I'm coming, Bertie,' she whispered. 'I'm going to find you, no matter what.'

7

MARTHA

Martha and Otto were led to the small customs office into which they had originally been taken from the train the previous evening.

At the desk sat the same moustachioed officer, regarding them with an expression of such intense hatred that her heart faltered. Another man, taller and with an authority that made her assume that he was the more senior, paced the floor and did not even acknowledge them as they entered.

They were not invited to sit and, in the silence that followed, Martha felt her legs trembling beneath her. Why had she believed the foreign office when they told her she could travel freely into what had so recently been enemy country? And why had she brought Otto with her on this insane adventure? She was ready to give up their quest and catch the next train back to Berlin.

Then she felt his hand tightly gripping hers, and knew that this was not a moment for capitulation. She must be strong for him, reminding herself that they had a legal right to enter Belgium. They had already travelled so far. It was too late to quit now.

Moustache-man began to fire questions, going over the same ground as before: where had they travelled from, could they prove their address, what was her occupation before, during and after the war, and who could they contact to prove it? And finally, why had they come here, to Belgium, so soon after the war had ended?

She tried to answer him clearly in her best French, but it was this last question that finally cracked her composure. 'My God, have you no pity?' she snapped. 'What more do you need from a grieving mother? I've already told you: we have come to find the grave of my elder son, the brother of my boy here, who died in the service of his country.'

'Who died in the service of invading our country,' the tall man hissed.

'We are just ordinary citizens, sir, and the war is over.'

'Espionage never sleeps,' he replied.

'Do we look like spies? A middle-aged woman and her twelve-year-old son?'

He walked towards her, stopping within just a couple of paces and looking her directly in the eyes. She straightened her shoulders, pulling herself up to her fullest height. His stare seemed to pierce her brain; it took every ounce of her courage to hold his gaze.

'Spies take many disguises, madam,' he whispered before finally turning away.

The questioning ended but their ordeal was not over. They were instructed to place their cases onto the desk and open them, watching as the men examined every personal item. Martha coloured with embarrassment as moustache-man picked out with disdainful fingers her shabby greying underwear, her few sparse pieces of clothing, pored through her washbag with its few sad bottles and ointments, opened her private wallet and counted the rapidly devaluing Deutschmarks from her father's legacy.

Otto, his jaw clenched with grim determination, shuffled uncomfortably when they discovered the ancient and balding toy rabbit, his comforter, the last vestige of his childish self, that always accompanied him. She heard his horrified gasp as moustache-man took out a pen knife and slit the rabbit's belly, pulling out the few sparse lumps of remaining stuffing before pushing his fat fingers upwards into its head and turning the empty sack of fabric inside out.

'For goodness' sake, is it really necessary to destroy a child's toy?' she cried in desperation.

'Spies employ all kinds of tricks,' the tall man said. 'We cannot be too careful.'

Once their belongings had been roughly stuffed back into their cases they were instructed to remove all of their outer clothing and turn out every pocket. Their humiliation was complete.

Finally they were allowed to get dressed and the tall man sat at the desk to sign the papers required to enter Belgium. The next train would leave in two hours, they were told. But yesterday's tickets were no longer valid; they would have to buy two more. They would simply have to cut back on spending when they got to Ypres.

'Well done,' she whispered to Otto as they waited on the platform. 'We're nearly there. Speak French only from now on, remember?'

He nodded in acknowledgement, studying the ground. She wanted to reach out a comforting hand but knew his self-control was so fragile that it might be shattered by the slightest gesture. She felt so proud of the mature way he had conducted himself, his stoicism even in the face of the men's cruelty. He was fast turning into a man.

She had never envisaged that Otto would want to come with her to Flanders but when he learned what she was planning he refused point blank to countenance being left behind. A close friend had offered to look after the boy while she was away. It would have been so much easier to travel without him, and she did her best to dissuade him, but he'd been insistent.

'I want to find Heiney just as much as you,' he insisted. She knew it to be true. He'd worshipped his elder brother.

'My darling, we cannot afford two fares.'

'Didn't Papa say we should use Grandpa's money?' He'd always had sharp ears, that boy.

Even though she feared what dangers might lurk beyond the border she sensed that a mother and son travelling together would be less likely to attract suspicion than a single woman travelling on her own.

There was one other problem. To deflect unnecessary questions she planned to present herself as a Swiss citizen travelling on behalf of her sister to find the grave of a nephew. She had worked as a nanny for a family in the Swiss Alps twenty-five years ago and had taught French ever since, so her language was still passable enough, she believed, to provide sufficient cover for just the few days of her stay. But Otto knew no French at all.

Finally, she relented. 'You can come with me, but on one condition. Before we go, you will learn basic words of

French. And after we enter Belgium we will speak only that language in public, or not talk at all. You understand?'

'Why go to all that trouble?'

'We do not want to attract attention.'

'But you said we are free to travel now.'

'That won't stop the Belgians hating us. Why would they not? We invaded their country.'

'But we did that to protect our Republic,' he fired back. 'That's what they told us in school. To serve God, the Emperor and the Fatherland. They tried to starve us to death and scooped out the eyes of our captured soldiers with their special knives.'

'And their schoolchildren were told that our soldiers killed innocent Belgian babies and spit-roasted them on their bayonets for dinner.'

'But that's all lies, isn't it?' he said, eyes darkening.

'Wars are full of lies, *mein Liebling*. Who knows what is the real truth?'

She saw him blanch. Silently chastising herself for her harsh words, she put an arm around him and pulled him into her warmth. At least he would still allow that, sometimes, her *bubeleh*, her dearest boy.

How could she tell him that his brother died for a cause that was spurious at best or, at worst, simply immoral and rotten at the heart? That wars cause atrocities on both sides? No one won, everyone lost. Every day she felt bone-weary with the terrible tragedy of it.

'Anyway, it doesn't matter now. It is finished. And we have a very good reason for going there, do we not? To find Heinrich's grave?'

He'd mumbled something unintelligible. But after that

he had willingly submitted to her teaching of basic French phrases and her insistence that he learned ten new words of vocabulary each day.

❧

Now at last they were into Belgium and on their way, exhausted and starving, crammed onto a hard bench in a cramped third-class railway compartment that smelled of rotting cabbage and unwashed bodies. She cast her eyes around the carriage, surreptitiously checking their fellow travellers; they all seemed to be engaged in their own worlds, reading, knitting, snoozing. As the sun rose in an immaculate blue sky the carriage became increasingly hot and stuffy, and she found her eyes closing once more.

The next thing she knew was the nudge of Otto's elbow in her ribs. He was pointing out of the window, his eyes wide as dinner plates. She turned to look, but it took several seconds for her brain to comprehend what she saw. The scenery they'd been passing for the past hour or so, ever since the border, the patchwork of evergreen forests and placid fields, the black and white cows, the long stands of poplar and the wide stripes of dykes, had disappeared.

Instead, beyond her own reflection distorted by the smeary glass, stretched an ocean of brown mud extending on either side as far as the eye could see, punctuated only by the blackened stumps of trees and water-filled shell holes. Her heart seemed to stop in her chest, her mouth dried. Here were the battlefields. This was the narrow strip of Belgium over which her country had been at war for four years, for which hundreds of thousands of German lives had been sacrificed.

Were it not for the warmth of Otto at her side and the grunts and snores of the other passengers she could easily have imagined herself dreaming once more, only this time it was *ein Alptraum*, a nightmare. As the reality became clear, she felt queasy all over again: somewhere out there, in that chaos of destruction, that vision of hell, was the body of her precious son.

'How much longer?' Otto mouthed, in German. His French did not stretch to whole sentences. 'Are we nearly there?'

As if in answer the brakes squealed and the train slowed as the devastated landscape gave way to the broken remains of a town. She had been told that Ypres was close to Langemarck and from there she could pick up a tourist bus to the cemetery. She planned to find a small *pension* where they could stay for a couple of nights, but so far they'd passed barely a single intact building, let alone a hotel.

The train jolted to a halt. 'Ypres, this is Ypres. Everyone out. Train terminates here,' came the porter's shout, first in Flemish and then repeated in French.

The station buildings were wrecked; it was a wonder the railway was still working. 'I thought you said we'd be staying here,' Otto whispered. 'There's nothing left.'

'We'll go to the town centre and ask,' she said, trying to sound confident even as the sick chill of anxiety gripped her once again.

It was just a short walk to the main square, along a street in which most buildings had been completely destroyed and even those still with four walls had lost roofs and windows. The sight of the square, when they reached it, was even more shocking. Small mountains of rubble lay where clearly there had once been grand municipal buildings and a cathedral, the jagged remains of which still reached perilously towards the sky. Not a single building had survived.

For several moments they stood, stunned into silence. Otto nudged her. 'This is crazy. Where on earth are we going to stay, Mama? And when are we going to eat? I'm starving.'

Martha scanned the scene, trying to find someone who looked kindly and reliable, someone educated who would probably speak French and not just the local Flemish. Her eye was caught by a man in his early thirties with a bold, handsome face. She watched him for a few moments, his brow furrowing as he studied the ruined buildings, making notes and sketches in his book.

Carefully, she manoeuvred herself until she was standing within earshot, and took a deep breath. It was time to try out her French. 'A dreadful sight, is it not, monsieur?'

He looked up with an easy smile. '*Oui, c'est terrible.* But I find my eye has grown sadly accustomed. Is it your first visit here?'

'Indeed it is.' She paused. 'We are just arrived. Would you know of somewhere my son and I could stay for a night or so?'

The idea evidently amused him. 'Madame, you cannot stay in Ypres. I am afraid there is not a single habitable building remaining.' He immediately added, more kindly, 'You could try Hoppestadt. It is not far, only seven kilometres. There are two hotels there, The Grand, and Hotel de la Paix.'

'I thank you, sir, for your helpful advice.'

She went in search of Otto, whom she'd left guarding their luggage near a coffee stall. His eyes were fixed hungrily on the vendor pouring batter into a waffle iron.

'Can we have one, Mama? Please?'

The delicious aroma of warm sugar and fresh coffee reminded her that they had eaten only half an egg and a crust of bread since yesterday. She ordered a waffle for each of them. Dusted with icing sugar like a light fall of snow, these crusty grids of golden batter were more delicious than she could have imagined. The coffee was stronger and smoother than any she had tasted in living memory.

'I'm in heaven,' Otto mumbled through a mouthful. 'I shall eat nothing but waffles the whole time we are here.' The joy of his smile filled her heart, sweeping away the discomfort and distress of the past twenty-four hours. *If he is happy, I can endure anything.*

An hour later they were still waiting for a taxi. When they checked again with the waffle seller he told them there were only eight serviceable motor cars in the whole town and all were engaged taking tourists to the battlefields.

'You need to get here early next time,' he added unhelpfully.

She was beginning to despair when she saw the man with the notebook approaching.

'You are still here, madame?'

'We are attempting to travel to Hoppestadt as you recommended, but all the cars seem to be engaged,' she said.

'It is obviously a good business being a taxi driver in this town.'

'I'll remember that, if I am out of work in future,' he replied, with a teasing smile that reminded her, just a little, of Heinrich's. He paused, turning away and then back to her. 'Madame, I am returning to Hoppestadt in my own car shortly. May I offer you a lift?'

Her immediate instinct was to refuse: it was far too risky to become familiar with this man who, given longer contact, might see through their subterfuge, their pretence of being Swiss. But he was so charming, his eyes so kind, and it could be several hours until a taxi became available. She heard herself accepting.

Ten minutes later he reappeared in a battered, dusty old Citroen without a roof or side windows. It spluttered to a halt, emitting a cloud of choking, oily smoke.

'She's no Rolls-Royce, I'm afraid,' he shouted over the clatter of the engine, leaping out to open the passenger door. 'But the war, you know . . .' He shrugged. 'Tanks were their priority. Still, she gets me from place to place.'

Otto climbed into the tiny back shelf, wedging himself beside their two small cases. She'd given him strict instructions not to utter a single word for the whole of the journey. The man held open the door as Martha lowered herself as gracefully as possible into the passenger seat – it was a long way down and she could feel her knees creaking – and folded in her skirt so that he could close it.

Surely no harm could come of travelling with a gentleman with such impeccable manners? It felt sweet to relax into the unaccustomed pleasure of handing over responsibility to another, if only for a brief while. She hadn't realised how exhausted she felt, after facing that gruelling interrogation on top of an uncomfortable and mostly sleepless night.

He climbed into the driver's seat and turned to her. 'Please let me introduce myself. Daniel Martens, at your service.'

'Martha Weber,' she said. 'And my son Otto.'

'Do I detect a Swiss accent?' he said, navigating the car carefully between piles of rubble.

She had rehearsed this moment over and over in the weeks before their departure. 'We are from Geneva, come to find the place where my nephew is buried.'

'I am sorry for your loss. Will you need to take a car from Hoppestadt? I recommend that you book early.'

With every exchange, Martha's confidence grew. Her story about being Swiss would provide, she hoped, a plausible excuse for any lapses in her pronunciation.

'If you have any trouble, the owner of the Hotel de la Paix will be able to help you: Monsieur Vermeulen. The name suits; when he gets excited he whirls his arms about just like a windmill.' The image made her giggle; there had been so little to laugh about lately. 'It is the most comfortable hotel, more reasonable than the other one, which is rather grand and full of businessmen, and Madame Vermeulen is an excellent chef. For a lady such as yourself, with a young boy, it is the place I would recommend.'

'You are really most kind. Thank you very much.'

'It is the least I can do, madame.'

The town of Hoppestadt turned out to be reassuringly intact, albeit rather down at heel. Only a few buildings showed signs of shelling. The main square was busy with shoppers and a cafe on the corner was open, parasols raised over terrace tables to protect against the harsh heat of the sun. It was a cheerful sight, reminding her of Berlin in the good old days, before the war.

Monsieur Martens stopped the car right outside the Hotel de la Paix, on the edge of the square.

'*Au revoir*, and a thousand thanks,' Martha said. 'You have been most kind.'

'*De rien*. It was nothing.'

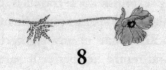

8

ALICE

When Alice cornered Major Wilson on the way into breakfast and explained her plan to leave the group and return to Hoppestadt his jaw slackened with incredulity. This was most irregular; troops were supposed to follow orders.

After a second or so he recovered, composing his features into an expression of polite concern and suggesting gently that it might be just a little unwise for a woman to travel alone, especially in a country so affected by recent turbulent times. Alice attempted to placate him with the news that Ruby would go with her and they would chaperone each other, but this seemed to have the opposite effect.

As his jaw now tightened she found herself distracted by the way the muscles in his closely shaved cheek rippled in a subcutaneous wave. 'I'm sorry, but I simply cannot allow that. I promised Mrs Barton's father-in-law that I would personally keep an eye on her. He especially requested it to be so. She has never travelled abroad before, you understand?'

He was not a tall man; in her heels Alice met him eye to eye.

'Please have no fear, Major,' she purred, assuming her most reassuring expression. 'I travelled on my own in Europe before the war, I speak French fluently and I promise not to let Ruby out of my sight. I will take full responsibility, and return her perfectly safe and well. Perhaps you could advise us on the best place to stay?'

'You're planning to stay *overnight*?' he gasped. 'What about your room here in Ostend, the meals and so on? We cannot make any refunds, I'm afraid. This really is most irregular, Miss Palmer.'

'Major Wilson.' She placed a carefully manicured hand on his arm, leaning forward and lowering her voice. 'I have money enough to cover all eventualities, for Miss Barton too, and we shall not be seeking any refunds. I am not to be dissuaded, I'm afraid. But please do not be concerned. We shall both be perfectly safe.'

Eventually, in the face of her insistence, he was forced to relent. 'I regret your decision, Miss Palmer,' he said. 'If you are determined to undertake this journey, I cannot prevent you. But please, at the very least, allow me to ensure that you travel with a respectable cab company. And if you insist on staying the night, then the most suitable hotel would be The Grand. It was a former officers' mess and the rooms are rather splendid. For what time shall I book your car?'

'As soon as possible, please. I really am most grateful, Major. We will telegraph to let you know that we have arrived safely, and when we will return to Ostend.' When she held out her hand he shook it with a grip so powerful it felt like a punishment.

Now, as they climbed into the cab, her stomach churned with a jumble of excitement and apprehension. Not only was she going to meet this enigmatic priest, with the chance – only a very slight one, she had to admit – that he might have known Sam, but there was also that other unfinished business.

His reply to her telegram was in her pocket: FORMID- ABLE STOP À LE GRAND HOTEL DEUX HEURES MARDI STOP

It had been six long years. They would both have changed, of course, she told herself, she must not expect too much. He was now a qualified architect with his own prac- tice in Lille, which was how Julia, with the help of embassy staff, had managed to trace him. 'Chances are he'll know people in Flanders who might be able to help you,' she said. 'No naughty business, though. Promise me?'

Alice had promised. She was no longer that gauche, timid girl, after all, out of depth as she struggled to under- stand the French language and culture, the girl who had once drunk far too much wine because she was so unaccus- tomed to it and had to be carried back to her lodging, to the disgust of their landlady. Her cheeks still burned at the memory.

No, she was a woman of society now, well known and respected in Washington for supporting her mother's tire- less work for charity and the arts, with her own handsome trust fund and soon to be married into one of the city's wealthiest families. But how could she come all this way to Belgium and not take this chance to see him just one more time? It was simple curiosity, she reassured Julia, nothing more. For old times' sake.

The church bells were already tolling midday as they drew up in the square at Hoppestadt, and Ginger was lowering the cafe's awning against a fierce sun that had burned away yesterday's clouds. The smell of malting barley still lingered, although less pungently than the previous day.

'Mam'selle Palmer! What a lovely surprise,' Ginger called, mopping the perspiration from her brow.

'We came back because I wanted to meet your Reverend Clayton. This is my friend Ruby Barton.'

'*Bonjour, mesdames.* You are both most welcome.'

'Where's the best place in town to stay a couple of nights, please? The major suggested The Grand. What do you think?'

The girl shrugged. 'Grand is not so friendly. Me, I would go there.' She pointed to a part-timbered building with Dutch gables immediately opposite the cafe. The sign outside read *Hotel de la Paix*. The Peace Hotel. It seemed so apt.

From the outside, the place did not look promising: the windows were shuttered, the paintwork peeling. 'Are you sure it's open for business?' Alice asked doubtfully.

'*Mais oui.* Tell Monsieur Vermeulen I send you, and he give you good rate. His wife excellent cook.' Ginger kissed her own fingertips in a gesture of approval that knew no language barriers.

The front door of the hotel yielded with a theatrical squeak into a wood-panelled hallway. As their eyes became accustomed to the dim light, they discovered a reception desk leading into an untidy office behind. Further along the corridor was a stairway with an ornately carved banister; opposite that a door into the formal dining room, its tables dressed with reassuringly crisp white linen. Mouth-watering smells of frying butter and garlic wafted from a door at the rear.

They exchanged glances; the place appeared deserted. Alice spied a small brass bell on the reception desk and pinged it, gently at first and then more firmly. After a moment, a man appeared from a further door at the end of the corridor – the bar, judging by the smell of beer that came with him. His brows and lashes were so pale they gave his face an expression of slight surprise; a stubble of ginger beard completed the impression of someone who had just woken up.

'Good afternoon,' he said. 'What can I do for a couple of beautiful young ladies?'

Surely this could not be the hotelier, speaking such fluent English? 'Am I speaking to Monsieur Vermeulen?'

'Dearie me, no, I'm just Freddie. Plain old Fred Smith. Left over from the war.' He called through the dining room doorway: 'Maurice! You got customers.'

'Are you from England, Mr Smith?' Ruby asked.

'Born within the sound of the Bow Bells. Can't you tell?'

'You're a true Londoner, then?'

'Got meself a Blighty one.' He indicated an empty sleeve. 'But Blighty didn't seem to want me: no work, no home, family all gone. I'm not bitter, it's just the way it goes. So I come back here. I like the people here, you see. They're gentle folk, the Belgians, and their beer is good and strong, not like the dribble they serve back home these days. Now I run a guide service to the cemeteries and battle-fields. Just get in touch if you need me.'

A tall, gaunt-looking man in his middle years, spectacles pushed up onto a pate of thinning grey hair, appeared from the office behind reception and introduced himself as Monsieur Vermeulen. He spoke French with a guttural accent that was at first difficult for Alice to grasp. 'How may I help you?'

'We require two rooms, for two or three nights. Would you show us the best available, please?'

He picked up two sets of keys and led them up the stairway to a wide landing, unlocking the door to room 1, first on the left. As he threw open the shutters the sun flooded in. The room was large and the decor homely and a little faded, but it reminded her of the family's cabin where they spent every summer of her childhood: her favourite reading corner with the view of the lake, Sam in his canoe, her father fishing, her mother cooking crab. The place had been abandoned since Sam disappeared. No one had ventured there. The memories were too painful.

A patchwork quilt covered the double-sized bed and the floorboards were scattered with colourful plaited rugs. She tested the bed springs with a discreet fist; they gave satis-factorily. The long windows looked out over the square – from here she would be able to see the all comings and goings of the town. Alice was charmed; the place was hardly deluxe, but she liked the atmosphere and it could not be more centrally located.

'It is good, *mesdames*?'

'It's lovely,' Ruby said. 'Nicer than that gloomy old room in Ostend.'

He led them to room 2, next door. It was much the same, with the double bed, the basin and the view over the square.

'Wherever did you learn such good French?' Ruby asked, after he'd gone to fetch their cases.

'I spent three months in Paris before the war. It's a bit rusty, but it's coming back.'

'You never cease to surprise me.'

'Is that a good thing? I can never tell whether you English are joking.'

'It means I'm quite impressed.'

'Quite?'

'Very impressed.'

'Thanks,' Alice laughed. 'I'll take that as a compliment, then. Shall we unpack and then go across to the cafe for lunch?'

'Good plan, I'm starving,' Ruby said.

※※※

Half an hour later, as they came downstairs, the Englishman was still lingering at the doorway to the bar. 'Nice rooms, eh, ladies? Overlooking the square, are you?'

'Very good, thank you. It's a very pleasant view,' Ruby said.

'How long are you staying?'

'Not long.'

'If you need anything, just get in touch,' he said, unfazed by Alice's curt reply. 'I know my way around and can give you pointers, if you get my drift. Help you search for names and the rest; they're turning up all the time. I can make enquiries and take you places.'

'Thanks. We'll certainly let you know,' Alice said.

'If I'm not here, just ask Maurice. He knows where to find me.'

'Don't you find that man a bit strange?' she whispered as they crossed the square to the cafe, blinking in the sunshine.

'He's just down on his luck, I think,' Ruby replied. 'I've seen plenty of his sort on street corners. It's wicked that they're treated so badly, after they've given everything for their country. I feel sorry for him.'

'I guess you're right.'

'You could ask him where you might look for Sam? He seems to know his way around the place and, for whatever reason, he's decided not to go home. He might just have clues about others who've done the same.'

'Good thinking, Rube. That's certainly worth a try. But first, lunch.'

They sought shade from the midday sun beneath the striped awning that had certainly seen better days. Across the square, stallholders were packing up their goods, and every now and then the cobbles echoed with the staccato rattle of blinds being lowered over shopfronts. The bar was filling with working men quenching their thirst with cold beer, reminding Alice of how seriously the French took their lunchtimes, and how they would then retire for a couple of hours' rest. She wondered whether Belgians followed the same custom.

After Ginger had taken their order, she asked, 'Do you know when we might expect the Reverend, Mr Clayton, whatever you call him?'

'Tomorrow, I think.'

'Will he agree to see us, do you think?'

Ginger followed Alice's lead and replied in broken English. 'Of course, he is good man. My boys love him.'

'Your boys?'

She rested a hand on her hip, an affectionate smile on her lips. 'That is what I call them, the soldiers. I miss them sometimes. They are so strong, fighting on the battlefields, but here they are like babies. All they want is food and drink, lots of drink, to help them forget. And women, of course.'

'You don't mean . . . ?'

The girl shrugged. '*Bien sûr*. The women must have food for the children, you understand. Five francs for ten minutes.'

Alice heard Ruby gasp beside her.

'But me, I give just smile, a joke, you know, a kiss on the cheek. For a little happiness.' Ginger smiled. 'This is a small thing when they give life for our country. Also is why Monsieur Clayton set up Talbot House, like a home.'

'Didn't you say there was a chapel, too?' Alice asked.

'*Mais oui*. In room under roof, what you call it?'

'The attic?' Ruby suggested.

'People say it fully to burst for service.'

Alice struggled to visualise a chapel in an attic. The only ones she'd known were solemn stone, hard and cold. Even though Sam's faith had been tested by Amelia's death she felt sure he would have sought out such a place, had he known about it.

'What was it like here, during the war?'

Ginger looked thoughtful. 'I am only thirteen when Germans come and my father and mother want to send me away but I stay. Then fighting come closer and shells fall and make us scared. There are sad boys, muddy and tired, who drink too much and my father send me upstairs to bed. But I am not afraid. It is only the ones who shake who frighten me most.'

'Shake?' Alice asked.

Ginger demonstrated, her hands trembling, her body juddering, face contorted.

'Shell shock, that's what we call it,' Ruby chipped in. 'It's from the trenches and the constant shelling. It is an illness; they cannot help themselves.'

'Many run away,' Ginger said. 'They hide in woods because they fear to be shot. They come at night and ask my father to help them. But what can we do?' She shrugged her shoulders.

'Even now, after the war is over?'

'A few, still.'

'What do you think?' Ruby asked, when the waitress had gone back to her duties.

'About what?'

'About those poor deserters. The ones still coming out of hiding?'

Alice shrugged. 'You never know. Don't *you* hold out hope? You said your Bertie had never been found.'

Ruby looked down at her hands. 'Of course I never give up hope. Who does?' she said in a whisper. 'But so much time has passed now. I can't help thinking that if Bertie was still alive he'd have moved heaven and earth to get back to us.'

'But somehow I'm not ready to accept that,' Alice said. 'Being here makes it feel so real, as though Sam could just appear, walking across the square.' She sighed. 'But hey, this is a pretty gloomy conversation for lunchtime. Let's decide what to eat.'

Although most of the customers around them were tucking into large plates of meat and potatoes, Alice preferred the American way: a light lunch with a larger meal at dinnertime. On the menu she spied *croque monsieur*, a French treat she'd enjoyed in Paris, and described to Ruby the fat slices of ham and gruyere toasted between slices of bread topped with a white sauce. They both ordered it, with two glasses of lemonade.

After lunch, they headed back to the hotel to find Freddie, but he seemed to have disappeared. As the church clock sounded two o'clock, Alice faked a yawn. 'I'm heading up to get unpacked and take a rest. Do you want to meet up later for tea? After that we can take a walk and explore the place,' she suggested. 'When the sun's not so hot, perhaps?'

She had decided not to confide in Ruby, not just yet. She'd be bound to disapprove and in any case, if this first rendezvous was a complete disaster, there would be no need for her to know. In her room she hurriedly changed out of her red travelling jacket; it was too warm for the weather and the colour she'd chosen for its cheerfulness now felt garish and inappropriate. Her coolest outfit was a calf-length green pencil skirt with a lightweight cotton blouse in white picked out with matching green embroidery on the cuffs and collar. Flattering, modest and not too formal, she thought approvingly.

She spent a few moments tweaking her bob into place, and, after some subtle rouging of her cheeks, a few pats of face powder and a fresh application of her trademark scarlet lipstick, she tried out her most alluring smile in the mirror, looking at herself sideways, tilting her head this way, then that.

This is either the best idea in the world, or the very worst, she said to herself, *but there is only one way to find out.* She slipped quietly from her room and tiptoed down the stairs.

9

RUBY

Ruby was grateful for a couple of hours' respite. Alice was exhausting company, always talking, always busily planning her next move. She was used to a slower pace, needing time to herself, to get her thoughts in order.

She tried to rest but the multiple impressions of the past couple of days passed through her mind like the insistent flickering of a kaleidoscope. She had resigned herself to living a quiet, unadventurous life, asking no questions, trying to bury the past and live behind a mask of normality. And yet, against all of her better instincts, she had agreed to cross the Channel and join a tour of the battlefields. That was crazy enough.

Now, somehow, she'd allowed herself to be persuaded to accompany a brash, bossy American woman to this small war-torn town in the remote hope of finding a single grave. Ginger's stories had made it so much more personal. Bertie could have been – probably was – one of those boys she'd spoken of, desperate for good food, a warm bath and an affectionate word. He'd certainly have enjoyed the strong Belgian beer; he loved his brew. Did he queue for ten minutes with a woman desperate to feed her children? She winced, quickly pushing the thought from her mind.

He'd never been religious and she doubted that he'd have visited the curious-sounding attic chapel, but he may have gone to read books in the library at this Talbot House place, and he'd certainly have enjoyed the musical entertainments Ginger spoke about.

She went to the window overlooking the now deserted square, trying to imagine what it had been like during the war, full of troops coming and going, men in the cafes and bars, trucks trundling through, smart, puffed-up-looking officer types marching to and from their important business at the Allied headquarters in the town hall, its tower still dominating the square. She shivered, despite the warmth of the sunshine, to think of the men who'd entered unwillingly through its stone gateway, facing punishment or even death for desertion or other misdemeanours.

It's all ruddy rules, Ruby, Bertie had written in one of his letters. *No one knows what they are till you get caught breaking them. Then they tell you, right enough.*

The memory of his words made her smile. And then, in a heartbeat, she could hear his voice in her head, his real voice, the voice that in the turmoil of her grief she'd found herself unable to recall, the voice she'd mourned for so long.

'You *were* here, Bertie, weren't you? I can hear you, my darling,' she whispered.

Now she could picture him clearly, sitting with his mates at a cafe table. He'd be ordering a large, cold beer, rolling a cigarette. He'd tell a joke and someone would tell another and as he laughed he'd carelessly lean the chair back onto its hind legs. She could almost hear his mother reprimanding him: *Don't do that Albert, you'll break the chair.* And he'd be running a hand through the tight curls that sprouted back so defiantly after each military haircut, determined never to be tamed.

From the day they learned he was missing Ruby had found herself unable to continue writing in her diary. No words written or spoken could ever express her pain. But his precious letters were tucked into the back of the notebook, along with the terrible notices they'd received from the army, and she took it with her everywhere.

She went to her case, still unpacked on the floor beside her bed, and found it. Seating herself at the small table beside the window, she flicked through to the first blank page, took up the pencil, licked the lead and held it to the paper, her fingers trembling. And then she began to write.

You were here in Hops, Bertie. I am certain of it. And now I'm here too, with you. If you asked me to describe what I've just experienced, I'd call it 'feeling your presence'. None of that spiritual guff – you know me well enough – and not as a spirit or a ghost, none of that nonsense, but just feeling close to you. Closer than I've felt for months.

She could feel her shoulders releasing, her sadness easing. Writing seemed to soothe her like a dock leaf rubbed on a nettle sting, or a cold paddle in the river on a hot day.

*Bertie my darling, I am doing my best to find your
grave, to honour the terrible sacrifice you made for our
country, to find a way of helping us face life without you.*

She sighed and began to write again, slowly, deliberately.

*I have not been a good wife to you, dearest Bertie, and I
don't think I can go on living unless I can admit it to
you and beg your forgiveness. While you were away so
bravely fighting, I did something terrible . . .*

The pencil seemed to freeze in her hand. How could she
have betrayed her beloved with that slick, smooth-talking
man?

When Bertie was at war she'd felt so lonely and lost without him. One evening, after he'd been away several months,
she went out with friends, drank too much and flirted with
a tall, snappily dressed man she barely knew. From the way
he bought rounds of drinks and offered his fancy cigarettes
to everyone at the table it was clear he had plenty of money,
and she found herself admiring his generosity.

Her friends went home early and they stayed on chatting
and laughing. He offered to walk her home and one thing
led to another: kissing and groping, a surge of animal desire
and a short, hasty coupling against a wall.

She had never seen him again but, even now, the
memory made her nauseous, stinging her throat with acid
bile. It was a moment of insanity for which she would never
forgive herself, let alone expect the forgiveness of anyone
else, alive or dead. She threw down the pencil and gazed

towards the window, watching the dust motes hanging in a shaft of sunlight.

It was then she saw the print, hanging on a wall in the shadows, a map of Flanders, in a dark-wood frame. Around its edges were small coloured illustrations of places of local interest: cathedrals, ancient buildings, famous landmarks and the like. Or at least, how they'd looked before the war.

She soon located Ypres, its magnificent medieval Cloth Hall intact, and the cathedral towering behind. More modestly, Hoppestadt was illustrated with a horse and cart carrying barrels to celebrate the town's brewing fame. What caught her eye next, with its familiar burden of horror and grief, was the word *Passchendaele*. The word made her fizz with impatience; she began to pace.

Now that she had felt Bertie's presence, finding his grave became even more urgent. All she needed was a few more hours at Tyne Cot. This was what she had come for; why else would she be here, if not to discover what had happened to him? She needed to confess, to say a proper goodbye and beg his forgiveness. Only then, perhaps, might she be able to cast off the pain of her guilt. You couldn't do that writing in a diary.

There was no reply from Alice's room. Pulling on her shoes, she went downstairs and into the simple bar area with doors open to the square. She didn't see him at first, sitting in the shadows, and the sound of his voice made her start. 'You looking for your friend, love? Yankee lady with the lipstick?'

The Cockney accent was unmistakeable. As her eyes adjusted she saw him more clearly: that unruly ginger hair and those disturbingly blond eyelashes and brows that gave him an expression of constant mild amusement.

She replied as politely as she could. 'Yes, I am looking for my friend, Miss Palmer. Have you seen her, by any chance?'

'Went that-away,' he said, ''Bout half an hour ago. *À propos* of very little,' he added, 'I'm waiting for a customer who booked a tour. Got the car and driver organised and everything. Lovely day for a trip, ain't it? But he hasn't turned up, the b . . .' He checked himself. 'Anyway, I've been on my loney-oh all afternoon. Care for a drink?'

'That is kind, but no thank you, not just now.'

She went back to her room and stood by the window looking out over the square, watching people come and go, feeling trapped and restless. The church bell chimed half past three. The afternoon was wearing on. Wherever could Alice have got to?

Then it came to her, a thought almost surprising in its simplicity. Mr Smith was a tour guide, short of a customer, and she was desperate to get to Tyne Cot. For all of Alice's doubts, she saw nothing wrong with the man. The days were long at this time of the year, there were still plenty of hours of light left, and it wasn't as though she had anything else to do, here in this little town. And what she most wanted, right now, was to find Bertie.

Uncertainties crowded in, but she pushed them away. *He's a soldier. One of your kind, Bertie. Can I trust him?* There was no answer, of course, but she knew what he *would* have said; it had become a kind of catchphrase for the pair of them: *C'mon, Ruby, take a chance.*

Swiftly, before she could change her mind, she ran

downstairs again. 'How much would you charge for a trip to Tyne Cot, please?'

'Ten francs plus five for the driver and the car,' Mr Smith responded promptly, his eyes twinkling. 'As it happens, I've booked the car for this afternoon but I've given up on the wretched man. How's about it, miss?'

There was an envelope of Belgian francs in her suitcase, as yet untouched, that Bertie's father had thrust into her hand at the last minute.

'That would suit me very well, Mr Smith,' she said.

'Freddie, please.'

'Then you must call me Ruby.'

❦

Half an hour later, she was sitting in the front seat of an ancient green motor van, with *Pain Frais* roughly stencilled on each door, beside a gaunt-faced middle-aged Belgian with the blue-grey bruises below his eyes of someone who has too little sleep. Freddie had introduced him as Monsieur Vermeulen – 'he only answers to Max' – the brother of the hotelier Maurice. Apparently he owned the best bakery in town, and the smell of fresh bread lingered deliciously from the morning's deliveries, mingled with the not unpleasant aroma of tobacco smoke from the cigarette that seemed to be a permanent fixture hanging on Max's lower lip. Freddie climbed into the back, seating himself on a couple of wooden bread crates. 'Don't you go worrying about me, darlin', I can put up with almost anything after them trenches,' he said.

Was it the Cockney accent, or the cheerful, irreverent

humour so like Bertie's, that made her warm to him? For some reason she felt safe in his presence. They'd had the briefest of conversations about where she wanted to go and how long it would take before she'd made up her mind, running back upstairs only to retrieve her hat and slip a note beneath the door of Alice's room.

As the van clattered through the streets Ruby felt an unusual lightness in her chest, a fluttering sensation as though her heart was dancing. Then she recognised it: this was the same feeling she'd experienced on the steamship, a mixture of nervous anticipation and excitement. Here she was, the girl who found it alarming to travel a new bus route in her home town, in a car with a couple of strangers in a foreign country. The heavy feeling of dread that had been lying in the pit of her stomach for so many months, even years, had somehow lifted.

Just look at me, Bertie. I'm on my way to find you. Taking a chance.

Despite the fact that Freddie apparently spoke no French or Flemish, and Max barely a word of English, the two men managed to maintain a fluent conversation of grunts, gestures and a few common words of 'Franglais' that provided them much amusement and helped distract Ruby from the alarming rattles and clunks of the van.

The journey took longer than she remembered from the previous day, and was certainly much further than the map on her bedroom wall had suggested, but they finally arrived at Tyne Cot, the great field of crosses laid out in every direction. As Max settled into his seat and closed his eyes for a snooze, she and Freddie climbed stiffly out of the van.

'Trust me, I done this plenty of times,' he said. 'We take an area each to make sure we don't miss anything. Then we'll take the next section and so on. I've found any number of graves the army swore blind were not on their records. So you never know, we might just get lucky.'

Buoyed by his optimism, Ruby set off across the field following the paths of baked mud, criss-crossing the area he'd indicated. A few rows away he was doing the same, walking slowly, checking every name. Between them, surely they would find her beloved.

Freddie spotted another Barton, and Ruby the cross of an A. Burton on which the lettering was badly worn. But then they noticed he was a sergeant, so it couldn't have been Bertie. A couple of further false alarms caused her heart to skip a beat but, as the time passed, her spirits began to flag. The sun was warm, and she found herself having to stop every few minutes to wipe her brow. There was no sign of Private Albert Barton.

'Is there much more to cover?'

He indicated a large area to their left. 'You take that side and I'll take the other,' he said. 'But I'm afraid we'll have to leave at five. Max has to be back in Hops in time to mix the dough and set it to prove. I give him a hand, some evenings. My uncle was a baker, back in the day, so I knows a bit about it.' He smiled a little ruefully. 'Keeps me out the bar and gives me wallet a treat.'

'What time is it now?'

He pulled a battered metal watch from his pocket. 'Half past four.'

Only half an hour left. Ruby began to walk more quickly, scanning the names without stopping. If only they could check every one, however briefly, she could be satisfied that she had done all she could to find him. But the time slipped by and she seemed to have read every name under the sun, except for *Private Albert Barton.* They met at the middle of the final section. 'Nothing?' he asked gently.

'Nothing.'

'I'm sorry, love, but I reckon we've covered everything now. You do know that he's probably here, even so?'

Dozens, no, hundreds, were simply marked *Known only unto God.* One of these could easily be him, but how would she ever know? She nodded, not trusting herself to speak, as he led the way back towards the van.

Just as they reached it, their attention was diverted by a lorry pulling up on the road close by. Around twenty men jumped down from the rear with spades and canvas bags slung over their shoulders and gathered in a group, awaiting orders. They looked Chinese, and she wondered what could have brought them to the battlefields of Europe.

A taller man in a captain's uniform appeared, shouting in English: 'Now, lads, you know what to do? We only have five hours of daylight left, so get to work. Stay within your marked area and dig very, very carefully. Take every scrap you find, and put it into your bag. Any bodies or body parts, call me at once.'

Now she understood that the pegs and string she'd noticed earlier demarcated a search zone just beyond the perimeter of the cemetery, and found her eyes drawn unwillingly to the men as they fanned out and began to dig in the mud. A small breeze brought to her nostrils the stench of sour earth, of decay. The smell of the aftermath.

'C'mon, Ruby, this ain't a good idea,' Freddie urged, taking her arm, but she held her ground.

'No, I have to,' she said, resisting his pressure. *It could be Bertie.*

Almost immediately, after just a few jabs with his spade, a man called out and the captain went over. He took the spade himself and dug a little more, carefully turning each clod of soil over to inspect before discarding it. Even from this distance she could see what they were uncovering: a body.

But not a body. She found herself mesmerised, unable to look away. Finally, they revealed what was clearly just a head and torso, still in uniform but with arms and legs missing. Torn between the desire to close her eyes and the need to continue watching, to bear witness, she found her feet fixed to the spot, her eyes unable to cease their seeing. She felt her legs go weak and begin to tremble. With the utmost tenderness three men lifted the remains and placed them gently, almost reverently, onto a white sheet laid on the ground. A shroud.

This mess of bloody, muddy, foul-smelling remains had once been a living, breathing, loving and much-loved man, a father, husband, son or brother.

It was then that she fully understood the sheer desolate hopelessness of her search. Bodies were everywhere. They were not confined to cemeteries or marked graves. This whole field, or fields, perhaps the whole area, was itself a graveyard. Wherever men had fought, there would be bodies. One of them might be Bertie. There were probably French, Belgian and even German bodies too.

In her mind's eye she could see layers and layers of them, laid end to end, some complete, and some just lumps of unidentifiable flesh, lying close beneath the ground, close beneath her own feet, right here, and reaching away as far as you could see.

The world tilted, there was a roaring sound in her ears and a dark gauze seemed to fall over her eyes before the world went black.

***

She felt arms around her, raising her from the ground, and heard Freddie's calm voice. 'Don't you worry, darlin'. Reckon you've had a bit of a turn. We'll get you back to the van and you'll soon feel better.'

She found herself shivering uncontrollably. He wrapped his jacket around her shoulders and handed her a less-than-clean white handkerchief. 'Come on now, let's get you up.' She tried, but even with his help she could not stand. Her legs felt like India rubber.

'I'm so sorry to have caused any trouble,' Ruby whispered. 'It was . . .'

'Nothing to be sorry for,' Freddie said. 'It's a shocking sight all right. Never get used to it meself. That's why I didn't want you to see it. Makes you realise how many they've yet to dig up. At least we know they are doing all they can to find people and give them a decent burial.'

At last, after several sips of brandy from his hip flask, she managed to summon the strength to stand and then, supported by Freddie, to walk unsteadily back to the van.

Max dropped them back at the hotel. 'Care to join me for a drink?'

'I'd better go and find my friend,' she said. 'Thank you for all your help this afternoon.'

'I'm sorry we didn't find your lad,' he said.

'You did your best. It was just that . . .'

'I'm sorry you had to see those Chinese fellas, too. Bit of a shocker, that one.'

How could she explain the darkness in her heart? Earlier this afternoon, she'd felt close to finding him, but now all she was left with was that grim vision of decomposing body parts being pulled from the ground. Any one of them could have been him.

'How do they identify them?'

'Identity discs, cap badges, pocket books. Lots of ways,' he said. 'They're finding people all the time.'

'Will they let the families know?'

'I expect so,' he said. 'Although I'm guessing it will take years to find everyone.' He looked up at her. 'Don't give up hope, Ruby.'

'I'll try not to,' she said.

Alice was not in her room, and Monsieur Vermeulen had not seen her, but Freddie was still in the bar. 'I hope it's not too late to take up your offer of a drink.'

'Nothing would please me more,' he said cheerfully,

pulling her a small glass of what he said was the local brew. 'This'll put hair on your chest.'

She took a tentative sip.

'Good?' he asked.

'Delicious.' Though light in colour, the beer was surprisingly deep in flavour, sweet and bitter all at the same time, and cold enough to make the outside of the glass sweat. From the first sip she could tell that it was much more alcoholic than the beers at home.

'Let me buy,' she said, opening her handbag.

'Nah. You owe me nothing, love. Maurice is happy for me to have a few glasses in return for the little jobs I do for him.' They were the only customers and he chose a table beside the doorway leading to the square. 'I like it here,' he said, settling into a chair. 'It gets a good breeze and you can watch who's going by.'

They sat in silence for a moment, watching the passers-by: men on their way from work, women carrying shopping or laundry, or hand in hand with small children, older children freed from school and out to play. Ordinary lives. People just carrying on, making the best of it, even with so many horrors lived through, and still being experienced right on their doorsteps.

'Your friend not back?'

'I'm sure she'll be here soon.'

'Bit of a one, isn't she, if you don't mind me saying?'

'She's American.'

'Explains a lot.' He grinned over his glass, eyes teasing behind the blond eyelashes.

'But she's very generous. We met on the ship coming over.'

'Where's she been today, then?'

'To be honest, I'm not entirely sure. We said we'd meet for tea.' She glanced up at the clock above the bar and shrugged.

He scoffed. 'Those Yanks think they can get away with anything after they won the war for us. Who's she looking for?'

'Her brother. He joined up to fight with the Canadians under a false name, she thinks.'

'Good lad. I take it he didn't come home?'

'It's been nearly nine months since the peace, and no news. She seems convinced that this army chaplain, a man called Clayton, can help her find him.'

Freddie's face lit up. 'Old Tubby? I knew him well. Good man, even if he is a God-botherer. I thought he'd gone home.'

'Apparently he's coming back here tomorrow. According to Ginger.' She took another sip, beginning to enjoy the taste.

'Sorry old business, ain't it?' he sighed, tracing a pattern in the condensation on the side of his glass. 'Sometimes I envy the ones who've gone. It's harder being left behind, knowing you'll live your life, even grow old, perhaps. And their lives are over, almost before they had a chance to begin.'

'How can you bear it, going back to those graveyards?'

'It's not easy to explain to anyone who wasn't there. Of course the war was effing awful, 'scuse my French: the mud, the lice, the rats, terrible rations, the stupid, pointless orders, living in utter bloody fear that every shell coming over is likely to blow you to kingdom come and every breath you take could be your last.'

He took a long swig, nearly emptying the glass. 'But what keeps you going, day in day out, is your mates. You trust 'em with your life, they trust you with theirs. You would die for them – many did. I dunno . . .' His voice cracked and he swallowed hard. She feared that he might be about to cry, but he carried on, the words tumbling from his mouth now.

'It's just that . . . I bloody loved those men, you know. More than I loved anyone, even me old lady, God rest her soul, though that's a different kind of love, I grant you. That friendship with your mates, when you're facing the enemy together, it's just . . . I don't have the words for it, I'm not an educated bloke. You feel alive like you've never felt before. It's a privilege to have known it. For all the grief and misery we went through, I wouldn't have missed it for the world.'

His cheeks flushed, discomfited at having expressed such strong emotions. She smiled back, reassuring, finding his words unexpectedly comforting. This must have been what Bertie had also experienced: that powerful bond of comradeship, that fierce love that sustained you, that made you feel brilliantly alive even in the face of death and destruction.

They sat in silence for a few seconds. 'Did they survive, your mates?' she asked gently.

'Some of 'em,' he said. 'We had a couple of get-togethers, once we got home, you know. But it was never the same. That's why I'm here. There's nothing left for me back there and life seems so drab now, after the war.'

'Do you have any family?'

He gave a long, weary sigh. 'The wife died of the cancer

just a few months after I got back. I couldn't get no work and was drinking that much her sister claimed I wasn't fit to bring up the kids. She was probably right, at the time, though I've mended my ways a bit since coming over here. At least she's giving them a proper family life. More than I could, anyway.'

'That's a sad story, Freddie. I'm so sorry.'

'Nah, girl, don't you worry about me.' The grin returned to his face. 'I'm a survivor. Nine lives and all that.' He stubbed out his cigarette and pushed his chair back. 'It's been a pleasure, but I'd better be on my way.'

'Thank you again for this afternoon,' she said. 'And for the beer. I'm quite taken with it.'

'The pleasure's been all mine, madame,' he said, with a mock-formal bow.

Dear Bertie, she wrote. *I may not be able to find your grave, but that doesn't seem to matter so much, now. That piece of land, the place where you gave your life with so many others, doing what you believed was right, will forever be in my heart. There is a kind man here called Freddie, who told me a bit about how it was, fighting with his mates, how they depended on each other, even loved each other. It gives me comfort to believe that this is what you experienced too.*

She would ask for his forgiveness another day.

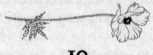

10

MARTHA

By the time they reached Hoppestadt, the town seemed to
be slumbering in the midday sun.

Martha hoped that now they had survived the journey
and the border interrogation the worst would be over but
she found herself once more wracked with nerves as Monsieur Martens pulled to a halt outside the Hotel de la Paix.
It looked distinctly unpromising, with its shuttered windows and neglected paintwork.

'Are you sure it is open?' she asked.

'Oh yes. It's just they haven't had time to smarten it up,
after the war, you know,' he said airily. 'It is very pretty
inside.'

She thanked him, offered him a few notes which he
refused and waved him goodbye. Then, taking a breath, she
steeled herself, calling once more on dwindling reserves of
courage, and pushed open the front door of the hotel.
Immediately, they were assailed by the most glorious smells
of frying butter and garlic.

'Yum,' Otto murmured, following her over the threshold
into the gloom of the hallway.

A wide, wood-panelled corridor lay ahead of them, furnished with cheerful woven rugs. It felt homely enough, just as Monsieur Martens had promised, but the place appeared deserted. She rang the brass bell at the reception desk but when no one appeared they moved cautiously along the corridor and opened a door labelled *Cafe/Bar*. Its only occupant was a young blond-haired man who appeared to be enjoying a liquid lunch.

'Good afternoon,' she said. 'Do you know the whereabouts of Monsieur Vermeulen, please? I wish to take a room.'

'Parlay no Frenchie,' was his reply, which she did not understand. Was it Flemish? Or perhaps her accent had confused him?

She tried again. 'Monsieur Vermeulen? I wish to take a room.'

The man peeled himself off the stool and shouted through a door at the back of the bar to someone called Maurice. It was then she realised that he was speaking English, which unsettled her even more. Of all their country's enemies, the English were the worst.

To her relief, Monsieur Vermeulen soon appeared. He seemed friendly enough, understood her French and displayed no tendency to windmill his arms, but the room rates he quoted were well out of her range. After some discussion he seemed to take pity on them, offering a price she could afford for what he called his 'budget' accommodation.

'It is nothing grand,' he said, leading them up the wide wooden staircase to another, narrower stairway twisting upwards into an attic. The room was small and dark, with sloping ceilings and just one double bed, but this didn't matter in the slightest: Otto often crept into hers at home, for warmth and comfort. Monsieur Vermeulen showed them the bathroom and toilet at the end of the corridor, and explained that as the only other bedroom on this floor was unoccupied these facilities would be for their sole use.

'This will do very nicely, thank you,' she said. 'May we take it for three nights, please?'

As she heard his footsteps descending the stairs she gave a deep sigh. At last she could relax. They were safe, away from prying ears, and could talk in German without fear of detection. Otto went to the dormer window and she moved behind him, resting her arms around his shoulders. Even in the two days since they left home he seemed to have grown taller; she had to peer around his head to see the view – a tangle of neglected gardens and derelict buildings at the rear of the hotel.

'Heinrich is out there somewhere,' he said quietly. 'Is it far away?'

'To Langemarck? I am not sure exactly. Perhaps half an hour?'

'When are we going to see him?'

'Tomorrow, I hope. When we can find someone to take us.'

They stood in silence for a few moments.

'I was so proud of you today, Otto,' she said gently. 'At the border.'

'They were just stupid, horrible people but we won, didn't we? We're here now.'

'I'll mend Rabbit when we get home. He'll be good as new.'

'It's okay, Ma, he doesn't really matter anymore. Can we go shopping now? I'm starving.'

'Half an hour. Then we'll go, promise.'

Martha opened her case, took out her washbag and went along to the bathroom. The fittings were clean and modern, the water gushed from the tap luxuriously hot. Later, she promised herself, she would take a long, deep bath, but for now she contented herself with a wash, cleaning her teeth and brushing her hair. Instructing Otto to follow suit, she unpacked and carefully refolded their few items of crumpled clothing into an enormous wardrobe that seemed to take up a full quarter of the room. Then she kicked off her shoes and fell onto the soft white bed, closing her eyes. She didn't even hear him return from the bathroom.

She was jolted awake when he bounced onto the bed beside her.

'Can we go before I die of starvation?' he grumbled.

Poor boy, not for five years had he seen a shop offering anything other than empty display tins and packets, faded and dusty reminders of past riches. Out of school hours, much of his time had been spent standing in queues for bread, sausage, potatoes, eggs, everything almost. While Martha could endure the constant ache in her own shrinking stomach, she could not bear to see her son hungry and would always give him the lion's share of any food they could find. She would gladly have starved herself had she believed it would relieve the boy's suffering. But since Karl died she'd discovered a renewed determination to maintain her own health and strength. She was all the family Otto had, after all; she must live for him.

Much as she was enjoying the comfort of this bed and

the safety of this little room, she could resist his pleadings no longer.

The square was busier now, the cafe terraces filled with men and women eating bread and sausage washed down with amber-coloured beer.

'This is what it used to be like in our city,' she whispered to Otto. 'You won't remember. But one day it will be like this again.' *Perhaps*, she added to herself. It saddened her to recall how Berlin was before the war, when she and Karl would meet after work and sit in a cafe, joined by friends and colleagues, and how they would drink and laugh and gossip, discussing the latest radical ideas and putting the world to rights long into the evening.

What heady days. The old order was on its way out and a bright future lay ahead for the country, they believed; a future which would see an end to rural poverty, would provide education for all, including women, and the vote for everyone over twenty-one, regardless of their income or gender.

How wrong they'd been. All they'd got was a crippling, devastating war.

Martha and Otto walked on, politely returning any greetings that came their way, trying to avoid eye contact and the curious glances. Much as she would have loved to have taken a seat in a cafe, to have tasted a beer, she feared being drawn into conversation. Their treatment at the hands of the border guards had been a harsh reminder: they might be protected by international peacetime law but how individual citizens would react should it be discovered that she and Otto were German, even just an ordinary mother travelling with her son, was anyone's guess.

She became uncomfortably aware of how unusual they must look: a tall middle-aged woman with a famished, war-weary face, and a gangly adolescent boy in his slightly too small sailor shirt, shorts and cap. She had unearthed from the recesses of the wardrobe her best serge jacket, a long skirt and hat – usually saved for interviews, or special days at the college where she taught. They were too warm for the time of year, but the moth holes were mostly well concealed and, besides, they were all she had. In Germany, no one had been able to buy new clothing since the start of the war. It was hardly surprising that they attracted a few stares.

They left the square and took the street they recognised from their journey into the town. Otto was the first to spot the bakery. 'Look,' he whispered. 'Just down there.' Even though the shelves were largely empty, this being mid-afternoon, an irresistible aroma of fresh-baked bread, sweet vanilla and warm sugar seemed to reach them even before they drew near.

They went into the shop and were greeted by a dumpy, dour-faced woman. 'Can I help you?'

'May I have some bread, please, and pastries?'

'I'll see what I've got left.' The woman disappeared through a door and returned with a basket of assorted bread rolls, a small tray of cakes and a box of round biscuits covered with sliced almonds. Martha chose four white bread rolls, two small gateaux topped with strawberries, and two squares of a yellow cake decorated with slices of crystallised lemon. Together they watched every move as the woman rolled up the bread in a page of newspaper, deftly folding a second page into a box for the cakes. Taking up a stub of pencil, she wrote the cost on the box.

Martha felt like laughing out loud: the transaction had been so straightforward. She could barely remember what it was like to buy food so easily. Yes, the woman had been a little surly at first but acknowledged her payment without a single suspicious glance and even, as they bid her farewell, with the hint of a smile. They hadn't had to queue for hours, to jostle with others or fight their way to the front only to have the vendor shout at them, grab the cash and then almost throw the unwrapped goods at them without a single courtesy.

With the packet of rolls under her arm, and Otto carrying the paper box of pastries like a precious sacrament, Martha finally felt her mood lightening, the anxiety lifting. They hurried back to the hotel and into the sanctuary of their little attic room, unwrapping the spoils of their excursion with the same joy and sense of anticipation as if they were Christmas gifts.

'Don't eat too much. You'll ruin your appetite.'

'If that's supposed to be a joke, it's not even slightly funny,' he retorted. The only times she'd ever seen Otto lose his appetite were after they'd told him of Heinrich's death and then, later, when his father had finally passed away.

Sometimes, they'd been grateful even if a meal consisted of bread alone. Occasionally they would visit Karl's brother in the countryside where his wife grew vegetables and kept secret supplies of eggs, meat and corn hidden away from the sequestering eyes of visiting officials keen to lay their hands on anything they could to feed the troops.

But as starvation became more widespread, their relationship had soured. She and Karl had never expected handouts and had always paid a fair rate for the food but now her in-laws became greedy, fleecing them just as they did the other city folk on 'hamster tours' – so-called because they returned with sacks bulging after bartering what they could for eggs, butter or even a scraggy chicken.

A beautiful carriage clock, inherited from her mother, had gone that way, as had the rather fine Persian carpet from the *Wohnzimmer*. For a week or so after each trip they had eaten well, even though their apartment felt increasingly bare. The visits ended abruptly after the wife had called them 'city scroungers' and refused to exchange a box of eggs for a brass lampshade worth many times more.

It saddened Martha to remember the good times they'd had with Karl's brother and his wife. The boys had loved their visits to the farm, had named all the cows, and the pigs, even the chickens. The last time they met was at Karl's funeral. Their murmurings of condolence, although perfectly polite, had been mechanical, even frosty, as though they held her responsible, in some way, for his death. She doubted she would see them again.

Otto had already wolfed down a bread roll before she could stop him, his eyes widening with delight at each mouthful. 'The crust, it's so delicious. Imagine how it would be with butter?'

'We shall have butter this evening, I am sure.'

'Can I have a pastry now?'

'It will be dinner in an hour or so. We'll share one and have the rest for dessert afterwards.'

He took a bite, rolling his eyes in ecstasy. 'It's got custard inside, Mama. Vanilla. Mmm. Food of the gods.'

'Whatever's made you come over so poetic all of a sudden?'

'Custard is my muse. I shall become famous for my poetry in praise of pastries.'

'Your books will sell like hot cakes.'

'I'll mix with the cream of society.'

'The girls will flock to you like bees around a honey pot.'

'Jam side up. That's me.'

They fell onto the bed giggling helplessly, intoxicated by sugar. The sound of his laughter, so rare these days, filled her heart. She pulled him into her arms. 'I love you, son,' she said, kissing his forehead.

'Don't be so soppy, Ma,' he grunted, pulling away.

❧

Encouraged by the success of their shopping trip, Martha suggested they venture out once more to find a taxi company or tourist agent who might arrange transport to Langemarck.

'Can't we find one tomorrow?'

'It's better if we can book something now, ready for tomorrow. Anyway, it's such a beautiful afternoon, too lovely to stay indoors.'

'You go. I want to stay here and read my book,' he said, snuggling into the bed.

She relented. He'd never been a studious boy but this particular novel, a translation of *Robinson Crusoe*, seemed to have gripped his attention and she was delighted to see him reading more.

'Very well then. Don't talk to anyone, and don't eat any more pastries.'

***

She made her way down the stairs and walked across the square. The sun was cooler now, slipping below the roof-tops, which was something of a relief. She was just entering a side street down which she could see what looked like more shops when she was approached by a small grizzled man in a jaunty beret.

'Good afternoon, madame.' He addressed her in heavily accented French. 'You visitor?'

She nodded cautiously and he moved closer, a little too close for comfort. She could smell the beer on his breath.

'You want battlefield tour? You take my leaflet.' He handed her a handwritten, well-thumbed piece of paper that scarcely merited the description.

'What transport do you have?' she asked.

'Motor car or coach for groups more than two persons. Where you want to go?'

'Just me and my son, twelve years old. We wish to visit Langemarck.'

Bloodshot eyes held hers with a stare. 'Langemarck? That is a *German* graveyard, madame.'

She could feel the sweat breaking out at the nape of her

neck, but she must keep calm. She had practised the story many times.

'We are Swiss, but my sister's son was unfortunately conscripted in Germany,' she said. 'It is regrettable, of course, but since she is unable to travel she begged me to visit his grave. I am sure you must understand. I cannot deny her.'

His eyes glinted. 'Forty francs.'

'That is too much for me, sir.'

'To Langemarck. German graveyard. Forty,' he said again.

He was blackmailing her. 'I cannot afford forty francs,' she said more firmly, and went to leave, but the man followed her. 'Thirty, madame?'

She shook her head again and continued walking. Surely there must be someone who would offer her a better deal?

He followed her, and she quickened her pace. 'Twenty?'

She considered a moment. Ten francs each, that was reasonable. She turned to him. 'We can go tomorrow morning?'

The man nodded. 'Certainly. Eleven o'clock.'

It was too good to resist. 'That would suit us, thank you.'

She held her breath as he muttered to himself for a second and then held out his hand. 'I must rent car. You pay ten now, ten tomorrow.' She pulled out a note from her bag and handed it to him before he could change his mind. He stashed it in the inside pocket of his grubby jacket. 'Where you stay?'

'The Hotel de la Paix.'

'See you tomorrow, madame. I come eleven.' He tipped his cap and was gone.

It was only after the man had disappeared that Martha realised he hadn't given her a receipt. She studied the piece of paper once more. Scruffy as it was, it did at least carry a name: *Monsieur G. Peeters.*

She could hardly wait to tell Otto the good news. At last, after all their saving and planning, after the long journey and terrifying ordeal at the border, they were on their way to Langemarck.

Not long to wait now, my darling Heiney. See you tomorrow.

II

ALICE

Alice tried to ignore the knowing glances of the stiffly polite receptionist at The Grand Hotel. Monsieur Martens had not yet returned. Would madame care to wait in the lounge and take a coffee, or a drink?

The place was certainly grand in that old-fashioned French way, but she was glad they'd chosen not to stay here. After the rustic charm of the Hotel de la Paix the place felt uncomfortably formal with its faux pillars, fancy plaster-work, highly patterned wallpaper, heavy curtains and ornate chairs. The major said that during the war it had been commandeered as an officers' mess and she could almost smell the sense of privilege, the cigars and whisky that they must have enjoyed while their men were sleeping in dormi-tories, or worse. Alone in the stuffy lounge, Alice found herself sympathising with the potted palms wilting in the heat, the tips of their leaves curling brown.

Her nerves were strung as tight as piano wire by the time Daniel rushed in, flustered and a full half hour late, with some story about a Swiss woman and her silent son whom he'd rescued in the square at Ypres. Standing to greet him, she found herself suddenly tongue-tied. He hadn't changed much in six years; though not overly tall, he was still an imposing figure, a man likely to attract attention in a crowd. A little thicker around the waist and jawline perhaps, but the hair was just as dark and unruly, and he still had that humorous glint lurking in his eyes when he smiled, that smile that made you feel as though you were the only person in the room.

He took both hands and kissed her cheeks three times. Then he stood back at arm's length, appraising her. Those eyes, the colour and grain of polished oak, were just as deep and unfathomable as ever.

'*Mon Dieu!* Always so beautiful, Aleese.' His pronunciation instantly transported her back to the day they first met. She'd been mesmerised as, with hands full of Gallic gesture, he'd talked about books and ideas, about the importance of good design in everything from chairs to cars, and how buildings affect people around them and who inhabit them. She'd thought him the most entrancing man in the world.

He summoned the waiter who'd been hovering in the doorway.

'What will you take? Tea? Or perhaps a *citron pressé*?'

She recalled the delicious sweet-sour drink, so refreshing on those sweltering days in Paris, long ago. 'That would be perfect.'

His gaze turned back to her face, fixing her eyes with his. 'It is true, the years have not passed for you.'

It was a lie, of course. She was under no illusion that the years had taken their toll, both physically and psychologically. She was already twenty-four and perfectly aware that the youthful bloom had started to fade from her cheeks, and that the tiny lines around her eyes and mouth resisted disguise. Her hair, once so long and lush, now rested in an ultra-fashionable bob just above her shoulders. That blithe, carefree spirit he'd first encountered, that girl with a child-like trust of strangers and an almost insatiable curiosity about the world, had been tempered and hardened by life and loss. She was now more sceptical and guarded, wiser and more composed.

The last time she'd seen him there had been tearful fare-wells and promises to meet again soon, perhaps the following summer. Their romance had been short but intense – the physical attraction was almost irresistible and on that last evening in Paris she'd come closer than ever before to intimacy.

They'd been with the crowd all evening, drinking carafe after carafe of cool rosé, until the group had dwindled. Julia claimed she was tired, and Daniel had promised to walk Alice back to their lodgings.

They'd talked and laughed until the last carafe was fin-ished, and left the cafe to walk home along the River Seine, glistening like a million diamonds in the light of the street lamps. Paris on a warm spring evening was so intoxicat-ingly beautiful that she almost forgot to breathe. The intensity of extreme happiness was dizzying, dreamlike. Just before they reached the lodging house Daniel turned to her, cupping her cheeks as though she were something infinitely precious, and kissed her intensely and intimately.

'*Chez moi?*' he murmured, as though there'd been some earlier, unspoken agreement. Desire made her carefree and rebellious, the blood coursing through her body like the current of the sparkling river.

But just as he went to take her hand and walk onwards, the small voice in the back of her head became more persistent: *Well-brought-up girls save themselves for a future husband.* Even through the rosy mist of infatuation she knew he would never be husband material; they were too young, being in Paris was too romantic, he flirted with all the girls. And what if she got pregnant? Her reputation would be ruined, marriage prospects damaged forever. Feeling wrong-footed and childish, she pulled away. 'Julia is waiting up for me.'

Once back in America she found herself physically yearning for him, regretting that she had not allowed herself to be fully loved by him. Just the once. She'd imagined it so many times. And now here he was in front of her once more, and she found herself without words.

Their drinks arrived, misty white juice diluted with water and clinking with ice, a slice of lemon wedged onto the edge of the glass. With them was an elegant silver bowl of finest white caster sugar and two long-handled spoons.

As the waiter left the room they both broke the silence, speaking at the same time. 'So, what have you been doing . . . ?' She laughed to cover her embarrassment.

'Ladies first,' he said. She had forgotten how fluent his English was.

Sipping her drink, Alice recounted how discontented she'd become at home after those carefree few months in Paris, how she'd rebelled against the innate conservatism of Washington society, the stultifying social round and the constraints of being a politician's daughter, of having to ensure that there was nothing, literally nothing, in your past that might sully his reputation in future.

'It's like living in a straitjacket.'

His lips pursed into a small moue of sympathy and the new lines at the corners of his eyes made the smile even more beguiling than ever before. She felt herself becoming seduced all over again.

'It is so wonderful to see you again, my dearest Aleese,' he breathed. 'But I sense that my good fortune is the result of a loss – that is what usually brings people here.'

She told him about her brother's disappearance, how she assumed that he must have signed up under a false name, and how she had defied her parents' wishes to come to the place where he'd last been heard of. She mentioned Tubby Clayton and how she hoped he might remember Sam at Talbot House.

'I was wondering if you know of anyone else I might ask?' she said.

'Ask?'

'About where I might look for Sam, to find out what happened to him, if he is alive or dead. There must be other people of all nationalities looking for their loved ones and I kind of hoped there might be local organisations helping them.'

He shrugged, his expression sceptical. 'So many have gone missing. So many are searching. But I can certainly try to find out for you.'

'If only I could find just a little clue, something to follow up, it would help the misery of not knowing . . .' She stopped herself. She knew nothing of what Daniel may have suffered. 'Of course, it is not the same as having your country invaded and shattered.'

'Losing a loved one is always terrible, wherever you are, whoever.'

There was a brief silence, filled with unsaid things.

'And what about you? I was so happy to get your reply to my letter. I thought you might have gone to fight and, of course, imagined the worst. I am so glad you . . .'

He sighed, a shadow crossing his face.

'If you'd rather not . . .'

'It is only that I feel a little ashamed,' he said quietly, 'because I did not have to fight. I enlisted, of course, but they sent me instead to the headquarters in Paris to help manage infrastructure and supplies. I suppose they thought that because I was training as an architect I'd know about building things.' He gave a harsh, scoffing laugh. 'Ordering thousands of concrete blocks, sandbags, that sort of thing. Hardly what I'd spent three years studying for.'

He added a precise, slightly heaped spoonful of sugar to his drink and stirred it until the grains dissolved. She recalled that gesture so well, sitting in the cafe in the Rue des Livres close to the college where they were studying; how she would find herself holding her breath through those enigmatic pauses, wondering what he would say next.

'I was angry, not being allowed to fight,' he went on. 'It made me feel like half a man. I begged them to let me go. Then my brother died, and my two cousins. Just about all the boys my age went the same way, either killed or coming back broken men, without limbs or with horrible scars. Of course, I was fortunate, but I felt so guilty.' He punched himself in the chest with a clenched fist, over the heart. 'My parents depended on me to stay alive. But that didn't stop me feeling as though I'd taken the cowards' way out.'

'You're no coward, Daniel. I'm sure of it. And I am so sorry about your brother.'

'I don't think my parents will ever recover, not properly.'

'I feel the same. It makes you feel so inadequate, being the last one left and not being able to make it better.'

He nodded, pensive again. After a few seconds he straightened up, took a breath and looked Alice directly in the eye. 'I have never forgotten our time in Paris, you know.'

She felt suddenly light-headed, as though the intensity of his gaze had sucked all the air from her lungs. 'Me neither.'

'You are still so beautiful.' As he leaned across and took her hand she felt the heat of it passing up her arm, drawing her towards him just as it used to do. She checked herself; this was moving too fast. Withdrawing her hand, she leaned back in her chair.

'There's something I need to tell you.'

'Go on.' The eyebrows quizzical, one side raised. She'd forgotten how much she loved the expressiveness of his face.

'I am engaged to be married.'

'Ah.' A pause, and then, 'Do you want to tell me about him?'

'Not really. What about you? Are you married?'

'I have a girlfriend. I've set up my own practice in Lille, did I tell you? I expect we'll marry once I get more established.'

In a way it was a relief, but that didn't stop her feeling just a little deflated somehow. All she knew was that she couldn't bear for this to be the last time they met. The church bell chimed.

'Five o'clock already? I must get back.'

'Why don't you join me for dinner tonight? The chef is already busy – can you smell it?'

She could and it was making her mouth water, but she couldn't abandon Ruby. 'My friend will be wondering where I've got to, and she'll be expecting me.'

'Your friend?'

'She's British, I met her on the ferry – she's looking for her husband's grave. Why don't you come for a drink at the Hotel de la Paix after dinner. You can meet her?'

She imagined introducing them. They would have a pleasant evening enjoying each other's company. He was just an old friend; there was nothing clandestine about their meeting, it was all perfectly normal. Whatever could be wrong with that?

He caught her eye with another questioning glance.

'Eight-ish?'

'Okay, okay, my American beaudy,' he said, mimicking. He took her hand and kissed it. 'See ya layder.'

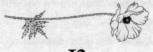

12

MARTHA

At the first sound of the dinner gong Otto leapt up from his chair, flinging the book to the floor. 'Dinner. Hurray. Let's go, Mama.'

Mouth-watering smells had been wafting through the hotel since late afternoon, seeping up the stairs and between the gaps in the floorboards: frying garlic and onions, meat being seared, pastry rising in the oven. All reminded Martha of home, before the war, when there was plentiful meat and butter, and real flour for baking.

Before leaving Berlin she'd visited the city library and taken out a guide to Belgium, dated 1910. *Whether in Wallonia, Flanders or Brussels you will always be able to enjoy a wide array of regional specialties, typical dishes or world-class gastronomy*, it said.

Yet now her appetite seemed to vanish. She felt the fears rising again, of being drawn into conversation, of being detected. The memory of their ordeal at the hands of the border guards – was it really only this morning? – was too fresh. Belgians, French, English and whoever knew what other nationalities would also be dining. Had she been travelling alone she might have asked for room service, but she knew how much Otto had been looking forward to eating in a proper restaurant with white linen and silver cutlery.

She went over the rules once more. 'No talking in German, not a word, not even a whisper. And your best table manners, please. We don't want to attract attention.'

'Yeah, yeah,' he muttered, his hand already on the door handle. 'Let's go.'

'Listen to me, Otto.' She grabbed his shoulder. 'It's important. Tell me why it is important, please?'

''Cos we don't want them to know we're Germans, 'cos they hate us.' He scowled, adding, 'Well, I hate *them* too.'

'If anyone asks you a question, smile pleasantly and turn to me. I will answer. Do you understand?'

'Yes, Mama.' He faked a smile. 'Now can we eat? I'm ravenous.'

❧❧❧

She was relieved to discover that they were the first to arrive in the dining room. Here, it seemed, punctuality was not so highly valued, and she tried to reassure herself that they might manage to avoid having to talk to anyone. She requested a table in the corner.

When the waitress brought the bread, Otto lunged at it like a starved animal, almost before she had left the table.

'Manners, boy,' she hissed.

'Look, butter,' he whispered, his eyes round as cartwheels. 'Do they eat it every day?'

'I expect so, nowadays. In the war they knew hunger like

us. It's just that they've had help from their friends the Americans,' she replied.

'They're all murdering pigs,' he muttered with his mouth full. 'But their butter is so good.'

'Shh, no more talking. French only, please. Remember what you promised.'

The meal arrived, generous portions of meatballs in a dark beer sauce served with delicious waxy yellow potatoes. She watched her son wolfing it down and envied his simple needs. Her own stomach, shrivelled through years of starvation, could not cope with the mound of rich food so soon after their pastry feast just a few hours ago. Discreetly, she exchanged her half-eaten plateful for the one that Otto had scraped clean. It too was soon empty.

The dining room filled with couples and small groups lively with conversation about the adventures of their day. They exchanged friendly greetings with Martha and, to her relief, did not engage her in conversation. But for all their friendliness, as Martha observed her fellow diners ordering food and tasting their wine, she began to experience a sense of growing resentment, even bitterness. They were so carefree, so at ease with their surroundings, chattering in a polyglot of languages: French, English, Flemish and other tongues she did not recognise.

They did not gobble their meals as Germans did, fearful they might never eat again, but lowered their faces to their plates to smell their food before tasting it in small experimental mouthfuls, exclaiming and discussing with each other the quality of the cuisine.

When the wine arrived, poured with great ceremony by Monsieur Vermeulen himself with a white napkin over his right arm and the other held behind his back, they would hold their glasses to the light, remarking on its colour before swirling it around the glass and taking tiny sips to savour it before approving with a polite nod of the head. What connoisseurs they were, so sophisticated, with such elegant manners.

Just one table remained unoccupied, the one closest to Martha and Otto. She prayed that it might remain so but before long a couple of young women entered the dining room. Sisters? But no, surely impossible. The one leading the way was tall and sharply dressed in a smart tailored red jacket with matching scarlet lipstick, her hair in a stylish bob like a star from the silent movies. The other, trailing a few steps behind, looked younger, probably young enough to be Martha's daughter. Shorter than her companion, she was really rather plain, her hair pulled back into an inexpert bun, her clothes ill-cut and unflattering.

The tall one spoke first. 'Good evening,' she said. 'How're you doing?'

'*Excusez-moi. Je ne parle pas Anglais,*' Martha replied. In fact, she did speak a few words of English, but she did not want to encourage conversation. The woman spoke again, this time in French with a sophisticated Parisian accent: 'I'm Alice Palmer, come all the way from America. Pleased to make your acquaintance. This is my friend Ruby Barton. She's English.' The other girl acknowledged her with a shy nod.

She did not want to appear impolite after this friendly overture. 'Good evening. I am Martha Weber.'

'And who is this handsome young man?'

'My son Otto. Say hello, Otto.'

'*Bonsoir, mesdames,*' he muttered awkwardly, the acne rash on his cheeks burning scarlet.

'And good evening to you, young sir,' the lipstick woman said to him, before turning once again to Martha. 'Tell me, Madame Weber, what did you eat tonight? Would you recommend it?'

'The meatballs. They were very good,' she replied, trying to calculate how soon they could leave the table without appearing rude.

'Meatballs, that's a good choice. Thanks for the recommendation. And what did you drink? Beer or wine?'

'Just water this evening,' Martha replied. 'After our long journey.'

'Just water. Have you travelled far?'

'From Switzerland.'

'Switzerland. How wonderful. I went there once. I just love your mountains. The Alps. Do you live in the mountains?'

'Not far away, in Geneva.'

'Geneva? Great lake you have there.' What a strange habit the woman had, of repeating everything she said. Perhaps it was an American thing? It felt more like an interrogation.

'Excuse me, I trust that you enjoyed your meal?' Madame Vermeulen, arriving at the table, nodded approvingly at the plates Otto had wiped clean and the empty bread basket.

'Very good, thank you,' Martha said. 'Delicious.'

The woman smiled with pride. 'The gravy is made from the beer we produce here in Hoppestadt,' she said. 'We are famous for it. Can I entice you to take dessert?'

It was the perfect excuse. 'Thank you, but we are so

weary from our journey. I think we will take a coffee and a hot chocolate in our room.'

'Of course, madame.'

She felt Otto tugging at her sleeve.

'We still have those pastries to finish,' she said, ruffling his hair, a gesture he was powerless to resist in company. She pushed back her chair and rose to her feet. 'Come, Otto. Good evening to you, ladies,' she said. 'Please enjoy your meal.'

'Good to meet you. Catch you tomorrow perhaps?' the American said.

I sincerely hope not, Martha thought to herself, forcing herself to return the smiles of other diners as they made their way to the door. What a curiously mismatched pair they seemed. The American woman was far too cheerful, chatty and nosy, the English girl so quiet and withdrawn, her skin sallow with grey thumbprints beneath her eyes, a face etched with a sadness that reminded Martha uncomfortably of her own loss.

❧

As the day of departure had drawn closer she had begun, despite her fears, to long for the moment of finding Heinrich's grave and leaving the letter and his great-grandfather's medal, of fulfilling her final promise to Karl. At least she would know where her son was buried, and would be able to say a proper goodbye. But now, as she lay in the dark between the white sheets of the bed with Otto snoring quietly beside her, the prospect felt frightening, even over-whelming.

She had no idea what to expect. From the chaos and devastation they had observed from the train it was impossible to imagine a cemetery such as they had at home, with close-mown grass paths and carefully tended flower beds between rows of crosses set in military precision. No, she must lower her expectations, steel herself for what would surely be a very different and probably rather terrifying place.

What would the grave look like? How would his name appear? She shivered involuntarily, causing Otto to stir slightly, as she imagined the lettering carved into wood or stone: *Kdt Heinrich Weber 1897 – 1915*. How could any mother respond, finding herself at the very place where her beloved son lay beneath the earth, the boy of her own flesh whose needs, both physical and emotional, she had tended for eighteen years, the bright, handsome young man for whom they had held such great hopes? She prayed she would be able to maintain her dignity, to stay brave for Otto when the moment came.

But then what if, after so many hopes and expectations, after this difficult and expensive journey, they weren't even able to find his grave? They'd still received no official confirmation, only the say-so of the families of Heinrich's friends and regimental colleagues to go on. Would she have to return to Germany with his great-grandfather's medal still in her bag? The prospect was too dismal to contemplate.

She sighed and turned onto her side, wrapping her arms around her sleeping son. His heavy warmth wove its usual magic: within minutes she was asleep.

13

RUBY

'What a strange pair,' Alice whispered across the table.

Ruby hadn't thought them particularly strange; she felt sorry for them, shocked by their hollowed cheeks and famished faces. The woman, her dark hair streaked with grey and pulled back into an unflattering bun, seemed to hold a sort of dullness, a layer of grief as fine as ash, just beneath the surface of her skin. She recognised it from her own mother's face, after her father had died.

The boy had barely uttered a single word, staring down at the tablecloth most of the time, and responding with a mumble only when his mother instructed him. He was around ten or eleven years old, she guessed, with eyes too large for his head, his face spotted with acne and his hair cut painfully short, exposing the vulnerable skull beneath. The woman was wearing a tweed jacket more suitable for winter, and his clothes seemed a couple of sizes too small: narrow wrists protruded from the sleeves of a quaint sailor-style smock.

'Did I hear her say she was from Geneva?'

'They're Swiss. I suppose that's why her accent's a bit

odd,' Alice replied. 'I wonder what brings them here? It's not like Switzerland was in the war.'

Ruby busied herself with buttering her bread as Alice chattered on. 'I'm not sure I'd bring a kid here, would you? Don't you think it might be a bit traumatic, at that age?'

'Maybe there's no one at home to look after him.'

'Did you see what she was wearing? Like something out of the last century. Wool serge in July! And putting him in that sailor suit. Poor kid.'

Ruby felt uncomfortable speculating about the woman and her son. 'So where did you get to this afternoon? I called for you at three, but you weren't there.'

'Sorry,' Alice said airily. 'I went to see a friend and it took longer than I'd planned.'

'A friend?' How could Alice have a *friend*, here in Hoppestadt?

'Someone I knew, long ago. It's a long story.'

'But I thought you'd come here to find your brother?'

'Of course I have. That's why I got in touch with this friend, because he lives in Lille and I thought he might know local people or organisations who could help.'

'And does he?'

'He's going to find out for me.' Ruby noticed for the first time a chink in the American girl's confidence. The lipstick had worn off, the loose hair was slightly awry, and there was a tiny tea stain on the front of her pretty white blouse.

'Is there something you're not telling me, Alice?'

'It's not what you think. I knew Daniel was in this area and I just thought that . . .'

Daniel? It was the fondness with which she spoke the name, like a verbal caress. There was obviously more to this 'friend' than Alice would admit. The wine arrived, dark red, aromatic and delicious.

Alice took a sip and put down her glass. 'Anyway, enough about me. What have you been up to?'

'I went to Tyne Cot.'

'Oh my goodness. Tyne Cot? However did you get there?'

'With Freddie. Mr Smith.'

'The Englishman? But how did he drive with only one arm?'

'A man called Max drove us in his baker's van. Freddie helped me and we searched and searched for an hour and a half, but didn't find any sign of Bertie, and then we saw a whole bunch of Chinese men digging up dead bodies from the mud.' She grimaced.

'How horrible. You should have waited for me to go with you. You're so brave, doing all that on your own.'

'It was a waste of time, I couldn't find him. But Freddie was very kind. Despite appearances he's a real gentleman, you know.'

'Poor you. Would it help if we went back again?'

Ruby shook her head, sighing. 'We looked pretty thoroughly. I just have to get used to the idea that there is no grave. Or he's buried somewhere else, heaven knows where.'

'Or perhaps he's alive?' Alice said.

'I'd love to believe that, but I have to be realistic. Where would he have been, all these months?'

'Anywhere, hiding out. Survivors are being found all the time.'

'Do you really believe your brother might . . . ?'

Alice sighed. 'He *has* to be. I couldn't bear it if he was dead. So he must be alive, and I'm going to find him.'

***

'It's been quite a day. I think we deserve a nightcap,' Alice said when they'd finished their meal. 'Daniel is going to drop by to meet you.'

Ruby's heart sank. She'd had visions of curling up on that big bed and perhaps writing in her diary before turning in for an early night, but she could hardly do so now without appearing rude. They sat by the open doors looking out at the square, busy with people strolling, conversing, enjoying beers in the cafe over the road. Swallows squealed in a sky still tinged pink and purple from the setting sun. It was hard to believe that only eight months ago the place had been the epicentre of Allied army activities, just a few miles back from the front. A place where Bertie would have sat and enjoyed a few beers himself, before being sent back to the mud and mayhem of the trenches, completely unaware of what his treacherous wife had been up to at home.

'Penny for your thoughts?' Alice said, returning with a whisky for herself and a coffee for Ruby.

'It's nothing. When are you expecting your friend?'

Alice laughed. 'Oh Ruby, there's no need to sound so suspicious.'

Ruby shrugged. 'I am a bit, if I'm honest.'

'Will it help if I explain? We had a bit of a fling, but that was six years ago, when we were both at the Sorbonne. I couldn't come all this way, to his home territory, and not catch up with him. I knew he was training to become an

architect so we looked him up in a French business directory – my friend Julia's father is a diplomat and knows how
to do things like that – and I sent him a telegram.'

'An old flame?'

'I suppose you could say so.'

She wasn't sure why, but it just came out: 'Old flames can
be dangerous.'

'Woah. That sounded a bit heartfelt.' Alice raised a
questioning eyebrow. 'What happened to you, then?'

Ruby shrugged. 'I got a bit burned, that's all. It was a
long time ago.'

'Go on.'

'I've never told anyone before.' *Why did I start this?*

'Only if you're sure.'

'Not much to tell, to be honest. It's the same old story:
just a one-night stand, so stupid, so unimportant. I was
lonely and he was charming and made me laugh and I
drank too much. But it wasn't long after that we got the
letter saying Bertie was missing. I saw it as some sort of
divine retribution, if you like. I've never got over the guilt.
It just eats away into you and never lets you go. In some
ways that's why I'm so desperate to find Bertie's grave, so I
can confess to him, ask his forgiveness.'

'Oh my goodness. You poor kid.'

'I can't help thinking that if I hadn't been unfaithful, Bertie
would still be alive.' Ruby swallowed, close to tears now.

Alice leaned across the table, put a hand on her arm.
'You know that's not how it works.'

Ruby sighed. 'That's how *my* mind works, though. I can't
help it.'

'I'll be careful, I promise,' Alice said.

As soon as they were introduced, Ruby appreciated exactly why Alice had been attracted to him. Daniel Martens was neither tall nor especially handsome in any classic kind of way, but he exuded confidence and an easy charm which made her feel instantly wary.

His eyes sparkled as, encouraged by Alice, he talked passionately in excellent English about his work, about how Belgians were outraged at the British suggestion that Ypres be left in ruins as a monument to the lives lost in the area, and how they were trying to persuade the authorities to let them rebuild the Cloth Hall just as it had been for six hundred years. 'It's where the heart of Ypres lies,' he said. 'There, and the cathedral. Putting them back together will be like a giant three-dimensional jigsaw puzzle. But it is such an exciting project. If only we can raise the money to do it.'

In his company, Alice's demeanour softened. Even the tone of her voice modulated, becoming sweeter, more feminine, less strident. The chemistry between the two of them was unmistakeable. As a second round of drinks was ordered the conversation became increasingly flirtatious. Ruby began to feel like a gooseberry. She had no trouble in summoning a polite yawn.

'Time for bed,' she said. 'Goodbye, Monsieur Martens, it was nice to meet you. See you at breakfast, Alice.'

Much later, when she'd been asleep for what felt like hours, she was woken by the creak of a floorboard in the corridor.

She assumed it was new guests arriving until she heard a single stifled giggle and a brief whispered expletive in an American accent, unmistakeably Alice.

She lay rigid in the bed, heart pounding, her ears finely tuned for further sounds: the deep timbre of a male voice, the squeak of a bed. She was shocked. Surely even Alice would not be so blatant as to invite that man into her hotel room?

But there was another feeling, one that Ruby couldn't name until her own body gave her away. In the silence her imagination began to embellish the scene: the increasingly passionate kisses, the slow removal of clothes. She found herself flushing hotly in the dark. She envied their intimacy. It had been so long that Ruby could barely remember what it felt like to kiss a man, let alone have his hands on her. Against all her better instincts, she began to feel desire.

It was such a long time ago – in a different lifetime, it now felt – but the persistent, agonising guilt of that reckless moment still haunted her today. It had left her feeling sickened with self-reproach, terrified of an unwanted pregnancy and disgusted with herself for betraying Bertie when he was facing dreadful hardships on the other side of the Channel. Not even two hundred miles away.

When the letter arrived telling her that Bertie was missing, all became clear: this was a punishment for her infidelity. *If only I had not been so weak*, she reproached herself, *perhaps Bertie would still be alive.* However much she'd tried to reason that there was no such thing as divine retribution, that Bertie's fate was pure coincidence, that it was nothing to do with her 'lapse', as she thought of it, she had been unable to rid herself of the corrosive guilt that was always in the back of her mind, tainting every memory.

It was her lowest moment. She believed herself to be worthless; she did not deserve to live. One dark day she went to the chemist and bought a bottle of aspirin; after her mother had gone to bed she grabbed from the kitchen cupboard an old bottle of her father's brandy, left over from before he died. Choking and gasping, she managed to down the lot.

The next thing she remembered was lying in a pool of her own vomit, her mother shaking her shoulders, keening and calling her name. She came round in hospital the next day and her mother was still there – a pale moon face peering into her own, holding her hand and promising that everything would be all right.

It was not, of course, but she was soon allowed home and deemed well enough, after a week, to return to work. 'Just a touch of the flu' was the official story. Neither she nor her mother ever spoke of it again. Grief sealed them into their own private worlds, tiptoeing around each other's rawness. Life went on, in its way.

❄

She held her breath, listening again, but could hear nothing more. Either Daniel had already left – although she heard no sound of a door opening or closing, no further creaks on the floorboards – or they were simply resting silently in each other's arms. She sat up and turned on the light, took out her diary and read what she had written earlier this afternoon and then scribbled out so furiously.

Then, taking up her pencil, she started a new paragraph. *Dearest Bertie, I have to tell you about something terrible that*

I did, long ago, when you were alive. You felt so far away and I was so lonely without you, you see, and I met someone who made me laugh, who made me feel special, and pretty . . .

Fifteen minutes later, she paused, reading back through what she had written. Then she added: *So, you see, Bertie, now you are dead I can't make up for it, or ask for your forgiveness.* She chewed the end of the pencil. *But I have to go on living because there is no alternative. And so the only option is to find some way of forgiving myself. I don't know how to do this, but coming here is helping me to make a start.*

14

ALICE

Alice woke with a sickening lurch, her mouth dry, her stomach churning. She became aware that she was lying on top of the bed fully clothed, shoes still on her feet. Sunlight sliced through the slats of the shutters.

Ruby called through the door. 'Are you coming for breakfast? We're meeting the chaplain at ten, remember?'

'Go on down. I'll be with you in fifteen minutes.' The effort of talking made her head throb. *Whatever was the time?*

Daniel had persuaded her to finish off the evening with a brandy – a drink she rarely touched – and it arrived in what looked like double measures, although it was hard to tell in those *ballons* the size of tennis balls. She'd already drunk two glasses of red wine at dinner followed by a whisky with Ruby, and then he'd insisted that she try the Belgian beer which, although light in colour, was strong in both taste and, she discovered, alcohol.

After this, the brandy was sweet and delicious, slipping down a treat. They ordered another. By now they were the only ones left in the bar except for Maurice, noisily washing up behind the counter.

'I should go to bed.' Her tongue felt too large for her mouth.

It was only when she stood up and discovered her head was spinning like a top, and realised she'd been so distracted by the pure enjoyment of being with Daniel again, all the serious conversation and light-hearted banter – she hadn't laughed so much in years – that she'd really overdone it.

'Whoops.' She felt his hand steadying her, steering her towards the open doorway.

'Come into the fresh air. It'll clear your head.'

They turned a corner into the shadows and, before she could figure out what was happening, he was holding her face in his hands, gazing into her eyes as though she were something infinitely precious. Then he pulled her to him, his lips on hers. For a few brief, delicious moments she responded, her lips opening, desire coursing through her body.

It was then that they heard ferocious barking and turned to see the dog haring across the square towards them: a thin, mangy cur the size of a wolf, with its hackles raised and teeth bared. 'Cripes, it's going to attack,' she yelped.

Daniel stepped boldly towards the creature, waving his arms and shouting loud French curses. Alice watched, her knees weak with relief as the animal retreated, growling, turned and trotted back across the square.

'Now, where were we?' he whispered, turning back to her.

Her heart was still pounding with the shock and she leaned in to him, at first, for the comfort of it. But when, after a few seconds, he put his finger beneath her chin, lifting her face for a kiss, she pulled away.

'We'd both regret it, Daniel.'

'I wouldn't.' He caressed her cheek with the lightest of touches before releasing her.

'It's been wonderful, seeing you again,' she said.

'And you too,' he whispered. 'What might have been, eh?'

They said goodbye at the door of the hotel and she made her way unsteadily up the stairs, clutching the banister for balance. At the door to her room she attempted to unlock the door and giggled, muttering to herself – *Get a grip, girl* – as she failed, several times, to get the key into the lock.

Finally she managed to open the door and fell onto the bed.

❦

Now, as she sat up in bed and sipped a glass of water, listening to the sounds of the hotel and smelling the delicious aroma of coffee from the dining room, she felt deflated. Daniel had promised to follow up her request for local contacts but wasn't particularly encouraging. 'So many died but have no graves, dearest Aleese,' he said. 'You must be realistic.' He made no mention of further meetings.

Thank heavens she'd come to her senses last night. And yet, try as she might to dismiss the thought, she couldn't help wondering what she was missing. Would she regret, for the rest of her life, not knowing? Had Julia been with her, they would have talked long into the night, weighing up the pros and cons. Here she only had Ruby, and she already knew what her views were.

✿✿✿

'Sorry to be so long. Glad you didn't wait for me.'

'So am I,' Ruby said. She wasn't smiling.

Pretty much what I deserve, I guess. Alice ordered coffee and a large glass of water. *She made it clear last night that she disapproved of Daniel. Not that I care.* 'I'm afraid I drank a bit too much last night. I never learn,' she said. A touch of British self-deprecation might ease the tension.

Ruby folded her napkin a little too carefully. 'He seemed nice. You were getting on like a house on fire.'

Cripes, another of those weird English sayings. 'Nothing happened, you know,' Alice said. 'We didn't burn down any houses.'

Ruby hesitated for a second and then, at last, she smiled. 'Well, that's a relief,' she said. 'We'd have been drummed out of town. Did he have any suggestions about who you might contact here in Hoppestadt?'

Alice shook her head. 'He wasn't very encouraging, to be honest. Said Talbot House is our best bet.'

'We'd better get a move on then,' Ruby said.

✿✿✿

The Reverend Philip Clayton lived up to his nickname. 'Call me Tubby, everyone else does,' he said, with a great booming laugh.

Shortish and generously upholstered, he had broad, restless

hands, an oversized head and an innocent expression. A strong, forward-leaning jaw suggested he liked to get his own way, albeit through charm and quiet determination.

His garb was an eccentric combination of religious and secular: the white dog collar and black cotton cassock, below the skirt of which could be seen scuffed brown brogues. Over this he wore a baggy tweed jacket with leather elbow patches that Alice recognised as the uniform for Englishmen of a certain intellectual leaning.

There was such a pent-up energy to the man, as though constantly bursting to pursue the next project. And yet, when he came to sit with them, and she began to describe her search for Sam, the quiet focus of his attention was so powerful that Alice could almost feel it as a physical sensation, like a beam of light.

Kindly brown eyes peered myopically through round, professorial spectacles; his hands were stilled into a clergyman's fold, his mouth set into an expression of deep thoughtfulness. Just being in his presence was calming, encouraging. As Alice told him about her brother, she felt her optimism returning.

He didn't respond at once. After a few moments, raising an index finger to loosen the dog collar from the folds of his neck as though trying to release himself from its bonds, he began to speak: a parson's tone, quiet, measured and reassuring.

'In my experience, when someone is determined to remain hidden, they can be extremely difficult to find, but that is not to say you should give up hope. Plenty of Canadians came to Talbot House – although my cloth ear for languages always failed to distinguish between true Canadians and Americans flying under the maple leaf flag, as it were. Let me put my thinking cap on.' Alice tried to picture what shape that cap might be.

'And what about you, my dear?' he said after a few moments, turning to Ruby.

'I've come in search of a grave,' she said quietly. 'My husband died at Passchendaele in 1917, but they never found his body.'

'I am so sorry to hear that,' he said. 'I am afraid you are by no means alone. What was his name?'

'Bertie. Albert Barton.'

The chaplain whispered the name to himself as he studied the empty coffee cup, twisting it around on the saucer. He shook his head. 'It doesn't spring to mind. Not that I remember the names of all those who came to Talbot House. And my memory is not what it was – I think war addles the brain. Was your husband a believer? I mean, a man of faith?'

Ruby shook her head with a rueful smile.

'Not that it matters a jot,' he added. 'Everyone was welcome at the house. It's just that I have a better recall for those who joined me in prayer.'

'What about your brother?' He turned back to Alice.

'My parents were – are – churchgoers,' she said. 'Sam too, although he seemed to lose his faith after his fiancée died on board the *Lusitania*. I remember him cursing God then, saying he'd been deserted.'

'That was not uncommon,' Tubby said. 'I have known it myself. But at least he felt there was someone to curse. Better than a void, I always think.' He tugged at the collar again, as though his own faith bothered him.

The church bell began to chime. 'Oh, dear me, is that the time already? I must be getting along, I'm afraid, ladies. I've an appointment at Talbot House to collect some of the bits and pieces we didn't manage to pack when we left. It was all very rushed, you understand. The owner will be waiting – a very punctual man, he is. Not like yours truly, who alas enjoys a regrettable reputation for tardiness.'

Alice's heart leapt. He was going to the house? 'Is there any chance we might come?'

'Oh my dears, I'm such a silly old fool. Of course,' he jumped in. 'I'm sure Monsieur Van Damme won't mind a couple of charming young ladies to leaven the dull company of my own good self. There's not much left there from the bad old days, I'm afraid, but there's still an atmosphere to the place, the air they all breathed. You may find something to give you solace. We might even climb the ladder to the chapel, send up a prayer or two to the Old Man.'

❦

The ornate cast-iron gates at the entrance to the house were open today, leading into a wide hallway. What had once been a gracious residence now felt sad and abandoned, musty and unloved, the ornate plasterwork on walls and ceilings felted with grey dust.

The hall was unfurnished apart from a scruffy Persian carpet but a blackboard still hung on the wall, with a notice handwritten in white chalk:

Welcome, to all who enter.

Ground Floor: Canteen & Rest Room

*1st Floor: Warden's Office (Don't be shy, he will be
pleased to see you)*

Friendship Corner

2nd Floor: Library & Writing Room

3rd Floor: The 'Upper Room'

Chapel with Sacred Altar, The Carpenter's Bench

Monsieur Van Damme arrived, a tall, well-built man in
a fine three-piece suit, every inch the prosperous member
of the local community. An impressive girth suggested
that he hadn't suffered overly much during the starvation
years.

They were duly introduced and he nodded his assent to
their being shown around. 'I will return in an hour, Father,
is that sufficient for you?' he said, taking out a pocket watch
on a chain that reminded Alice of the rabbit in *Alice in
Wonderland*. It was her favourite childhood book, of course,
and she completely identified with its eponymous heroine,
after whom, her mother said, she had been named.

'We are most fortunate,' Tubby whispered, after he left.
'Word was he became so irritated with visitors clamouring
to see the old place that he put his foot down, so to speak,
which was a shame, because people gain much solace from
such a pilgrimage. But there you go. It was only ours on
loan – we can't claim it forever.'

Even though the rooms were echoing and empty, Alice
felt she could still sense the presence of soldiers who had

come here for rest, friendship and solace. Jokey notices still adorned the walls. By the front door, a sign read: *To pessimists, way out!* Another, at the foot of the stairs: *Owing to the descent of a meteorite upon the electric lighting plant, the House is temporarily reduced to the oil and grease expedients of a bygone age.*

'We had a bit of bad luck in the winter of 1917,' Tubby explained. 'The Germans found their range and we thought we'd be blown to kingdom come.'

'My old office is up here,' he said, panting a little as they mounted the stairs. Above its door hung another sign in painted lettering: *All rank abandon, ye who enter here.*

'I like that,' Ruby said. 'When my Bertie was in training he said they hated the captains, how you always had to salute them and they got the best food and a clean bed to sleep in. But after a bit he wrote that they were mostly good chaps, once you got to know them.'

'Nothing pleased me more than to see them getting along man to man, like normal human beings,' Tubby replied.

A single piece of furniture remained in the former office: an enormous dark oak desk. 'We had to leave in a hurry and, like a fool, I left all my papers inside, so please forgive me while I look for them, ladies. I won't be long.' He began to pull open drawers, rummaging through bundles of paperwork and notebooks with small yelps of recognition. 'Feel free to explore while you're waiting.'

Rooms were still identified with hand-lettered signs. The library was echoing and empty save for the dusty shelves, but the reading room felt cosy, like an Edwardian lady's drawing room with its floral wallpaper, mahogany desk and a small stove in the fireplace, a large enamel kettle atop it.

'There's something about this place, isn't there?' Alice said. 'Those men having a few hours of normal life before going back to the trenches.' She could visualise large sofas and easy chairs, and Sam sitting with a book, his legs crossed, his eyebrows furrowed in concentration, the small crease forming between, just as it always did. When she was six and he only four she'd taught him the alphabet, and then how to read. After that she'd felt a great sense of pride every time she'd seen him with his nose in a book.

After ten minutes or so Tubby emerged from the office with a wide grin on his face, puffing slightly, the shabby leather case now so crammed that it appeared in imminent danger of splitting at the seams. The thought came to Alice with a suddenness that felt like a physical blow. 'I don't suppose, among that paperwork, you have any kind of record of the people who came here?' she asked.

'Of course!' He hit his forehead with the heel of his palm. 'What a dolt I am. Whyever didn't I think of that before? That is exactly what I've come back for – our visitors' books.' He put the case to the floor and opened it to show five green leather-backed books.

Beside her, Ruby sighed. 'Oh! Just imagine . . . what if?'

'And in here somewhere, I'm sure' – he rummaged further – 'are some of the notices people put up when they were searching for friends.' As he pulled out a fat buff folder, scraps of paper escaped and fluttered like confetti to the floor. 'Here they are,' he muttered, scrambling to gather them up. 'I knew there must be more. I've been trying to get in touch with everyone who came here to see whether they would support a new organisation in London. We want to try and keep that wonderful spirit alive, that spirit of comradeship, I mean, that we witnessed here in war but which seems to have disappeared in peacetime.'

He paused, the scraps of paper now safely gathered, his eyes taking on a faraway look. 'And to remember those who didn't come home.'

Alice's fingers were itching. 'I don't suppose you would let us have a look at them, Reverend Clayton?'

'Of course, of course. Please call me Tubby, I can never get used to being called Reverend. Here I am wittering on about my plans and what you most want is news of your loved ones. Tell you what, ladies, why don't we take them back to the cafe? We could have a drink – my goodness, I could do with one.' He took out a handkerchief and wiped a brow shining with sweat from his exertions. 'That way you can take your time looking through them.'

'That is most generous,' Alice said.

'But first, I have in mind to say a final prayer in the chapel, before I leave the place for good. Would you care to join me?'

❦

'Mind your step, ladies,' he called, his ponderous form disappearing up a steep flight of wooden steps, more of a ladder in reality. At the top they emerged into a large and airy attic space that smelled of incense and dried leaves, its sloping whitewashed walls reflecting the light from windows at either end.

'This room was originally used for drying hops,' Tubby

explained. 'When we suggested it might make a good chapel they told us it was unsafe, not suitable for more than a few people at a time. But with His help and a few more joists put in by some of the lads we proved them wrong. There must have been more than a hundred up here sometimes.' He wandered slowly around, examining each corner of the room and cleaning with a squeaking finger the glass of a semi-circular window, one of a pair set either side of the chimney breast, to peer into the gardens below.

'My goodness, it's marvellous to be here again,' he sighed. 'You should have seen it, in all its simple glory, my dears. We received so many generous gifts: a great gilt candelabrum hanging from up there.' He pointed to a broad king beam. 'And a pair of magnificent candlesticks made out of carved bedposts either side of the altar over here. We used a carpenter's bench for the altar itself. Very apt, don't you think?'

'I won't be long,' he said. 'Join me, if you wish.' He crossed himself and lowered heavily to one knee. Instinctively, Alice followed. In the silence, she noticed the rise and fall of her own breath and a sense of serenity, like a light silk shawl floating down over her shoulders, soothing the constant thrum of anxiety. Ruby came to kneel beside her, still and quiet. The only sound was the trill of songbirds from the gardens.

Tubby began to pray in the most comforting, mellifluous voice she had ever heard, taking long, reflective pauses between each phrase: 'Dear Father. Bless this house and keep it safe, in memory of all those who found sanctuary here and in particular those who gave their lives so that we may find peace. Bless this country and its countrymen, who suffered so sorely, that they may in time recover. And finally, Lord, please bless these two young women so that they may find some kind of solace after their losses. Amen.'

When he began reciting the Lord's Prayer, Alice joined him. Beside her Ruby muttered the words, hesitantly at first, and then more confidently: *'Forgive us our trespasses, as we forgive them that trespass against us . . .'*

At the end was another long moment of stillness.

'I am so glad you are with me,' Alice whispered.

'I am glad you brought me here,' Ruby whispered back.

Scanning the names in the visitors' books was a slow business. Many had been so hastily scribbled that they were almost illegible, others partly erased by spills of something liquid. Coffee or tea, Alice assumed. No alcohol was served, Tubby had told them. 'Plenty of that to be had elsewhere.' There were other marks, too, darker brown stains, of mud, or even perhaps dried blood, smeared across some of the pages. Even in the peace of Talbot House, the signatories of these books carried with them signs of the war from which they had been taking a brief moment of respite.

Each time she saw an entry listing the Canadian Corps, often decorated with rough renditions of their maple leaf symbol, Alice's heart seemed to skip a beat. She read these with special attention, trying to imagine the men who had written them. Even if they weren't Sam, these Canadians may have been his comrades. If only she could talk to them. She considered, briefly, writing down the names so that she could track them down once she got back home, but the brutal truth was that many of them would now be dead. Each time she reached the end of a page her confidence seemed to dip a little further.

'Any luck?' she asked Ruby, at the next table, scanning other books, while Tubby sat nearby, sorting his papers.

'Nope. Not a dicky bird.'

'Dicky bird?'

'There are entries from men who were in Bertie's regiment but there's not a single name I recognise. It's like looking for a needle in a haystack.'

Alice laughed. Two more quaint English phrases.

She had just opened the fifth and final book when an entry on the first page caught her eye. *Lance Corp. Samuel Pilgrim, 3rd Canadian Division, 3rd February 1917.* What really arrested her attention was the comment that followed: *A little haven in a hellish war.* These were the exact words Sam had used in his letter.

'Can I show you something?'

'Of course, my dear,' Tubby said, rising from his chair. 'What is it?'

Fingers trembling, she showed him the entry and then took out Sam's letter, pointing out the same phrase. 'Is that something people commonly said about Talbot House? I haven't seen it anywhere else.'

Tubby took off his spectacles, and rubbed his eyes. 'I *have* heard it said and even seen it written, I think. I take it your brother is not Samuel Pilgrim?'

'No, he's Sam Palmer.'

Tubby put on his specs again, peering at the signature. 'That's curious. Palmer, Pilgrim. They have the same meaning, you know? A palmer was someone who carried palm leaves to prove that he'd been on a pilgrimage.'

The realisation seemed to knock the breath from her chest. It was so obvious: Sam must have been hiding himself in plain sight. She inhaled slowly, deeply, deliberately trying to remain calm. 'But the handwriting is so different.' The letters were much larger, looser, more forward-leaning and less carefully formed than Sam's usually neat hand.

Ruby leaned over. 'May I see?'

Ruby studied the signature on the letter intently, comparing it with the entry in the Talbot House book. 'Do you know, I can see definite similarities,' she said quietly. 'The loops on the letter G are just the same. And the uprights on the H letters are a bit loose, like an upturned V. It's not really surprising that it looks different when you consider the circumstances these men were in.'

'Wow, Rube. Where'd you learn all that stuff?'

'It's just a thing schoolgirls used to do,' Ruby replied. 'Trying to analyse your boyfriend's writing to find out his character and whether you are compatible. There's a special word.' She shook her head. 'I even borrowed a book about it from the library.'

'Graphology?' Tubby suggested.

'That's the one.'

Alice rubbed the tip of her finger gently over the script. The idea that her brother might have written these very words tingled all the way up her arm, and she could feel the tears welling up. 'You think this could really be my Sam?'

'It's a bit of a coincidence, isn't it?' Ruby said. 'The timing is right, the name has the same meaning, he uses the same phrase here as in the letter and the writing has quite a few of the same characteristics.'

'But how can I prove it?'

'My dear,' Tubby said quietly. 'There is only one way to find out. You need to contact the Canadian authorities.'

'We've asked them time and again. They say that without a name . . .' She stopped herself. 'But now, oh my goodness, I *do* have a name!' Her head spinning with excitement, she began to gather her coat and bag. 'Where's the post office? I'm going to telegraph my father. Back soon.'

15

MARTHA

At a quarter to eleven they were waiting in the hotel lobby for Monsieur Peeters.

Martha had slept restlessly, despite the warmth of Otto, the comfort of the soft mattress and the clean white linen. Her belly was heavy with so much rich food, her mind filled with too many anxieties.

In a small shoulder bag clutched close to her chest was a hat for herself and one for Otto. He'd never wear it but she felt it a mother's duty at least to try to protect her boy from the harsh sunshine. Folded carefully inside was a linen napkin containing a couple of bread rolls and an apple that she'd surreptitiously secreted from the dining room at breakfast.

Tucked carefully away in a secure inside pocket was the medal in its green leather box and an envelope addressed to *Mein Liebling Heinrich*.

My dearest Heinrich, the letter inside it said.
You were, and still are, our precious, greatly loved first-born son. In your hands you held our hopes, our dreams and our future.

*The world is a sad, grey place without you and we
can hardly bear to believe that we shall not see you
again until, God willing, we will join you in heaven
when our own time comes.*

*But we know that you died doing what you wanted
– upholding the honour of our great country – and we
could not be more proud of your courage and your
determination to do what you felt was right.*

Sleep well, our darling boy.

Mama, Papa and your little brother Otto.

Otto sighed impatiently. 'When is this man coming, Ma?'

'Any moment now,' she said, trying to reassure herself as much as him. Silently, she berated herself for being so trusting; she had no receipt for her ten-franc deposit, nor an address for Monsieur Peeters should they need to contact him. What if he should fail to show up? And would he know where to go? Langemarck was just a name; she had no idea whether it was a village, an area, a battlefield or a cemetery. She'd read that the villages of Poelcapelle and Langemarck had been taken and retaken several times throughout the war. Surely, if that was the case, there must be more than one burial place in the area?

But then, even if Monsieur Peeters took her to the right graveyard, would she be able to find the place where the *Kindermort* were buried? Even then, what were their chances of finding a single name among so many thousands?

By half past eleven, for lack of anything else to do, they had already eaten their bread rolls; Otto had stopped asking and Martha was beginning to lose hope. Sun-warmed air wafted in through the open door of the hotel, carrying the heavy-sweet aroma of roasting malt.

The pale-eyed Englishman wandered past. 'Still here?' he asked kindly. 'Who are you waiting for?'

She shook her head, pretending not to understand. It was simpler that way.

'I'll get Maurice,' he said.

When the hotelier appeared she explained her predicament, describing the man in the square, and showing him the leaflet she'd been given.

'I know Geert Peeters,' Monsieur Vermeulen said, nodding affably. 'He uses the van belonging to my brother Max, the baker. I'm sure there's no problem. Perhaps the deliveries were running late today. Cécile wants me to collect more bread for lunch, so I will find out for you.'

She thanked him and settled down to wait some more.

Twenty minutes later he reappeared, puffing slightly from his walk across the square and clutching three large loaves of bread, wrapped in newspaper. He took them into the kitchen and returned, mopping his brow with a handkerchief. His smile had disappeared, replaced with a dark, disconcerting frown.

'Is there a problem?' she asked.

'Would you mind stepping into the office, madame?' His eyes slipped sideways at Otto. 'Let the boy stay here, if you don't mind. I think it best if we speak alone. We'll only be a few minutes.'

'What is it, Mama?' Otto whispered, grabbing her hand.

His brow was crumpled with alarm. The metallic tang of fear – that taste she knew so well – seared her mouth, making it hard to form words. 'It's probably just about the bill,' she managed to reply, squeezing his hand before following the hotelier down the corridor.

The office was so chaotic she wondered how he ever managed to track their bookings or produce any accounts, and furnished with just a couple of rickety old chairs and a table entirely covered with books and folders. He took the desk chair but did not invite her to sit; indeed, there was nowhere for her to do so as the only other stool was piled high with paperwork.

She waited, now almost light-headed with anxiety, while he searched beneath the piles of correspondence, magazines and newspapers. Finally he unearthed a packet and extracted from it a slightly crumpled cigarette which he straightened out and lit with a match scratched on the underside of the table.

He cleared his throat. 'Mrs Weber, I am most pained to have to ask you, but my brother Max tells me that Geert agreed to take you to the cemetery at Langemarck.' The word came out as a growl. 'Is this correct?'

'Indeed, that is so, monsieur. As you know, my son and I are Swiss, but we have come at the request of my sister, who is unable to travel herself, to visit the grave of my nephew.' She felt sure he must be able to hear her heart hammering against her chest.

'You are aware, are you not, that the cemetery at Langemarck is for *German* soldiers?' In a narrow ray of sunshine slicing through a broken shutter, swirls of cigarette smoke reeled and dispersed into a blue haze.

'I am aware of that, sir.'

'So you acknowledge that you were planning to visit a German grave?'

'Indeed I do, sir. I made no secret of this to Monsieur Peeters.'

He took another long pull on the cigarette. It flared slightly and a small pile of ash scattered onto the papers in front of him. He appeared not to notice, or to care.

'Do you not appreciate, madame, that this plan of yours could cause offence in our country? Your nephew was fighting for the enemy, who invaded our land and who were responsible for the deaths of many thousands of our citizens.'

Martha took a breath, raising herself to her fullest height, pulling back her shoulders and lifting her chin, meeting his gaze just as she'd learned to do when, so many times, she'd had to face military guards or the *Polizei*.

'I am sure you will appreciate, monsieur, that this poor young man, my nephew, was not *personally* responsible for all those deaths. He was doing his duty like all soldiers, like the Belgian, French and English boys. And he died doing it. My sister's only desire, and it is surely a modest enough request, is for me to place a gift and a stone at his grave, as she is unable to travel here for herself. Is that such a wrong thing to ask?'

'You are right, madame, war makes all men guilty. It is most surely true that we should honour the dead for their sacrifice, whatever side they were on.' Monsieur Vermeulen sighed heavily and rubbed his thinning hair. 'But such high-mindedness will not help to solve today's problem. Max cannot allow Geert to use his van not because he has any personal objection – he understands just as I do – but because he is afraid his customers will notice and take their trade elsewhere. His name is written on the outside of the van for all to see. What if it should be observed at a German graveyard?'

'Then it can be explained, as I have done for you. I am a visitor from a neutral country and have a perfectly logical reason for visiting Langemarck. Surely no one could find that offensive?'

Monsieur Vermeulen cleared his throat and lowered his voice. 'What you seem not to understand is the terrible fear in our community, even now we are at peace, of German infiltrators. To put it plainly, of *spies*.' He spat out the word with a venomous hiss. 'Those fears turn into whispers, whispers soon become rumours, rumours fuel suspicions, suspicions lead to official accusations.'

The smoke-filled air in the little room hung close and heavy.

Martha took a breath and tried once more. 'I have come all the way from my home in Switzerland, monsieur, to carry out my sister's wishes,' she said, trying to summon a voice as deep and authoritative as she could muster. 'Your countryman Monsieur Peeters agreed to the deal and has taken ten francs of my money as a deposit. If your brother feels unable to lend his van, then surely it is Monsieur Peeters' responsibility to arrange alternative transport or to refund my money?'

The discussion had reached neutral ground, and the hotelier seemed to relax now that the responsibility had shifted. 'You are right, of course. But my brother tells me

Geert stormed out of the bakery after they rowed over the matter, and he has not been seen since.'

'Do you have an address for him? I will seek him out myself.'

His face twisted into a wry smile. 'On your behalf I visited his house en route from the bakery. However, Madame Peeters informed me that her husband has not been home all morning. She was – how shall I say? – in an ill temper. Indeed she gave me an earful about his misdoings. She is a formidable woman. I would not recommend that you visit her, not today.'

She would not be defeated. 'Then what am I to do? I would welcome your advice, Monsieur Vermeulen. At the very least I must retrieve my deposit from this man. And I would appreciate it if you could direct me to someone else who is prepared to transport me.'

He shrugged. 'I regret I cannot assist you further with your plan to go to Langemarck. It is a problem for which I am unable to suggest a solution. But I will do my best to trace old Peeters. I am sure he will return in a day or so.'

A day or so! The old hatred rose up, burning her throat like the bitter bile unleashed by hunger. She tried to speak calmly but could hear the anger in her voice anyway. 'That will not do, sir. I must retrieve my deposit so that I can secure another guide so that I can make this visit today, or tomorrow at the latest, as our return train is booked for Friday.'

Monsieur Vermeulen sighed, crushing the remains of his cigarette onto a small plate already overflowing with butts. 'I have done what I can. I am sure you will appreciate that. I am sorry for this inconvenience.'

He stood, holding out his hand towards the door. She felt her eyes welling as the hopelessness of her situation began to dawn. Surely she could not have travelled all this way only to fail at the last few kilometres?

'Please, you must help me, sir,' she began and then, to her utter dismay, found herself falling to her knees before him, her palms outstretched in supplication. 'Surely it is not too great a thing to ask? I have barely any money left and I must find this grave; I have promised my sister.'

The hotelier stared for a moment, embarrassed and uncertain, before putting a hand to her elbow and helping her to her feet. 'Madame, please get up. You must pull yourself together. There is nothing more I can do for the moment.' He waited while she gathered herself, sought a handkerchief from her bag, wiped her eyes and blew her nose.

'Now I must return to the kitchen to help my wife,' he said. 'Or she will accuse me of shirking. Will you be taking lunch?'

'I think not, in the circumstances, Monsieur Vermeulen.'

He opened the door and, holding her head high, she moved past him into the corridor. Then she walked, placing one foot consciously and carefully in front of the other, back to Otto. She had not a single thought in her head except the desire to get out of this hotel, to find a quiet place where she could recover her dignity. Without a word, and ignoring the boy's puzzled expression, she took his hand and led him out of the hotel into the burning sunlight.

'You're hurting me, Mama,' he whispered, trying to wriggle his hand free from her grip. 'What's happened? I thought we were waiting for the man to take us—'

'Shush,' she interrupted fiercely. 'We are going to the cafe for coffee and then we shall go to the baker and ask where we can find the man who has promised to take us to Langemarck. As he has not seen fit to come to us, we shall go to him.'

16

RUBY

Such a weight of sorrow seemed freighted between the scuffed and torn pages of the Talbot House visitors' books: the script of shaky hands, the smudges of ink, mud stains and smells of wood smoke, sweat and old tea leaves. What had happened to all these young men? Had any of them survived and, if so, were they injured, struggling to make sense of life after war? Where were they now?

After Alice left for the post office Ruby turned back to scan, without any particular expectation, the columns of names, dates, ranks and regiments. She studied especially the half dozen names she found from Bertie's regiment. None were familiar, but might they have known him? Were they perhaps together at Talbot House with him? Did they witness his final hours?

What saddened her most were the comments of strained jollity, belying the terror the men must surely have felt at the prospect of returning to those terrifying battlefields. *Back to beat up the Boche once again*, one wrote. *May he go to hell in a hand cart.* Some made her smile: *This farce promises to be a great success and a long run is expected.* Others made her want to cry: *While I have the strength I will fight to save my country*, or: *If I go to heaven, let it be like Talbot House.*

She reached the final page of the final book and the last entry dated 11th November 1918 in the chaplain's bold, open-looped hand: *It is over at last. Pray God we never forget all those who suffered and died. P. Clayton.*

As she closed the book she felt his eyes on her. 'No sign of your Bertie?'

She shook her head, too choked to speak.

'My dear, I understand how hard this must be.'

Tubby took out a large white handkerchief and gave it to her. Somehow just being in his presence was comforting, and his calm, patient listening seemed to unlock something; the words began to tumble out in a stream.

'People talk about heroes' deaths, of their souls still being with us, or being in some place called heaven, but it doesn't mean anything to me. I just can't get out of my head the fact that he may have died alone and probably in dreadful pain, among all that terrible destruction.' A sob escaped. 'Oh God, I don't think I can face this any more . . . The mud and the mess and the thousands of crosses at the cemetery. I've seen them pulling bits of men from the mud, but we'll never have a body to mourn.' She sniffed and wiped her eyes. 'I need to talk to him, Tubby. I need his forgiveness. Otherwise I'll never be able to get on with my own life. I might just as well be dead.'

She stopped, embarrassed, fearing that she'd said too much. Any moment now he would ask her what there was to forgive, and she would have to confess her shameful secret. But all he did was take her hand and sit quietly beside her, waiting for the storm to pass.

'My dear, I have few words of consolation, I'm afraid,' he said at last. 'We are all sinners, and being able to forgive ourselves is the hardest lesson we face in life. But as for your Bertie, what I know from my own encounters with so many brave men over the past few years is that even in the most extreme circumstances, in conditions that no human, not even any animal, should be expected to bear, they took comfort from two important things.'

She looked up into his face, hungry for the balm of his words.

'The first was comradeship. Men learned to depend on each other in ways those of us who have never experienced front line combat will never understand. Those friendships were powerful and profound. To experience that real camaraderie, that absolute trust of knowing that someone would give their life for you, or you for them, is a rare and precious thing. I observed it at the House and when I went to give Sunday services in the trenches, and even envied them for it.'

'That's what Freddie talked about, the comradeship,' she said, eager to understand more. 'About how the war was hell, but he wouldn't have missed it for the world because of that experience. He called it love.'

Tubby nodded, smiling. 'I have also heard it called that before, many times. But that was not the only thing that kept them going. For the fortunate ones, like your Bertie, the most important thing was knowing that they were also loved, deeply loved, by those at home. They knew that they were playing their part, however small and ineffectual it might have seemed at the time, to protect those who loved them, and whom they loved.'

As her tears began afresh, he sat beside her, quietly waiting. Eventually, she gathered herself, clearing her throat enough to speak. 'Thank you.'

'I wish I had more to offer.'

She sighed, glancing around the cafe as it filled up with lunchtime customers. Somehow, the world carried on, but she felt altered: reassured and calmed. The importance of loving and being loved.

'I hope your friend reached the post office before they closed for lunch,' he said. 'Talking of which, I'm feeling a tad peckish, are you?'

'A little,' she admitted.

'Shall we get sandwiches? And some lemonade – I love it with fresh lemon juice. I can't be long, mind, because I have to get off to the hospital shortly. They've asked me to visit an English patient who's arrived there without papers.'

An English patient? Ruby's heart seemed to leap into her throat. 'A Tommie?'

He nodded. 'I believe so. Apparently he's confused and doesn't even know his own name – or at least he's not telling.'

'When you find out, you will let me know, won't you?' She heard her own voice, thin and pleading.

'Dear heart,' he placed his hand on hers. 'Of course I will.'

As Tubby went to the bar to order their food, she struggled to stifle the thoughts in her head: what if the English patient really was, by some blessed miracle, Bertie? After all, it was here in Hoppestadt that she'd felt his presence for the first time in months, even years. What could account for that? Silently, she chided herself; it was absurd even to imagine, the chance so slim. But Tubby's casual remark had rekindled a flame that refused to be extinguished by reasoning. Then she remembered what Auntie Flo had said when she came back from the séance. The medium told her that Bertie was recovering *in hospital*.

An English patient, in a hospital in Hoppestadt? She was about to ask Tubby to take her to him *right now*, when she was distracted by the arrival of the Swiss woman, dragging her son by the hand. Her eyes unfocused, her face pale and distorted with strain, greying hair awry, she appeared not to see Ruby, or at least chose not to acknowledge her. Ginger tried to offer a table by the window but she moved purposefully into the shadows at the rear of the cafe.

Ruby stole a glance. They sat, heads bent together. The woman muttered something inaudible, the boy answered back and then she turned her mouth to his ear, apparently whispering a longer explanation. He began to speak again but she put a finger to her lips, peering around as though fearful of being overheard. But what struck Ruby, even more than this curious behaviour, was the look on the woman's face: it was the expression of a hunted animal.

The next time she managed to catch a glimpse, she was sitting stiff-backed, staring at the wall, a single tear glinting on her cheek that she made no move to wipe away. Such silent suffering was almost unbearable to witness.

'My dear, is something troubling you?' Tubby asked, arriving back at the table.

She gave a single nod. 'There's a woman behind you, with her young son. They're Swiss; we met her last night at the hotel. But she seems so dreadfully distressed. I'm not sure what to do.'

He tugged at his dog collar and peered over his shoulder. After a few seconds he looked again. Then he stood, pushing back his chair. 'Give me a moment.'

She heard him address the woman in English, and then in French; saw him offer his hand. The woman shook her head and turned her face away. But he stayed at her side and said a few more words until she made a slight, reluctant nod, and he took a seat at her table. After her initial sense of alarm at his bold intervention Ruby began to understand: this is what chaplains do. The white collar gives them licence; they are trained in offering solace.

Alice's shout startled her. 'Hi there! How's it going? Any luck?' she asked, gesturing towards the Talbot House books, now piled neatly at the side.

Ruby shook her head. 'Not a sign.'

'Tubby made a new friend?' Alice tipped her head towards the interior of the cafe.

Ruby put a finger to her lips. 'They're in some kind of trouble and he's trying to help her,' she whispered. 'I thought it best to keep out of it. Did you manage to send your telegram?'

'Yup, in the end. But what a kerfuffle. I had to fill in forms and have the right coins, all the rest. But it's gone off now and we just have to hope that Pa manages to get some sense out of the Canucks.'

Tubby returned to the table and beckoned to Ginger. 'I think we might need your help, my dear,' he said in a low voice. 'I have just been speaking to Mrs Weber, over there. As far as I can tell, with my terrible French, she wishes to visit the grave of her nephew. She booked a guide, a man called Geert Peeters, but the van he was going to use is apparently not available any more. It seems the person who owns it – the baker – is not willing to lend it for visiting a German graveyard. Now this Mr Peeters has disappeared with her deposit, and she is desperate to find another way of getting there. She has to leave on the train the day after tomorrow, back home to Switzerland. Do you or your father know anyone who could help?'

'She wants to visit a *German* graveyard?'

'I believe so,' Tubby said.

Ginger frowned. 'This is problem.'

'She has come all this way. We really must try to help her.' Tubby scratched his head. 'Anyone got any ideas?'

'Could we call a taxi, from Ypres?' Ruby asked.

'They are usually booked up days in advance,' Tubby said. 'But she mentioned a kind man who brought her from Ypres. A Monsieur Martens. Do you know of him?'

Ruby nudged Alice. 'Isn't that . . . ?'

Alice frowned, shaking her head. 'For Christ's sake,' she hissed. 'Don't interfere.'

'But why not? Surely he—' Ruby felt her arm gripped like a vice. Before she knew it, she'd been pulled from the chair, steered away from the table and out of the cafe into the open air.

'You're hurting me,' she gasped, pulling her arm free. 'Whatever is the matter?'

'Don't get involved, Ruby.'

'Whyever not? She needs help, poor woman.'

'You don't get it, do you?' Alice hissed. 'She wants to visit a *German* grave, for heaven's sake. In a *German* graveyard. Of course no one wants to help her. And if you think I'm going to ask Daniel . . .' She shook her head, pivoted on her heel and marched off towards the hotel.

Ruby took a few breaths of fresh air, trying to order her thoughts. Glancing towards the cafe, she saw Ginger placing a cup of coffee and a glass of lemonade in front of Mrs Weber, and Tubby reaching into his pocket for some coins. He said something to the boy, who responded with a weak smile. *What a good Samaritan.* This was nothing to do with war, or who was right or wrong, or even about Christian forgiveness. It was a matter of being human, of being kind to other humans; it was that love Tubby spoke about, that she and Bertie felt for each other, that he must have experienced with his fellow soldiers.

Ruby wasn't sure where this new sense of strength came from but it fizzed powerfully in her head – exhilarating and liberating all at once. *So what if the woman's nephew was German? She's lost someone she loved, just like I've lost my husband, and Alice has lost her brother. It's not our fault that our countries decided to go to war, not the fault of those boys who were only doing their duty. It's the Kaiser we should blame for their deaths, not ordinary women like her. To hell with what anyone thinks, to hell with Alice. Aren't Christians supposed to forgive?*

She ran back into the cafe. 'I want to help. Does she know how far it is?'

'About fifteen kilometres from here, close to a place called Poelcapelle.'

The woman's eyes fixed on her, huge in her famished face. 'Please can you tell her I'm going to ask Freddie? He took me to Tyne Cot yesterday and he may know of other cars. I will do what I can.'

Freddie was in his usual place at the hotel bar.

'So that's what was going on,' he said, after Ruby explained the Swiss woman's predicament. 'I did wonder. She was talking to Maurice and he went off and returned with a face like a thundercloud.'

'Can you help me help her, Freddie? Please? All she wants is to get to her nephew's grave.'

'Well,' he said, grinning now. 'Just for you, lovely Ruby, I might be able to lay my hands on a vehicle, if you ask very nicely. Where is it?'

'Lange . . . something. Only a few miles away, she said.'

'Langemarck?'

'That's the one.'

His face darkened. 'But that's a *German* cemetery.'

'She's Swiss. It's her nephew's grave.'

He frowned, scratching the day's growth of gingery beard on his chin. 'Let me get this straight. You want me to drive her to a Kraut grave?'

'It's just that she seemed so distressed. I'll pay.'

He raised his pale eyes, and then looked away. 'Look, Rube, I'd like to help, honest I would. 'Specially since it's you. But frankly, I went past that place once and I had to get out and spit on the ground. A grave's the best place for a Kraut, as we always used to say, but I don't think I could bring myself to go there again.'

Ruby steeled herself, shocked by the intensity of his hatred. Persuading him to help was going to be harder than she thought. 'But Martha's done nothing wrong. You should see her, honestly. She's desperate.'

Freddie shook his head again. 'Can't they get a cab from Ypres?'

'Apparently they're booked up days in advance. Oh please, Freddie?' she pleaded. 'Look at that poor laddie, come all this way for his cousin. He's around the same age as your boy, isn't he? You'd help if it was him, wouldn't you?'

Freddie snorted. 'By God, you're determined, aren't you? I'll have a think.'

She leaned forward to give a quick peck on his cheek.

'Easy, girl,' he stuttered, colouring beneath the pale stubble. 'You'll go giving me ideas.'

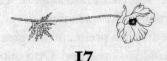

17

MARTHA

Buoyed by the sympathy of strangers, Martha felt her courage returning.

The English chaplain didn't spout any Christian platitudes and God wasn't mentioned, not even once. All he did was listen quietly and offer a few words of solace in that slow, thoughtful voice of his, before seeking help from the waitress and the English girl. His words had calmed her, restored her sense of reason. She would not give up hope; there would be other ways of getting to Langemarck, she was sure.

Otto responded with disbelief when she told him the full story. 'What? They're afraid to let us see Germans even when they're in the ground? What idiots!' But even he seemed to have recovered his sense of humour. 'We'll take a donkey if that's the only thing on offer, Ma,' he said.

The sad-faced English girl had been a revelation, too. Her American friend obviously tried to warn her off, but she'd come back into the cafe offering to do what she could to help.

First things first, though: she needed to retrieve her

money from Geert Peeters. The baker should surely feel some sense of responsibility for her plight and would direct her to him. It would not be a pleasant conversation, of that she felt sure, but she could not think of any other way of recovering the money she was owed.

Thanking the English priest and the ginger-haired waitress for their kindness, she and Otto set off across the square. At the southern corner, in the shade of the buildings, was a small group of food stalls where housewives gathered, clutching purses and baskets. As they passed a butcher's table Otto halted in his tracks with mouth agape. Martha stopped beside him, equally transfixed. She had not seen such bounty for many a year. There was enough fresh meat to feed an army: enormous hunks of mutton, pork, veal and beef, its flesh gleaming freshly red and streaked with creamy yellow fat. From the awnings above, dead chickens, ducks and smaller birds she did not recognise hung by their feet. A short way beyond were stalls laden with trays of shimmering silvery fish, eels, fresh brown prawns and a large bucket of shiny blue-black mussels.

Artistic pyramids of fruit and vegetables were piled in a rainbow of colours: salads in a range of greens, brilliant orange carrots, pale chicory, dark beetroot, aromatic celery, early-season potatoes with their sweet white flesh peeking through the covering of dusty brown soil, ruby plums, russet apples. Once again they came to a standstill, captivated by the sight of so many delicacies.

Otto pulled at her sleeve. 'Can we buy apples, Ma?' he whispered. 'Or plums?'

She hadn't tasted a plum for three, perhaps even four years, and her mouth watered at the thought of sinking her teeth into the sweet, yielding flesh, the juice dripping down her chin.

Only when they joined the queue did she begin to sense the furtive glances, the whisperings behind hands. She tried to ignore them; she had just as much right to stand in this queue as anyone and only wanted a few plums, after all. Women elbowed past her and, for a while, Martha tolerated it patiently. But, after several minutes of being jostled aside, she decided to stand her ground, holding out her hand, just as the others did, to display the coins in her palm. *My francs are just as good as theirs*, she told herself.

Even then, the stallholder refused to catch her eye and a cold fear began to creep into her heart. Had word already spread? 'Excuse me,' she said loudly, in her best French. 'May I have half a kilo of plums, please?'

Heads turned, the hum of conversation in the crowd ceased. For a long moment the stallholder hesitated, caught in the gaze of his customers, unsure how to respond. At last he moved, grabbed a handful of fruit, wrapped them in a cone of newspaper and held it out to her.

'Twenty cents,' he said curtly.

The crowd stood aside to allow her to pass as she nudged Otto forward, out of the queue. As they walked away she could hear the hubbub of their chatter resuming with renewed vigour. She quickened her pace, fearful of overhearing what they might be saying.

***

Now, as they approached the bakery, her stomach began to churn once more. Would they recognise her as the woman who'd come to visit a German grave? Through the window she could see a man serving other customers. She held back, pretending to study the window display, until they had left.

When they'd visited the shop before, the shelves were empty. This time she was astonished by the variety of loaves and rolls: round, rectangular, long and fat, short and narrow, white, wholemeal, pumpernickel or rye, and covered with flour, oatmeal flakes, sesame seeds or poppy seeds.

On a low marble shelf was a display of pastries even more astonishing than the bread: waffles, croissants, apple turnovers, cherry tarts, *viennoises*, éclairs, French horns filled with cream, colourful macaroons and every shape and size of biscuit.

'More pastries, Mama?' Otto pleaded. 'Please?'

'Wait and see,' she whispered.

At last, when the shop emptied, she told Otto to wait outside. As she entered, the baker turned. He was so like his brother the hotelier – tall and gaunt, only with a little more hair – that she found her stomach contracting with the memory of how, just an hour or so ago, she'd fallen to her knees, weeping and begging, all dignity disappearing in her distress.

'Good morning, how may I help you?' he said, smiling pleasantly.

'I would like two poppy seed rolls, please, and one of those pastries,' she said, composing her face into a reciprocal smile.

Just as before, the rolls and pastry were carefully packaged into newspaper. 'That will be fifteen cents.'

As she handed over the coins, she steeled herself. 'Monsieur Vermeulen?'

He nodded, looking up with a quizzical smile.

'My name is Martha Weber,' she said. 'I am looking for a man called Geert Peeters. He owes me ten francs, a deposit against a visit to the cemeteries.'

The smile vanished in an instant. 'I know nothing about this man,' he muttered.

'But he borrows your van,' she said. 'You must know something.' She was determined to have an answer.

He shook his head. 'I have not seen him. Since three days.'

'Then may I have his address, please? Where does he live?'

'Sorry, I do not know his address.'

'I believe you *do*, sir.' She took a breath and tried to look him directly in the eye. He turned away, pretending to busy himself with something below the counter.

'Monsieur Vermeulen,' she said firmly. 'I believe you to be an honourable man, and I know you can help me. I must get my money back before we leave the day after tomorrow.' His jaw jutted, his expression truculent and unrelenting. She smiled as charmingly as she could. 'By the way, your bread and pastries are so delicious, the best I have ever tasted. You know we have come from Switzerland? Our bakers are famous around the world but I declare that yours are even better.'

Perhaps it was the reassurance of the word Switzerland or the appeal to his professional vanity, but his face softened and she held her breath as he hesitated, still unsure where to place his gaze. Then, furtively glancing around to make sure he was not being observed, he took up a pencil stub, scribbled something onto a corner of newspaper, tore it off and gave it to her.

'Tell no one I gave you this,' he said under his breath. 'Especially not Peeters. Now I must ask you to leave.'

At Otto's insistence they returned to the hotel room and ate a delicious lunch of pastries and plums. After the nervous tension of the morning she felt exhausted, barely able to move a muscle, let alone able to summon the courage to face Monsieur Peeters.

At two o'clock they set out once more. She suggested that he should stay behind at the hotel but Otto insisted on coming and she was glad of his company as they found themselves becoming lost in the back streets of Hoppestadt. They had to ask for directions several times, and by the time they found the street Monsieur Vermeulen had written on the scrap of newspaper she was beginning to sweat uncomfortably.

It was clear that this eastern quarter had been more badly damaged by shelling than the rest of the town. Many of the houses appeared derelict and unoccupied, including the one outside which they found themselves. Fearing that the baker had fobbed them off with a false address, she knocked, politely at first, and then more loudly and insistently.

This raised a holler from inside the house, a woman's voice shouting something unintelligible and certainly ill-tempered. Soon enough, they heard bolts being drawn and the door was flung open to reveal a dumpy, red-faced woman in an overall, frowning and wiping her hands on a grubby dishrag. She looked extremely displeased.

'What is it?' She spoke Flemish but Martha could understand the gist well enough.

'I am looking for your husband, Monsieur Geert Peeters.'

The woman shook her head, scowling even more. 'He's not here.'

Otto nudged his mother in the ribs. 'He *is*, Ma. He's up there,' he whispered, pointing to an upper window. 'I just saw a face.'

Martha looked up just in time to see the shutters being jammed shut, and heard the clatter of the lock. 'I believe that your husband *is* at home, Madame Peeters,' she said. 'We have just seen him.'

The woman shook her head, fiercely repeating her denial, and was about to close the door when, from the corridor behind her, they heard a harsh cough and the burly figure of Geert Peeters appeared. He shouldered his wife aside and stepped out onto the street, swaying slightly on splayed legs.

'What you want?' he slurred. Even from two metres away Martha could smell the sour combination of alcohol and stale sweat.

'You promised to take me to Langemarck and took my ten francs as a deposit, monsieur.' She pulled from her pocket the scruffy leaflet he had given her. 'You did not come to my hotel at eleven o'clock as you promised. So I would like my money back, please.'

Geert took the paper and squinted at it, swaying slightly on his feet. 'I not give you this.'

'You *did*, sir. When you took my money. Ten-franc deposit, ten more after the tour, that's what we agreed.'

He looked up, attempting to focus. 'Not me, madame.'

'It *was* you – look.' She pointed at the leaflet. 'Geert Peeters?'

'I not Geert.'

'Sir, you are lying,' she cried, exasperated. 'I know your face. You are the man who approached me in the street, offered to take me to the cemetery and took my ten francs as a deposit. If you do not return it to me, I will go to the police.'

At this, the door behind him reopened and the wife stepped out, her face puce and distorted. The overall had gone, and a battered felt hat was plonked firmly onto her head. She shouted something that sounded obscene, slapped his cheek and pushed him to one side before striding towards Martha.

'Go away,' she spat. 'Kraut murderer!'

Martha gasped and felt Otto tensing beside her.

'I am not German, I am Swiss,' she said, standing her ground, trying to keep her voice calm even though her legs were trembling.

'You visit Kraut grave so you Kraut. Go home or we kill you. Like you kill our son.'

Out of the corner of her eye, Martha saw Otto stepping forward with his fists raised and she leapt sideways to reach him before he could take action. Then horror struck: at that very moment she glimpsed the terrifying glint of steel in the woman's hand.

'No! Stay back, Otto. She's got a knife,' she shouted as the woman lurched towards them once more. Otto tried to stand his ground but she managed to grab his arm more firmly, and summoned all her strength to drag him out of harm's way to the other side of the street.

'Go away and no come back,' the woman jeered, hauling her husband to the doorway. She pushed him inside and followed, slamming the door with such ferocity that the house seemed to rock. A broken tile slipped from the roof and shattered onto the street in front of them.

Now that the immediate threat had been removed, Martha's legs began to shake uncontrollably, until they could no longer support her. She sank to the ground against a wall, careless of the dust and rubble beneath her, folded her face into her arms and began to weep. Otto crouched by her side, putting his arm around her shoulders.

'It's all right, Ma.' His voice cracked and she heard for the first time the deep bass tones of an adult man. 'They're crazy people. Let's just leave it. It's only ten francs; not worth getting into a fight for. I don't mind if we haven't enough money for food tomorrow. We're used to it, aren't we? We'll be okay.' He rested his head on hers. 'Please stop crying, Ma. We need to get out of here.'

18

ALICE

Alice was still fuming.

She was so naive, that girl, poking her nose into other people's business without any notion of the trouble it could create. She'd seemed such a timid little thing, no trouble to anyone, but now she was becoming a liability. Trying to help someone visit a German grave, for Pete's sake! And she'd had the cheek to go all preachy about human kindness.

To calm her jangling nerves, Alice decided to take a stroll, but it wasn't long before she began to regret it. Walking on cobbles was tiresome; the streets were hot and dusty, and the sweat soon began to break out on her forehead, prickling her scalp. Beyond the square there was little of interest; just a few months ago the town must have been buzzing with activity but now the army had gone, everything seemed abandoned and the place was deserted.

The only sign of life she encountered was a group of three elderly women, all dressed in black, sitting on stools in doorways at the side of the street, heads bent over small cushions on which were pinned white threads held by a dozen brightly coloured sticks, which they flicked with such speed that their fingers became a blur.

The sight was a welcome distraction. '*Bonjour*,' she said. 'Your lace is very beautiful.'

Three gnarled faces looked up, their fingers momentarily stilled, their expressions confused and guarded. Much as she longed to ask about the lace making, perhaps even to enquire whether it was for sale, she knew that there was little point in trying to hold such a complicated conversation with Flemish speakers in French. Alice watched for a while longer, then smiled sweetly and went on her way.

Further along the street she found a small shop doorway. In the window was a dusty display of what she took to be Belgian delicacies: tins of goose pâté, bottles of beer in a presentation case, packets of waffles in cellophane tied with a red ribbon, and a small bottle of brandy. She was reminded of her promise to take presents back to Julia's family in London as thanks for their hospitality.

As she entered the dark interior a hunched old lady took to her feet. 'Madame?' Alice purchased a tin of pâté, a packet of waffles and, as a final thought, a bottle of brandy.

At the end of the street she found a small park beside a stream, the grass parched and neglected, the flower beds overgrown, the spars of the single bench long since stolen, probably for firewood. But it was shady here, under a willow tree. She took off her jacket and sat down to rest her aching feet. Before long, her head began to feel heavy – the hangover catching up with her. She stretched out on the grass and closed her eyes.

She must have dozed, because when she checked her watch again an hour had passed. Scrambling to her feet, she began trying to retrace her steps back to the square. But she must have taken a wrong turn because she found herself in a completely unfamiliar area, a run-down part of the town she'd not seen before, where many of the houses were shell-shattered and derelict. She couldn't even see the spire of the church any more, nor the tower of the town hall.

Trying to navigate by the position of the sun, she passed a junction and heard raised voices. She turned to glance down the side street and glimpsed in the distance an argument playing out in the street. A short, dumpy woman pushed an old man aside so forcefully that he stumbled and nearly fell to the ground, all the while bellowing abuse at another couple. Unwilling to be drawn into what looked like a domestic altercation, she began to walk on.

It was the word 'Kraut' being shouted that stopped her in her tracks. Looking more carefully, she recognised the couple as the Swiss woman and her son. Still she wavered, reluctant to become involved. This was the woman who wanted to visit a German grave, after all.

She watched with growing alarm as the confrontation seemed to escalate. Mother and son retreated to the other side of the street and the woman collapsed against a wall while the old crone who'd been shouting at her grabbed the man and dragged him inside the house. The boy leaned over his mother, reaching out a comforting hand.

Alice could ignore them no longer. She found herself running down the street towards them, calling out in French, 'Are you all right?'

The woman's eyes were wide with fear. 'They have stolen my money,' she sobbed. 'She has a knife.'

Behind them, a shutter creaked open with a further furious shout: 'Go home, Kraut murderer!'

'Come on, I'll buy you a coffee,' she said, placing a hand beneath the woman's elbow, trying to raise her from the ground. It was no use, her legs seemed to buckle beneath her.

'Get her arm on the other side, we can lift her together,' she ordered the boy. He stared, apparently uncomprehending, until she gestured to him. At last, after much pulling, they managed to bring Martha to her feet. Placing her arms over their shoulders to support her, they took one step and then another until, with agonisingly slow progress, they reached the main street. Through the buildings she could now catch a glimpse of the church tower, and navigated in that direction until they reached the square.

Ginger led them to the table the Swiss couple had vacated earlier, deep in the shadows at the rear of the cafe. 'You look as though you've all had a terrible fright,' she said. 'What can I get you?'

'Two coffees and a lemonade,' Alice said. 'And some biscuits, perhaps, or pastries? Something sweet?' She turned to the woman. 'Mrs Weber? Martha, isn't it, and Otto? You'd better tell me what was going on.'

'I was only trying to get my money back,' Martha said, her face still as pale as paper. 'But she threatened us with a knife. I was so afraid.'

'She threatened you?'

'Otto too.' Between ragged breaths, Martha began to recount the story of how she'd been trying to recover the ten-franc deposit from the man who had refused to take her to her nephew's grave. Ginger arrived with drinks and pastries. The woman ignored her food while the boy started to eat ravenously. Alice began to wonder whether he was actually a bit stupid – he didn't seem to understand much of what she said to him. But at other times he'd seemed bright enough, and she'd observed him gabbling away to his mother when they were out of earshot.

They really were a strange pair – so secretive. She couldn't quite put her finger on why, even after such brief acquaintance, she felt so wary of them, so convinced that they were hiding something. She'd noticed from the start that the woman had a curious accent, and now she remembered: it reminded her of some family friends back in the US, immigrants originally from Germany, with whose children she'd played as a girl. They were good people but she recalled now how different the parents were from her own: strangely formal and old-fashioned. Heaven knows what had happened to them since the war.

It had been tough for Germans, even those who had lived in America for most of their lives, during the war. Thousands had been interned, including half the players of the famous symphony orchestra in her home city. Even after the war ended and the detainees released, they were still shunned and treated with suspicion.

Why, only a few weeks ago a woman claiming to be Swiss had applied in response to her mother's advertisement for a housekeeper. 'I am a good worker, very honest,' she'd told Alice's mother. 'I was a nurse before the war, but it is so difficult to find a job now.' On investigation she turned out to have been schooled in Germany and Alice's father declared, with his usual tone of finality, 'I'm not having Krauts in my house.' So the woman, by far the best qualified of all the applicants, was turned away.

She'd felt sorry for those people back home but now she had seen the terrible devastation and death the Germans had caused, she understood why they were so reviled. She hated the Germans for taking away Amelia, and Sam, and so many other young men she knew. It was natural, wasn't it? Yet here she was, helping a woman who she strongly suspected was German and, like the would-be housekeeper, only pretending to be Swiss. What else could she have done, when they were being threatened by a madwoman? It was so confusing.

She scrabbled in her pocket book and found a note. She needed to buy off her conscience. 'This may help a little,' she said, placing it on the table. 'It's not worth putting yourself in danger for ten francs.'

The woman shook her head. Alice pushed it back. 'Please. It will help you find your nephew. And now I must go.'

Martha's hand slipped out discreetly and the note disappeared. 'Bless you,' she said.

❈

Standing in the queue at the post office once more, waiting to see whether there was any response from her father, Alice listened idly to the townsfolk gossiping around her. Everyone seemed to have some fresh news to exchange with each other, and with the man behind the counter, slowing even further his deliberate, unhurried delivery. Under normal circumstances Alice would have fidgeted impatiently, sighing and muttering about poor service and inefficient bureaucracy, but she found herself distracted by their little exchanges.

'Did you see the price of those tomatoes?'

'They're bringing them all the way from Spain, would you believe?'

'Time we rebuilt our own glasshouses, I'd say. So we can grow our own earlies.'

'Need to mend our homes first.'

'Have you heard Churchill's suggested leaving Ypres as a monument?'

Alice's ears pricked up.

'You mean, not rebuilding the Cloth Hall?'

'Not rebuilding anything. Leaving it as a memorial.'

'But where would people live?'

'It's bloody ridiculous, if you ask me.'

'Our government won't let them get away with it.'

'There are architects already making plans.'

'Thank the good Lord for that. Now we just have to get the money to pay for it.'

Just as she was drawing close to the front of the queue the gossip took a different turn. She caught the name Vermeulen and listened more carefully – this was the baker, brother of their hotelier. Then she heard mention of someone called Peeters. It seemed he was the despair of his wife, drinking away any money he managed to earn from fleecing the tourists. This must be the couple she'd seen threatening Martha and her son.

'Can I help you?' the post office man repeated, first in Flemish, then in French. She'd been so absorbed in the conversation that she'd failed to notice that she'd reached the counter.

'Have you a telegram for Alice Palmer, please?' She did not really expect anything but it was just possible that, if he'd acted quickly and the Canadians had responded equally promptly, her father might already have heard back. So it was with some astonishment that she saw him reach into the pigeonhole marked with a 'P' and pull out a yellow envelope.

'Sign here, please.'

Outside, with trembling hands, Alice ripped open the envelope. Anticipating a negative response, or at the very least a 'no news yet' message, she could scarcely believe what she read: CANUCKS SAY SAMUEL PILGRIM ADDRESS UNKNOWN BUT SAME DOB SO LIKELY OUR SAM STOP DIED 30 OCT 1917 WE ARE DEVASTATED WILL CONFIRM WHERE BURIED TOMORROW PA STOP

Her head was spinning. What was a DOB? Some kind of acronym; a military term, perhaps? She ran through in her head words beginning with D. Then it came to her: Date Of Birth. That must be it. When he registered with the Canadians, Sam had given a false address but hadn't bothered to change his birthdate. So it *must* be him: same writing, same birthdate, a name that had the same meaning. She gave a little whoop. She'd found him, at last.

Only on reading it again did the words properly sink in: *Died 30 Oct 1917*. If this was her Sam, it meant that he was definitely not alive. Sam was dead. The shock made her gasp and she found herself bent over, struggling for breath. While his disappearance remained a mystery she'd been able to cling to the slim possibility that he might still be alive somewhere, perhaps shell-shocked, or simply ashamed, afraid to return home to face his future without his beloved Amelia, or perhaps just because he didn't have the money for the transatlantic crossing. There could be any number of reasons.

So, for the past three years, every day, almost every hour, she'd thought of him, cherishing the chink of hope that she might, somehow, find him alive. It wasn't entirely deluded, she told herself. Look at the man Tubby went off to visit at the hospital. Look at Freddie, hiding away from his future here, in a place dominated by his traumatic past.

She had rehearsed these and any number of other scenarios over the past few months. But now, none of them applied. If Sam Pilgrim really *was* her brother, and the coincidences were just too great to imagine that he was not, then the remote hope that had sustained her for all these years was extinguished for good.

Staggering to a lamp post for support, she rested her head against the cold metal as the old anger welled up once more. How could he have been so selfish, going off to war, getting himself killed? And to leave without saying any proper goodbyes, taking a false name, covering his tracks so thoroughly that they might never have found out what happened to him? How could she ever forgive him for putting them all through such heartache?

Now he was gone. Forever. She would never see him again, never have those midnight chats, those evenings of drinking too much of Pa's port and sharing unwise confidences, never watch him grow into a man, fall in love again, have children, even grandchildren. She couldn't imagine a life without him, her little brother, always there.

She was still too shocked to cry. Like a wounded animal, her instinct was to hide away, alone. She would go back to the hotel, take refuge in her room and crack open that bottle of brandy, holding the grief close to her heart until she could face the world again.

Nothing else mattered any more.

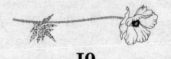

19

RUBY

Ruby had been in a fervour of anticipation ever since Tubby mentioned the Englishman in the hospital.

Now, waiting restlessly in the hotel lobby as the clock chimed three and the minutes passed, she could hardly breathe for the suspense. It was a million-to-one chance, of course, perhaps even less. She scarcely dared to hope, but now she was about to find out.

What must it be like, lying there in the hospital bed, injured and in pain, possibly confused and unable to communicate, terrified about what might happen next? What horrors must he have seen? What terrifying ordeals had he endured? If he was a deserter, how must it have felt to be so fearful of punishment that you would run away, even knowing that being caught might lead to being shot by your own countrymen?

And what had happened to him since? She tried to imagine the people who must have taken him in, cared for him, given him shelter, shared their own meagre food supplies with him, probably risking their own safety. What saints, these anonymous people.

At last Tubby arrived, flustered and red in the face, sweating and apologising profusely for being late. 'Please don't worry,' she said. 'I know you are a busy man.'

'Are you ready to meet my bearded friend? He's in a bit of a pickle, you know. Shell shock. You need to be prepared,' he said, as they set out across the square.

'I scarcely dare ask,' she panted, struggling to keep up with the chaplain's brisk pace. 'But what does he look like?'

'Hard to tell beneath the beard, I'm afraid. He's dreadfully thin, of course.'

'Does he have any physical injuries?'

'Nothing obvious,' Tubby said. 'No bandages. He's lost the top of a finger somewhere along the line, but it looks like an old wound.'

The top of a finger! The shock knocked the breath out of her so sharply that she had to stop walking. Tubby turned back to her. 'My dear, you've gone white as a sheet. Here . . .' He walked back to her, putting a supportive hand to her elbow. 'Take a few deep breaths. That's right. Slowly now. Was it something I said?'

'Which finger?' she gasped.

He looked puzzled. 'I cannot precisely remember, my dear. Why do you ask?'

'My husband, Bertie. He lost a finger falling off a friend's motorbike. The left index finger. Do you think it could possibly be . . . ?'

'There's only one way to find out,' Tubby said. 'Here, take my arm. It's not far now.'

She could see it so clearly now, with such certainty. It *must* be him. His face would light up with recognition as he looked up and saw her approaching down the hospital ward. She would fall into his arms, weeping and crying. *I'm coming, Bertie.*

❄❄❄

The convent building had a forbidding air, all grey stone and gothic windows, like a Victorian church. At the top of the steps, under an imposing arched doorway, Tubby yanked the rusty chain and a bell echoed through distant corridors while Ruby tried to keep herself from fidgeting. *Keep calm, take deep breaths*, she told herself.

After several almost unbearably long minutes the door was opened by a crisply wimpled nun, tiny and bent, supporting herself with a stick. She peered up at them suspiciously at first but then, on recognising Tubby, the dark little eyes brightened. She welcomed them, leading them at an agonisingly slow pace along three corridors and up a double flight of stone stairs. The further they walked, the more utterly convinced Ruby became that the man in the bed would be Bertie, and the more terrified she became of discovering that it was not.

Apart from the almost overwhelming smell of coal tar soap and disinfectant, it was unlike any hospital she had ever visited: no nurses carrying covered enamel dishes, no doctors with white coats flapping as they rushed importantly to the next emergency, no anxious-faced relatives crowding the hallway. She saw no staff, and they seemed to be the only visitors. From the first-floor landing, through open doorways leading to the right, left and straight ahead, were long wards lined on each side by hospital beds, all made up with sparkling white sheets, all unoccupied.

'The nuns did a wonderful job during the war,' Tubby whispered. 'There are a further three wards like this on the top floor and they could care for nearly three hundred at a time. But now, thank the good Lord, they hardly have any customers, just locals and the occasional Allied malingerer, like our man. He's along here.'

Ruby's feet seemed to move of their own accord, carrying her forwards as though she were floating. Now that she was about to meet him, her mind had gone blank. Ahead of them, at the end of the long white ward, was an occupied bed.

Even before she could make out his face, the chill of disappointment settled on her shoulders. The man, now clean-shaven with his hair cut and combed, was propped up in bed sitting perfectly still, hands folded over the sheet in front of him. But she knew, oh so intimately, how Bertie sat, how he held his head, how he placed his hands, how his shoulders sat on his body. And this was not him.

The disappointment was like a hammer blow; she felt dizzy and nauseous, tempted to run away, out of the ward, out of the hospital, away from all her foolish hopes, her naive, ridiculous imaginings, away from Hoppestadt altogether. It was so unfair – she had believed so powerfully that she was close to finding Bertie alive. And now here was this stranger in front of her, and she had no idea how to respond.

As they arrived at his bedside, he seemed barely to notice them. His eyes, open and unnaturally wide, stared into space, his expression was somehow inhuman.

'Good morning, sir. How are you today?' Tubby asked.

The man started, eyes blinking furiously. The muscles in

his jaw worked as he tried to speak – 'Uh, uh, uh' – and his body became racked with the effort, his head jerking, hands wringing the sheet. She could see now that it was the top of the little finger on his right hand that was missing.

Tubby sat beside the bed and placed his broad, fleshy hand over the man's clenched fist. 'It's all right, my friend. Don't try to talk. Just nod or shake your head, if you can. Your speech will come back soon enough.' After a moment the man's hands stilled, and his body seemed to relax, his expression returning to that blank, unfocused stare.

Ruby took the chair on the other side. As his gaze shifted slowly towards her she saw that, against the fresh-shaven pallor, his eyes were clear and bright, a surprising cornflower blue. It would have been a handsome face had it not been so distorted with mental anguish, and she could see now, even through her own disappointment, the human being inside.

This man might not be Bertie but he was surely the son, brother or husband of a family back home who were even now going about their daily business, unaware that he was still alive. He must have been much loved and greatly mourned when they learned that he was missing. But now here he was with a future ahead of him, having survived against all odds. Imagine their joy when they learned the news? The important thing now was to trace them, and get him home as soon as possible.

'Hello,' she said, keeping her voice slow and even, emulating the chaplain's soothing tone. 'Can you tell us your name?'

He seemed to gather himself, taking a deep breath and trying to force his lips around the words but all that came out was 'jee jee'. He struggled for a few moments and then gave up, gasping with frustration. Ruby smiled at him again, trying to read his face.

'Have you any family at home? Someone we could contact?' Tubby asked.

The man shook his head wildly, accompanied by a number of involuntary twitches and shudders which then stilled suddenly, his gaze distracted and shifting beyond Tubby, towards the doorway. They turned to see an older gentleman, short and burly, accompanied by a woman dressed entirely in black, being prevented by the tiny nun from entering the ward.

Tubby rose and strode towards them, asked some questions and remonstrated with the nun. After a moment it became clear that he'd managed to make himself understood, because she seemed to relent.

He brought them to the bedside. 'These excellent people are farmers, and they've been sheltering our friend,' he explained. 'When he disappeared, a few weeks ago, they were too frightened for their own safety to look for him. I've reassured them we won't do anything to harm the lad.'

Ruby shook their hands in turn.

'They've brought this.' Tubby held out a simple brown octagonal tag, just like Bertie's. He examined it, squinting through his thick round glasses. After turning it over and squinting some more, he held it out to Ruby.

'It's no good. You have a go. Your eyesight's probably better than mine.'

She peered at the rough, unevenly stamped lettering. *PVT J CATCHPOLE*. It was when he handed it to her that she could now see the part that Tubby's fingers had been covering, and her heart seemed to stop. Across the top of the tag, separated by the hole for the string, it read *SFK RGT*. She gasped. Bertie's regiment.

She gathered herself to ask, and heard the shake in her voice: 'Is this you, Private Catchpole? You were in the Suffolks?' The answer was more of a tilting of the head than a full affirmative, but it was enough.

'I'm from Suffolk too.' The glimmer of a smile turned up the corners of his mouth.

'You're safe now, Private Catchpole,' Tubby said. 'We will contact your family and try to get you home.' The smile evaporated instantly, and his head began to twist violently from side to side, his limbs trembling.

'Nnn, nnn, nnn,' the man stuttered, clasping the tag to his chest with whitened knuckles, violently shaking his head. Tubby mouthed, 'Deserter.'

'Don't worry,' he added quickly. 'We won't do anything you don't want us to do. I promise.'

After a brief conversation with the old man and his wife, Tubby translated for Ruby: 'Private Catchpole turned up in October last year, raving and exhausted, with some minor injuries which they tended to. They took him in and fed him, let him use their barn to sleep in, but he would not tell them who he was. Just a few days ago they discovered that he'd gone, leaving a note of thanks saying he was going to try to make it back home.

'It was only after that they found the tag he had left behind in a bag under the straw he'd used as a bed. They were very worried for his safety as they were pretty sure he was a deserter and everyone knows what happens if they're caught. Then yesterday they learned about a soldier who'd turned up here, and felt they must come to make sure he was safe. They've been travelling since dawn.'

'What kind people.'

'Their own son was killed,' Tubby added, in simple explanation.

They returned to the man's bedside. 'What does the J. stand for on your tag? Is it John?' she asked.

He shook his head.

'Joseph?' He seemed to hesitate, but then shook his head again. She hoped it wasn't going to be an obscure name like Jeremiah or Jeffrey. They could be here for hours.

'James, then?'

At last, an affirmative nod. Ruby and Tubby exchanged triumphant smiles.

'Do they call you Jimmy?'

Tears glittered in the corner of his eyes. Ruby leaned forward again, taking his hands in hers. Her touch seemed to calm his tremors. 'You want to go home, Jimmy, don't you, to your family? But we need to know your address. Can you try to tell us?'

He breathed in, and sighed out, 'Umb, umb, huh.'

'Take another breath and try again,' she urged.

'Umb, umb, baa. Umb baah.'

She nodded encouragingly. 'You're nearly there.'

But he shook his head and closed his eyes, resting his head back on the pillow. It was too much effort. Reaching into his briefcase, Tubby pulled out a pencil and an old envelope. 'Perhaps you could try to write it down?'

The effort of controlling the pencil was clearly exhausting as the tics took it off into wild loops and arcs, but eventually some legible numbers and words appeared.

'A hundred and thirty-four Humber Lane? In Ipswich?'

'Is that your parents' address?' Tubby asked.

~~Another slow nod.~~

'Then we shall get in touch with them as soon as we can. You're going home, laddie.'

This time it was not a distorted grimace but an almost natural smile. Tubby explained to the Belgian couple, and their weather-beaten faces became wreathed in smiles as they shook the chaplain's hand, and then Ruby's. '*Merci, monsieur, mam'selle, merci mille fois.*' The man clapped Jimmy on the shoulder with a gruff '*Bonne chance, mon vieux.*' She watched them trying to control their emotions as they turned and walked slowly away down the long ward.

'Where are we going, Tubby?' Once more Ruby found herself skipping to keep up with his purposeful stride.

'We're going to telephone the Ipswich exchange and ask directory enquiries. If there's no number, we'll get them to send a telegram. It'll be quicker that way, we'll avoid the Belgian authorities and there'll be fewer eyes to read it.'

'We can telephone, across the Channel?'

'They set up the lines under the sea during the war, and there's a link to the town hall here, because it was the Allied headquarters,' he said. 'The army's all gone now, of course, but I know the mayor, and he owes me a few favours.'

She recalled Major Wilson telling them what else the town hall had been used for. 'Do you really think he's a deserter?'

'Sure as I can be, from his reaction,' Tubby said. 'They

didn't look kindly on men with shell shock. Just told them to pull themselves together and sent them back into battle. If he'd been caught, he'd probably have been shot. I did my best, but the high-ups didn't usually listen.'

She sensed it from the passion of his words. 'Was that something you had to get involved in, Tubby?'

He strode onward, his jaw working.

'I'm sorry, I shouldn't have asked.'

There was a longer silence. Then he stopped and turned to her. 'It was the worst duty of all for an army chaplain and I prayed I would not be called on, but it came to me once. Just the once, thank the good Lord, but that was enough.' He wiped the sweat from his brow. 'They had to have a chaplain to spend the night with the poor bastard in the cell before the execution. I snuck in a bottle of brandy that night, to make it a little easier for him. It was a long night, I can tell you. Some of them used to like to sing hymns, they said, but my laddie just wept and wept, and cried out for his mother. The army said it was all about setting an example. Typical of their ruddy blinkered thinking, 'scuse my French. I can't think of a worse example of man's inhumanity to man.' He sighed, starting to walk on. 'War's a brutal thing, Ruby, whichever way you look at it. It tests your faith to hell and back.'

She didn't know much about faith but she'd certainly been tested to hell and back. And still there were no answers, none of the 'making sense of it all' the major had promised.

The mayor welcomed Tubby like a long-lost friend. They jabbered in French for a while before he ushered them into a stuffy cubbyhole just large enough for a couple of chairs and a desk on which sat a large black Bakelite telephone. On the wall was an empty board peppered with the marks of drawing pins that, she imagined, must once have held vitally important communiqués.

It took several minutes for the operator to contact the London exchange. Tubby asked them to put him through to Ipswich and then handed the receiver to Ruby. 'You speak to them,' he said. 'You know his address.' Moments passed as the line crackled and creaked. She imagined the cable, threading through the mud and seaweed deep beneath the grey waters of the English Channel. What critically important information had these lines carried, throughout the war?

A voice answered, a soft, distant voice with that gentle Suffolk lilt so familiar that it gave her a pang of homesickness. What a miracle to be talking to someone in her home town from so far away.

'Ipswich exchange 'ere. Can oi help you?'

She gathered herself to speak. 'We are looking for the telephone number of a Mr Catchpole who lives at one-three-four Humber Lane, please.'

Another long pause, more crackles and creaks. The operator returned. 'We've got a J. Catchpole at that address. Would that be the one?'

It was all Ruby could do to contain her delight. *You're going home, Jimmy*, she said to herself, giving Tubby the thumbs up. 'That's right.'

'No telephone number, miss.'

'Then could you send a telegram, please?'

Tubby handed her a piece of paper on which he had hastily written: PVT J CATCHPOLE SAFE HOPPESTADT HOSPITAL STOP SEND FAMILY MEMBER ASAP REV P CLAYTON STOP

As she read it out, slowly enough for the operator to write it down at the other end, Ruby allowed herself to imagine the reaction of the people receiving these words: shock, astonishment, disbelief, a slow understanding, followed by excitement and pure joy.

It was not her Bertie. But at least someone's son, brother, perhaps even husband, was alive.

❧

'Let's have a beer to celebrate,' Tubby suggested as they walked back across the square. 'I think we've made a family very happy today.'

'How do you think Jimmy will fare, when he gets back home?' she asked. 'I keep wondering whether his family have seen the telegram yet, and what it must be like in their household, getting that news. I'm envious, I suppose.'

He paused for a second. 'His family will wrap him in love and creature comforts, but after all these months of living rough, hand to mouth, he'll find it very difficult to adjust.'

'I hope they'll be patient with him.'

'He'll need it. But at least he's been given a second chance.'

'If he doesn't get caught.'

'To be honest, what with all the other things they've got

on, demobilisation, repatriation, dealing with the wounded, war pensions and the like, the army has greater problems than chasing up deserters these days. I reckon that if he lies low for a year or so, they'll just forget all about him. He'll miss out on the war pension, of course, but I suppose that's a small price to pay for his freedom.'

'How wonderful if he could just go back to a normal life, perhaps get married and have children.'

They sat in companionable silence as the sun lowered in the sky, leaving the square in shadow, watching the lights going on, one by one, in the windows. Ruby couldn't help being reminded of her own village, where few drew their curtains of an evening except against the cold. Lights in windows signified home, family, safety.

Being away in this foreign place had made her all the more appreciative of those things she'd failed to value while so consumed by her own grief: the love and generosity of her mother, the support of Bertie's family, her friends, her colleagues at work.

She wasn't sure where it sprang from but the question – that question which, looking back at that moment years hence, would change her life – seemed to come out before she'd had time to think about it.

'That organisation you're setting up to help returning soldiers?' she asked. 'Is there anything I can do to help, once we're back home, do you think? I have a job to go back to, of course, but in my spare time . . .'

Tubby's grin seemed to split his face in two. 'My dearest child, we would welcome you with open arms. I feel so strongly that we must help those who survived, to bring them together and help them find a way forward in life.

We owe it to the memories of those who didn't make it. I have a day job too, of course, but this is what I plan to dedicate my life to in the future. And there is so much to do: writing letters, knocking on doors, raising funds, organising events. Would that sort of thing appeal?'

'It appeals very much, thank you.' She felt flooded with excitement, with a sense of purpose that she seemed to have lost since Bertie died.

A figure emerged out of the dusk. 'Appeals very much? S'pose that's me you're talking about.'

She laughed. 'Not you, nosy parker. Stop picking up fag ends.'

Freddie's eyes twinkled with mischief. 'Shame. Thought I might be in the running.'

'Come and join us,' Tubby said.

'Don't mind if I do,' Freddie said. 'I'll just get in a pint. Another one, Ruby? Reverend?'

While he was at the bar, Tubby whispered, 'Don't say anything about Jimmy, will you? The fewer people who know, the better.'

Freddie returned, Ginger arrived with the drinks and they all raised their glasses.

'Cheers,' Tubby said.

'Here's to peace,' Ruby said.

'About ruddy time,' Freddie said, taking a long draught.

'And forgiveness in our hearts,' Tubby added.

Ruby told Freddie she was planning to help Tubby with his new association to support returning soldiers and Freddie said he'd be happy to get involved too, 'so long as I don't have to turn up in church'. Tubby laughed and promised there'd be no expectations. Then, after a brief lull in the conversation, he said, almost musing to himself, 'I wonder whatever happened to that poor Swiss woman?'

Ruby could have kissed him. As far as she was aware he had no idea that Freddie had proved unwilling to help – certainly she had not mentioned it – but he seemed to know, from careful observation, listening and intuition, how to ask just the right question at exactly the right time. Freddie remained silent, apparently engaged in reading the advertisement for a beer company engraved into the side of his glass.

'I suppose no one wants to be seen at a German grave-yard for fear they might be considered sympathisers,' she said, playing Devil's advocate.

'Or just 'cos they hate Germans,' Freddie muttered.

Tubby folded his hands together and closed his eyes, chin resting on steepled fingers. *Here's the church, here's the steeple, open the doors and here are all the people*, Ruby recited silently to herself. 'It is time for reconciliation,' he said, quietly but firmly. 'If we don't start forgiving each other, we will never find peace in our hearts.'

In the long, weighty silence that followed, she caught Freddie's eye. He flushed and grinned back, a little sheep-ishly. Then he cleared his throat. 'It might . . .' He faltered, and stopped.

Tubby opened his eyes. 'Go on.'

'It's just possible . . .' They waited, while he gathered himself, clearing his throat again. 'There's a vehicle I might be able to borrow.'

She beamed a grateful smile.

'I'm not promising anything,' he said, blushing more. 'Can I let you know tomorrow?'

She leaned forward and took his hand. 'Thank you, Freddie. You're a . . .' She struggled for the right words.

'A diamond geezer?' Tubby suggested.

'One of those, with bells on,' she said.

20

MARTHA

Martha slumped onto the bed and closed her eyes, miserable and defeated. Monsieur Vermeulen's words, so eloquent in his evident hatred, rang in her head: *fears turn into whispers, whispers soon become rumours, rumours fuel suspicions, suspicions lead to official accusations.* The image appeared before her eyes of Madame Peeter's ravaged face, red and distorted with fury: *Kraut murderer.*

She understood why they were so angry, especially now that she'd seen for herself the state of their country, their wrecked towns, the mud and destruction and the countless graves. But at least things were improving here. Food imports were easing their hunger, businesses were starting to recover, farms beginning to increase production, plans for rebuilding the towns and villages underway. These people could imagine a future.

But it was hard to imagine a future for her beloved Germany, which would be saddled with debt for decades to come under the terms agreed by their treacherous politicians at Versailles. Whatever sort of country would it be for Otto as he grew up? Its people were so crushed, so hungry, so poverty-stricken, so locked in revolution and rebellion. The old order was broken but no one knew what the new order, enshrined in the constitution over which they'd been battling in Weimar for months, might bring.

It was only now that she began to understand that her sense of urgency, her burning need to come here just as soon as travel restrictions were lifted, was more to do with resolving something inside herself, trying to find her own peace of mind, than any sense of duty towards her husband or her dead son.

Life in Germany was so grindingly miserable, so lacking in any hope. She'd been driven by the belief that seeing Heinrich's grave would bring her heart some ease, and perhaps allow her to plan for her own future, and Otto's.

Yet, however difficult this trip was turning out, she did not regret coming. They may have endured suspicion and even the threat of violence, but had also, she reminded herself, encountered great kindness from people whose countries she'd learned to hate. The English chaplain and the girl, even the American woman who had at first seemed so hostile, had freely demonstrated their compassion, comforted them, given food and money.

It was so different at home. In Berlin, everyone was afraid of everyone else, and violent gangs roamed the streets. Hardship and misery had left no room for considering the plight of others.

She glanced at Otto, sitting on a chair by the open window, reading his book and swinging his legs as though nothing untoward had happened. His cheeks were lightly pocked with the scars of an earlier outbreak of acne, a soft fluff covered his chin. How mature he had shown himself to be this afternoon, keeping his head and remaining calm, trying to comfort her when she'd broken down and wept in that desolate street. She prayed that he was not too traumatised by the experience of seeing his mother so humiliated and helpless.

Her heart ached with love and fear for him. All too soon her boy would become an adult, keen to leave home and forge his own way in the world. Thank heavens the war was over and he would not feel he had to fight, like his brother.

A knock at the door made her stomach lurch. Was it the hotelier, with more bad news? Or, worse, the police come to arrest and deport them? Otto looked up, his face pale in the gloom of the room, his eyes wide as wagon wheels, sensing her fear. She put her finger to her lips.

The knock came again, louder this time, and then a woman's voice: 'Mrs Weber?'

Martha put on her shoes and smoothed her hair before going to the door, opening it cautiously, just a crack at first. It was the English girl, Ruby.

'May I come in for a moment?' she asked.

Martha hesitated, gesturing with a raised finger for the girl to wait. Even now, after the kindness this girl had shown her, she found it difficult to trust anyone.

'Hurry, Otto. Put your book away, tidy up your things.' She straightened the bed quilt, pulled the bolster into place, threw their scattered shoes and clothing into the wardrobe before returning to the door. She let Ruby in, and closed the door behind her. There was only one chair, and she could hardly invite a stranger to sit on the bed, so the three of them stood, uncomfortably close to each other, in the small space between the bed and the door.

Ruby began speaking slowly and carefully, in English.

'I think I might have found someone to take you to Langemarck.'

Heaven be praised. 'Langemarck?'

The girl nodded. 'To find your nephew.'

'*Mais . . . ?*' she gestured with hands outstretched, palms raised.

'You know Mr Smith? Freddie?'

Martha shook her head.

'Englishman. In the bar downstairs?' The girl mimicked lifting an imaginary drink to her lips, her hands gripping around the handle of a *Stein* of beer. Now it was clear that she was referring to the rather dishevelled Englishman who seemed to inhabit the hotel bar whose blond eyelashes gave him a slightly disreputable look; the fellow to whom Otto had taken such an immediate dislike. Martha pointed to her own left arm, the one that Freddie had missing.

'That's the one. He is going to try to find a car or something.' Ruby gestured driving, with two hands on an imaginary steering wheel. There was no explanation as to how, with this disability, the man might be able to drive, and there was another problem. She held out her palm, touched it with the fingers of the other hand. 'How much?'

'Don't worry. I don't think Freddie wants money. Only for fuel, perhaps.'

Martha shook her head, not understanding.

'For petrol,' Ruby tried again. 'Petroleum.'

It was the same word in German. God be praised, it

might really be happening. Martha smiled, offering her hand. As they touched, for a brief, charged moment, their eyes met. The girl's, a pale speckled hazel, seemed to radiate the deep sorrow that Martha had sensed when they first met. Of course she, like them all, was only here because she had lost someone. A husband, a brother, a father or a lover?

Feeling the warmth of the other woman, Martha longed to ask her, to offer her sympathy, to soothe her grief; feeling a surge of that powerful motherly desire that would lead you to give anything, even your own life, if only it could take away your child's pain.

The girl smiled back and the sadness was spirited away in that instant, in that moment of mutual friendship and understanding that seemed to breach all barriers of language or national enmity. *She's a survivor*, Martha said to herself. *She will find happiness in future, just as we will all survive this, and find some kind of happiness, just so long as we remember to show kindness to each other.*

The moment passed, their hands parted. 'Good. See you tomorrow then.' Martha thanked her again, said goodbye and closed the door, resting her back against it, eyes closed, dizzy with relief.

'What was all that about, Ma?' Otto whispered.

'She's going to help us get to Langemarck.'

'To Heiney's grave?'

'To Heiney's grave. At last.'

'How? Who is driving?'

'Does it matter, Otto? At least we are going to get there.'

'I heard her say Freddie. That Englishman from the bar with the creepy eyes?'

'Now you're being silly. Whatever have his eyes got to do

with it? I am sure anything she organises will be perfectly safe.'

'Not with him driving with only one arm it won't.'

'For heaven's sake, Otto, let's just wait and see, shall we?' she snapped. 'We're going. At last. That's the most important thing.'

She sat down heavily on the bed, trying to order her thoughts, and after a few minutes Otto came to join her, sitting close and resting his head on her shoulder. The intimacy of the gesture took her by surprise: it was so long since he'd voluntarily sought physical contact with her. She pulled him to her.

'What is it, *mein Liebling*?'

'I'm scared, Ma.'

'What of, boy?' She turned and took his face in her hands. His fear was hardly surprising after the difficult events of the day. She expected him to say he was afraid of the horrible people in this town, or of being driven by a one-armed man. These she could deal with. But what he said instead shook her to the core.

'Of having to live the rest of my life.'

'What do you mean? Now we are at peace there's so much for you to look forward to.'

'Without Heiney.' The tears began to well again, in grief for her living son as much as for the dead one. She'd been so focused on her concerns about travelling, of finding a way to get to the grave, that she hadn't really considered the effect it must be having on Otto.

'Are you worried about seeing Heiney's grave?'

He nodded.

'Me too, my darling. But it's something we have to do,

don't you see? So we can tell him we love him. And say goodbye, properly.'

'I don't *want* to say goodbye.' His voice cracked. 'I'm scared of knowing, really knowing, that he won't come back any more. That he's gone for good.'

She struggled for words, but failed to find any. All she could hope for was that finding the grave might help both herself and Otto find a way to live the rest of their lives without him.

21

ALICE

In the lobby of the Hotel de la Paix, Cécile Vermeulen took up a wooden mallet and struck the gong hanging from its frame by the reception desk. Five strikes in rapid succession on the beaten brass sent up deep reverberations sufficient to rouse guests from every corner of the hotel. She preferred her customers to arrive for dinner in an orderly fashion: not all at once, which made it stressful in the kitchen, but never late or the food might spoil and her hard work go to waste.

Fearsomely proud of what she saw as 'her' hotel – Cécile was raised in the flat above the historic cafe and helped her parents turn these rooms into *chambres d'hôtes* before the war – she was now determined to transform it into the premier destination for pilgrims visiting the nearby cemeteries and battlefields. She and Maurice would soon make their fortune, of that she was certain.

Up in her room, Alice sat huddled in her quilt, sipping from the bottle of brandy that she'd bought as a gift for Julia's family and chiding herself for feeling so miserable. She'd known Sam was dead, right? Otherwise he'd have been home long ago, stupid. All the telegram had done was to confirm it. She had achieved what she'd set out to do in coming here. All they needed was the photograph finally to confirm his identity and soon enough she would find out where he was buried. Then she would be able to visit, to tell him she loved him, to explain how guilty she felt allowing him to leave, to make her peace.

Somehow none of this felt like any consolation.

The sound of the gong made her feel suddenly hungry. She'd missed lunch. Unravelling herself, she went to the basin to wash her face and hands, making a smile, and then a frown, at herself in the mirror. Both expressions reminded her of Sam, always had, always would. There were so many family likenesses. 'You're a part of me,' she whispered to the reflection. 'You will be with me for the rest of my life.'

She shook herself. *What you need is a hearty dinner and some cheerful company*. There was no answer from Ruby's door, so she went down to the bar. It was empty. She stood at the doorway, peering across to the cafe. No sign. Then, just as she was resigning herself to dining alone, she heard the squeal of brakes.

'Aleese?' Daniel looked impossibly dashing at the wheel of his rusty green coupé. 'Come to Lille with me? I have to deliver some orders.'

'Lille? That's miles away.' She didn't feel ready to see him again, somehow, not after this afternoon's revelations. It would mean putting on a brave face, being the charming, witty Alice he'd come to expect.

'Only about fifty kays. An hour and a half, perhaps? We'll get there in time to eat.' He patted the seat beside him. 'She's no Rolls-Royce, but she goes well and it's a good road once you get away from the battlefields. I just have to drop in to the office, and we can go to my favourite restaurant. What do you think?'

A dozen doubts flooded her mind but the rumbling of her stomach quickly dismissed them. What better distraction could she ask for than a trip in that car and the promise of dinner with Daniel? 'Just give me a moment.'

She raced up to her room and changed into her prettiest dress, the one with the green flowered silk with the flattering lace border around collar and cuffs, and carefully pulled on a clean pair of silk stockings. She reapplied lipstick, powdered her nose, dabbed her neck with eau de cologne and brushed her hair into place. *That'll have to do*, she said to herself, pulling in her tummy as she posed in front of the long oval mirror. *You may not be eighteen any more, but he's no spring chicken either.*

She grabbed a scarf and the light green linen jacket that matched the dress so well, and was about to rush downstairs when she remembered Ruby. On a piece of hotel notepaper she wrote a note and pushed it under her door. *Out with Daniel. Back later, A.*

For the first few miles he listened quietly, sympathetically, manoeuvring the car around the potholes in the road as she poured out her heart, telling him about this afternoon's telegram from her father and her devastation on discovering that her hopes of finding her brother alive had been so completely dashed. He was almost certainly dead, and buried who knew where.

At last she could no longer hold back the tears. He pulled up the car and put his arm around her as she sobbed. 'My sweet, dear Aleese,' he murmured. 'You are so brave to come here and I'm sorry there was not a happier result. But maybe you will find his grave, and that may be some consolation, no?' After a while she took a few deep breaths, wiped her face and declared that she was okay now.

He seemed determined to cheer her, as they drove on, recalling their time in Paris and their friends there. He told her what had happened to him and his family during the war, and talked about his work, the people he worked with and his new apartment. She was grateful for the distraction. His girlfriend was never once mentioned. She imagined someone impossibly glamorous, a more mature version of those girls he used to hang around with in Paris: beautiful, languid, fashionably dressed and devastatingly clever. He deserved her.

Whatever Alice had expected Lille to be like – Brussels, perhaps, or a small version of Paris – was soon replaced by reality.

'Poor devils had a rough time in the war,' Daniel observed drily, as he steered the car through streets of shelled and fire-damaged buildings. 'Thank heavens I was in Paris when the Germans rolled in; they didn't leave till the liberation last November.'

Even in those streets not obviously damaged by shell-fire the buildings appeared in danger of collapse through neglect. Small signs of life – a geranium growing in a window box, washing hung on lines strung across the street, a bowed, black-clad woman sitting on a step – only served to emphasise the struggle that people must have endured.

'It must have been grim, living under German rule,' she said.

'It was. They took people's food, furniture and pretty much everything from the shops and factories for their troops. The place was packed with soldiers – most people had Germans billeted in their homes. The starvation was terrible. And the regulations, *mon Dieu!* My neighbour says they had to have a form for everything, even for travel to another part of the city. People were forced to work in the fields and factories and anyone who got sick was deported. It was miserable.'

'I had no idea,' Alice said.

'It was not good to be a woman here, either. The orphanages are full of Boche babies.'

She fell silent, finding it hard to imagine what it must have been like, at the absolute mercy of a brutal, ruthless enemy.

In the central square – La Grande Place, Daniel called it – the buildings, although in desperate need of repair, seemed relatively untouched by the shelling. It was five in the afternoon and the place was bustling – shops were open and cafes were filled with workers quenching their thirst. Dominating the square was a tall stone tower that reminded Alice of Nelson's Column in London, only this one was topped with the statue of a woman.

'She's the Goddess,' Daniel said, 'memorial to another war, another occupation long ago. Poor old Lille, she gets it every time.'

He turned into a side road, pulled up and switched off the engine. 'My office is just around the corner. I'll be as quick as I can.' He tweaked her cheek affectionately and dashed away. As she waited, she repaired her make-up. *Brave face, Alice. Allow yourself a little fun.* Soon, he was back. 'Business over. Now, how about that dinner? I'm starving.'

The restaurant was in a cellar, its low, brick-arched ceiling supported by columns, their table in a corner carefully chosen by Daniel because – she now understood – it was unobserved by other customers. The *maître d'hôtel* had welcomed him like a long-lost friend, glancing at Alice with the look of someone who understood exactly the nature of their engagement.

From the menu it was hard to imagine the city had ever suffered food shortages. 'It's your country we have to thank for this.' Daniel explained how American loans to rebuild farm production and the fishing industry were already taking effect.

'You choose for me. Anything but beef stew,' she said, laughing. 'I've eaten enough of that to last a lifetime.'

'You do not adore our *carbonnade*?' He pulled a teasing face. '*Quel dommage.*'

Black-clad waiters with stiffly starched aprons went about their work with the Belgian formality she'd come to admire, taking seriously the business of good service. He ordered *moules* for both of them, followed by a *carbonnade* for him and, for her, *lapin à la gueuze*.

'I'm not sure I can eat a fluffy bunny with a clear conscience.'

'It's delicious, you'll see.'

When the *sommelier* arrived Daniel tasted the wine with great seriousness. Once approved, their glasses filled, he raised his. 'To the memory of your brother.'

'To Sam,' she said shakily, before taking a long sip. The wine was delicious. She took another.

'Now, let us enjoy our meal. I guarantee you will feel better once you have eaten,' he said, with a sweet smile.

After a tentative start, she discovered that she quite enjoyed the mussels, and most of all the delicious cream and wine sauce. Daniel showed her how to use an empty shell to pinch out the chewy orange morsels. It seemed a wonderfully sensual way of eating, although she was grateful for the dish of warm water with a floating slice of lemon, provided for rinsing her hands.

He refilled her glass several times, ordering another bottle when the main course arrived. The tender flesh of rabbit in its gravy of light beer was a delightful surprise. She watched him as he concentrated on his food, the thick dark hair falling over his eyes, and wished that this moment would never end. He leaned across the table, taking her hand.

'I am pleased you could confide in me,' he said. 'It feels so natural between us, *n'est-ce pas?*' He spread her fingers, stroking the sensitive skin between them. It was the most exquisite sensation, resonating up her arm and throughout her whole body. Giddy from the wine, warmed by the good food, weary from her sorrows, it made her feel reckless.

Poor Sam, his life taken when he was only twenty-one, will never again have the chance to enjoy these pleasures. You only have one life, she said to herself. *You might as well live it to the full.*

'I suppose we should head back before long. I just have to call in at my apartment to pick up some clean clothes,' he said as they finished their coffee. 'Maybe you would like to see it?' he added, almost as a throwaway.

In the ladies' she combed her hair, powdered her shiny nose and reapplied her lipstick. For a fleeting second she saw in the corner of her eye a vision of Lloyd beside her, looking up from his wheelchair like a devoted spaniel. Handsome as he was, he'd never been flirtatious, let alone seductive, and she was almost certain that he, like her, was still a virgin. She recalled their tentative fumblings on the settee after her parents had gone to bed – lots of kissing, heavy breathing and intimate touching – but after his accident even that had become constrained by his self-consciousness about the leg. Her feelings had never come close to the kind of desire that she experienced for Daniel: that melting, overwhelming wave that left her giddy and breathless.

She turned from the mirror, blinking away the image.

22

RUBY

Ruby called out and knocked again, pressing her ear to the side of the door.

At last she heard a faint groan. 'Just having a lie-in. Go without me.'

In truth, Ruby felt relieved. She still felt so angry that she wasn't entirely sure how she would react when they met again. Alice's snarl still resonated in her head: *Just don't get involved, Ruby*. Well, it was too late, she was already involved with the Swiss pair, and even if it turned out to have been the wrong thing to do, at least she would have tried to help.

And then there was this business of Daniel. It still left a bitter taste, the lingering feeling that she was being used as a pawn in some pre-arranged game. Although she'd only met him for a short while Daniel reminded her, uncomfortably, of the man she'd met in the pub that night: good-looking, amusing and charming in a way that made you feel like the most beautiful woman in the world. She feared it would not end well for Alice.

On her way to the dining room, Monsieur Vermeulen

handed her an envelope. 'For you, madame.' She tore it open and pulled out a scrappy piece of paper on which was roughly drawn a map that she recognised as the centre of Hoppestadt. An arrow pointed to a street junction, marked with a cross. Written in block capitals in a childish hand were the words *Meet heer with Swiss 2 p.m. tooday. Fred.*

Immediately, she felt cheered. The diamond geezer had come good.

The Swiss pair were at their usual table. 'Good morning,' she said. 'I hope you slept well?'

Martha gave a cautious smile. '*Bonjour,*' she said. The boy looked down at his plate.

'I have good news,' Ruby said. She imitated the movement of steering a vehicle.

The woman's eyes widened. 'Today?' She lowered her voice to a whisper. 'Langemarck?'

Ruby pointed to the clock on the wall, holding up two fingers. 'Meet me here. Two o'clock.'

Martha nodded, and whispered something to the boy. A sweet, shy smile illuminated for a brief moment the tender boyishness beneath his usual dour expression. It would all be worth it, Ruby thought, if only to see that smile more often.

After breakfast she waited for Tubby in the lobby, as they had arranged. He arrived only five minutes late, red in the face and puffing slightly. As well as the usual briefcase, a small canvas bag hung from a strap around his shoulder.

'On a tight schedule today,' he panted. 'I have to leave by

eleven to catch the evening ferry from Ostend. Better get along to the hospital now, if you don't mind?'

When they arrived, Jimmy was out of bed and sitting on a chair, washed and shaved, although still in his hospital robe.

'Here you go, laddie,' Tubby said, handing him the canvas bag. 'They told me your clothes weren't worth laundering, so I've brought you some more.'

'Tha tha tha,' Jimmy stuttered, clutching the bag to his chest.

'Don't tell anyone,' Tubby said, in a stagey whisper, 'or they'll all want some. There's a bar of chocolate in there too.' The twitching features were stilled momentarily by the hint of a smile. 'We've sent your family a telegraph. I'm sure someone will come soon.'

'Ah, ah, ah.' Jimmy's brow furrowed with frustration.

'Sorry, almost forgot this.' Tubby pulled from his pocket a small notebook with a pencil attached to it by a short length of string. Jimmy struggled to hold it at first but he soon began to scribble, the letters emerging slowly from his trembling hand.

IMPORTANT. Please do not tell anyone I am here.

'Don't worry, we understand,' Tubby said, placing a broad hand on his shoulder. 'We asked your family not to tell anyone.'

Jimmy scribbled some more. *Thank you. Want to go home.*

'You will stay here until someone from your family comes for you,' Tubby reassured him. 'It may be later today, or tomorrow. But I am sure they will come.' Jimmy nodded, and then dropped his face into his hands. Ruby feared he might be crying.

'Now, laddie, why don't you get yourself changed?' Tubby said briskly. 'We need to get you presentable. The trousers are hardly the height of fashion but at least you won't look like a Tommie.'

As they pulled screens around the bed, and moved to a discreet distance. Tubby glanced at the clock on the wall. 'Goodness me, is it that time already? I'll have to leave soon.'

Ruby felt suddenly bereft, realising for the first time how much she had come to depend on this man. 'I'll miss you, Tubby. Don't forget to leave me your address. Remember what we talked about?'

'Yes, of course,' he said, taking out a scrap of paper and scribbling on it. 'And you must let me know how your friend gets on with the search for her brother. I'm only sorry we couldn't help find your Bertie, too.'

'So am I.' She paused. 'But I seem to have found something else here in Hoppestadt. I don't know why, but I feel so much more optimistic about the future than I ever did before. I've surprised myself, to be honest. I was all wrapped up in my own misery before I came out here, afraid that if I let go I'd fall apart somehow.'

She'd barely articulated these thoughts to herself and now here she was, sharing intimate feelings with someone she'd only just met. Except that Tubby didn't feel like a stranger at all. He was more like a father, a man she could trust with her life.

'Dearest child, I am sure you will find a new way of living. You are stronger than you believe yourself to be. Write when you get home and we'll see how you can help with my new association.'

'I promise. Thank you for everything, Tubby.'

'May the Lord bless you and keep you safe, my dear,' he said, placing a gentle hand on her head.

Her family had never been churchgoers, and the few times she'd been Ruby had felt uncomfortable with the ceremony and what she thought of as 'mumbo-jumbo', but this simple act, the warmth of Tubby's hand radiating through her scalp, seemed to calm her, making her feel truly blessed.

They heard the clatter of the screen, and Jimmy emerged with a self-conscious smile. The shirt was over-large, the trousers too wide and the legs too short – Tubby's proportions. Even so, what she saw now was a tall, handsome man barely recognisable from the pale, trembling wreck, prematurely aged by mental strain, whom they'd met the day before. His dark hair, even though barbered by an inexpert nun, seemed to provide the perfect frame for his face, high cheekbones, a determined jaw and intense blue eyes set wide beneath lightly arched brows.

'You look terrific,' she said.

He lowered himself onto the bed, reached for his notebook, scribbled something and handed it to her. *Hope my girlfriend thinks so too!*

'Now, laddie,' Tubby said. 'It's time for me to be off, I've a boat to catch this evening. You can find your way back to the hotel, Ruby?' She nodded, and he turned back to Jimmy. 'Ruby will stay for the moment and with a bit of luck you'll have some more visitors later. I wish you every blessing in the rest of your life.'

After Tubby left Jimmy rested his head back on the pillow, apparently overtaken by the exhaustion of bringing himself back into the world.

'Shall I leave you to sleep?' Ruby asked.

He shook his head, but closed his eyes anyway.

She felt a rush of tenderness, trying to imagine the moment of shock and disbelief when his family received the telegram. They might even have thought it was a hoax, or a case of mistaken identity. She hoped they would come quickly, before rumours could reach the authorities. The thought brought her to her feet: she must warn the nuns not to admit anyone except for his family.

Just as she reached the top of the stairs, she heard conversation below. Peering over the stone banister, she could see the top of the nun's wimple, animated as she apparently spoke to someone else, out of sight. It took her a few seconds to realise that the words were in English.

It couldn't be Jimmy's family, not yet. But who else, other than she and Tubby, was likely to speak English in this hospital? It could only be someone from the military authorities. Had word spread so fast? She rushed back to the ward and shook Jimmy by the shoulder, shushing him with a finger to her lips.

'Come with me, quickly, we need to disappear,' she whispered, pulling him to his feet and, pausing briefly to tidy the bed and hide the abandoned hospital robe under a pillow, dragging him to the far end of the ward where a door led into another corridor. He moved frustratingly slowly, his limbs uncoordinated and unaccustomed to this level of activity. *Let the door be unlocked*, she prayed, urging him along. It was, and they scurried through and around another corner, out of sight. His face was as white as a sheet, twitching and grimacing harder than before, his limbs trembling so much she was afraid he'd fall. She held firmly onto his hand. 'Take deep breaths. They'll be gone soon.'

They could hear voices on the ward: the deep baritone of the man and then, louder, the high-pitched voice of a young woman. Without warning, Jimmy pulled free of her hand, lurching towards the door muttering something that sounded like 'Eed, Eed.' Heart in mouth, she followed close behind him. As they rounded the corner a young woman sprinted towards them with her arms outstretched, eyes streaming with tears. Her face was vaguely familiar. Jimmy folded into the young woman's embrace, crooning unintelligibly.

It was the man limping behind, in danger of tripping in his haste, that Ruby recognised first: the man with the eye patch she'd seen that first day of the tour, with the strawberry-haired girl she'd taken to be his wife, who was now sobbing in Jimmy's arms.

'Oh my good Lord. Is it really you?' The eye-patch man's voice cracked with emotion as he flung his arms around the entwined couple. 'Great God, it really *is* you. What a bloody miracle. You're alive!'

Ruby found that she'd stopped breathing; it really was a miracle, unfolding in front of her eyes. Behind them stood the little nun, wiping the corners of her eyes with a sleeve. Finally, the man pulled away, releasing his hold. He caught sight of Ruby and held out his hand. 'Hello, I'm Joseph, Jimmy's brother. Unless I am much mistaken, we met in Ostend, didn't we? You were on the tour too? But you disappeared after the first day.'

He was perhaps a couple of years older than Jimmy, she guessed, and it was clear that he too had suffered: as well as the limp and the eye patch, a livid scar ran diagonally across one cheek. But in all other respects he could have been Jimmy's twin.

'And this is his fiancée, Edith, if they ever stop kissing . . .' he laughed.

'Hello, Mr Catchpole, I am very pleased to meet you. I'm Ruby. Ruby Barton. I had no idea . . .'

'Nor did we. All we knew was that he was missing. We came on the tour hoping to find his grave and now . . .' The couple had released their grasp and were whispering to each other.

'But the telegram went to an address in Ipswich.'

'My father immediately forwarded it to us at the hotel in Ostend. Crazy, isn't it? It arrived this morning at breakfast. Thank heavens we were still here in Belgium and could get here so quickly. We were convinced it was some kind of cruel joke, but I'd heard of the Reverend Clayton and knew he wouldn't do such a thing.'

'I'm afraid you just missed him. He's on his way back to England, today. '

'But how did you . . . ?'

'It's a long story. I was looking for someone too,' she started.

'And you thought it might . . . ?' His words faded away. 'I am so sorry.'

'I'm just so grateful you have found him,' she said, taking a breath. 'He's been through a tough time. You know he's very anxious about the authorities?'

'Yes, we shall have to be cautious. '

The young woman had disentangled herself from Jimmy's arms. 'Oh dear, I must look such a mess,' she said, laughing as she tried to straighten her hat. Her face was lit up with the most ecstatic smile Ruby could remember seeing for a very long time. Jimmy, too, had been transformed. The frowns, tics and grimaces were gone, his face a dazed, beatific beam.

'Come, we should let him rest,' Ruby said, leading them towards his bed. 'He finds it difficult to talk.' She picked up the notebook and handed it to him. 'Writing things down works best.' She pulled up chairs for the two of them, either side of the bed, and hovered for a few moments, reluctant to leave but anxious to avoid intruding on their reunion.

'I'm going back to our hotel, the Hotel de la Paix in the square. If you need anything, you will be able to find me there.'

'You have been so kind,' Joseph said.

'It's been lovely to meet you. Bye, Jimmy. I'll see you before you go.' She grasped his hand. He looked up, grinning, and returned the squeeze.

'This is the best day of my life,' Edith whispered. 'I can never thank you enough.'

※❀※

Ruby descended the stone steps and headed out into the street, trying to hold on to their joy and suppress the bitter feeling of envy, but she couldn't help it: *I wish it was me, at Bertie's bedside, making plans for our future. I have to go home and admit to his parents that I have failed to find any sign of their son.*

Then she remembered her promise to help Tubby. *But I have something to look forward to now, a purpose for my life, a way of honouring Bertie's memory. I will make him so proud of me.* She took a deep breath, wiped the tears from her cheeks, pulled back her shoulders and walked briskly back towards the square.

23

ALICE

They'd left Lille in the early hours of the morning and the first glimmers of dawn were already lighting the horizon as they approached Hoppestadt. Daniel had pulled up the car and rested his arm along the back of the seat, his hand caressing her shoulder. As they sat in comfortable silence watching the pink and orange sunrise dissolving the darkness, Alice felt flooded with a sense of pure, uncomplicated joy. It was like a fairy tale.

The evening had been more extraordinary, more magical, than she'd ever allowed herself to imagine. His flat, on the second floor of an old building just outside the city centre, was modest, just two spacious rooms with high ceilings, sparsely furnished but in the most elegant taste: wooden floorboards with Persian carpets, large pieces of dark-wood furniture set against simple white walls.

'Another quick drink before we head home?' he'd asked, closing the heavy shutters and returning from the tiny, old-fashioned kitchen brandishing a bottle of red wine. 'This one's a rather special Burgundy from my father's cellar.'

She happily agreed. America and Lloyd seemed to be on some far distant planet, well out of the reach of her conscience. They drank, talked and laughed, then drank some more. He pulled her up from the chair and began to dance with her, humming a Belgian folk song: *The night is young and the world is ours.* Before long, he lowered his face and they were kissing, her lips bruising against his. She felt consumed with desire.

For a brief moment, as they moved towards the bedroom and the ornate brass bed with its plain white coverlet, she sensed a pang of guilt – for Lloyd, for Daniel's girlfriend. She hesitated. 'Daniel, I don't think—'

'Do not worry, my darling. We will do nothing that you do not want to do.' He was so solicitous for her welfare, so patient and thoughtful, that she allowed herself to be carried away by the moment. He made her feel – and she utterly believed it – like the most desirable woman in the world.

Afterwards he smoked, and she lay in the crook of his arm, listening to his voice rumbling in his chest. 'That was your first time?'

'Uh-huh.'

'It was good?'

'It was so much more than good.' He lowered his face to kiss her, and her body melted for him all over again. A little later she slipped into sleep, and the next thing she knew was his whisper in her ear.

'You are so beautiful when you are sleeping,' he said, kissing her forehead. 'I would like to stay here with you forever, darling Aleese, but I must be at work in Ypres by eight.'

She could not bear for it to end. 'Just a few more minutes,' she said, snuggling into his shoulder, but he pulled away from her and sat up.

'It is time to go, *ma chérie.*'

❧

She woke to hear the church clock chiming eleven and, with a sinking heart, she remembered. Her father had promised to telegraph her just as soon as he had further confirmation of Sam Pilgrim's identity from the Canadian authorities. She dressed hurriedly and bought a reviving coffee at the cafe before making her way along the familiar streets to the post office.

Time was running short now. They must return to Ostend tomorrow evening; the group was booked on a cross-Channel steamer first thing on Saturday morning and the transatlantic liner would leave Southampton on Monday, just four days away. If there was news of where Sam was buried, she had one last day to visit his grave.

Once again, as she waited in the queue, she found herself eavesdropping on conversations. One exchange taking place behind her, in low voices that she had to strain to hear, was particularly intriguing.

'Did you hear about Geert's wife, threatening that Swiss woman?'

'Bloody cheek, though, come here to visit a German grave. Deserved it, they did.'

'Even so, Geert should return the money. That sort of thing gets our town a bad reputation.'

'Germans already have a bad reputation.'

'They're Swiss, not German.'

'Do you believe that?'

'Even if she is, it's not her fault.'

'We want visitors to come and spend their money.'

'Me, I'm not touching their filthy Deutschmarks.'

'You're stupid, then. Tourists are our future, you mark my words.'

❦

The postmaster welcomed her with a friendly smile. 'Good morning, Miss Palmer. Two for you today.'

She took a deep breath and opened the first.

YOUR PA TOLD ME ABOUT SAM STOP SO SORRY STOP MISSING YOU VERY MUCH STOP I LOVE YOU LLOYD STOP

She crumpled the paper into her pocket and ripped open the second.

PHOTO SAM PILGRIM DEFINITELY OUR SAM STOP DIED CORFU FARM HOPE YOU CAN FIND HIS GRAVE STOP SO PROUD OF YOU FATHER STOP

Ruby was not at the cafe; she ran across to the hotel. Freddie was in his usual place in the bar. 'Have you seen Ruby?' she panted.

'With the Reverend, I think. They were going back to the hospital. What's up?'

'I've found my brother . . . or at least, where he's buried.'

The smile slipped from his face. 'I am sorry for your loss.'

'It's somewhere called Corfu Farm. Do you know it?'

'Of course. That's where I ended up. It's a field hospital where they took you from the clearing station, if you survived long enough. It was close to the rail lines so once they'd patched us up we got shipped back to the coast.'

Oh Sam. You were so close to safety, ready to be brought home. You so nearly made it.

'What date did you say he died?' Freddie asked.

'October 1917.'

'Chances are he'll have copped it at Passchendaele.'

'Passchendaele? How do you know?'

'That was when the Canadians came in, at the height of the fighting around there. By God we was pleased to see them. The good news is, though,' he went on, 'if he died in hospital, at least they knew who he was, and his grave will be marked.'

'Then where would he have been buried?'

'Lazyhook, the cemetery next door, most likely.' Freddie took a sip of his beer.

'Is it far, this place?'

'Not far. You could get there in twenty minutes.'

So close. 'Would you be able to take me, Freddie, can we borrow the baker's van?'

He glanced away as though discomfited by something he did not want to admit. 'Sorry, I'm tied up this afternoon.'

Frantic now, she pulled out a handful of notes. 'Would this make any difference? Please? It's really important to me.'

Freddie looked at her with an amused expression – or

was it just those pale eyelashes? Either way, it left her feeling awkward. 'Sorry, love, no can do, not today. Not even for all that cash. How's about tomorrow?'

'It *has* to be today. We go back to Ostend tomorrow.'

He scratched his stubbly chin. 'What about your French friend, the one with the sports car? Surely he'd give you a lift?'

* * *

She'd been reluctant to ask Daniel – he'd told her last night about the amount of work he had on this week – but she was left with no choice. The receptionist at his hotel raised an eyebrow. 'You wish me to pass this note to Monsieur Martens?'

'Yes please. As soon as he returns.'

'Would you wish to give it to him yourself, madame?' He gestured towards the lounge.

She found Daniel at the long table, papers and charts strewn around him.

'*Bonjour, Aleese.* This is a pleasant surprise.' Behind the smile was a guarded look she had not seen before.

'I am sorry to interrupt your work,' she said, flustered now. 'But I really need your help. I've discovered where my brother is buried, and it's just down the road from here, at Lazyhook.'

He frowned. 'I do not know this place.'

'Near a military hospital they called Corfu Farm – that's what Freddie said.'

The frown cleared. 'You mean *Lijssenthoek.* Yes, it is just a few kilometres away.'

'Would you be able to drive me, Daniel? It's really important.'

He paused for a beat before his face softened. 'Of course, *ma chérie*. In one hour or so?'

'Thank you so much,' she whispered gratefully, reaching for him.

'See you at half past three.' He caressed her cheek with the lightest of touches. 'And now I must return to my work.'

Just as Freddie had promised, it took only twenty minutes to reach the place that turned out to be spelled, according to the signpost, Lijssenthoek. All those consonants! No wonder the Brits had such trouble getting their tongues around it. A small settlement of traditional single-storey Belgian cottages had been swamped on one side by a large railway depot and, on the other, dozens of wooden huts, stretching into the distance, row on row. In the sunshine they looked almost cheerful, like a holiday camp by the seaside.

Daniel turned off the engine. 'This was the field hospital they called Corfu Farm,' he said, into the silence. 'The cemetery is over the other side.'

'I never imagined it could be so enormous,' Alice breathed. 'It's like a whole village.'

The place had evidently been evacuated in a great hurry. A badly damaged ambulance lay rusting on the roadside and the area in front of the huts was littered with the abandoned debris of war: coils of barbed wire, wheel rims and other vehicle parts, rubber tyres, wooden sleepers and planking, and crates stencilled with hieroglyphics of military code.

In contrast the huts, linked by gravel pathways, looked quaint, almost homey. Although now strangled with weeds, you could tell that once upon a time the spaces between the pathways had been dug and planted as flower beds.

They peered cautiously into the first empty hut: metal camp beds still remained in rows, their white paint peeling where rust had broken through. Stretchers were piled against one wall, torn canvases hanging from them in a pale cascade. Three pot-bellied stoves were ranged along the centre of the hut, metal flues leading upwards to chimneys in the ceiling. A Union Jack flag hung forlornly from the wall above the nursing station, which was arrayed with trays and bedpans; an enamel cup still contained tea leaves, as if the nurse drinking from it had just left the room. The floor was stained with what looked like mud but could just as easily have been dried blood, Alice thought with a shiver.

'It's like a ghost hospital,' she whispered, as if afraid that the spirits would hear. It wouldn't have surprised her to see a nurse appear through the door, or a patient being carried in on a stretcher.

Yet it was curiously reassuring, reminding her of the illustrations she'd seen in the illustrated magazines: long tents with rows of metal beds, nurses in spotless starched white headdresses. At least in his last hours or days Sam would have been looked after and made as comfortable as possible. There would have been people to comfort him, to give him water and talk to him. He would not have suffered alone in some muddy battlefield.

When they emerged from the hut the sun had gone in,

obscured by heavy clouds that seemed to have appeared from nowhere.

'Better get on with it. Looks like rain,' Daniel said, as they followed the path to the cemetery past a dozen more huts and through a small copse at the edge of the encampment. The sight, as they emerged, seemed to punch the breath out of her: field after field of wooden crosses, separated by wide walkways, stretching away towards the horizon as far as the eye could see.

'I had no idea,' she gasped.

'It is one of the largest cemeteries after Tyne Cot.'

But it was nothing like Tyne Cot. This place was well ordered, with graves in neat rows between paths of parched grass, set with hedges and mature trees. In places, people had even attempted to create flower beds in which a few rangy rose bushes still managed to bloom despite the choking bindweed. Poppies and ragged robin flowered in abundance along the hedgerows and, above them, larks were singing. *Bravely* singing, Alice remembered. She'd have thought the place beautiful had she not been so painfully aware of its terrible history.

Sam would have been evacuated here away from the front line on one of the trains which still lay rusting in the railway sidings. There would have been time to dig the graves in a more orderly way, to give them a proper burial, possibly even with some kind of a short service as they were interred.

After half an hour her eyes were aching from reading so many names and dates. Just as she was beginning to despair she came upon a group of graves, dozens of them, dated October 1917. Walking more slowly now, reading every name with the utmost care, she found herself concentrating so hard that she almost forgot to breathe. But the dates moved on: November, December, even into 1918, and her feet felt heavy with disappointment.

Then she heard Daniel's call from a hundred yards away in a corner beside the hedge. 'Over here, Alice.' As she approached the letters swam into her vision: *In Memory of Pvt S. Pilgrim, Canadian Corps, injured in action, died 29th October 1917. R.I.P.*

She stared at it for a long moment before the ground started to shift beneath her; she began to feel dizzy and unsteady. Falling to her knees, she grasped with both hands the base of the tall white wooden cross. 'You stupid, stupid boy,' she heard herself shouting. 'Why did you have to go and get yourself killed? *Why?*'

Resting her face against the rough soil, she barely noticed the stones pressing into her cheek, the harsh scratch of grass and thistles. Thunder rumbled in the distance and then she became aware of raindrops falling onto the parched ground, throwing up small puffs of dust as they landed. She began to sob quietly, the tears mingling with the rain as it fell onto her brother's grave.

Too soon, she felt Daniel's strong hands pulling her up, pressing a handkerchief into her hand. 'Come on, we're getting soaked. I must get back to the car. I left the hood open.'

She remembered the letter she had written, and now pulled it from her pocket and laid it at the foot of the cross, carefully choosing four smooth stones to hold it down, one at each corner. Then she hesitated; there was something she hadn't done. She pulled away from him, running towards the hedgerow, pulling up handfuls of red campion, corn-flower and poppy. Splitting the flowers into two bunches and binding their stalks with strands of grass, she laid one of them on the grave. The other she would press, and give to her parents.

Kneeling at the foot of the cross once more, she traced her finger over the carved letters. *We will never forget you, Sam, my dearest, sweetest baby brother. How can I leave you here, in this sad, quiet place? You were only nineteen and all your dreams are over. Oh Sam, how could you do this to us?*

When she finally looked up again, Daniel was far in the distance, striding back to the car, scarcely visible through the pall of rain.

24

MARTHA

She could barely believe that they were on their way to visit Heinrich's grave. At last.

Ruby met them in the lobby with commendable promptness and they set off to navigate the streets according to a scrappy map apparently provided by Freddie. Martha was surprised at how calm she felt, given that she had taken such a leap of faith, placing their fate in the hands of virtual strangers. But this was the long-planned-for moment; a meeting with her destiny. What happened now was out of her control.

Partway along a deserted, dusty side street they found the place, a small corrugated-iron building with green metal double doors, padlocked with a sturdy metal chain. They waited ten minutes, then another five. Otto fidgeted impatiently, kicking at small stones, while Martha stood alongside Ruby, feeling awkward once again that they had no words of a common language.

At last Freddie appeared, waving in his hand what looked like an enormous malign insect but was in fact a black Bakelite cup with wires sprouting from it. After struggling with the padlock for a few moments, he managed to release the chain and wrenched open the metal doors with a creak so loud they must have been undisturbed for years. Inside was what Martha at first took for an army lorry: a large vehicle in the same green as the garage doors, only considerably rustier. It had definitely seen better days.

He folded back the engine cover and fiddled with the cup, clicking it into place and linking up the wires. Task completed, he closed the cover and climbed up onto the wide bench seat that straddled the width of the cab. He stretched his arm beneath the dashboard and pressed a button. Nothing happened. He cursed and pressed several times more but despite making heavy grinding noises, the engine failed to come to life. After many further curses the engine finally started with a deafening roar, filling the garage with a choking cloud of black smoke.

'Eureka!' he shouted. 'Climb in.'

Ruby went first, next to Freddie, then Otto. Martha climbed in last. It was only then, as she was about to pull herself up, that she noticed, painted on the side of the canvas covering the back of the lorry, a bright red cross. She found herself smiling: these English were full of surprises. And here was another one: Freddie trying to teach the English girl how to manipulate the gears. Martha suspected she'd never driven anything before, let alone an Allied army ambulance.

Ruby managed to find reverse gear and he manoeuvred the ambulance out of the garage. Then she crunched into first and they set off down the street accompanied by his shouts: 'Second. No, down to second. Try again.' She jiggled the stick into the right position. Then another shout:

'Up, across and up again, into third, now! Up again! Oh, here.' Freddie took his hand off the wheel, steering unsteadily with the stump of his left arm while leaning across to help her find the gear. At last, after much cursing and laughter, the girl got the hang of it, and they progressed more smoothly.

It could be one of her more surreal dreams were it not for the powerful realities: solid tyres hammering so hard on the cobbles that it made her teeth rattle, the trail of black smoke behind them, the discomfort of being squeezed onto the hard bench seat, the way she had to cling on for dear life when they turned a right-handed corner to stop herself falling out onto the road. And all in the company of two English people.

For five long years the English had been the enemy, the worst of the worst in her book: a nation who lied and cheated, who reneged on their promises, instigated the cruel food blockade that caused so many thousands of ordinary German citizens and children to die of starvation. It was the English who unleashed deadly poison gases causing untold suffering among their troops; the English who tunnelled underground and blew thousands of unsuspecting Germans into a million smithereens.

And yet here she was on her way to finding her son's grave thanks to the generosity and compassion of two English people. She wished she had the words to express her appreciation properly.

'What an adventure,' she said to Otto, speaking in French. Sandwiched between herself and Ruby, he seemed to find it hilarious when the girl crunched the gears once more, earning herself further good-humoured curses. It was such a joy to hear him laugh. There had been so little of that lately.

'*Nous arrivons*, Heiney,' he said. It didn't matter that he'd used the wrong French word, she knew what he meant. *We're coming.* Bittersweet tears stung her eyes: how he missed his brother.

As they left Hoppestadt she plucked up the courage to ask, 'How far? How long?'

Freddie said something about kilometres and the girl held up her hands, opening the fingers on both hands and then again: twenty. She showed the palm of her hand, drawing with her index finger a clock hand travelling through three-quarters of a circle. Forty-five minutes.

They drove straight through Ypres, past the main square with its piles of rubble and devastated buildings, the broken tower of the cathedral pointing to the sky as if to summon God's wrath. The road worsened as they left the town and their progress slowed as Freddie manoeuvred the clumsy vehicle around countless potholes and diversions.

Martha had already witnessed through the train windows the devastation of no-man's land, the mud-brown landscape, the trenches, the shell holes, the broken guns, tanks and other machinery, the shattered trees and the barbed wire rolling over the land like rusty surf. But driving right through it, at the same level, the destruction was even more starkly shocking.

Otto's face paled as they passed the first group of roadside graves: dozens, even hundreds of crosses, mostly simple constructions of wood with hastily scrawled lettering, or slabs of stone flat on the mud. She took his hand and he squeezed hers back. By the time they had passed five, ten, and then twenty such graveyards, they had become accustomed to the sight. Crosses were just another part of this strange, sickening landscape of war.

After what seemed like hours of lurching and bumping, Freddie announced that the piles of rubble and timber through which they were passing was what had once been the village of Poelcappelle. She heard the bitterness in his voice as he pointed out the skeleton of stonework at the crossroads that was once the village church, and her face burned when he spat out the word *Kraut* not just once, but several times.

Although she could not follow every word his meaning was clear: these had once been homes, where villagers had lived peacefully and happily until the Germans came. And now all that had been destroyed by her nation's guns. She shivered: if they ever learned her true nationality, these good people, they would never forgive her.

Within a few minutes, they were rattling into the ghost of another village, at the centre of which was an even larger pile of stone and timber. 'Langemarck Church,' Freddie announced. Shortly afterwards, he pulled off the road and drew the ambulance to a stop.

'The German cemetery.'

Although the area was largely flat they seemed to be at a high point, with the land falling away in every direction. On the horizon, heavy grey clouds piled one upon another into menacing stacks. The air was still and almost silent save for the raucous calls of crows, black scavengers who seemed to be the only birds brave enough to return. Otherwise, the place was deserted.

To one side of the road was nothing but crosses and flat

stone grave-markers, reaching away into the distance. Martha felt her heart falter as she struggled to contemplate the scale, the immensity of human tragedy. Under every scrap of this vast piece of land lay men, thousands of them. How would they ever find Heinrich among so many?

Into her mind flooded the memory of a mural she'd once seen on the wall of a Catholic church: hundreds of naked bodies trying to scramble upwards out of the earth in their desperation to reach heaven. Here, on this ordinary field of Belgian mud, the Day of Judgement had arrived. How would she and her country be judged?

'We'll wait for you in the van,' Ruby said. 'Take your time.'

At first, they wandered randomly between the crosses, taking turns to read names out loud as though, with each utterance, they were paying respect to the memory of the men they named. But after twenty, thirty, forty names, it became just too difficult, too repetitive, too painful.

'At this rate we'll never find Heiney,' Otto said, peering across the immense field. 'Why don't we split up? You go that way, I will go along here.'

'You don't mind going on your own? Are you sure?'

In his smile she saw once more the young man fast overtaking the child. 'I'm fine, Mama,' he said, his voice breaking into the bass register that no longer seemed to take him by surprise. 'We just have to find him. That's why we're here, no?'

After a while the names seemed to blur into one. *Müller,*

Schmidt, Schneider, Fischer, Meyer, Wagner, Becker, Schulz, Hoffmann, Schäfer, Koch, Bauer, Richter, Neumann, Klein, Wolf . . . Martha paused to stretch, scanning the great field of crosses, her eyes narrowing, unwilling to accept its harsh reality. These men were fathers, brothers, sons, all of them individuals whose families had loved them, and now they were left to rot beneath this black, foreign earth. *Dust to dust.* That dismal sentence. Nothing could be more final.

A hundred metres away Otto walked slowly and intently, his eyes scanning to left and right with fierce concentration, discharging his sombre task with the utmost attention. From this distance he looked taller, broader, his silhouette reminiscent of Heinrich's.

Martha resumed her own search. Each time she read Weber – it was common enough and there were dozens of them here – her heart seemed to stop in her chest. Each time she saw that it was not Heinrich she felt simultaneously relieved and disappointed.

She heard Otto shouting: 'Mama! Over here.' With a pounding heart she walked as swiftly as she could over the uneven duckboards. In front of him was a tall wall of rough wooden planks set upright into the ground stretching twenty metres or so to either side. Slowly, her eyes adjusted and she saw that, covering each plank from top to bottom, were scratched names: dozens, hundreds, perhaps even thousands, of them. At the top was written: *Kindermort, April 1915.*

The blood seemed to congeal in her veins. It was a mass grave.

With the fierce concentration of a hawk tracking its prey, Otto had already begun to scan names, starting at the top of each plank and reading to the bottom before moving to the next. She took a deep breath and forced herself to follow his example, starting at the other end. As she read familiar names – of boys that Heinrich had been to school or college with, whose mothers had shared her grief when the dreaded news had arrived – a great weight of sorrow seemed to press down on her shoulders.

A single scratched name among so many others seemed to leap out against the dark wood. 'Oh my dear Lord, it's Hans.'

It was their neighbour's son, the oldest of four, three of whom had died in the war, a small blond lad with a smile so endearing that it was hard to resist cuddling him. This was the boy who had spent so many hours in their home, passing winter evenings with chess games by the fire, or the long summer hours kicking a football around the garden. He'd been Heinrich's best friend until their lives had taken separate paths: Heinrich to the *Gymnasium* for academic boys, Hans to the vocational school to become a carpenter.

And now they were together once more, joined by death, the great leveller. Pinning her gaze to the name, she whispered a short prayer for the boy she'd once known, promising that she would visit his mother just as soon as they arrived home. It would be comforting for her to hear of his resting place. She took up a small stone and rested it at the foot of the plank.

Surely Heinrich must be close by? She hungered for that moment of recognition as much as she feared it, but it did not arrive. Her eyes scoured the names until they burned, but there was no sign.

Heinrich was such a clever boy, as good at his lessons as he was in sports. After a late growth spurt he'd blossomed into a tall, handsome young man, popular with his friends and much admired by the girls. She would observe from a safe distance, with a mixture of apprehension and maternal pride, how they gathered round him giggling and flicking their plaits, fearing that he might fall in love and become distracted from his studies. They had such high hopes for him but, at seventeen, he seemed determined to defy their wishes and gave up his college place to join the army cadets.

'Is it so wrong to want a bit of excitement?' he'd shouted defiantly. 'Who needs an education anyway? It's just dull old books and libraries. I can do my learning in the real world.' *So you got your excitement, my darling Heinrich, right here, in the mud of Flanders.* But where was he now? Otto looked up and shrugged, his face pale as chalk. 'He's not here, Mama.'

But if Hans was here, Dieter, Christian and Peter, all those bright-eyed college boys who had joined up with him, surely Heinrich must be here too? Had he died somewhere else? But her neighbour had been so sure . . . She forced her mind back to the task in hand. Patting the bag hanging from her shoulder, feeling the bulge of the small leather pouch, she remembered her vow to Karl.

'Let's search for a little longer, so we can be absolutely sure. We've come all this way.'

It was when they'd started again, in another section of the graveyard, that she saw in the distance a large black four-seater car pulling up by the side of the road at the far end of the cemetery. For all their civilian summer wear of pale linen jackets and green felt alpine hats she knew at once from their upright bearing and the way the three men jumped to attention when the boss barked his orders that these were either policemen or soldiers, probably officer class, in plain clothes. Whatever had brought them here? Had they come to arrest her for spying?

But they showed no interest in her or Otto. In fact, they barely glanced in their direction, and after a few moments she allowed herself to breathe again. Two of the men, holding clipboards, set off along the boardwalks and seemed to be writing down names from the crosses and grave markers. The other went with the boss, who had a pronounced limp and walked with a stick. Otto, whose ears were sharper than her own, whispered, 'I swear they're speaking German, Ma.'

'Just ignore them.' She was not going to be deflected from her task now, not after coming all this way, not after the trials they'd been through to get here. They turned back to their search, but after a few minutes she became aware of footsteps approaching along the boardwalk behind her.

'Good afternoon, madame.' He spoke French but with a clearly detectable German accent in a tone that, while friendly enough, was clearly not to be denied.

'Sir?' she said, turning to greet him.

The man took off his hat and made a small bow. 'If it is not too bold, may I enquire as to the purpose of your visit?'

'My son and I are seeking the grave of my nephew, whom we believe to be buried here,' she replied.

'Aha.' He stroked his moustache, distracted for a moment. 'What regiment was he in?'

She hesitated. 'May I ask why you wish to know, sir?'

A slight smile tipped the corners of his mouth. 'Forgive me, madame. I should have explained my purpose. We have been given permission by the Belgian government to visit on behalf of a new charity, the *Volksbund*, which is being set up to make a formal record of German war graves. Our aim is to trace all those who gave their lives in this conflict and to ensure that their sacrifice is properly commemorated.'

'You are from Germany?'

He saluted, clipping his heels. 'Commandant Johan Albrecht, at your service,' he said in German.

Otto tugged at her arm. 'Ask him to help us find Heiney.'

'Your nephew?'

She nodded. No point in admitting the deception now.

'We can certainly check if we have any record.'

'I am Martha Weber, and this is my son Otto,' she said, even now uneasy speaking in her own language in public, for the first time since entering the country.

'We have some files in the car, if you would care to accompany me?' he said.

As they followed him, Otto took her hand and squeezed it. 'They'll find him for us, won't they, Ma?'

'I hope so,' she whispered back.

One of the other men – the one with a neatly trimmed ginger beard – was summoned to the car and ordered to open the capacious rear compartment. Inside, they could see several dozen ring-binder files in military grey.

'Please tell us the name and regiment of your nephew, and the date of his death if you know it.'

She told him all the details she knew, and explained that her sister had never received formal notice of his death, so she did not know a specific date. The two men turned back to the car, sorting through the files until he found the one marked on its spine *V–Z*.

He laid it on the bonnet of the car and began to flick

through the pages. Each side of paper held typed columns of names, hundreds on each sheet. The list of Webers, when he reached it, seemed to occupy several pages. 'Do you have a second name and date of birth, please?' He returned to the search, running his index finger briskly down each column.

As his finger stopped she felt her heart stop with it. He paused for an agonising moment before saying to his boss, 'Please take a look at this, sir.' The pair of them peered at the entry for a few seconds before Herr Albrecht cleared his throat and turned to her with a surprising smile on his face.

'Frau Weber, your nephew may not be dead after all. Our records show that he was captured by the French in September 1915. He would almost certainly have been taken to a prisoner-of-war camp, where he would have stayed for the rest of the war.'

'Captured?' What did this mean?

'He's alive!' Otto's shout, close beside her, made her start. 'Heiney's alive, Mama!' It made no sense. Could it really be? Not dead? Was this another of her crazy dreams?

'But his letters were returned . . .'

'Didn't you hear what the man said, Ma? He wasn't killed, he was *captured*,' Otto shouted, jumping up and down beside her. 'So he *must* be alive, somewhere.'

'But if that's the case, where?' She held out upturned palms, pleading for an answer.

'Please, Frau Weber, you must understand. The chaos of war may take years to sort out.'

'We have already waited. For four long years,' her voice cracked. She swallowed hard.

'You will have to ask the authorities once you return home,' he said, shaking his head.

'But I don't understand. If he was taken prisoner, surely someone would know? Why were his family not informed?' Martha asked, desperate now for someone to tell her the truth. Was he alive, or was he not?

'May I make a suggestion, sir,' ginger-beard murmured.

'Speak up, man.'

He stepped forward, clearing his throat. 'As you are aware, I was also held in a French camp, sir, so I know from experience. They were often overwhelmed by the numbers and their records were chaotic. I also know that some of our men were so traumatised that they lost their minds; didn't even know their own names. So it would follow that they are probably still assumed to be missing.'

By now the other two men had joined them; one nodded in affirmation.

'What are you saying, man?' the boss interjected. 'If you had no papers and couldn't even remember . . . ?'

'That is what I am saying, sir. My point, precisely. Some prisoners were taken alive but could not even identify themselves.'

'Then where would they be now?'

'In a sanatorium, sir, being treated. We can surely put this lady in touch with the right authorities.'

Otto tugged at her arm once more. 'Do you hear, Ma? Heiney could be in a hospital somewhere.' She had only been once to such a place, visiting Karl's grandmother, bless her soul, in her last days. She remembered the patients bound to their beds, torsos wasted, skulls skeletal and eyes vacant, like lost souls. She could not bring herself to visualise Heiney like that. But where there was life, surely there was a glimmer of hope, however small? If only they could find him and bring him home, they might be able to nurse him back to health.

'But what is it that they suffered, that they do not even know their own names? Is there no cure?' she managed to ask.

One of the minions asked permission to speak.

'Sergeant Stein, at your service.' He made a small bow. 'I too was in a prisoner-of-war camp with other enlisted men. With us were some who, they said, had suffered what they called shell shock. It does strange things to the brain but so long as some parts of it are still functioning, the doctors believe that, with time, they might recover their faculties. My comrade played chess with a young man each day whose mind seemed completely gone; he couldn't speak and his hands shook so much he kept knocking over the pieces, but he was still a brilliant player. None of us understood it.'

The clearest vision appeared in Martha's head: her husband Karl and ten-year-old Heinrich at the table by the window, the sunlight glinting off the boy's blond hair like a halo. She'd been enjoying this perfect scene when Heiney had suddenly jumped up, scattering the board and pieces onto the floor. 'I hate chess,' he'd shouted, and stomped off upstairs. Later, he became a keen player, but then so did almost every boy at his age. They played between lessons and after school, neglecting their homework.

'What did he look like, this chess player?' Otto's voice squeaked with urgency.

'Like all the rest of us, son. We were worked so hard and

had so little to eat, our hair fell out, our cheeks fell in. I suppose we may never know who he was, or whether he ever recovered.'

'All boys play chess. It would be too much of a coincidence,' Martha said, trying to ignore the way her heart fluttered in her own chest. Could it possibly be?

'I am afraid there is not much more we can tell you,' Herr Albrecht said.

The sergeant was scribbling on a scrap of paper, which he handed to her. 'This is a sanatorium you might try,' he said.

'Thank you, gentlemen, you have all been most helpful,' Martha said.

From the corner of her eye she could see Freddie and Ruby standing by the ambulance at the other end of the cemetery, looking in their direction. 'But our friends are waiting and we must leave you now.'

They had walked a hundred metres or so when Otto asked to see the address.

'Not now,' she whispered. 'They are waiting.'

But he refused to move any further until she relented. He read the words on the scrap of paper and then, before she could stop him, turned and sprinted back along the boardwalk towards the men still waiting by the car. Within moments he had returned to her side, panting heavily, and grinning from ear to ear.

'What was all that about?' she whispered.

'Tell you later,' he said.

25

RUBY

'Quite a little tonic this, looking at all these dead Germans.'

'Freddie! For heaven's sake.' He was trying to pass it off as a joke, but she knew he meant it. 'She's very brave to come all this way for her sister. I hope they find him.'

They sat in silence, watching Martha and Otto criss-crossing the graveyard. He pulled out a tobacco pouch and a packet of papers. 'Could you make me one of your excellent roll-ups?' She rolled it and lit it with a match from the crumpled box he'd handed her. In the still air, the cloud of exhaled smoke drifted slowly around their heads and the smell of it conjured up a powerful, painful presence, as though it were Bertie and not Freddie by her side.

A longer silence this time. 'You got me thinking, you know,' he said.

'What do you mean?'

He looked away sheepishly.

'C'mon, Freddie. You aren't usually this mysterious.'

'Well . . .' He paused, took another drag and began again. 'It might be time to go home. Get on with my life instead of burying my head in the past.'

'That's a big decision.'

'Made for me, really, by this old bird.' He thumped the steering wheel. 'Gotta get her home.'

'I thought you said you were just looking after it for someone else?'

'Yeah, but the secret's out now, and my mate'll get clobbered when they hear about it back home, as they surely will. He was given orders to bring her back across the Channel, but he hid her away and told them she was lost, stolen or summat. I think he had an idea to give her a new livery and plates, you know, use her for tourist trips. Anyway, that never worked out – he had trouble getting the plates and raising the cash to get her repainted. Then his pa got ill and he had to rush home. But now she's out and about someone will report it, sure as eggs are eggs. Rumours spread like a rash in these parts. I'll have to deliver her back to the UK sharpish so he don't get arrested for theft.'

'That makes it stolen goods, Freddie! You decided to risk that?'

'It was for you, really,' he said, with a crooked smile.

'How are you going to drive with just one arm?'

'Holding the wheel with me knees while I change gear,' he said breezily. 'No problem.'

'Sounds dangerous to me,' she said, realising too late how stupid she sounded. Nothing could ever be more dangerous than what he and his mates had been through on the battlefields.

Half an hour passed in companionable chatter, and then a further quarter of an hour.

'Wonder where they've got to?' Freddie said, twisting in

his seat. And then, 'Hang on a sec. Who the hell are they talking to?'

She peered past him to see, in the distance, a full quarter of a mile away, a large black car beside which were standing four men, from whom Martha and Otto were apparently taking their leave. 'Look, they're heading back. We'll soon find out.'

Then, 'Now where's the boy going, for heaven's sake?'

'He's a good little runner, I'll say that for him.'

As the couple arrived back, the boy looked very pleased with himself.

'Did you find your nephew's grave? Who were those men?' Ruby asked.

Something about Martha's demeanour made her seem years younger, even girlish, with a smile that lit up the whole of her face. 'No grave. Prison.'

'He was a *prisoner of war*?' Freddie spluttered. 'After all that?'

'Is that what those men told you?' Ruby asked, astonished. 'He is alive?'

'We hope.'

'Goodness. Why didn't they tell your sister?'

Martha shrugged.

Freddie walked away to the back of the ambulance and Ruby joined him. 'Doesn't that just take the effing biscuit?' he cursed. 'We bust a gut to get them here and now we find the bastard is still alive somewhere, when frankly he doesn't deserve to be. I'd rather he was in the ruddy ground, Rube. That's where the buggers belong, 'scuse my French.'

She couldn't help being glad for the Swiss pair but this didn't prevent the queasy sensation in her stomach, a feeling she recognised from yesterday when Jimmy's family turned up: that almost visceral envy that wouldn't be quashed.

'There's no rhyme or reason, no justice,' she said, taking a breath. 'Life just isn't fair. You know that better than anyone, Fred. You just have to get on with what it gives you – or takes away.' She shivered. 'Come on, let's get going.'

The journey home was much smoother. Ruby was by now so practised that she could predict from the sound of the engine when it would be necessary to change gear, even before Freddie needed to ask.

As he steered around the potholes, he described the battles that had raged over each of the places they passed. They were returning a slightly different route, she noticed; the landscape was unfamiliar. He slowed and pulled up the ambulance on a high verge.

'Is there a problem?'

'I just thought you might like to see where I was stationed, those last few weeks.'

She followed his finger towards a network of trenches zigzagging into the distance: a web of deep ditches lined with rough wooden planks and sandbags in an ocean of mud and barbed wire.

Somehow, she'd imagined that trenches would be the width of a man's shoulders a few feet deep and just a few yards long at the most, like the holes they dug in the road to lay water mains. But these were wide enough for three men to pass, and deep enough for a man to stand upright and still not be visible, with duckboard walkways and steps at various intervals. She had no idea they would be so extensive, like the streets of a small town dug deep into the mud.

She gazed and gazed, trying to make sense of it all, trying to imagine how men had managed to survive here, under the constant barrage of shells and with the fear and stench of death all around them.

'It wasn't so bad, you know,' Freddie said. 'At least we was always with our mates and you knew they'd look out for you. You trusted them with your life, and they trusted you too. We lived together, slept in each other's arms for warmth.'

He paused a moment. 'Never known anything like that outside the army. It just ain't the same in ordinary life. We got so's we'd know the sound of a shell and whether it was coming our way and we'd know from the wind direction whether they were likely to try and gas us so we was already prepared. We even got used to the sound of shells. The only thing we never got used to was the lice and the rats.'

In his letters, Bertie had never described his living conditions, and now she knew why. Somehow she'd imagined that they would go out each day to fight and then come back to a barracks, or at least tents, where they could wash and eat at mess tables, just as he'd described his first training camp. But not here, on the battlefield. Here, they ate, slept and survived in these muddy trenches with little cover from the elements – or from enemy shells, gas and the like – going forward each day for their shift in the front-line trenches. It was almost unimaginable. How had Bertie, who loved his creature comforts and always needed an extra blanket on his bed, endured this terrible place?

Freddie pointed to a row of trees about three hundred

yards away. 'That's the German line. On a quiet night we could hear them talking, just like we was neighbours in the street. Singing, sometimes, or playing harmonicas. Fritz sang all the time, just like we did. Trying to keep our spirits up, I suppose. We even used to shout at each other across no-man's land – sleep well, give us a fag, all that. But then come daylight we'd be shelling the hell out of each other. Like everything else, you got used to it.'

Ruby had imagined a more heroic picture, men charging with their bayonets fixed, and the terrified enemy running for their lives. Or perhaps that was just what the *Illustrated London News* wanted you to believe. 'And all for a few miles of Belgian farmland,' she whispered.

'Less than that, sometimes,' Freddie said. 'We'd push forward and take their trenches and then get shoved back and back till we'd find ourselves where we'd first started three weeks before.'

'It must be hard, seeing this place again.'

He sighed, straightening his shoulders. 'I just wanted to remember the men what didn't get the chance to come home. They'll bulldoze this place before long, turn it back into farmland, and everyone will forget.'

It was then they heard the first rumble of thunder; above the German line to the east was an ominous purple-black cloud with shards of rain already slanting to the ground.

'Let's get going before these roads turn to mud,' Freddie said, starting up the engine.

Brilliant flashes of lightning illuminated the terrible scene they were leaving behind. Wet mud glimmered eerily against the darkened sky; broken trees and coils of barbed wire were reduced to black outlines set against a horizon where, already, the storm clouds had parted to reveal an unlikely stripe of brilliant blue.

By the time they reached Hoppestadt the rain was falling steadily and heavily, filling the gutters and puddling into lakes in the square. After dropping Martha and Otto outside the hotel, they drove on to the garage. 'I shall be sorry to say goodbye to this old thing,' Freddie said as he killed the engine. 'It's one of these and her crew I have to thank for my life.'

'Your arm . . . ?'

'Uh-huh.'

'Tell me, Freddie. Tell me what happened.'

There was a long pause. 'Don't worry, if you don't want to . . .'

He sighed. 'It was like this. The pair of us was trapped by enemy fire in a shell hole – enormous it was, deep with steep muddy sides and a ruddy great pond full of stinking bodies – sorry to say it like that, but that's how it was.'

She steeled herself. 'Go on.'

'Christ, it'd rained, like this, every day. Day after day after bloody day, filling the trenches and turning the mud into glue. My mate Charlie got it in the leg and me in the arm but we reckoned we'd a good chance of making it back to our line when the firing stopped. We was even beginning to celebrate 'cos we'd both caught a Blighty one, and as we waited we'd tell each other what we'd do when we got home – how much we'd drink and eat, where we'd go. You know, soldiers' talk.

'So we waited and waited, hanging on with our fingers and trying not to slip down the sides into the mud. Every time we stuck our heads over the top they fired – we must have been pretty close to enemy lines 'cos they was flipping accurate and it really wasn't worth risking. The night passed, and another day. More bloody rain, more shelling. Our water bottles were empty and we took to lying with our mouths open to catch the rainwater. By the second night Charlie was moaning and starting to talk rubbish. I had to put my hand over his mouth 'cos they'd have heard us and given us hell. But by the morning he'd stopped moaning.'

'He was dead?'

'He was one of the best, Rube. We'd been together all the way through, nearly three years, and got convinced that if we could stick with each other, neither of us would cop it. Turns out we was wrong.'

'What happened to you?'

'I sort of gave up. I'm ashamed to admit it now, but that's how I felt. What was the bloody use, shells flying all round and the rats and the stinking filth? I reckoned it'd be better to die alongside Charlie. And then, the third night came on and the shelling stopped. When I heard a noise I pulled out my gun – if it was a Kraut, at least I was going to take him with me. But then he whispered in English, telling me not to fire. He was going to get me back.

'I told him to eff off, that I was quite happy here, thank you, but he insisted, reaching down into that ruddy hole and pulling me up by my jacket. It was all I could do not to cry out, I tell you. I didn't care about my life but he was the one out in the open, who'd have copped it if I'd made any noise. So eventually he dragged me back to the line and they bundled me off to the field hospital, in one of these.' He thumped the steering wheel.

'I was back in Blighty six weeks later, just in time to hear that the Krauts had surrendered, but by then I'd got the gangrene and they had to cut my arm off.'

'Did you ever find out who he was, the man who rescued you?'

'Nah, I was pretty much out of it by the time he got me back and then I was on the stretcher. Never thought to ask. But it was the thought of him what got me through the next few months, and all that time in hospital. He'd risked his life for me so I reckoned I owed it to him to make the best of the life he'd saved.'

He relit his cigarette and took a deep draw of smoke. 'So here I am.'

'And I'm glad of it,' she said. 'And I'm glad I met you.'

'Me too. I needed a right kick up the backside, and you gave me it.' He thumped the wheel again. 'Me and this old girl are off back to Blighty, just as soon as we can get some more fuel.'

'Will you go to see your children?'

Freddie jumped out of the cab, burying his head beneath the engine cover.

'Freddie?'

'What?'

'I asked if you would go to see your children.'

'Yup, 'spect so.' His face popped up from under the bonnet, grinning. 'Not so sure about me sister-in-law.'

'She'll come round,' she said. 'Surely she'll see that they need their dad?'

'Perhaps if you come and help me persuade her?'

'It's a deal, Fred. The least I can do.'

26

MARTHA

'Now you can tell me why you ran back to those men,' she said, kicking off her shoes and lying back on the bed. 'And why you've been grinning like a monkey all the way home.'

Otto's laugh, a deep bass note followed by a series of boyish squeaks, sounded to her fond ears like a peal of bells. His brown eyes were shining. 'Heiney is alive!'

'It is wonderful news, my dearest. But we don't know that for certain. We still have to find him.'

'I know where he is!' he persisted.

She shook her head. 'How can you know this, my darling? We cannot find out until we get home. Now go and wash your face.'

'I do, Ma. *Really*. Remember what the man told us about the chess player?'

'What about it? Everyone plays chess. You too.'

'They said there were lots of sanatoriums, didn't they?'

She nodded, puzzled.

'Then why did they give us only the address of one in Berlin?'

'I don't know, for heaven's sake. Perhaps because his regiment came from Berlin?'

''Cos the chess player came from Berlin.'

She sat up, taking Otto's hand. 'You don't *know* that, my darling,' she said gently.

'But I *do* know it.' Otto stood up and began to pace the small space between the bed and the door. 'I ran back to ask how they knew he came from Berlin, if he couldn't talk. The man told me he had a tattoo on his arm with a heart and the word Berlin written on it. So it was Heiney, don't you see?'

The boy seemed to be slipping into a fantasy world. 'Heiney didn't have a tattoo.'

Otto stopped. 'But he *did*, Ma,' he shouted, before remembering to lower his voice. 'I saw it when he was washing, the morning he left. He shouted at me for barging in. And he made me swear not to tell you or Papa about it, because you'd be so angry.'

Martha gasped. 'You mean . . .'

'Don't you get it? That man was playing chess with Heiney.'

'No, that is too much of a coincidence.' She shook her head and rubbed her eyes, trying to make sense of it all. 'Anyway, why didn't they tell us?'

'He couldn't even remember his own name, remember? How could they have known who he was?'

All of a sudden, his reasoning made sense. 'Great God.' She took his hands and held them, looking up into his face. 'You might be right.'

'Of course I'm right,' he sighed, exasperated. 'Who else could it be?'

The information was dizzying.

'You won't be cross with him about the tattoo, will you? He got it with his mates when they were away on training.'

It was only then that she allowed herself to imagine the moment of recognition, their first embrace, and her chest seemed to burst with utter joy. Laughing almost uncontrollably, she pulled Otto onto the bed and wrapped her arms around him. 'My darling boy, I love you so much. You and your sharp eyes! Of course I don't care about the wretched tattoo. I don't care about anything so long as your brother is alive.'

How could she have imagined, setting off in the ambulance just a few hours ago, that they would be giggling on the bed together, talking about what they would do when they found him? How they would bring him home and cook meals of the freshest, most nutritious foods they could find to help his poor body and mind to recover. Otto would play chess with him, take him to the football ground for a kick-around when he was ready. They would hire the best doctors to treat him, to restore his mind to its old self, whatever it took, no matter the cost. Tonight she would spend a little of the money Alice had given her on a carafe of wine with their last dinner in Belgium, Martha promised, and yes, Otto could have a small glass too. What she'd expected to be a solemn wake would be an opportunity to celebrate.

※

A sharp rap on the door made them both jump.

'Madame Weber?'

She knew the voice: the hotelier, Monsieur Vermeulen.

Perhaps he had recovered the money Geert Peeters owed her – she felt so euphoric right now that she barely cared. But as she opened the door she knew it was not good news. His face was even grimmer than usual, heavy eyebrows knitted in a scowl.

'I must speak with you, madame,' he said.

She would not let him spoil this moment of pure happiness. 'We have been out all afternoon and we need to change in time for dinner, Monsieur Vermeulen. May we come in ten minutes?'

He shook his head. 'No. Leave the boy. I wish to speak to you alone. Now.'

Irritated at his insistence, she turned to Otto: 'Have a wash and change your clothes for dinner. I'll be with you in a few moments.'

Monsieur Vermeulen led her down the stairs and into his study, just as before. As before, he did not invite her to sit. From the untidy desk, he picked up a book that she immediately recognised as Otto's – the German translation of *Robinson Crusoe*. The boy had loved this story, asking more than once whether they could go to a deserted island just to find out whether it would be possible to survive. She'd read it too, loved the way it transported her to a place where no one else could trouble you; where you could be entirely self-reliant, not dependent on food tickets, or queues, or men who wanted to wage war or foment rebellions.

'The chambermaid found this in your room, Madame Weber. Can you confirm that it belongs to your son?' She nodded and smiled. What on earth could be wrong with that?

He opened it at the inside front page and held it out to her. Written in Otto's teenage hand were the words:

This book belongs to Otto Karl Weber

Apt 25, Mittenstrasse 324

Berlin

Republic of Germany

The World

The Universe

SPACE

Even now, Martha refused to be cowed. So what if her subterfuge had been uncovered? It hardly mattered any more. She had just received news that she could never have dreamed of. Heiney was alive.

'Monsieur, you are right. Please forgive me for the mistruth I felt compelled to tell to protect myself and my son. We are indeed originally from Berlin, but we are only human beings like you, and we come in peace. Our only wish in coming here, like your other visitors, was to honour our dead with a small act of remembrance. '

'And the grave you were seeking?' he asked. 'Not your nephew but in fact your own son, I assume?' The scowl had not eased a jot.

'I was carrying out my husband's dying wish, Monsieur Vermeulen. When he lay on his deathbed he made me promise that, as soon as it was possible, I would take his grandfather's bravery medal and lay it on our son's grave. That is why we came here.'

The hotelier took out a cigarette and lit it, as before, with a match scratched into flame on the underside of his desk. He sighed out the first breath of smoke, and took another drag. 'Madame Weber, I am afraid I have no choice. I cannot allow you to stay in my hotel.'

'That is no problem,' she replied. 'We are leaving tomorrow morning anyway. In fact, I was going to ask you to book a taxi for seven o'clock, please.'

'You misunderstand me.' He fixed her with a steely glare. 'You must leave immediately.'

She struggled to understand. 'What do you mean, *immediately*?'

'I mean *now*. Otherwise I will be obliged to call the police.'

'The *police*?' She could hardly believe her ears. 'But we have done nothing wrong. We are here perfectly legally, and have all the correct papers.'

'You have lied to us about your nationality and we are obliged to inform the police if there is any suspicion of spying.'

She gasped. 'Surely you are not serious? This is outrageous. I have a right—'

'You must leave tonight,' he was saying. '*Tonight*. Do you understand me?'

'Surely . . . just one more night? Please, Monsieur Vermeulen, it is pouring with rain. I have the boy with me. We will take dinner in our room so we don't trouble your other guests.'

'I cannot allow it. I am sorry . . . my wife, Cécile' – he waved his hands vaguely in the direction of the dining room – 'it was she who found the book and she will not allow Germans in our hotel, any Germans, on principle. You see . . .' He struggled some more, trying to form the words, his voice breaking. 'Our sons, they both died. Pieter and Jan. Good boys too. You understand?'

Now Martha understood. Further pleading would only make matters worse. She would go to the other hotel, perhaps, that Mr Martens had spoken about?

'May we have half an hour to change and pack our bags?'

He checked his watch. 'Cécile is in the kitchen now, but you must be gone before she starts serving dinner. By seven o'clock. Twenty minutes.'

It was only later that Martha remembered that she had paid him in advance for three nights' stay, and should have asked for a refund.

But by then it was too late.

27

RUBY

The rain was still hammering on the tin roof of the garage. Freddie went to the back of the ambulance, returning with a couple of heavy green army blankets. 'Here, these'll keep the worst off. Let's run for it.'

As they passed, Ginger beckoned to them from the doorway of the cafe. 'Miss Ruby, please come. There is more trouble.'

'What trouble?' Ruby panted, glad to be out of the rain. Her feet were soaking.

'The lady and her son. She not Swiss, but German. Maurice not want Germans in his hotel. He say they spies and he call police.'

'The lying witch,' Freddie muttered beside her.

She'd had her suspicions, of course, ever since Alice had suggested it, but she'd pushed them from her mind. How could she have been so naive? Contradictory emotions clashed in her head: annoyance that she'd been deceived, embarrassment that she'd persuaded Freddie to help her, against his better instincts, and sadness for Martha that she'd felt compelled to lie.

'However did Maurice find out?'

'Cécile – Madame Vermeulen – clean their room and find a book. Inside is boy's name and address. In Berlin. So Maurice, when they get back, he show it and ask them and woman tells him yes it is true. And it is son they look for, not nephew. They German, not Swiss like she say. So they must leave hotel, he say. For other guests, you understand?'

'Why can't he let them stay? It's only one night. They leave tomorrow.'

Ginger shrugged, shook her head. 'Maurice two sons killed. No one want Germans here. We remember too much what they did.'

'Perhaps they can stay at The Grand?'

Ginger shook her head. 'Same problem. Word travels fast.'

It was then they spied Martha and Otto stepping out uncertainly from the door of the hotel carrying their small, battered cases, cowering from the soaking rain. The boy held his mother's hand, glancing up at her anxiously, looking suddenly much younger than his twelve years. They were human beings who just happened to have been on the other side of this wretched war. German or no, this was still the same woman with whom they had shared the afternoon, who had responded so warmly towards herself and Freddie, the mother who clearly loved her boy deeply, who had, just this afternoon, experienced the joy of discovering that her elder son was probably alive. She couldn't abandon them now.

She beckoned to them from the cafe doorway. 'Come over here, quickly. You'll get soaked.'

As they took shelter, Martha said, 'Is not worry. We go Grand Hotel.'

'Ginger, can you explain?'

The girl spoke quickly in French. As understanding dawned, Martha's face seemed to collapse and her shoulders sagged. Glancing nervously towards the bar, Ginger said to Ruby, 'My father is watching me. I must go back to work and they must leave. I so sorry.'

Ruby thanked her with a sinking heart and turned to Freddie, but he was no longer there. He was walking away through the rain under his blanket, already halfway across the square.

'Hey,' she yelled, running after him and grabbing his shoulder. 'Where are you going?'

'Count me out, Rube,' he muttered.

She held on to his arm. 'Don't let me down now, Freddie. Please? You heard what Ginger said, nowhere else will have them. They could even get arrested. At the very least we should try to find them somewhere safe to stay.'

'I wouldn't shed a tear if the whole effing German nation got itself wiped off the face of the earth,' he said.

'But what about the boy? We can't let him spend the night on the streets in this rain,' she persisted. 'Or worse, in prison. What if it was your son? Would you walk away then?'

'How come you've turned the good Samaritan?' he said, sullenly scratching his cheek. 'Those Krauts killed your man, remember?'

'I can't find it in myself to blame her, Freddie. She's just a normal human being trying to do her best.'

Still he refused to move.

'For heaven's sake,' she shouted, exasperated. The rain was trickling down her neck. 'If you won't do it for them, do it for me? *Please*. I really need your help.'

He hesitated a few further seconds, and then his face softened. 'Blimey, Rube, you're getting soaked. Get under this blanket, will you. Let's go to the church, they don't lock up till later. At least we can get out of this ruddy rain while we think what to do next.'

❦

Inside, the church smelled of dust and musty prayer books, but at least it was dry. Martha lowered herself wearily onto a pew. 'I sorry,' she kept repeating. 'Sorry for trouble.'

Freddie fidgeted, pacing the aisle.

'Please stop,' Ruby said. 'You're getting on my nerves.'

'All this God stuff makes me uncomfortable,' he muttered.

'So what are we going to do? Perhaps I could sneak them up to my room?'

'Maurice would throw you all out. Then where would we be?'

'What about your place?'

He snorted. 'Give me a break. There's hardly space for me, let alone those two. And my landlady would hit the roof.'

'Any other ideas?' The rain was still driving against the church windows. Ruby turned to Martha. 'What time does your train leave in the morning?'

Martha wrote the figure nine on her palm.

'Nine o'clock? From Ypres?'

'I could take them in the ambulance,' Freddie said after a moment.

'To Ypres? At this time of night?'

'I've driven in worse. No shells flying about, at least.'

'Where would they stay?'

He scratched his stubble, frowning. 'They could sleep in the back, and I could drive them to Ypres in the morning.'

'In the back of the ambulance?' She struggled to imagine it, sleeping on those narrow canvas stretchers that had carried so many desperately injured men, perhaps even corpses.

'It'd be warm and dry, at least. And the police would never think to look there.'

It was the only idea they could come up with and the more she thought about it, the less crazy it seemed. She tried to explain it to Martha, who frowned with confusion before Otto began to giggle, whispering excitedly to his mother. At last she appeared to understand and nodded, seeming to be too weary to resist.

Freddie picked up a handful of votive candles from the stand, shoving them into his pockets and dropping a few coins into the money box. 'Always thought there ought to be a better use for these,' he said with a grin. 'Come on, the pastor will be here soon. I'll take them to the ambulance.'

'I'll come with you,' she said.

'Nah. Let me take them. Best not to have too many comings and goings at the garage.'

The church clock chimed seven and Ruby suddenly realised that she was starving. Dinner would be being served. She tried once more to persuade him, but he insisted.

'Okay, if you think that's best. Thank you, Freddie.' She reached into her pocket and pulled out a few coins. 'Can I ask one last favour?'

'You can ask.'

'Buy them some hot chocolate and a few things to eat, if you can. And take them some water to wash with. A few creature comforts for the poor things.'

'You don't ask for much, do you, missy?' he said, taking the money with a broad smile. 'Me, helping Germans,' he whispered. 'You'd never credit it.'

'Do it for me then?'

'Just for you, Mrs B. Just for you.'

She wanted to give him a hug but it would not be appropriate, here in the church with Martha and Otto looking on. An awkward silence fell between them.

'Well, I suppose that's it then,' he said. 'We'll be off first thing in the morning. Have a safe journey home.'

'What? Won't I see you when you get back?' She felt suddenly bereft. It was too sudden, too soon to say goodbye.

He shifted from foot to foot. 'I was thinking I'd carry straight on from Ypres to Calais. It's on the way. No point hanging around now I've made up me mind.'

'You really are leaving tomorrow, going back to England? To your family?'

'Reckon.' He looked down at his feet.

'I'll miss you, Fred.'

He glanced up again, cheeks colouring. 'When are you off?'

'We're supposed to be back in Ostend tomorrow but I haven't seen hide nor hair of Alice since yesterday, so I haven't a clue what she's got planned, whether she's ordered a cab or anything.'

'Ostend, eh?' His face cracked into a broad grin. 'How'd you fancy a ride in the old jalopy? For old time's sake?'

'In the ambulance? But I thought you were going to Calais?'

'I'd go via Ostend anyway, along the coast road.'

'Is there room for all of us? Alice too?'

'Of course. Those things carry twenty walking wounded, remember? Not in any great comfort, mind, but we can have a laugh. Besides, it'd be easier with you helping with the gears – safer than steering with me knees all the way.'

'I'll have to ask Alice, but I'd be up for it. Talk about travelling in style.'

He tipped an imaginary cap, and bowed extravagantly. 'Your carriage will call just after eight, madame. Will that suit?'

'That will do nicely, Jeeves.' He laughed. 'See you tomorrow.'

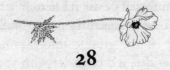

28

ALICE

Alice looked at herself in the mirror of her hotel room and shuddered.

Her face was streaked with muddy tears, and she winced as she recalled how she had prostrated herself on the ground in the rain at Sam's grave. Why had she made such a spectacle of herself in front of Daniel?

They'd shared few words on the short return drive – how could she explain how brittle and empty she felt, how hollowed out? Memories of her brother would always end in that lonely place, with a plain white cross in a forest of so many thousands of others. It broke her heart: tomorrow she must start the long journey home, leaving Sam behind.

'I cannot thank you enough,' she said, as they arrived back outside the Hotel de la Paix. 'This has meant the world to me. But I guess it's goodbye. We leave tomorrow morning.'

'So soon?' He appeared genuinely shocked. 'You cannot leave without dining with me one last time. Or at the very least, a quick drink.'

She was about to refuse, remembering Ruby, and the fact

that she needed to book a car for the morning and pack her suitcase. But the prospect of dining with Daniel, one last time, was impossible to resist – why not? She would be back at the hotel before ten. She found herself accepting, agreeing to join him after changing from her muddy clothes.

His back was turned as she approached the bar of the Grand Hotel, but the set of his shoulders, the way he held himself, the hair curling over his collar, was now so familiar, it felt as though she had known him forever. As she said his name he looked round, pushing back the lick of hair from his forehead and raising a single eyebrow in that sweet, amused look of his, then stood to kiss her cheeks: right, left and right again.

'Darling Aleese, you look wonderful. A new woman. What can I get you? We shall make a toast to your brave brother.'

The wine was aromatic and comforting, flowing warmly into her stomach, easing the raw emotions of the day. *You came here to find him and, against all the odds, that is what you have achieved*, she said to herself. *You know what happened to him and where he lies. It will give Ma and Pa solace to know that you have been there and to have the flowers from his graveside. Now it's time to get on with the rest of your life.*

He recommended the wild duck. 'So rare these days; the soldiers saw them as fair game.' The meal, when it arrived, tasted delicious and Daniel was at his most entertaining; he ordered another bottle and refilled her glass several times.

Warmed by the wine, Alice began to relax, to enjoy herself

once more. She would miss Daniel so much, his lively conversation, his seductive smile, the informality and freedom from convention. No one knew her here; she could do as she wished. How different it was from straight-laced Washington, where appearances were everything and any kind of non-conformity meant risking being cold-shouldered and whispered about or, worse, endangering her father's political career? She dreaded returning to that life: of pinning on the smiles, pretending to enjoy herself at dreary rounds of fundraisers, dinner parties, tennis tournaments and teas.

He leaned across the table, putting his hand on hers. The intensity of his gaze made her feel like the only person in the world.

'Nightcap in my room?'

She shook her head, steeling herself. 'No. I really shouldn't. We're leaving for Ostend first thing tomorrow morning.'

'*Quel dommage*,' he said, with an exaggerated pout. 'But as you choose, my darling Aleese.' She felt herself weakening. His lips were full and wine-stained; how could she resist one last kiss?

'But perhaps . . .'

'A lady is allowed to change her mind,' he whispered, as they left the dining room.

❈

He leaned up on an elbow, holding her gaze with those deep brown eyes and stroking her cheek. Alice had never felt like this before, not with Lloyd, not with anyone else. Lying with their limbs entangled, her fingers tracing the skein of dark hairs that strayed down his chest, he mur-mured, 'My beautiful girl, it is no wonder I fell in love with you. It's a shame you have to leave.'

She did not want to leave. Sam was here, Daniel was here. The idea was enticing, thrilling, crazy, overwhelming: what if she stayed, just a little longer? A few weeks, perhaps a month or so? She would visit Sam's grave every day, spend every evening with Daniel.

She began to fantasise: she could take a job in an office – she had little idea of what went on in an office, but surely it couldn't be that difficult? Or she could teach English; there would be plenty of people wanting to learn, just as she'd travelled to Paris to learn French. Or perhaps they could both move to Paris, and take a flat together. Paris! What a dream come true that would be. No, it was absurd.

She looked into his eyes. 'I don't want to leave. I'd like to stay here forever.'

He laughed. 'But you are to be married, no?'

'I'm not sure I want that life anymore.' There, she'd admitted it. 'Truly, I'd like to stay here, in Hoppestadt. Forever.'

'You crazy woman! What would you do in Belgium? There is no money, no work. The country is in pieces, the economy is a mess. And you have no family here.'

She stopped his words with a kiss, which instantly caught fire. 'You are such a wicked girl,' he murmured. 'Quite adorable, and quite impossible to resist.'

'That's the thing.' She fell back onto the bed, looking up at the cracks in the ornate plasterwork above. 'How would it be if we decided not to resist?'

She held her breath, waiting for his answer.

'You mean . . . ? Don't tease me, Aleese.'

'If we could spend every night together, like this.'

He sighed. 'My precious one. We have had a wonderful time, have we not? It has been a great adventure, discovering what we missed when we were younger.' Withdrawing his arm from beneath her neck, he sat up and lit a cigarette, blowing artful smoke rings towards the ceiling.

'And you fell in love with me,' she said. 'That's what you said just now.'

'But it is not real life, is it? You are engaged to be married, and I too, in all but the name,' he purred, stroking her cheek. 'My girlfriend knows that although I play around, I have given my word.'

It was as though she'd been dashed with cold water, sobering her up in an instant. She sat up in bed, drawing the sheet around herself to cover the nakedness that felt suddenly vulnerable. 'Not real life? Play around?'

He shrugged and took another drag on his cigarette. 'Ma chère Aleese,' he murmured.

'Play around?' she said again, feeling nauseous now. She was just a plaything to him, a cheap toy he'd been having fun with. And all the while she'd thought it something they both believed was beautiful, precious.

Disgusted with herself, and with him, she scrambled from the bed and grabbed her clothes, pulling them on as fast as she could, ignoring his protests. 'I'm so sorry . . . Please don't let us part like this.'

She turned on him. 'You bastard,' she hissed. 'You've been using me. You seduced me . . .'

'I seduced you?' His eyebrows raised in genuine surprise. 'I thought it was the other way around.'

Her head spun; perhaps he was right? She was the one who'd instigated this reunion in the first place. It was her decision to go to his apartment in Lille and again to his room this evening. At no point had he forced her hand. Bitter, self-pitying tears stung her eyes. She was a naive, stupid idiot and had made an utter fool of herself, like a doe-eyed schoolgirl living in a fantasy world, mistaking intimacy for love.

Now she must try to retain some level of dignity until she could get away. He made no move to prevent her. She snatched up her handbag, ran from the room and slammed the door, not caring who heard.

Only when she reached her room at the Hotel de la Paix did she allow herself to weep.

29

MARTHA

Martha had been prepared to spend the night in the church. Although it was chilly and rather musty-smelling, it was at least dry and out of the rain. But never, in her wildest imaginings, her darkest nightmares, could she have dreamed that she would find herself preparing to sleep in a British army ambulance in a tin garage hidden away in the town's deserted back streets.

Yet, as Freddie secured the doors she felt relieved, safe again. At least if Monsieur Vermeulen had called the police or should any crazy citizens take it on themselves to go spy-hunting, they would never think to look here. By the light of the torch Freddie had miraculously produced she was cheered to discover that the rear of the ambulance was surprisingly spacious, furnished with three tiers of khaki canvas stretchers on either side of a central gangway. A woollen blanket, folded with military precision, lay on each bunk.

Freddie unhooked the two sets of upper bunks, leaving just a single tier on either side. 'You won't be needing these,' he said, rolling them up and standing them in the corner of the garage. He folded two blankets lengthways and laid them out on each stretcher to make a kind of mattress, placing the spares at the head ends.

Martha clambered up the steps. She sniffed suspiciously, fearing she might smell blood or worse but, apart from being a little musty, the cabin appeared to be dry and, as far as she could tell, surprisingly clean.

Otto leapt onto a bunk and lay down immediately, apparently enchanted. 'It's like camping. Just wait till I tell them at school.'

❧❧❧

After Freddie left they bolted the garage doors from the inside, just as he instructed. On a wide wooden shelf just behind the cab, probably once intended for dressings and medicines, she placed the votive candles he had brought from the church and lit them with the matches he'd also provided. They would save the torch for emergencies.

'Come, Otto,' she said. 'Let us give our thanks for saving your brother, and say Kaddish for your father.' Together they murmured, '*May His great name grow exalted and sanctified . . . in the world that He created as He willed . . .*' The words were so familiar that their meaning became subsumed into the rhythm, the pitch rising and falling like a chant, calming and comforting, like a warm blanket wrapping itself around them.

❧❧❧

A loud hammering on the garage doors made them both jump. Dread lurched in her stomach once more. Who had betrayed them? Surely not Freddie or Ruby? But who else knew they were here? Not that sweet girl Ginger?

The knocking came again.

'Who is it?' she shouted, deepening her voice to sound gruff and manly.

The familiar voice was reassuring. 'It's me, Freddie. Back again. Bad penny and all that.'

She reached for the torch and slipped down to open the door.

The rain had ceased now and he stood there holding out a jug wrapped in a towel, and two enamel cups. 'Hot chocolate,' he said, his cheeks colouring. From under his jacket he produced a loaf of bread and a large chunk of cheese wrapped in greaseproof paper. Handing these over, he turned and picked up a bucket of water, steaming in the misty air. 'For washing,' he explained, pulling from his pocket a small bar of soap.

After saying Kaddish, inviting him in as a guest was the perfectly natural thing to do. 'Come,' she said, beckoning him in.

He shook his head. 'No, I don't think so.'

'Come,' she insisted until, reluctantly, he followed her.

She relit the candles and they sat opposite each other in their gentle light as she poured the creamy, delicious-smelling drink from the jug and handed a cup to Freddie. When he hesitated, she indicated that she and Otto would share.

'*Prost!*' she replied, chinking hers against his and taking a sip. 'Is good.'

'You have hot chocolate in Germany?'

'No in war.'

For a few uncomfortable moments all they could do was smile shyly at each other.

She tried again. 'You have child?'

'Two. The boy's a bit younger than Otto, about seven I should think.' He held up his five fingers outstretched, then closed them and held out two more. 'Jack, we call him. The girl, Elsie, is . . .'

He frowned at his hand, holding out five fingers, then three more, then added one. Nine. Hearing the tenderness in his voice, she wondered why he was still here in Belgium, months after the end of the war, but she hoped that he could return home to his family soon. He deserved them, they deserved him. But this was all far too complicated for her limited English vocabulary, so she contented herself with silently willing him good fortune.

Freddie drained his cup and seemed about to leave. But then, almost as an afterthought, he reached into his inside pocket and pulled out something small and silver. Martha flinched, thinking for a fleeting, terrifying moment that it was a pistol.

He put the harmonica – for that is what it was – to his mouth and began to play a hauntingly familiar tune. A German tune: '*Lieb Vaterland*'. Tears sprang to her eyes. How hollow it sounded now, that marching song once so full of hope and enthusiasm for the future of their new, prosperous and powerful Fatherland. These days, in the cafes of Berlin, this same tune would be sung as an ironic refrain, a mournful requiem for their lost youth and derelict country.

'*Nein, nein,*' she said, stopping him with an upheld hand. 'Play English.'

He began another tune, stamping out the jaunty rhythm with his foot onto the wooden floor. It was almost impossible to resist; she and Otto joined in, tapping their feet along with him. Freddie took the harmonica from his lips and sang: 'Pack up your troubles in an old kit bag and smile, smile, smile. While you've a lucifer to light your fag, smile, boys, that's the style.'

He resumed the tune on the harmonica and, when it ended, held it out to Otto. 'Want to give it a go, laddie? It's easy. You suck in like this.' He demonstrated. 'And then you blow out.' He moved his lips along the holes, producing a scale of notes, and then jumped between them, making a tune. 'You can play soft,' he said, with a gentle breath. 'Or hard.' He blasted into the holes, producing a harsh chord almost as loud as a church organ on full stops. He wiped the mouthpiece and held it out once more.

Otto shook his head, reddening to the tips of his ears.

'Go on, boy,' his mother whispered. Slowly, cautiously, he took the little instrument in his hand, studied it for a moment and showed it to her.

'Look, Ma.' On it was engraved the familiar logo *Hohner*, the most famous of German instrument makers.

'Give it a go then, Otto. There's a good man,' Freddie said.

Otto put the harmonica to his lips and blew a swooping scale. He tried playing separate notes by pursing his lips, as Freddie had done, blowing into individual holes. After a few stumbling attempts, he managed to produce a vague tune. Flushing as they applauded his newfound prowess, he went to hand the harmonica back.

Freddie shook his head. 'You keep it, boy,' he said.

'*Nein, nein,*' Martha said, holding out her hand.

But Otto smiled, whispering simply, '*Vielen Dank.*'

'You are very welcome. And now I must be off,' Freddie said. 'Eight o'clock tomorrow morning.' He drew a clock face on his knee.

Martha shook his hand. 'You good man, Monsieur Freddie,' she said. 'We thank you. Many, many.'

※※※

After he'd gone they finished the hot chocolate, wiping their mugs and even the inside of the jug with bread, so as not to waste the last remaining delicious drips. They washed their faces and hands in the still-warm water and dried themselves on a spare blanket before settling onto their bunks. Martha leaned across to kiss Otto's cheek.

'Sleep now, son,' she said. 'We have an early start to catch the train tomorrow.'

After a few moments he piped up, 'D'you know, I think I like Mr Freddie after all, Ma. He's different from what I expected an Englishman to be.'

'I agree,' she said. 'He is a kind man, a true *Mensch*. The English are not all monsters. Let's try to look forward to the future, shall we? We will find your brother and make him well; in time our country will be healed as well.'

'No more wars?'

'No more wars.'

'You promise?'

'I promise. Now go to sleep.'

She blew out the candles and lay back on the bunk. As her eyes became accustomed to the half-light she could make out the metal arches holding up the battered green canvas roof. She thought of the hundreds, perhaps thousands, of gravely wounded and dying men who must have looked up at the same view, glad to be out of the fray but also probably in pain, wondering whether they would survive the injuries they'd sustained.

She tried not to think of the many desperate Allied soldiers, wounded and dying, who must have travelled in this ambulance, or the corpses laid out on their way to the cemeteries, or of the German shells, bullets and gas that would have put them here in the first place. Were their souls still lurking here? She cursed the Kaiser and his politicians: how could they have been so blind as to believe that a few thousand square kilometres of territory was worth such losses, such inhumanity to man?

Seeing the trenches today had brought it home to her, especially when Freddie had pointed out the German lines just a few hundred yards away. She had never imagined that Heinrich's life and that of his pals might have been so mundane, struggling under such harsh conditions with so few creature comforts. And all the while within hearing distance of men on the enemy side enduring equally difficult times, trying to exist from day to day, eating, sleeping, keeping themselves clean as best they could and yet in constant fear of shellfire and snipers' bullets. No wonder so many had lost their minds.

The face of the hotelier, distorted and red with rage, loomed before her eyes. She did not blame him; any English, French, Belgian or American would have been treated the same way in Berlin. She felt no bitterness; the wounds were still so raw. Their country, until then perfectly peaceable, had been invaded and destroyed by her countrymen. They had lost so many of their loved ones. It was hardly surprising that they hated the Germans. Discovering her lie must have sharpened their resentment and suspicions, leading them to wild, unlikely assumptions.

Before the war, anyone could travel widely throughout Europe, welcome in any country. Now, as a result of her country's misplaced national pride, all that was lost and in its place had been left death, devastation and a legacy of mutual hatred. What she felt, mostly, was a deep, dark sense of shame that made her skin flush beneath the prickly blanket.

Then she remembered: what did anything else matter, now that Heiney was alive? After all these years of grieving they would be back in Berlin tomorrow, and could begin their search for him. As she drifted off to sleep, she allowed herself to imagine the moment of their first meeting, their first embrace, his arrival home, their little family reunited at last and able to look forward to a future of peace and prosperity.

30

RUBY

Alice was nowhere to be found, but she couldn't wait any longer; Cécile would stop serving dinner soon.

On her way downstairs she heard English voices.

Edith was the first to spot her. 'Hello again,' she said sweetly. 'What a charming place. They've got two rooms for us and we couldn't be more delighted.' Beside her stood Jimmy supporting himself on two walking sticks, his face still as pale as paper, eyes anxious and forehead furrowed with worry lines. But the disturbing twitches and tics that had plagued him earlier still seemed to have abated, at least for the moment. 'We're going home tomorrow, my darling, aren't we?'

Joseph, who had been at the desk with Monsieur Vermeulen, now recognised her, his face lighting up with that crooked smile. 'Ah, Miss Barton. We didn't have a chance to thank you properly.'

'He looks better.'

'Can we buy you a drink later? Seems the least we can do.'

'I'm going for dinner right now. But perhaps afterwards?'

She went to the dining room and sat in the usual place but Martha and Otto's empty table made her wonder how they were faring. At least they were safe, and it was only for one night. Had Freddie managed to overcome his hatred of Germans and taken the things she'd asked him to? She felt sure that he would have done – she'd already seen him softening towards the boy. Tomorrow the couple would be on their way home – perhaps to a joyful reunion with her elder son.

A figure appeared at the table, breaking her reverie. 'May I join you?' It was Joseph Catchpole.

'Please. Are you on your own?'

'We thought it better to be discreet,' he said quietly. 'We don't want to draw attention to him, and Edith didn't want to leave him alone, so they've ordered room service. I felt it was important to give them some time together, so here I am.'

Cécile came to take his order, and he studied the wine list.

'Aren't you drinking?' She gestured to her water glass. 'Do you like red?' The wine arrived and she watched, impressed, as he sniffed and tasted it carefully before approving it, like an expert.

'Thank you again,' he said, raising his glass to hers. 'For the best gift in the world, bringing my brother back to us.'

'I did nothing, honestly. It was Tubby Clayton. You should write to him when you get home. I've got his address.'

The scar on Joseph's cheek lent him an endearingly jaunty expression. When he smiled, his single eye twinkled brightly enough for two. She'd seen quite a few returning soldiers with terrible facial injuries and imagined it might sometimes be worse than losing a leg or an arm. But Joseph behaved as though the scar and eye patch simply weren't there and, after a while, she stopped noticing too.

'Tell me . . .' They both spoke at the same moment, and then stopped, awkwardly.

'Ladies first,' he said, laughing.

'I hardly know where to start,' she said. 'What have you been doing since we saw you in Ostend?'

'Major Wilson told us the next day that you and Miss Palmer had returned to Ypres and, after a day in Bruges, we realised that's exactly what we ought to do too. Visiting tourist sights wasn't going to help us find Jimmy. The only thing we knew was that he'd gone missing in November last year at Passchendaele and Edie insisted that we come back to Tyne Cot to have another look. We took a car and spent the whole day there. It's depressing, isn't it, knowing that for every grave that's marked there are hundreds still hidden in the mud?'

'I went back there, too,' Ruby said. 'To look for my husband's grave. But I couldn't find anything. Not a sign.'

His easy manner faltered. 'I'm so sorry. I noticed the wedding ring, but didn't like to ask.'

'Finish your story first.'

'Well, the whole thing was just too much for Edie – she was devastated by not being able to find his grave. She couldn't stop weeping and wouldn't get out of bed the next day, while I hung around the hotel feeling guilty and fretting about whether we should ever have come here in the first place. It was that evening we got the telegram.'

'You must have been so excited.'

'To be honest, I couldn't get my head round it. I didn't tell Edie at first – I was concerned for her state of mind, and if it was some kind of sick joke, it might just push her over the edge. But then I read it again and realised the original telegram to my family had been sent by the Reverend Clayton, so it must have some credibility. So I ordered a car for the morning, and told Edie at breakfast. And just a few hours later, there he was. Extraordinary.' He shook his head, as though still trying to believe it.

'It is a kind of miracle, isn't it?' she said.

'I still have to pinch myself.' He lowered his voice. 'There is a problem, though, of course.'

'A problem?'

He straightened his cutlery on the white linen table-cloth. 'The truth is that he's alive because he was too afraid to carry on.'

'You know that's not true,' she said, wishing she could still those uneasy fingers. 'The fighting injured his brain. He's ill, that's perfectly obvious and, just like any physical injury, he'll take a long time to recover.'

Joseph's voice cracked. 'I know these things, of course I do. But I still haven't worked out how to explain it to our parents. They'll be devastated when they learn he's a deserter.'

'Do you have to tell them? Won't they be so thrilled to have him back that it won't cross their minds to ask?'

His face darkened. 'We could lie, of course. It might be the kindest way.'

The arrival of food interrupted their conversation. For some minutes neither spoke save for murmurs of appreciation.

'Delicious,' he said, refilling their glasses. 'Now it's your turn, if you want to tell me.'

'Not much to tell, I'm afraid,' Ruby said. 'My husband went missing in action at Passchendaele. I've searched Tyne Cot, twice, and there's no sign. He may be buried somewhere else but you could spend a lifetime looking. I have to accept that I may never have a grave to visit.'

'I am so sorry.' So often this simple phrase came across as empty words. But his tone of voice, balancing sympathy and acceptance, made her believe that he properly, deeply understood what she was feeling.

'I wouldn't even have dreamed of coming but it was his parents – my parents-in-law – who insisted and paid for the trip. I've got nothing to take home to them except some dried flowers from the roadside. But I'm glad I came, all the same. I've got a sense of the place where he spent some time when not at the front. I've even discovered that I remember him better, being here. And at least I tried my best.'

The dining room was clearing, the waiters pulling off tablecloths and starting to stack chairs. 'Shall we finish the bottle in the bar?' he suggested.

She gladly agreed. She was enjoying their conversation, the way he spoke with such refreshing honesty, and the fact that he listened, properly listened, and made the right responses. The bar was deserted and it seemed odd, without Freddie. They took his usual table in the corner.

'It must have been difficult for you today, when we found Jimmy,' he said.

She took a gulp of wine. 'When Tubby told me there was a man in the hospital I thought for a moment, just a very brief moment, that it might have been my husband. And when I learned that your Jimmy was in the same regiment . . .'

'The Suffolks?'

She nodded, not trusting her voice.

'My regiment too. What was his name, if you don't mind me asking?'

She took a deep breath. Curiously, it didn't hurt so much as she'd feared. In fact, pronouncing it gave her a deep sense of pride. She loved him, always would. 'Bertie. Private Albert Barton.'

It was as though she'd given him an electric shock. Joseph slapped a hand to his brow. 'Bertie Barton? Great heavens!'

'You knew him?' Her heart leapt. What a strange and wonderful coincidence.

'My goodness. I'm so sorry he didn't make it.' She noticed his hand trembling as he picked up his glass. 'He was one of the best.'

'You *knew* my Bertie?' She could scarcely believe it.

'No, not really, although I wish I had. He was the bravest man I knew. I owe him my life.'

Was she dreaming? 'Tell me, what happened?'

Ruby found herself hardly daring to breathe as he began to speak. 'We were out on a recce. It was a dark night, perfect for it, and I had the best men with me, people I knew and trusted completely. But someone stumbled on an unexploded shell and the next moment all hell broke loose. I got a piece of shrapnel through the eye and into my brain, and I was pretty much out of it. All I remember is trying not to moan too much or Fritz would come over and finish us all off.' Joseph paused, wiped his brow with a napkin and took a sip of his wine.

'I must have passed out because the next thing I knew it was daylight and some crazy idiot was lying next to me in the mud, whispering in my ear. "Shut up you so-and-so," although it was a bit riper than that, you understand? "Just shut up for a moment so we can get you back without getting us both killed."'

'That was my Bertie?'

He smiled. 'The very same. He had what I'd call a highly developed vocabulary.'

She laughed, fondly remembering the inventive curses Bertie used to come out with.

'But by Christ that man was brave,' Joseph went on. 'He'd crawled out through the mud across no-man's land in broad daylight to save me. No one in their right mind would do that, but he did.'

'So how did he get you back?'

'He pulled me, very, very slowly, inch by inch, till we got to a hollow, and we stayed there till it got dark. I was pretty delirious by this time but he had water and rum, which quietened me down a little. I just remember him telling me to hang on in there, how we were going to make it, and when we got home how he was going to treat me to several beers at his local.'

'The King's Head?'

'That's the one. And how there were so many beautiful girls there . . .'

'Cheeky so-and-so.' She could hear Bertie saying it. 'What happened in the end?'

'He dragged me back to the trench and handed me over

to the stretcher bearers, telling me to give his love to Blighty when I got there. He called me a "lucky bastard" – those were his last words to me – although anyone could see that my head was all smashed in and my eye was missing and I don't suppose anyone thought I'd make it. But his words gave me hope and all through my recovery I thought of him, telling me that I was lucky. I had to prove him right. And I *am* lucky. I'm alive, and we've just found my brother. What more could a man ask for? And it's all thanks to your Bertie.'

She could not speak for the lump in her throat, but in any case how could she adequately thank this man for the gift he had just given her: a final, wonderful, lasting memory of her funny, loving husband, who had put his life in mortal danger to save one of his fellow soldiers? The tears began, big fat drops falling silently from her eyes. She sniffed and fumbled in her handbag. 'Sorry, so sorry. I must look a mess.'

'Don't apologise. I understand.' From his pocket he produced a pristine white linen handkerchief. 'Here, will this help?'

'I'm crying with happiness, really. What you've just told me about Bertie means the world to me. I cannot thank you enough.'

She imagined the moment of sharing the news with Bertie's parents. She might even invite Joseph to meet them so he could tell them in person; a living testament to Bertie's extraordinary courage. They would be so proud. Ivy would weep, but the knowledge of her son's bravery would sustain her in the future, help her eventually to recover. Albert would bluster to hide his emotions but would relish recounting the story to friends at the bridge club and on the golf course: 'My Bertie saved a man's life, you know. He was a hero.'

As for herself, she would cherish this knowledge forever. It was better than any gravestone, any words of memorial.

31

ALICE

Alice slipped off her heels and crept past the reception desk at the Hotel de la Paix.

It was late, well after eleven, although for once she hadn't heard the bells. Consumed with humiliation and anguish, she scarcely noticed anything as she fled down the street from The Grand. Tiptoeing up to her room, she tried to avoid the creakiest stairs and floorboards, and managed to turn the key without its usual clunk.

Everything was just the same as she had left it only a few hours ago: muddy clothes strewn across the bed along with a damp, grubby towel, dusty shoes discarded in the corner, her partly unpacked suitcase still overflowing its unruly contents over the floor.

Dismayed by this scene of disarray, she nearly missed the note.

Dear Alice,
Hope you had a nice evening. Freddie's offered to take us back to Ostend in the ambulance, leaving eight o'clock in the morning. I hope this is okay with you? Mme.

Vermeulen is making breakfast picnics and says we can settle up in the morning.
  Love, Ruby

On the dressing table lay the small bunch of flowers from Lazyhook. Moving almost automatically, she spread out the wilting blooms, placed them between a folded page of blotter and weighted it with the Bible from the bedside drawer, leaning on it with an elbow for a moment. Then she pulled away, horrified. It was like pressing down on a grave. A powerful wave of grief crashed over her, leaving her almost breathless.

Sam was gone, forever. The earth pressing down.

Now, all she faced was the dismal prospect of leaving this place, this place that belonged to him, of journeying back to Ostend and being reunited with those gloomy couples on the Thomas Cook tour, then travelling to London and having to admit to Julia how right she'd been to warn her: *Don't for heaven's sake fall in love with him all over again. Promise?*

Yet that was exactly what she had so foolishly done, and everything had gone so badly wrong. She'd allowed herself to become caught up in the whirlwind of Daniel's magic as though it could somehow replace her sorrow with something wonderful. Along the line she'd lost touch with reality, imagining that he was serious about her. How could she have been so stupid?

She felt used and somehow dirty, and yet she still wanted him, or at least the idea of him. His smell was still on her and she breathed it in greedily, *Gitane* cigarettes mixed with the cologne that he splashed onto his face after shaving. The confusion was overwhelming.

Whatever had happened to the old Alice, the self-assured young woman who came to Flanders with all the confidence in the world, who'd rekindled that old flame never imagining for one moment that it might be she who would get burned? The sobs tightened in her throat and shook her shoulders with paroxysms of tears; great wracking howls she couldn't control.

There was a soft knock at the door. 'Alice?' She gulped and tried to speak normally. 'I got your note, thanks. That's all fine. See you in the morning.'

'You're not fine. I can hear you crying.'

'Please, Ruby. Just go away,' she croaked.

'You're obviously upset. Let me in.'

She sighed, wiped her face on her sleeve and opened the door.

'Goodness, whatever happened to you?'

'Long story.' Alice slumped onto the bed, resting her head in her hands.

'I'm listening.'

'Pa got confirmation from the Canadians that Sam died at a field hospital and we went there this afternoon.'

'Heavens! I'm so sorry. Where's "there"? And who's "we"? I haven't seen you since yesterday morning. Start at the beginning.'

'Hang on a sec.' Alice went to the cabinet and took out the half-full bottle of brandy. 'I need a drink. What about you?' She rinsed two tooth mugs in the sink and poured an inch into both of them, relishing the way the fiery liquid burned her throat. Then she began.

She'd reached the part where Daniel helped her find her brother's grave when she faltered, hating the sound of her own half-truths; describing a dignified, reverential moment at the graveside, supported by the man she loved. How could she admit that she had fallen to her knees and howled, prostrating herself in the mud? Or that Daniel, irritated and impatient to get out of the rain, had rushed her away as soon as he possibly could? How, after that, she had cravenly sought the comfort of his bed, only to be rejected like a plaything of which he had become bored?

'Oh God, Ruby. I've been such a fool over Daniel.'

'Don't blame yourself, Alice. I've made some terrible mistakes in the past, too.'

Alice looked up. 'Ah, yes, I remember. Your one-night stand. What a pair we are.'

'A pair of blooming idiots,' Ruby said, laughing.

Alice poured more brandy. 'I'm sorry you didn't find your Bertie, Ruby.'

Ruby sighed. 'I know. But I'm still really glad I came. More than I ever imagined. You'll never guess . . .'

'What's that?'

'Tonight I learned that Bertie saved a man's life.'

'My goodness! How amazing. How d'you find out?'

'The man he saved is right here in the hotel,' Ruby said, beaming. 'He's Joseph Catchpole, the eye-patch man from the train, whose brother turned up at the hospital. I had dinner with him tonight, and we discovered the connection.'

'Woah, slow down. The man with the eye patch is here? The man with the tour group in Ostend? You're gonna have to start at the beginning.'

Ruby recounted how she and Tubby had telegrammed Jimmy's family, and how his brother Joseph and fiancée Edith turned up, and what Joseph had told her over dinner.

'Phew. That is really something. What a hero. You must be so proud.'

'You cannot imagine just *how* proud. It means the world to me.' As Ruby smiled Alice could see how the grief, the mask that had always seemed to shadow her face, had lifted. The meek, mousy girl she first met had flowered into a pretty young woman, glowing not only from the brandy but with some kind of inner strength that hadn't been there before.

'You were so kind to that Swiss woman, you and Freddie,' she said now. 'I felt so ratty afterwards, refusing to help her that day.'

'Ginger told us how you rescued her from that man who stole her deposit when his wife pulled a knife on her. She said you'd been very generous, giving her money, too.'

'It was what anyone would have done. She was in real danger from those vile people. And you were right, you know, about helping fellow human beings. I was wrong.'

'But *you* were right too about one thing, Alice. It turns out she is German after all. The nephew she was looking for is actually her son. I know you suspected it all along.'

Alice was too weary to feel angry any more. 'I ruddy knew it, you know. Lying cow.'

'She's just a mother trying to do her best, not so different from us,' Ruby went on. 'Now all she wants is a better future for her sons.'

'Sons? I thought the other one had died.'

'When we took her to Langemarck some men she met told her that her elder son was taken prisoner of war.'

'My God.' Alice drained her glass, her emotions churning, trying to process this latest twist. 'That really takes the biscuit. Why did it have to be one of the bad guys who got to have a future? Why not Sam, or Bertie?'

'I feel the same. But you can't spend the rest of your life feeling bitter, can you?'

'You're right. I guess we ought to feel pleased for her.' Alice sighed, picking up the bottle and peering through the heavy brown glass. It was nearly empty. 'Just enough for a little snifter each. One more for the road?'

'I don't think so, thanks.' Ruby stifled a yawn. 'It's only a few hours before we have to get up again.'

'What's this about Freddie taking us to Ostend?'

'He's driving the ambulance back to England and on the way he'll give Martha and Otto a lift to catch their train in Ypres. He's asked me to go along because it's easier to have someone changing gear, at least for most of the journey. Can you forgive her enough to share a ride with them?'

'Oh hell,' Alice found herself saying. 'Why not give it a whirl?'

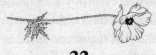

32

MARTHA, ALICE & RUBY

Martha could tell it was morning by the chinks of light coming through the cracks in the corrugated iron. The knock came again, and the sound of Freddie's voice.

She shook her slumbering son by the shoulder and went to unbolt the doors; the sun had already risen, the sky was blue and the air bright and refreshing as though last night's downpour had washed it clean. Three smiling faces greeted her: Freddie with a bucket of steaming hot water, Ruby with a brown paper bag that she thrust into Martha's hand. The American woman spoke in good French: 'There's water for washing, and food and drink for your breakfast on the train. We'll wait out here while you get ready.'

She returned to the ambulance, handing Otto the bucket. 'Here, wash your face. And look' – she peered into the paper bag – 'there's apples, bread and pastries to eat on our way.'

'Shall I travel in back with them?' Alice asked, as they waited outside. 'There's not room for all of us up front and Freddie will need you to change gear.'

Ruby looked at her, eyebrows questioning.

In the dark, sleepless hours, Alice had determined that it was time to make peace; the one small act of redemption she could achieve before leaving Belgium was to present a friendly face to the German woman.

'You can't go on hating people for what is passed, can you?' she said.

'Good for you.' Ruby's smile was genuine. Alice felt forgiven.

They folded the blankets onto the bunks to make them more comfortable for sitting on, and rolled up the canvas at the rear so that they could see out. Alice clambered into the back with Martha and Otto; Ruby sat next to Freddie in the cab. Then, with some grinding of gears, several bunny hops and much laughter from the front they were on their way, watching the road unfurl behind them and the little town of Hoppestadt recede into the distance.

'Are you looking forward to going home, Otto?' Alice asked. The boy nudged his mother.

'I am sorry, he does not understand French,' Martha said. 'Only the few words I taught him.'

'But you speak it so fluently.'

Martha's smile was gracious. 'Many years ago I worked as a nanny for a family in the Swiss Alps. And I taught French at a college in Berlin.'

'A teacher?' Alice was impressed.

'Not any more. The college closed.' Her eyes darkened. 'Berlin is not the place it once was. But to answer your question, we are of course very excited to be going home. Perhaps you know that we have some hopeful news about my son, Heinrich?'

Alice nodded, forcing as gracious a smile as she could muster. She couldn't help feeling bitter. How much more deserving of a future life were Sam, who went to fight for the love of his girl, or Bertie, the hero who saved a man's life? But watching Martha's face infused with joy as she talked about her beloved son and her hopes that they would find him alive, it was difficult to begrudge a mother such happiness. The suffering previously so clearly etched in every crease and frown line had lifted; she looked ten years younger.

'We have been warned that he is unwell,' Martha said, tapping her head. 'There is a long road ahead of us.'

'Have you no husband, or other family to help you?'

'My husband is dead. I have a brother, but he lives far away. In your country.'

'In the US? Whereabouts?'

'In Chicago. He is an engineer.'

'The windy city. I went there once with my father. It's a great place. Have you visited?'

Martha shook her head. 'Since the war he has not replied to my letters.'

Immediately Alice understood: he would have been arrested and interned as an enemy alien, heaven knows where. She chose her words carefully. 'I am afraid that America did not treat your people very well during the war. Many lost their jobs and were sent to live in secure camps.'

'So my brother may have been taken away and never had the chance to tell me? How will I ever find him again?'

'I'll do my best to trace him for you when I get home,' Alice said. 'Please don't worry. My father is an influential man and has good contacts. Here.' She handed over her notebook, opened at an empty page. 'Write his name and his last address. Your address, too.' Then she took out her wallet and found the five twenty-dollar notes that she'd secreted for emergencies. When Martha returned the diary she tore out another empty page, folded the notes into it, and wrote her own address on the front. 'This may help with what you need for your son's recovery. Or if you ever want to visit America.'

Martha unfolded the paper, gasped quietly and refolded it. 'No. This is too much. I cannot take it.' Her eyes were bright with tears.

Alice pushed her hand away. 'It is the least I can do.'

❦

Even though the train was not due for fifteen minutes, the platform was already packed with people. *Everyone seems to be on the move today*, Martha thought to herself, anxiously hoping they would be able to secure two seats together, or indeed any seats at all.

'Why don't you give us a tune while we wait?' Freddie mimicked playing the harmonica. Otto shook his head, embarrassed.

'He's been so kind, it's the least you can do,' she whispered. After hesitating a moment more Otto took out the little silver instrument, blowing a few slow, tentative notes at first and then stringing them together into something resembling the soldier song Freddie had taught him.

Freddie began to sing along, Ruby and Alice too: '*Pack up your troubles in your old kit bag, and smile, smile, smile! While you've a Lucifer to light your fag, smile, boys, that's the style. What's the use of worrying, it never was worthwhile. Sooo, pack up your troubles in your old kit bag, and smile, smile, smile!*' Before long others on the platform had joined in. As it came to an end, a spontaneous round of applause erupted around them.

'See, music makes everyone happy,' Freddie said, laughing.

'Where on earth did he learn that?' Ruby asked.

'We had a little sing-song last night, didn't we, boy?' He ruffled Otto's hair.

Martha whispered in her son's ear. 'Now, say what I taught you.'

'Thank you, Mr Freddie,' the boy said, in English.

'You're welcome, lad. Hope you get lots of fun with it like I did.'

Frustrated by lack of words, Martha held her hand to her heart. 'I thank you, all of you, for everything.'

※

Thinking about it later, Ruby couldn't remember what prompted her to put an arm around Martha's shoulder. The woman stood unyielding at first, surprised and unsure how to react, but after a second or two she leaned in and pulled Otto towards her to join the embrace.

Ruby felt their warmth, thawing the cold hatred she'd held in her heart for those who caused Bertie's death. In its place she sensed a growing glimmer of forgiveness. They were, all of them, just ordinary human beings unlucky

343

enough to have been caught up in the bloodiest war in history. Now all they could do, she said to herself, was carry on living, doing their best to make sure those sacrifices were not in vain. Little by little, out of the chaos of contradictory emotions, she was beginning to experience an unfamiliar feeling. One of peace.

Until now the word 'peace' had had little real meaning to her other than the bleak emptiness of loss. She'd gone through the motions of celebration, of course, helping with the street party: sewing yards of bunting, buttering dozens of sandwiches and brewing hundreds of cups of tea. But all she could really remember was how it rained and everyone got soaked while pretending to be cheerful. The only ones enjoying themselves were the children playing tag, organising skipping games, jumping in puddles. If anything, evidence of normal life resuming only served to re-emphasise the pain of her loss.

The notion of reconciliation was even harder. It meant truly forgiving those who had harmed you and your family, and that had always felt like a step too far. But coming here, meeting Martha, she'd been forced to face it: there could be no peace without forgiveness.

Alice nudged her and she opened her arms to fold her in. Then she felt Freddie's hand on her shoulder. For several moments the five of them – two Brits, two Germans and an American – held this unlikely embrace, listening to each other's breathing and feeling each other's warmth, saying not a word. No words were needed.

Only when they heard the train arriving, the stationmaster's whistle and his shout of 'All aboard, please', did they pull apart.

Freddie insisted on carrying their modest cases on board, shouldering his way through the crowd to secure two seats and swinging the luggage into an overhead rack before making a hasty retreat to the platform as the guard slammed doors and blew his whistle again. Martha pulled down the window with its leather loop and leaned out, waving, hearing their calls of 'Have a good journey' and 'Good luck' as the train began to move and the station disappeared into a cloud of steam.

'How are you, *Liebchen*?' she whispered, slipping into her seat beside Otto.

'I can't wait to see Heiney, Ma.'

'You did well with the harmonica. Like Freddie said, music makes everyone feel better.' Otto's response was a grunt, but she could tell he was proud of himself. 'We are fortunate to have met such kind people. Do you not think so?'

'When can we have breakfast?'

'Now, if you like.' She handed him the paper bag and he began immediately to devour a pastry, dropping crumbs down his front and onto the floor. She did not have the heart to tell him off.

As the train jolted along the much-repaired tracks, the rhythm of the English song echoed in her head and it made her smile all over again. Through the windows on either side the bleak landscape of mud, craters and broken trees rolled past but now, since the rains, everything seemed tinted with a green shimmer of new growth. Nature would soon heal the scars men had brought to this land.

Martha rested her head against the seat and closed her eyes. How her life had changed, in just a few days. She still found it hard to believe that her precious son might be alive, and had to pinch herself each time she thought of it to prove that she was not simply dreaming. She prayed that they would be able to find him and that, with home comforts and family love, they would be able to restore him to health and his old cheerful self. Patting the bag clutched on her lap that still contained Karl's grandfather's medal, and the letter they had written to Heiney, she smiled at the prospect of presenting them to him, in person.

Settling into her seat with Otto's comforting warmth at her side, Martha made a solemn promise to herself. With no work and dwindling savings the months to come would be hard, she knew, but she would try not to spend those precious dollars, now safely tucked into the inside pocket of her jacket.

Then, if Alice managed to trace him, they could use the money to visit her brother in America. From what she'd read, there was work for everyone there, plenty of food and housing. Once upon a time she would have scoffed at the notion of leaving Germany, but this journey had opened her eyes to other possibilities. She had the future of her two boys to consider.

'It was an inspiration, giving him that harmonica. Such a kind gesture. It'll keep him happy for hours,' Alice said, as they climbed back into the ambulance, the three of them up on the front bench seat.

'Even if it sends his poor mum up the wall,' Ruby said. They all laughed.

They left Ypres heading north towards Ostend through the landscape that had become so depressingly familiar: earth, craters, stumps and rusting barbed wire, barren and bleak. And the blackened trees were already showing signs of life: small sprigs clung bravely to shattered branches and, here and there, clumps of yellow dandelions and butter-cups, pink ragged robin and bright red poppies brought a splash of colour to the roadside.

'Don't suppose you'll be sorry to leave this behind, Fred-die,' Alice said.

He took a few moments to reply and she feared that she'd touched a raw nerve. 'It's the right time,' he said at last. 'I've got the two little'uns, you know? It was something Rube said about the importance of family what's made me realise that's where I ought to be, where my future is.'

Family. Future. Alice patted her pocket; the crumpled envelope was still there. This morning, as she put on her jacket, she'd found the telegram. MISSING YOU VERY MUCH STOP I LOVE YOU LLOYD STOP. Remorse washed over her. Lloyd must never discover how utterly she had betrayed him. But *she* would always know it, of course; what a fool she'd been, how weak, how utterly immoral.

With a sudden urgency she wanted very much to see him again, to hold him in her arms and reassure him of her love, to thank him for his understanding, his honesty, his generosity and his utter, unquestioning loyalty. In her head she composed her reply: TEN MORE DAYS AND WE WILL BE TOGETHER FOREVER ALL MY LOVE ALICE

'Nearly there, girls,' Freddie announced, as they entered the outskirts of Ostend.

Ruby was dreading the moment of parting, when he would leave them at the hotel in Ostend to continue his journey to Calais. He'd become such a good mate; it felt as though they'd known each other for a lifetime. 'You've been a brick,' she said. 'I really don't know what I'd have done without you.'

'Don't go all sentimental on me now, Rube.'

'Will you stop for a coffee with us?'

'Nah,' he said. 'Think I'll head off right away. Not good at goodbyes.'

'You will keep in touch, won't you? Let me know how you get on with your sister-in-law, and meeting your children again. If she needs any persuasion, I'd be glad to testify to your reformed character.'

'Reformed, eh? Not so sure about that. Chances are they won't even recognise me.'

'Don't be so silly. They need you, Freddie. You need them. Remember that.'

'Anything to please you, Mrs B.' He smiled. 'Now, make yourself useful before we get there, would you, and roll me a few ciggies for the road?'

Fifteen minutes later Ruby and Alice found themselves standing outside the hotel with their cases, watching the ambulance disappear in a haze of oily smoke.

'I'm going to miss him,' Ruby mused, as they turned to go inside. 'He's been a good friend. As Tubby said, a diamond geezer.'

On an easel in the lobby was displayed the photograph taken that first day.

A memento of your pilgrimage. Just 1/- per 8" x 6" print

Order by 11 o'clock for delivery before departure

There was Major Wilson at the centre, jovial and determined, surrounded by solemn-faced couples valiantly attempting to raise smiles for the cameraman. Alice was at the side, tall and conspicuous in her bold jacket and hat, in front of her a pale-faced Edith with Joe, piratical with his eye patch and crooked grin. Ruby, shyly hiding behind the others, was barely visible.

'It feels like a lifetime ago,' Alice said. 'Not just four days.'

'I hardly recognise myself,' Ruby replied. 'I look as though I'm scared of my own shadow.'

'And whatever was I doing wearing that hat to the battlefields?' Alice said, pointing at herself.

'You were so bold, so confident. I was in awe of you.'

'And such a bonehead, as it turns out,' Alice said quietly. 'Too bold for my own good.'

'Ah well, that's all behind us, now. You found Sam, and his grave. That's something, isn't it?'

'And you learned that your Bertie was a hero.'

'And that's something I'll cherish for the rest of my life.'

It was a curious feeling, returning to that huge, gloomy room with its enormous double bed, dark furniture and tapestries of medieval knights and dragons. Was it only five days ago they had arrived? So much had happened since then it really felt, as Alice said, like a lifetime ago. Out of it all she had emerged a new, surprisingly confident version of herself, who had promised to honour Bertie's memory by helping those who had survived forge new lives for themselves. She liked this new Ruby, felt proud of her, hoped she would stick around.

Although she had not found a grave she felt sure that one day Bertie's body – or at least some indicator of his identity – would be discovered and when that happened he would surely receive the dignified burial that he deserved. But having a grave to visit had, in the end, turned out not to be the most significant thing. Far more vital was the sense of his presence that she'd rediscovered and the forgiveness she had allowed herself.

Ruby opened her case, took out her diary and turned to where she had slipped the pressed flowers from Tyne Cot between its pages. Memories flooded back sharp as cut glass: the dusty paths, the sea of crosses lit with bright sunlight.

Dear Bertie, she wrote. *Last night, Joe Catchpole told me how you risked your own life to save his, dragging him back to safety even though he was desperately wounded. You probably never knew that he survived. But he is alive, and he is a lovely man.*

Hearing this has made me so proud of you, Bertie Barton. More than words can say. I love you, and will love you forever, my dearest one.

The writing swam in front of her weary eyes and she put the diary down.

Outside, blinking in the sunshine, she walked the few yards down to the promenade with its curve of damaged hotels like jagged teeth against the blue of the sea and the sky. The air was so crisp and clear that if she peered long enough at the horizon she might even be able to see the white cliffs of Dover.

Now, to her surprise, Ruby discovered that she was actually looking forward to going home. Somehow, she was beginning to make sense of it all.